The Fire Portrait

By Barbara Mutch

The Girl from Simon's Bay
The Fire Portrait

a&b

The Fire Portrait

BARBARA MUTCH

Allison & Busby Limited
11 Wardour Mews
London W1F 8AN
allisonandbusby.com

irst published in Great Britain by Allison & Busby in 2021.
This paperback edition published by Allison & Busby in 2022.

A CIP catalogue record for this book is available from
the British Library.

10 9 8 7 6 5 4 3 2 1

ISBN 978-0-7490-2679-0

Typeset in 10/15 pt Sabon LT Pro by
Allison & Busby Ltd

FSC
www.fsc.org
MIX
Paper from
responsible sources
FSC® C171272

Printed and bound by
CPI Group (UK) Ltd, Croydon, CR0 4YY

For E, R and Z

Prologue

This may be my last entry.

It is curious the way one's mind turns back to the beginning.

Mother said spring came early the year I was born.

Pale daffodils burst from the ground and opened their trumpets to the rising sun, swung their faces west to miss nothing of its afternoon passage, and then drooped for the night.

You couldn't get enough of them, even as a baby, Mother used to muse.

You'd struggle out of your father's arms and run into their midst.

I've left the daffodils behind.

Now, I race to capture the diverse colours of Africa.

The orange of Namaqualand daisies, the blue-rose of dawn, the gritty ochre of desert.

The fleeting jewel of a kingfisher's wing.

Sometimes I get it right, sometimes my colours wander across the paper like a random smear. Father says it's about the soul, my teacher says it's about technique and my husband says it's all in the eye of the beholder anyway, and I should not agonise so much.

But I do, because I am the beholder, and if my work cannot speak to me then I have failed.

How strange that I should find fame outside the area where I practised for so long.

And in a single work.

The portrait of a human face.

Chapter One

Embury St David's, England, 1921

When I was a sober ten-year-old, I fell head first out of an oak tree and nearly died.

Nothing was ever the same again. Not me, and not the world I crashed into. I should, various relatives complained, have realised there'd been enough dying and shown more sense.

My father's prized binoculars, slung around my neck, flipped over my head and smashed to the ground. I remember the calamitous sound of breaking glass but nothing at all from my own collision with the earth. It wasn't my fault, I cried to my parents when I later came to, it was because I was distracted by a woodpecker on a nearby branch and failed to watch my feet as I descended.

'Call an ambulance!' Gerald Whittington had shouted while he loosened his daughter's collar.

Emily Whittington knelt on the ground and mopped at the blood with her lace handkerchief and tried to clear the vicinity of lens glass. The clang-clang of the approaching ambulance brought out a crowd from the terraced houses. The Ferguson toddlers, attracted by the noise, had to be hauled out of the vehicle's anticipated path by their mother; the Atkinses' hosepipe, left running, flooded their tiny garden and ruined Mrs A's prize phlox while the Hodgson family – mother, father, three teenagers, visiting grandparents – rushed to form a circle around the inert body. Emily Whittington appeared to be praying over her daughter, which was only to be expected of a mother, especially one who'd lost so much already.

The ambulance ground to a halt, scattering the onlookers and silencing a pair of barking dogs.

A bottle was waved beneath Frances's nose and her eyelids began to flutter.

Why do male birds have different feathers from females? For courtship? Maybe to avoid mix-ups . . .

'She's alive!' yelled Mr Atkins. He'd arrived on the scene after he heard the thud.

'She's alive!' repeated the crowd.

Confused, lovesick birds fluttered across my brain. And something else . . .

A gust of wind shook the oak from where Frances had fallen. Folk exchanged glances. Frances was known to spend a lot of time up trees, more than the most adventurous neighbourhood boys. Maybe the oak had got tired of being climbed and tipped the invader out. Even Mrs Whittington had once confessed to Mrs Ferguson that she found her daughter's behaviour . . . unusual. It was the Great War, replied Mrs Ferguson. And then the Spanish Flu. Nothing would ever be the same again. Even girls.

The ambulancemen lifted Frances onto a stretcher, slid her into their vehicle and lurched off. Her parents followed more slowly in the family motor car, bought only a year ago and the first one on the street. Gerald Whittington was a coming man. 'Make soup,' Mr Atkins instructed his wife before shooing the neighbours away. 'They'll want something warm when they get back.'

By the time the ambulance arrived at the hospital, I'd regained consciousness and it seemed I wouldn't die from my moment of distraction. The binoculars, however, were ruined and that was the worst outcome. They were my extra eyes, the windows to a world I was sure no one else noticed. How would I see the way feathers layered along a bird's wing and caught the light?

'No more climbing for a while,' said Dr Evans, the emergency doctor, after he'd examined my skull and made me watch a moving pencil without shifting my head. 'Next time you may not be so lucky. Bed rest for five days. Lots of fluids.' He unrolled a bandage and wound it around my head.

'Her hands, Doctor?' Mother looked in horror at my scratched palms. Mother was particular; the sight of abraded skin was an insult to her careful management of the household. And she wasn't wearing a hat. Mother rarely left the house without a hat.

'They'll heal up soon enough. Nurse will clean them and put on dressings.'

I looked away and caught a glimpse of myself in a mirror opposite the hospital bed. Was that really me? Pale face, green eyes with a fleck of ginger, wild, titian hair scraped away from a large head bandage; a tear in my cotton blouse through which poked bruised skin.

'Frances? Are you listening?' Wind rattled against the ward windows and brought a speckle of raindrops to the glass. 'You need to tell your parents if your headache persists in the coming days.'

'Yes, sir, I will.'

'What if it does, Doctor?' This, nervously, from Mother as she plucked at my crumpled cardigan.

Mother was always well ironed, in contrast to Father's gangly untidiness. Maybe the combination of order and disarray was the correct mix where marriage was concerned.

'Then we'll investigate further. But I'm confident your daughter's injuries will heal swiftly.'

The woodpecker I'd spotted, the one that caused my fall, did he see me and wonder if I'd live? Do birds have brains that notice life and death in species other than their own?

'When can I go home, Doctor?'

'As soon as your cuts have been dressed. And, young lady,' he wagged a finger, 'no more outdoor adventures, rather take up reading or embroidery.'

'Thank you, Doctor,' said Father hurriedly, and shot me a warning glance. Embroidery!

'Why,' Mother asked later, after she'd helped me into the motor car, 'must you climb? Why won't you play on the ground like other girls? Like your friend Susan?'

'Emily,' murmured Father, putting a hand on her arm, 'Fran's had enough of a fright.'

He glanced at me in the rear-view mirror and closed one eye in a slow wink.

Father understood.

In a way, he was also to blame.

He'd first taken me up the oak as a child. Father said vantage points were the only way to gain a proper view of the world. Mother protested that climbing was an unrefined pastime for girls, but he said if Frances wanted to do so then why shouldn't she? He'd shown me how to use the glasses to trace the winding road that led to Eastleigh, and notice how the

12

land fell into folds as if liquid turned to solid. To match him, I'd learnt the names of the birds that played about the oak and some that didn't, and I'd recite them until Father covered his ears: cardinal woodpeckers, raucous magpies, friendly robins, scarlet macaws from the Amazon, unmistakably . . .

But for Father, the view was about more than pretty scenery and a sense of proportion. It was about money. Borrowed landscape opened up a crowded island and a buyer's pocket. 'Look,' he'd murmur, waving at the vista, 'it's ours, little one. We paid for it fair and square and it will surely appreciate with time. One day it'll be yours.' He must have known, even then, that I'd be an only child. And Embury, like Father, was known to be a place on the up: close enough to the cathedral cities of Salisbury and Winchester to provide business opportunities and religious solace, and also to Southampton from where the Empire was in reach for the making of a fortune. Father bought our house after the Anglo-Boer War. 'Mark my words,' he used to say, 'there'll be another set-to out there. Nothing was truly settled.' Queen Victoria died towards the end and some said it was only her passing that encouraged the two sides to look up from battle and make reluctant peace. The fact that Father's sister, Mary, lived at the Cape of Good Hope meant he took an interest in that part of the world.

My mind is unbound, darting from oaks to houses to distant wars . . .

We crept along the road towards our home, Father driving the motor car extra slowly to avoid jarring my bandaged head. Mother did not initially share Father's view about Embury. She would've preferred Winchester, even if it meant a cramped semi rather than a detached house. But Father persisted and

Mother conceded. After all, she was lucky to have a husband, let alone a house. Many of her friends had only framed photographs of men in uniform and bunches of letters tied with ribbons; unsatisfactory lives eked out alongside elderly parents.

Light broke from behind the Atkinses' curtains. Someone was watching for our return. A cat scuttled away, its eyes reflecting in Father's headlamps as he parked. The terraced houses shifted closer, looming overhead. I felt a tremor and touched a hand to the bandage. Maybe the injury was playing with my eyes. And somewhere out there, beneath the oak, were the splinters of Father's binoculars.

Do trees have a kind of consciousness? Do they know who climbs them? Who falls out of them?

And what kind of birds live in oak trees in Africa?

'Mind her sore hands, Gerald,' Mother said as Father opened my door.

Even with his helping hand around my shoulder, it took an age to reach my bedroom. Mother had wanted me to have dark curtains but I wanted voile so I could see outside at night. Father had said I could have any kind I fancied. Mother wondered how I'd manage to sleep with moonlight streaming in but eventually agreed and ordered them from France as a special treat. No one else on the street had foreign curtains.

'I'm sorry I fell,' I said later, when she kissed me goodnight.

'I wish you'd be sensible,' she murmured. 'You ruined your green cardigan. And your father didn't show it but you gave him a tremendous shock. He thought he'd lost you.'

And you, Mother?

I caught the words before they left my lips.

So often I see detachment on Mother's face. Perhaps it

14

was the Great War? Mother had lost her brother and nearly her husband but for a lucky avoidance of the Somme. Maybe emotion was a weakness that, like a creased blouse, should never be displayed.

Even so . . .

If I was the only child she'd ever have, surely she'd want to hold me closer, love me more openly?

'It's been a long day.' Father appeared at Mother's shoulder. 'Let's get you to sleep.' He leant down and kissed me, his beard tickling my cheek, his watch chain glinting in the lamplight. Father might be a little untidy but he valued quality. A good watch. A tweed suit. Expensive binoculars . . .

'I'm sorry, Father. About the glasses. I'll save my pocket money—'

'Hush.' He put his finger to his lips before leading Mother away.

Father was never detached. He'd laugh ruefully after he'd revealed something it would've been better to conceal – like his opinion of the King, who was nothing like the late Victoria in terms of decorum or ending wars – and say he couldn't lie to a child's trusting face. He also said it was foolish to store all your assets in one place, whether it was money or influence. I didn't understand him at the time but he said it didn't matter as long as I remembered the words when I was older.

Risk, whatever that was, must be spread.

I stared out of the window. It felt as if my voile curtains were being torn aside to expose the world in all its rawness. With each tug I saw more clearly, understood more sharply. Mother's indifference might reach to the bedroom she shared with Father. I wasn't clear how babies came about but I sensed you needed both parents to take part. That was why – not a medical reason, as I'd believed – there was no brother or sister. Mother didn't want another child. One was enough. Or maybe, at times, too much.

Through the open window came a trilling, bubbling song.

A nightingale, I registered, as my eyes closed.

A secretive bird, not often seen. Perhaps I'd missed it in the oak.

Chapter Two

The tremor in my head disappeared but the new sharpness didn't leave me the next day, or the next. I couldn't work out whether this fresh awareness sprang from outside of me or from within.

Had the world changed in my moment of collision with the earth, or was it only me?

'Is the sun too strong?' Mother fussed with the thin curtains. 'Are you chilly?'

Mother's detachment now veered into constant surveillance. She wouldn't let me draw or read in case such exertion placed too great a burden on my scrambled brain. She patrolled regularly to prevent me sneaking out of bed and falling prey to a delayed seizure.

'It's too soon, Frances. We must be careful.'

'But—'

'No buts, my dear. Remember what the doctor said.'

Mrs Atkins delivered soup and a fruit cake – I heard the door knocker – of which I was allowed to eat small portions, and Susan's mother called to say that Sue would love to visit and promised not to make me laugh if doing so might hurt my head. Aunt Rosemary from Exeter offered to come up by train to child-sit. Mrs Ferguson sent over a copy of *Crafts for Girls*.

Mother repelled them all. In my solitude I began to speculate about Jesus. I only knew Him from Sundays, where He resided on a cross at the centre of St David's Church, ready to forgive us for what we had done to Him, provided we sinned no more. Did He choose to cushion my fall instead of letting me die . . . and then cruelly decree that boredom should be my punishment? But I don't believe He noticed my moment of distraction in the midst of all the other upheavals that vied for His attention that day. Jesus couldn't possibly save every mouse from the fangs of a snake, or every sober child from an unfortunate slip. It was luck that spared me, not Divine Intervention. I realised these were probably heretical thoughts and should not be shared.

'How are you feeling, Frances?' Mother, again. 'Have you drunk your beef tea?'

'I hate beef tea.'

Mother was wearing a pink twinset and a navy skirt, and her hair was carefully set. I've never seen Mother un-set. Even in bed, she wears a hairnet to tamp down the possibility of stray curls.

'You will drink it, Frances. You need building up. And then you must rest.'

Susan says her mother winds her hair on pins every night. Isn't that sinful? Putting outward appearance above a holy heart? I've read about tribes who pierce their noses with skewers but that is for their Lord's benefit not for their husband's or random visitors—

'Frances?'

'Yes, Mother. I'll drink it.'

The only distraction – and I was shamefully aware that

distraction had brought me to this low point – was when Father returned from work and peered lankily round my door.

'Please, Father.' I wriggled to the edge of the bed. 'Take me outside! Please? A drive to the sea?'

'Next week. For the moment,' he fixed me with a mock stern glance, 'we will escape via the exercise of our brains, most particularly what may be left of yours. Let me see.' He cast his eyes upwards. 'If one caterpillar takes half a day to eat three leaves, how many leaves will four caterpillars eat in a week?'

'Father!' I giggled. 'I'm sure you don't know yourself!'

'I'll read to you instead, if you like.' He ran a skinny finger along my bookshelf. 'Some Shakespeare. "The Taming of the Shrew"?' He shot me a merry glance. 'Just the ticket. And if you don't fall out of any trees in the next fortnight, I'll take you to Southampton to see the mail ship.'

'Does it hurt?' Susan inspected my head as we sat in the playground of St David's School a week later. I'd been allowed to attend without my hat in case it restricted circulation to my brain. So there was no hiding the purple bruise which had spread across my forehead and around my eyes like a pagan adornment or the result, Father winked at me, of a barroom brawl. Phyllis Carter said I looked like a clown. Felicity Chalmers said Phyllis was a disgrace to make fun of me and Julie Eastman said her brother had once fallen out of a tree and was never the same again. Several boys laughed at me and shouted: did I think I was a monkey to be climbing like one?

'At least the doctor didn't cut off your hair to see the wounds.' Susan opened her lunchbox and poked through her sandwiches. 'That would have been much worse.'

'Sue! I could have died!'

Susan snorted. Her own hair was thin whereas I had enough – and of a distinctive colour – for both of us. And there it was, flowing freely while everyone else had to keep theirs unflatteringly bundled beneath school panamas. 'Did you see stars? When you fell? Fran?'

'I didn't see stars but I felt strange afterwards.'

'Whatever do you mean?'

'Everything was clearer.' I hesitated. 'I could understand things I hadn't been able to before.'

Susan halted with her jam sandwich halfway to her mouth. 'What things?'

But there was no time to explain because the bell rang.

'Good morning young ladies,' shouted Mr Cadwaller from the front of the art studio. 'Today we're going to study perspective. Does anyone know what it means?'

'It's when a road far away looks narrower,' Phyllis Carter said smugly. 'Or trees look smaller.'

Or, I caught my breath, when your view of the world is transformed by a blow to the head.

'So, if we want to entice our viewer into believing the distance we're creating,' Cadwaller's moustache twitched, 'we draw objects smaller. One sheet each!' He brandished a pile of paper.

I sharpened my pencil and held it above the paper.

The woodpecker in the oak, just before the fall.

My hand began to fly across the page. A slender head with a dominant beak emerged atop a striped breast, feathers ruffling slightly in the breeze, the afternoon sun falling sideways.

'Frances,' Mr Cadwaller murmured at my shoulder, 'that is charming but where is the perspective?'

20

'Coming, sir.'

I sketched the looming houses in the background, then roughed out a second, smaller tree with another bird poised on its trunk. The first bird seemed to be looking at the second and would not normally tolerate a rival close by, but if I made it seem too far away to be competition and yet just close enough to be clearly male . . .

'My,' Cadwaller raised his bushy eyebrows, 'have you been practising while you've been at home?'

'No, sir. I wasn't allowed to draw. And I smashed my binoculars so now I have to look for myself.'

'Yet perhaps that is not such a tragedy?'

Does he know?

Can he tell I'm seeing the world more clearly without magnification?

'Binoculars are valuable, Frances, but they're only tools. They can be replaced. A critical first glance at your subject cannot. It will never reappear.'

'But—' I'd always believed first impressions were flawed, lacking essential detail: the layered hues of a bird's wing, the intricate tracery of chestnut blooms.

'Draw what's in front of you, as you've done here.' He tapped the sketch. 'Reflect what the eye sees.'

By the end, most girls had created roads disappearing into the distance, lined by ever-diminishing trees.

'Quick!' muttered Susan. 'While Cadwaller's not looking, draw something for me, Fran!'

When the sketches were collected, my pair of birds was the clear winner, followed by Susan's surprisingly good triangular kites flown by distant figures on an otherwise deserted pebble beach.

'Are they us?' she whispered. 'Last summer? Before you swam out beyond the breakers?'

Father had shouted for me to come back, but the sea was flat and I could have floated all the way to the Isle of Wight, where there are gardens with plants from Africa that must be familiar to Aunt Mary.

'Excellent work, class!' Cadwaller shouted. 'Look for perspective every day, young ladies!'

When I was allowed back into the garden, the sky hid beneath lowering clouds. No flowers opened their faces, no drumming woodpeckers tempted me from the oak. The only presence was a strange absence, as if the world were waiting for something to happen.

A storm? Another fall?

'Miss is better?' Lionel Jacobs croaked, looking up from weeding around the roses. Father said we had a duty. Mr Jacobs had lost a limb in the war. He often touched a hand against his pinned-up trouser where the leg once was. They say soldiers who lose limbs can still feel them, still sense their flesh.

'I'm fine, sir, thank you.' I knelt down and began to search for stray bits of Father's binoculars in case they might stab my bare feet in the summer.

Mr Jacobs sat back on his one good heel and squinted up into the oak.

'The tree sees everything, miss.'

'What do you mean?'

Jacobs talked about birds and plants as if they were his friends.

'The tree sees the grown-ups' sadness. Miss must be careful.'

I felt a tremor, like when I came back from the hospital and the roofs leant over me. I remember a nightingale singing as I fell asleep. And then later – the same night, the next night? – a dream woke me, gasping, in the darkness.

Mr Jacobs wasn't talking about my fall.

Perhaps the detachment that comes over Mother's face has nothing to do with me at all.

Chapter Three

'One day we'll take a trip!' Father waved to no one in particular on the Union-Castle liner tied up to the quay in Southampton harbour. Father loved boats, even stationary ones without passengers. He loved the bustle of the docks, the aproned men swarming up gangplanks bearing boxes of unknown contents, a lighter curving through the water from an anchored barge. 'It's good to see such purpose, Fran. Such intent! Remember that, my dear.'

He raised his hat to a group of sailors marching by, their bell-bottom trousers flapping.

In honour of the visit, I was wearing a blue linen dress, white gloves and black patent shoes that pinched. 'One can't be too careful, Frances,' Mother had warned when I asked for easier footwear. 'The wrong accessories can betray the best of backgrounds.'

Father's necktie broke free of his waistcoat and flapped up into his face.

'Hold my hand,' he said, stuffing it back. 'We can't have any more accidents.'

'Mr Whittington?'

I gazed upwards as a motor car, carefully suspended from

the hook of a crane, swung slowly over the deck of the liner. 'We'll watch a bit longer,' Father leant down to me, 'then we'll go for tea.'

'When does she sail for the Cape, Father?'

'Today and every Thursday, 4 p.m. on the dot.'

'Mr Whittington?'

We turned. A young man stood before us, smiling nervously, and carrying a battered suitcase.

'I'm Julian McDonald, sir. You knew my parents.'

Father gasped and took off his hat. 'Would you believe it?' He reached out to grasp the young man's hand. 'Julian McDonald! The last time I saw you, you were Frances's age!'

The man offered his hand to me as well. He had fair hair and pale eyes and a strange habit of clasping and reclasping the case as if he were worried it would be snatched from him. I turned back to the ship, noting the sweep of her lavender hull, the raked angle of her red-and-black funnels, a row of dots for portholes. Mr Cadwaller was right. If I found a quiet spot and set up a folding chair and put a piece of paper on a clipboard, I could quickly sketch—

'What brings you to Southampton, Julian? Your parents . . .' Father rested a hand on his shoulder, 'I'm so sorry. Emily and I were shocked.'

'I've become a teacher,' he said hastily. 'I was supposed to leave today, but there's been a delay.'

'Come.' Father began to head down the quay. 'Walk with us. Where are you staying?'

'Well, the delay was unexpected. I should find a small hotel.' He looked about uncertainly. I wondered if he was short of money.

'Nonsense!' Father clapped a hand on the young man's

shoulder. 'You shall stay with us. I won't hear another word. Do you have any more luggage?' He glanced down at Julian's meagre case.

'That's awfully kind. I wouldn't want to be any trouble. I could—'

'We have a spare room, Mr McDonald,' I put in, feeling sorry for him. 'It'll be no trouble.'

And a visitor would successfully divert Mother, who was still monitoring my every move.

'Indeed,' Father beamed. 'Ah, there's a Lyon's tea room. Let's have a cup before we motor back.'

'Thank you, sir. That's very kind.'

'Frances,' said Father in due course, over a fat slice of Bakewell tart, 'I have a gift for you. I want to encourage a hobby that will keep you on terra firma. As does your mother.' He delved into his coat pocket and produced a package.

I tore open the wrapping to reveal a set of coloured drawing pencils in a decorated tin.

'Oh, Father! Thank you!'

He winked in Mr McDonald's direction. 'Frances fell out of a tree recently, Julian.'

I fingered the tin and glanced out of the window, back at the ship.

'Have you seen the other item, my dear?'

It was a book bound in leather, but not one that would teach me lessons in life like the Shakespeare Father teasingly employed. The pages were blank, lined in pale blue and edged with delicate gold. This was a book for me to fill with my own words.

'Why, Father?'

But he didn't need to answer. Father knew something inside

me had changed since the fall. He was giving me a place to record whatever sprang, unbidden, into my head; thoughts that couldn't be drawn or spoken out loud.

I reached over and kissed him.

'A diary is a friend, Frances. You can tell it anything you like.'

It turned out that Julian McDonald's nervousness was because of the Great War.

War and loss, in my youth, was a topic that lurked beneath every grown-up's conversation.

'Where is your school, Julian?' asked Mother over dinner. She was used to Father making acquaintances on docksides or at the railway station. They could become clients, Father would say. Accountants needed a ready supply because old ones died or lost their fortunes and that was of no help. But I doubted Mr McDonald had enough money to make him a worthwhile customer.

'In Africa, Mrs Whittington. The Hex River valley.'

'Ah,' said Mother, whose geography south of the equator was hazy.

'Near the Cape, Mother. Where Aunt Mary lives. What happened to your parents, Mr McDonald?'

'Frances!' Mother paled and put out a hand to stop me.

'It's all right.' Julian McDonald gave a faint smile. 'My parents died of Spanish Flu at the end of the war.'

'I'm so sorry. You didn't catch the Flu, Mr McDonald?'

'That's quite enough, Frances!' Mother shot a despairing glance at Father. 'Julian, please forgive Frances. She's had a bang on the head and it's made her a little . . . insensitive.'

'I was recovering from a wound,' Julian McDonald turned

and faced me, 'when my parents became ill. They passed away before I returned home.'

'Well,' said Father sombrely, leaning back in his chair, 'your parents were fine people. Now,' he crumpled his napkin, 'if you will excuse us, ladies, Julian and I will take a brandy and talk about Africa.'

I glanced outside. Tomorrow, provided it was dry, I'd get up early and take my new pencils and draw the rose that was in bloom at the bottom of the garden. Maybe I'd see Mr Jacobs and ask him again why Mother and Father were sad underneath. I sensed his answer might somehow involve me but not in a way I could understand. I wasn't at the centre of whatever it turned out to be, but rather looking on from the side. Like the dream that kept returning only to disappear before I could catch it; like smoke from a ship's funnel slipping past my fingers.

'I don't know what's come over you,' Mother murmured as we cleared the table. 'Ever since you fell out of that tree you've been in a strange mood. Perhaps,' she looked at me more carefully, 'perhaps we should get a second opinion. You're not yourself.'

But I am, Mother, I'm more myself than I ever was before.

I understand more.

And I see more, I see something that I can't quite make out—

Chapter Four

It's taken me a while to write my first diary entry.

That's because I was worried someone would find it and read what I've written and be upset.

You can never tell what will upset parents.

So I waited until my twelfth birthday, which is today, and until I found a safe hiding place.

It's two years since I fell out of the oak and I still see life sharply. Nothing has faded.

Maybe it's a coincidence or maybe I was ready to understand more of the world anyway, and the bang on my head made it happen sooner?

Could be.

I like this new version of me.

Susan says we're growing up and so everything in our lives will change, from our bodies – Sue is already endowed – to our minds, and that I shouldn't fuss. And I know I'm loved even if Mother sometimes doesn't see me at all.

I climb the oak when she's out, and I go just as high as before.

I want to see as far as Africa.

Father taught me to swim in the sea – he used to be

a champion – and he says I'm reckless to go beyond the breakers but he understands why. I like the edge it brings.

I still don't know what Mr Jacobs meant when he said the tree saw everything and that the grown-ups were sad. I asked him again last week but he shook his head and picked his teeth and repeated that only the Good Lord knew and I should pray. But I only pray when we're in church and I can't avoid it. Any spare time I have, I'm busy drawing. It takes away the tremor I sometimes still feel and lets me see what God has made, if it was Him who did so. Although, that's not what Mr Charles Darwin says.

Father said my diary would be my friend, and that I could tell it anything.

The dream has come back to me regularly and each time I see a little more, although it's still elusive.

There is a child in the garden. But it's not me.

I haven't said anything to Mother or Father yet.

The hiding place is my secret.

If I should fall out of another tree, these pages will never be found.

Chapter Five

Last night I dreamt again. Not of the unknown child in the garden but of young men going to war and never returning.

'What were they fighting over, in the Boer War?' I'd once asked Father when we were up the oak.

'Gold and diamonds, of course! No one cared about the Boer republics with their backcountry Dutch until riches were found beneath their feet! Remember, Frances, money greases the wheels of power.'

'But wasn't that unfair, Father?' I nudged him, but not too hard that he might fall. 'To fight a war only because you wanted to take someone else's riches? Isn't that a sort of burglary?'

'Indeed, but the world is ruled by the Great Powers, child. That's what mostly keeps the peace. Young upstart nations can't be allowed to get above themselves – especially as a result of lucky geology.'

'I don't understand,' I said to our history teacher a year after Julian McDonald's visit, 'why all those boys needed to die in the trenches? What did the Allies win?'

The Great War wasn't about gold or diamonds or upstart nations.

My classmates exchanged glances. Perhaps, I could hear

them thinking, Frances did indeed lose her mind in that fall. But she'd always asked odd questions, even before she fell out of the tree.

'The corridors of power, Frances Whittington, are not open for judgement by ourselves!' Mrs Beatrice Andrews retorted. We called her 'Beagle' on account of her oversized ears and ability to discern covert snacking beneath a raised desktop. 'Our leaders explore every avenue to avoid war until such a path becomes unavoidable. Now,' she gave me a quelling look, 'the Great War is not our focus until next year; let us turn our attention back to the voyages of discovery. Columbus and the New World. The sea route around Africa.'

I stared out of the window and pictured the Dutch in their wooden sailing ships, anchoring beneath the gaze of a flat-topped mountain and wondering what lay on the alien shore, just as Columbus and his men must have thought on arriving in the Americas. Might they be hit by poisonous arrows from local tribes? Would they die from eating strange fruits?

There were consequences of my question to the Beagle.

'Your teachers say you're very outspoken, Frances,' Mother observed, coming into the dining room after a parent–teacher meeting and unpinning her hat.

'Quite right, too,' put in Father, following her to the table where I was doing my homework. 'We've taught Fran to engage. Not to be afraid to ask questions. It's part of her education.'

'But perhaps not so . . . argumentatively?' Mother folded her gloves and placed them beside her hat.

'I won't say anything, any more.' I scowled at my open textbook, *Cross, Castle and Compass: Their Role in History*. 'I'll be completely quiet.'

'No, Frances,' Mother sighed, 'we don't want you to be completely silent. But you should think before you speak. Questioning the conduct of the Great War is not appropriate for a youngster.'

For Mother, it was less about education and more about bad manners, especially in a girl. Like wearing plain shoes to Southampton instead of patent leather.

'Art,' said Mr Cadwaller a few weeks later, wagging a stained finger at me, 'is a journey. It requires planning. You cannot simply trust to instinct or hope for fair weather. Eighty per cent is acquired technique, twenty per cent is talent. If you wish to progress, Frances, you must hone your technique.'

He spread out the sketches I'd brought in.

A pale pink rose, a lavender-hulled liner with a funnel in black and red, a fragile dandelion. If my pictures were no good, Mr Cadwaller would say so – unlike dear Father who said everything I drew was beautiful and showed a pleasing sense of soul.

'I see you're not over-detailing,' he arched an eyebrow, 'at the expense of the overall effect.'

'When should I start to use paint, sir?'

'Not just yet. This rose is well done.'

'Mr Cadwaller,' I felt a frisson of excitement, 'do you think I could be an artist?'

'Anyone can be an artist! Anyone!' He spread his arms wide as if to embrace the entire village, perhaps even the entire country, as if the gift were universal and simply needed to be uncovered. 'Are you asking me whether you could make a living from it?'

'Yes, sir.' I hesitated and then plunged. 'I'd like to make it

33

my career.'

None of my friends talked of careers. They only wanted to find boys to marry. 'What else is there?' asked Phyllis, teasing a kiss curl over her forehead. 'You'd be an old maid, otherwise.'

'Frances?'

Wasn't settling on a husband like putting all your assets into one basket, as Father had advised against?

I blushed. A truly heretical thought.

'Are you prepared to devote yourself, Frances? To fail, and try again?'

'I know Van Gogh went mad, sir. And Vermeer died poor. So did some of the great music composers.'

'Now, now!' Mr Cadwaller puffed out a breath. 'Self-sacrifice is not required.'

'Sorry, sir.'

'You could become an educated admirer of other people's work, like the Masters you've just mentioned. There's no shame in that.' His lips twitched. Now he was goading me. 'You could ask your parents to take you to London to view the National Gallery.'

'I don't want to study art, sir, I want to make it myself.'

Are there pencil strokes that can capture the thrill of a vantage point? I asked my diary later. *The risk of being up a mountain or a tree, precariously, looking down on the world?*

Father was in his study when I got home. I rapped on the door.

'Come in!'

He looked up from his desk as I closed the door behind me.

'Father, can I interrupt? Mr Cadwaller says I might be good enough to be an artist if I work hard!'

'Does he now,' Father leant back and regarded me. 'You

34

mean instead of an ornithologist, my dear? After all, you can list every bird in the garden by name and family.'

'Don't tease, Father. Could you pay for me to take private lessons?'

'I don't see why not.' He winked. 'Our shares are doing well!'

When I'd first asked where the money came from to buy our home, he'd said from the railways in America and I'd shouted 'choof, choof!' and it became our private joke.

I went around the desk to hug him. 'It's because I broke the binoculars. I learnt I could see well enough on my own to draw a picture - but I need to get better.'

He nodded and I saw his hand shake for a moment. Father didn't like to be reminded of my fall. It brought back memories of the war across the Channel and the soldiers who fell beside him.

'You promised to tell me one day about this man,' I pointed to a small, framed poster tucked away on a side wall, of a man in military uniform pointing a finger at his audience. Mother disapproved, as did relatives who came at Christmas, and particularly one visitor from overseas. 'After the internment camps, Gerald! The scorched earth! How can you bear to have him on your wall?'

And Father had replied, 'As a warning, dear chap. A warning.'

He stood up and took my hand and led me to the picture. 'That is Lord Kitchener, a famous British soldier. He was the hero or the scourge of the Boer War, depending which side you were on. Ten years later, he was exhorting the same young men to follow him and sign up for the Great War.'

'So why do you keep him here, Father?'

He hesitated.

'As a reminder and an omen. That a person can be an enemy one moment, and an ally the next. And that powerful men must be held to account, Fran. Whether they're Kitchener or the Kaiser.'

'I thought the Great War started because the Archduke was shot.'

'Yes it did, and one thing led to another. It became a matter of honouring alliances. We were obliged to uphold previous treaties and stop the Kaiser's ambitions in Europe.'

'Before he gathered too much power for himself?

He smiled. 'Indeed. Talking of power, shall we tell Mother you plan to be the greatest female artist in England?'

'Father?' I stopped him at the door. 'Mr Jacobs says you and Mother are sad.'

He put an arm about my shoulder. 'Poor Jacobs also thinks plants have feelings, my dear. A sweet notion. Don't listen to his nonsense.'

Chapter Six

The year of my fifteenth birthday was a stormy one. Winds from the Atlantic delivered gusts strong enough to bring down several branches from the oak and forced me to climb a more perilous route to my vantage point. Rainwater sluiced along our roads, filling the River Itchen with a muddy torrent that emptied itself into the Solent as a brown stain I fancied I could see in the distance. I tried to draw the bubbling streams but they were too fast, too unpredictable. Roses let you copy each delicate stage from bud to bloom but water tears past you before you can catch it.

Is love, I asked my diary after I clambered down the tree, *like water? Life-giving but erratic? Too changeable to be pinned down?*

I don't want to give my love too easily in case it runs away from me.

'How,' I asked Mr Cadwaller, 'do you draw something that is never still?'

'You choose one moment, Frances, you capture it as you see it,' he clapped his hands together, as if imprisoning the image between his palms, 'and fix it upon your mind! Then draw it just so.'

I walked on Embury Common with my sketchbook and my folding stool and an umbrella, and drew whatever was fleetingly in front of me. Shifting skies, windblown daisies, flitting sparrows. 'Rather come with us,' Sue and Julie would urge on their way to the bus stop, skirts swinging. 'Don't waste an afternoon in the damp! We're going to the pictures!' When I hear their bus depart, I close my eyes and conjure up foreign blooms and darting birds with coloured feathers that I copy from my imagination. Mother says it's unseemly to lust after what one can't have. Yet nature, whether real or imagined, is surely God's artwork? Even Mr Darwin might be prepared to agree.

'Excellent, Frances! Such diligence to record specimens in the rough. These sketches,' Mr Cadwaller flourished one to the class, 'show the challenge of working outdoors. Beware, young ladies! Rain will surely fall, sparrows will surely fly away! You will rarely have the luxury of time!'

'Now, Frances,' said Mr Cadwaller to me privately, 'shall we consider watercolours?'

I painted a line of cobalt blue at the top of the page and then lifted the paper vertically. Blue colour bled downwards like shards of rain. Or tears. I placed the paper flat, dipped my brush in the water and stroked it over the colour, lightening it, fading it. Too much water, though, and the effect became insipid; too little and the sky possessed a garishness that nature would never recognise. This wash of soft shades and meandering lines is the opposite of my precise flower drawings. The effect they create is like a dream, the blurry chase of a child in the garden.

Perhaps, one day, I'll be able to paint what I can't quite see.

'Mother?'

She looked up from her knitting.

'Did I have a brother? I see him in my dreams—'

Her face paled as readily as if I'd performed the same watercolour fade on her skin.

'It was a long time ago. I'd prefer not to talk about it, my dear.'

'But—'

She set aside her knitting, stood up and walked away to her bedroom. I flung down my brush, jumped up, ready to put my arms around her, but she closed the door behind her. I waited for a moment. I should have opened it, broken through her reserve. When I knocked an hour later she said she had a headache. I went outside and climbed the oak tree to the highest, most dangerous perch and looked towards the sea. Did anyone else know, apart from Mr Jacobs and our neighbours and extended family now keeping silent? Those neighbours, seeing me fall, must have feared that history might be about to repeat itself.

Mother will not allow me in, I wrote later.

She won't allow me to comfort her in her loss.

She doesn't realise that, in some strange way, I've lost someone, too.

I want to know the boy's name, and how he died. I would like to draw him. But I could ask nothing further because Mother emerged the following morning with her face powdered and her hair immaculate and her lips closed. I could almost understand if her withdrawal were a way to protect herself. How much, after all, could a mother weep before her heart ran dry?

I don't want to give away my love too easily either.

Mother and I may be more alike than I realise.

I began to paint pictures for the brother I never knew. Did he like bright colours? Roses in shades of yellow with a sweep of viridian green for their leaves; bougainvillea blossoms in indigo and rose madder. A navy swallow with a rufous throat and sleek wings made for thousands of miles of flight.

'My,' said Father, 'how bold, my dear. Mr Cadwaller will surely be impressed.'

Chapter Seven

I'm not regarded as a tree-climbing monkey any more.
Perhaps the outspokenness Mother tried to curb and
Father likes to applaud is refreshing for boys brought
up with girls who mostly giggle and agree with what
they say.

Or maybe it's because I read the papers more than
my friends. I know about Aboriginal tribes in Australia
and buildings in New York that are so tall they are
called skyscrapers.

I don't think the young men are interested in what I
know. Or in my painting.

I like to be with them. They're not as silly as girls,
Susan excepted.

When I turned seventeen I was invited to my first formal dance
by Brian Harris. Julie said he was a catch and if I ever tired of
him to let her know first. Brian was a tall boy with blond hair
that flopped over his forehead in an engaging way. Phyllis said
he'd inherit a tidy fortune from his solicitor father who, in his
spare time, bred horses that had won at Cheltenham.

'Lucky you!' chortled Sue as we pored over the invitation
in the privacy of my bedroom. 'Will you wear pink? They say

it's the colour of the season. With fringing on the hem, flapper style. A headband?'

'White or, at most, cream,' countered Mother over dinner. 'Demureness for your first outing, Frances! A plain slide in your hair. You don't want to appear worldly.'

Mother and I have said no more about my brother. Instead, she's taken up in my new-found popularity.

'I say,' exclaimed Brian when he fetched me in his father's motor car, 'the prettiest girl in town!'

'Only in town?'

He coloured, shot me a glance and then grinned. 'Alright then, prettiest in the world!'

'That's better,' I said, taking his arm and swinging my hips just a little, so that the tiny fringe Mother and I had compromised on could swish against my knees.

'No speeding, young man,' ordered Father, following us out to the motor car. He removed his watch from his waistcoat and tapped it. 'Back by ten-thirty, please.'

The hall was decked with paper flower garlands, the band played the latest American jazz, candles flickered on the tables and I danced all evening. Mostly with Brian, occasionally with other boys who cut in. Maybe it was the flapper dress? Whatever the reason, a string of admirers soon beat a path to our door. Mother insisted I should agree to their invitations in strict rotation.

'So you don't favour one over another. Not yet, at least.'

Mother believed a daughter who attracted widespread attention was an asset to be carefully managed.

'Who do you fancy?' whispered Susan, eyeing the crush. 'They're all crazy for you!'

The wooing accelerated when Brian invited me to watch

the arrival of the next mail ship along with his parents. Mother advised pink-and-cream stripes, and a cloche hat. I was on parade, as were all the ladies on the quay, some waiting for a loved one's return, others perhaps hoping to catch the eye of a foreign diamond magnate.

'You're fulfilling your talent, Frances,' Mr Cadwaller said, viewing my latest work: skeletal beech trees against a winter sky. 'Watercolours have added a new dimension.'

I stared out of the studio window. Brian Harris didn't see me as a true partner. If I was brave enough to wait, I might find someone who did, and if money happened to come in the same package, and the young man appreciated art . . .

'Frances?'

I was, I realised with a flash of guilt, making a calculation.

Mother had made it and it might suit me, too, but on my own terms.

'If I marry well, Mr Cadwaller, I'll have the freedom to continue with my art.'

'How so?'

'I'd have the means to ensure my family were well looked after – while I—'

He threw back his head and let out a giant guffaw. 'While you headed off and travelled the world and painted it? Come, come, Frances! I admire your strategy, but that will be a stretch! And if you don't find the paragon you're seeking? What then?'

'Then I shall stay single, sir. And I'll need my art to support me.'

'And your father? How would he feel if he were to know your plans?'

'I suspect he wouldn't be surprised, sir. Disconcerted,

perhaps, not surprised.'

But Father was recently too distracted to consider my burgeoning social life and was happy to leave the matter to Mother until a clear favourite emerged. I blamed Joseph Currie and Anthony Darby, who came to our house regularly, holding fat briefcases over their heads to shield themselves from the winter downpours as they ran from their motor cars to our front door.

'Won't you stay for drinks, gentlemen?' Mother would say when they emerged from the study after another lengthy conference.

'Thank you, no,' they would reply, and make the excuse of another engagement.

Mother was told that economies would have to be made in the running of the house.

'Just for a while,' Father said, affecting a nonchalant air. 'Nothing to worry about.'

I finished school top of my class and Mother proposed secretarial training if I insisted on an occupation before the leap into marriage. But rather than either of those, I joined Mr Cadwaller's evening classes: still-life drawing, watercolours, pencil sketches. 'Wise decision, Frances! Practise! Practise! That way lies mastery of technique!' If I made sufficient progress, he'd promised me an introduction to the Royal Botanic Garden's illustration section.

On the perimeter, a posse of young men vetted by Mother circled. I smiled and flirted and no one guessed my hesitation. Julie and Phyllis and Sue paired off with local boys and began planning summer weddings. All agreed that I, Frances, had bagged the best fellow. It was just a matter of the proposal and setting the date. Brian's family would buy us a house in Eastleigh and I would be taken up with producing a family and supporting my husband and occasionally drawing.

What more could Frances want, they asked themselves.

As my eighteenth birthday approached, the future was as clear as the colours in my paintbox.

The only clouds in my sky were ones I chose to conjure up myself.

Chapter Eight

'Good morning, Mr Whittington.' The secretary looked up. 'The partners are in the meeting room.'

'Thank you, Miss Fisk. Will you show my daughter to the spare office? It has a good view.'

'Of course, sir.'

I unpacked my small easel and set it up on the desk. The cathedral rose up, elbowing aside the smaller buildings around it. Brian was planning to take me up to its highest point for my birthday, chaperoned – only at a distance, hopefully – by his parents. I was certain he intended to propose and I still didn't know how I would respond.

That first critical glance, I told myself, remembering Mr Cadwaller's words.

I sharpened my coloured pencils.

A door further away opened and closed.

Draw what you see, Frances.

I picked up the grey pencil and began to sketch.

First the outline, the angles, then the great west façade emerging like a ship out of fog. The flying buttresses, just seen, the stained glass of the West Window, hinted at . . .

A door opened and voices swept out, talking over each

other, some shouting.

'There's no choice! We have to liquidate!'

Tiny jewel colours for the window segments, although I couldn't be sure without binoculars. Greyish-cream for the stone.

'How much are you exposed?'

A light blue for the sky, arcing overhead. Filaments of cloud.

'I warned you, gentlemen, but no one heeded me.'

'Everything.'

'It's all very well for you!'

'Surely not, Gerald—'

I glanced from the real cathedral to the copy and back again. Swiftly drawn lines, a bold cross-hatching of straight and diagonal, and the paper version had sprung to life! Yet within an hour the cloudy filaments might thicken into rain, veiling the sharp corners, smudging the bold lines—

'Fran?' Father peered in. His face was unusually flushed. 'We're going home, my dear.'

'So soon? A little longer, please Father?' I clipped up a fresh sheet. 'I must do one more!'

He shook his head. 'Another time. Gather your pencils, please.'

One of the men who may have been shouting earlier hurried by, ignoring Father as he stood in the doorway. Another came past more slowly and put a hand on Father's shoulder.

I stared at Father but he wouldn't meet my eyes. I folded my easel and packed my pencils into their tin.

Miss Fisk bent over her typewriter and didn't look up as we left.

'Read all about it,' shouted a paperboy on the corner as we motored home in silence. 'Big Crash!'

'Millions lost! Read all about it!'

Cloud dived over the hills and swallowed the cathedral.

'Splendid!' enthused Mr Cadwaller, when I showed him my sketch. 'Now try it with watercolours from the same vantage point – if your Father will allow you?'

'Have you heard?' Brian asked idly over tea, when the first whispers of collapsing shares began to circulate, 'there's been an issue on the New York Stock Exchange.' He shrugged, and took my hand and kissed it while my parents were speaking to Mr Jacobs in the garden. 'I don't think it's anything to worry about. Our family never took a big position in American stocks. What name,' he squeezed my fingers, 'shall we give our new filly? She's a beauty, and I have naming rights. I rather fancy Chestnut Delight.'

'I think my father may have some American shares,' I said, slowly, watching Father with Jacobs.

'Well, I hope he's covered against a loss. How about Fran's Fancy?'

The word blowing from New York to London to Winchester to Embury was that no one could have seen the Crash coming. Certainly, those besuited men striding jauntily down Wall Street between the skyscrapers one morning, and then slinking home with the contents of their desks in cardboard boxes in the afternoon, hadn't seen it coming: the ticker tape chattering madly, stock prices tumbling, fortunes dissipating like smoke in the unforgiving air. The newspapers with their shouted headlines were wise after the event, but there'd been no warnings in the paper that thudded into our postbox every day. And no warning from Father that such misfortune might cross an ocean.

'How much have we lost, Father?'

Mother was at church. Would our village Jesus see the Crash as born of usury? Or simply bad luck—

'How much, Father?'

He met my eyes reluctantly. 'A great deal, I'm afraid.'

'But we must have some money left!' I stared around the study: the walnut desk, the brass paperweight, the evidence of a successful life that surely couldn't vanish and leave behind no crumbs. Father was, after all, no longer a coming man. He'd arrived.

'Not enough, my dear.'

'Did you put it all in one basket?' I tried not to shout. 'That's what you warned me about! You said it was foolish to put all your assets in one place!'

Spread the risk, he'd insisted. That way you'll never be caught, or lose the power to shape your future.

'I'm sorry, Fran. More than I can say.'

'The railway shares? That paid for this house? For my art lessons?'

'Largely worthless, I'm afraid.'

Choof, choof! I'd shouted as a child, about the magic power of those shares.

'What will we do, Father?'

'We'll economise further. Cut our cloth more simply. Move to a smaller property.'

I grabbed the curtains that framed the window. While I might secretly long to go further afield, or ignore the young man who was the best catch, this place was my inheritance. Look, Father had proclaimed from the oak, one day it'll be yours.

'I'm so sorry, my dear.' He took his watch from his waistcoat pocket, put it back without looking at its face, then took it out again. 'We'll have to sell.'

The clouds parted, and a weak sun broke through.

The oak stood tall and impassive, soon to belong to someone else.

'If other people have been equally affected, Father, then we won't get the price we deserve.'

Father didn't reply but came over and put his arm around me. We stared at the garden.

'I had a brother,' I whispered. 'Here. In this house. We'll lose him, too.'

Father lifted a thin hand to cover his eyes. 'Not now, please, Frances. And never with your mother.'

Briefly, to my diary.

Father, so careful not to trust powerful men blindly, or take chances . . .

I once believed he was as wise in real life as he was in his advice about it.

I was wrong. He never followed his own teaching.

And not only for ourselves: Aunt Rosemary, from Exeter, refuses to forgive him for losing part of her fortune. She's withdrawn her remaining savings from her account, keeps the notes under her mattress and has ignored Father's telephone calls for weeks.

Mother is devastated on my behalf. She berates herself that she didn't hurry my romance. Have I lost my chance? Surely Brian will not back away.

But is this crisis pushing me in a direction I never wanted to go? Is money and a settled status enough – without love and partnership?

* * *

50

The Crash, it turned out, was another kind of fall. A fresh sharpening.

It came about not from my own distraction – or a sneaking desire for danger – but from a crisis over which I had no control. Our house was put up for sale and bought at a knock-down price by a man wanting to move from his terrace row. We could have waited for a higher price but Father wasn't sure we'd have done any better given the number of properties newly on the market.

'Sometimes it's best to take a loss and move on,' he said to me, out of earshot of Mother, 'rather than advertise your situation by hanging on for a buyer who may not come.' Rather accept an offer now, than wait for one that will not come.

But I was no longer in demand. A talent for conversation, titian hair and a slim ankle beneath a flapper frock were not, it appeared, enough to compensate for a lack of fortune or a reasonable standing in the community. My eighteenth birthday came and went without public celebration or a trip to Winchester Cathedral with Brian and the expected proposal. He stopped calling altogether. Susan said it proved he wasn't worth it, but then she hugged her own beau, Peter, and fingered her engagement ring. I was even delicately shunned in my art classes, which I'd cut from daily to weekly to save Father the expense. 'Shame,' I overheard Susan Currie say without regret, 'she won't get any further, now.'

The newspapers began to show hard, industrial images.

'Don't look away, Frances!' Mr Cadwaller urged. 'Express yourself in art!'

I copied the pictures in grey pencil: families queueing at soup kitchens or outside silent mills; men and women scrambling over mine waste dumps for stray pieces of coal to heat their homes. Yet my fingers misbehaved. Lines wavered or became unaccountably jagged, sketches lost their accuracy and I tore up more than I kept. Mother saw my struggle and said nothing. She didn't embrace me or murmur that she was sorry my romance had died, that life dealt blows that were not always fair. Instead she looked away from my latest failed picture, quietly left the room and closed the door behind her as she'd done before. Perhaps that was the only way she knew.

I took to coming downstairs early every morning to see Father before he left the house.

'Where is it today?' I asked on one occasion as he set off in the grey dawn wearing his best tweed suit.

'To the bus station, Frances.' He forced a smile. 'For Southampton. The mail ship.'

He kissed me and let himself out quietly. Our motor car had been sold so it had to be the bus – in fact, several buses. I willed the new arrivals to notice Father's smile and raised hat, and accept his offer of accounting services, assistance with housing, tax representation . . .

If we'd lived in a big city our plight might have been less visible but in a small village like Embury, any reduction in circumstances stood out. Father was no longer considered as having arrived and we, his family, retreated with him. While the neighbours watched – the Atkinses, the Fergusons, the Hodgsons – we moved to a terraced house with no outlook, no roses for Mr Jacobs to prune – even if we could have managed to keep him on. For Mother, it was the worst outcome. Our home had been her version of the oak tree, her vantage point over village society.

I watched her face as we left, the mechanical smile above the carefully ironed blouse, and caught her final rearwards glance from the taxi. It would have been easier if we'd made a complete break, to a place where no one knew our background. But I suspect Mother didn't want to go far away.

I know why.

I've not dreamt of my brother since we moved.

He's gone and I'm oddly lost without him. For Mother, it must be close to a betrayal, an abandonment of her son, the grass he ran over, the sound of his voice on the stairs.

My parents sit in our cramped lounge in the evening and say little. Father's forays to Southampton and his tireless local trawling have produced nothing in return. He won't be able to support me if I don't marry. And no one wants me.

Even though I'm struggling to draw, I sometimes feel I'm the only one thinking clearly.

Capture the moment . . .

'Father? I have an idea.'

Chapter Nine

Have you ever seized a dream? I asked my diary, in the hope it might answer back, one friend to another, and give me guidance.

> *And is it wrong – unseemly – to turn a crisis into an opportunity?*
> *Because I see one and I want to grasp it.*
> *Fresh colours on my palette, new scents on my nose . . .*

'You can't go all that way on your own, Frances! Tell her, Gerald! It's out of the question!' Mother swept a hand across her un-coiffed hair.

From outside came the clatter of bins. Our too-close neighbours clattered bins night and day with no regard to the disturbance. And they showed no particular respect towards Mother.

'It's an option,' said Father, with an appraising rub of his beard. I've noticed that Father is careful not to contradict Mother outright. He's failed her and therefore has no right to assume his views should be trusted or take precedence. I'm starting to appreciate that marriage is a tricky two-step. You must yield to the music and your partner – but also to the history between you.

'You've always said Aunt Mary needed a companion, Father,' I went on. 'I can be that person.'

Once a year we received a picture postcard of the Cape, showing rearing mountains or strange flowers – I copied one – and a peremptory message asking why, with Gerald's means, he'd yet to bring his family to visit. Hurry up, tardy brother! None of us is getting any younger.

'The only question,' I leant forward, 'is whether we can afford the fare. I'd go third class.'

'Third class!' Mother gasped. 'You will not! And nothing has been decided yet!'

'Emily,' Father murmured, reaching out a hand to her. 'Please. It is worth discussing.'

I waited in the chair opposite. The second sofa had been sold. We could only host two visitors at a time.

'What will we do, Gerald, without Frances?'

The words burst out of Mother as if they'd been held, mutely, for too long. I felt a chill around my heart. There were matters here that touched me but were not mine to resolve.

Is there so little left between them that I am the necessary glue? I wrote later in my diary.

I jumped up and went over to Mother and wrapped my arms around her. 'You have Father,' I murmured against her hair, 'and your friends. And the church. Mother,' I disengaged gently, 'please look at me.'

Her eyes were dry but red-rimmed.

'This is my chance. Don't you see, Mother? If you wish me to marry, my prospects are better there than here. No one will know my circumstances. It'll be a fresh start.'

Her grey eyes roamed over my face, like the way she'd

looked at me while fingering my bloody cardigan after the fall, as if she couldn't believe I was her child and had done something so unlike her.

'I will always be your daughter, Mother. You will always have me.'

As with the sale of the house, events moved fast. Father wrote to his sister and received a telegrammed reply.

DELIGHTED HAVE FRANCES STOP SEND HARRODS TEA STOP
MARY

Mother held her head up around the village and made out that the opportunity for Frances had come out of the blue and was in no way an act of rescue or desperation.

'Fancy that,' said Mrs Atkins with a quick glance at Mother's deportment. 'A benefactor!'

Mrs Ferguson said the colonies were exciting but surely ungodly places for a susceptible girl. It was as well that Gerald had respectable family abroad to protect her from temptation.

While I packed up my paints and pencils, Mother threw herself into preparations for my modest wardrobe: light dresses plus a wrap to protect me from the sea breezes; two hats of varying brim size to be worn in response to the ferocity of the elements; two pairs of silk stockings to be reserved for dinner at the captain's table – should I be so fortunate as to be chosen – or for the horse races in Cape Town, should I be invited. Father bought an outbound second-class ticket, a brass-cornered trunk, and, pressed by Mother, found a Scottish missionary and his wife to be chaperones.

'But I might find a millionaire, Mother, returning to his gold mines!'

'Don't be flippant, Frances. Reverend Campbell will take his responsibilities seriously.'

The attitude of my friends began to change. I was now the object of casual curiosity and even a measure of grudging envy, though Phyllis made sure to mention how savage I would find my destination. 'Those Boer farmers,' she observed, 'are hardly civilised.'

'But how do you know? You've never been there!'

She added that Africa would ruin my complexion and dry out my hair if I forgot to wear a hat and veil.

'Africa!' Sue whispered. 'When will I see you again?'

Mr Cadwaller viewed my emigration as a career move.

'Frances,' he leant towards me, 'I insist you send me new work! I have connections at Kew, as you know.'

'I will. And thank you, sir. This is for you.'

I laid in front of him a watercolour painting.

An oak. Dark-boughed, green-leaved, reaching into a pale sky. And clinging to the trunk – if you looked closely – a woodpecker.

'Thirteen thousand tons!' shouted Father at the Union-Castle Royal Mail Steamer, *Edinburgh Castle*.

Mother clung to my arm. My leaving has unleashed the fugitive warmth she's kept in check all my life.

'You'll be able to draw, Frances,' she murmured, 'wherever you go—'

'All aboard! All aboard, I say!' Smartly dressed officers chivvied the crowds.

I embraced my parents, kept a firm grip on my case – the

brass-cornered trunk was already on board – and stepped onto the gangplank.

'Wave your scarf!' Father called. 'We'll see you!'

I found my small cabin – to be shared, it turned out, with a quiet nun who prayed nightly for us both – deposited my case, hurried on deck and elbowed my way to a space at the rail. A tapestry of coloured streamers drifted down to the quayside. Hands reached up and grabbed for them. I flung mine over the side and watched it unfurl. Somewhere, a band was playing and snatches of a march, eddied through the shouts of fellow passengers. The ship's horn sounded, long and deep. Smoke curled from the funnel and the deck thrummed beneath my feet as the ship began to ease away from the quay. The streamers stretched, went taut, then snapped, their ends fluttering into the sea, the link between ship and shore severed. Another boom from the horn. I waved again, for the joy of it.

'Frances!' Reverend Campbell fought his way to my side, excusing himself to left and right. 'Do not be sad, my dear. A great adventure is in store.'

'I'm not sad, Reverend! I can't wait!'

He lifted a conservative Scottish eyebrow. 'We are always available for spiritual guidance.'

It seemed a young woman going abroad was forever deemed to be at risk of falling into sinful ways. Our vicar had been of a similar mind. 'Let Jesus,' he pointed to the Cross, 'be your compass, Frances, in an alien land. Do not be tempted by false prophets. Or unseemly materialism.'

The rhythm of the ship changed.

I craned over the side to see a wave curving against the graceful hull. The reverend lifted his hat and went to find his wife. The crowd drifted away. I leant on the rail and laughed out loud at the expanse of sky and wheeling seagulls, the qualms of the clergy . . . and the irony of a young woman setting out on a journey she would never have undertaken if her father had retained his fortune.

Southampton faded to a smudge.

A coal barge chugged past in the opposite direction under a balloon of smoke.

A crewman waved.

I waved back.

The air blew cool against my cheek, and I fancied I smelt the first heady scent of freedom.

Chapter Ten

I didn't expect to find such inspiration in the ocean, its colour and mood, its infinite vastness – nothing like the fickle streams I battled to capture as a novice. While my fellow passengers played deck quoits or lay in the sun with their eyes closed, I painted: the sea at dawn in shades of blue-rose, the sea at midday in blinding turquoise, the sea at dusk in silver and grey. Sometimes rocky islets appeared to break up the expanse of it, and gulls dived into its midst, but mostly it stretched from horizon to horizon, oblivious of our passage.

Freckles are appearing on my nose despite Mother's generously brimmed hats.

A few of the young men have tried their luck and I've danced with them, or taken tea, but I prefer to paint. The reverend and his wife have little to do other than keep a distant lookout. When we reach the Cape I shall borrow Aunt Mary's status to find a social circle – and admit to no misfortune back home.

'Are you a professional, madam?' a gentleman asked one day after we'd crossed the equator in a riot of high jinks. I see him most days when I'm painting my dawn pictures. He tips his hat to me as he passes on his morning constitutional. This is the first time he's addressed me. 'Do you sell your work?'

'Not yet, sir,' I laughed. 'Soon, I hope.'

He reached into his waistcoat pocket and withdrew a card and handed it to me. 'A very good morning.' He lifted his hat and continued on his way.

I fingered the card.

A. R. J. COMPTON.
KIRSTENBOSCH.

The captain encouraged us to rise early for the arrival into Cape Town.

It was still grey as I stepped on deck with a blanket wrapped around my disembarkation clothes, and set up my small easel near the bow, and waited.

How will it be? I'd written before I packed away my diary.

Is the vicar correct to call this place alien?

Will this be where my art becomes my career?

Might I discover love, perhaps, as well? The kind that will make me catch my breath?

So many questions . . .

Today there were languid swells. Yesterday, a chop of white water that I strained to copy. Brightening stained the east. Other passengers were coming on deck, now. They smiled and nodded.

There! A black ridge resolved itself against a slowly flushing sky. At first it was only an outline: the top of the famous Table, ruler-straight; two peaks, sentinel-like, at either end. The wind rose and foam began to whip off the tops of the swells. The ship's funnels caught the brightening light. I clipped up a fresh sheet. This time, a notch in the flat table, some kind of gorge.

61

And the left-hand outrider was bulky, while the right-hand one actually consisted of two peaks, the front one a low hill, the rear one looming above it in the shape of an upturned V.

'May I call on you, Miss Whittington?' A young man called Phillip Edwards, in a striped jacket, hovered over me. He'd escorted me to the Crossing the Line ceremony at the equator.

'Maybe,' I smiled. 'You'll have to find me, first.'

I've told no one my exact final destination. I could even stay on board, give my chaperones the slip, head up the coast to one of the other cities. I have a little money of my own, passed to me by Mother . . .

The city came into focus, shining beneath the famous mountain. But Aunt Mary would be waiting. And a house called Protea Rise. My fresh start.

Ropes snaked over the side as the *Edinburgh Castle* was nudged by a pair of tugs towards its mooring. A band on the quayside struck up a brisk version of 'Rule Britannia' that waxed and waned in the lively breeze. I felt the heat burn on my skin. And the light! Dancing on the water, glancing off the white buildings at the end of the pier, picking out the grey strata of the soaring mountain.

Whoever arranged for a mountain in the midst of a city?

'Good luck, Frances!' My pious nun offered her hand. 'Put your faith in the Lord.'

We lower-deckers waited while first-class passengers filed down the gangplank. Most of the men wore formal suits and bow ties, and carried furled umbrellas despite clear sky and significant heat. I struggled not to giggle. Yet perhaps it bore out Mother's insistence about the link between accessories and status. 'Look!' shouted a girl alongside me. A sailor was leading an Irish wolfhound down the gangplank. Behind the hound, several gentlemen hovered as if loath to leave the sanctuary of the ship. Maybe, I speculated from my lesser queue, they were well-dressed fugitives from the law, worried they might be arrested. For their part, the disembarking ladies were clad as if for Ascot, one with a hat of teetering ostrich feathers. Children in smocked dresses or sailor suits followed them, shepherded by nannies. 'It's flat,' one boy cried, pointing at the mountain. 'Flat as a pancake!'

I fixed my simple hat hard onto my head, hefted my suitcase and stepped down the gangplank.

An impatient crowd shouted and surged against the roped walkway that led to the immigration building.

'Millicent, over here!'

'Joseph!'

'Mother dear!'

'Grandfather!'

The band swung into a boisterous version of 'Roll Out the Barrel'.

'Taxi? Best taxi service!' a brown man yelled, waving a carboard placard. The call was taken up by several other vendors, also with handmade signs.

'Best price hotel! Quiet rooms! Car to the station!'

A barefoot urchin ducked under the rope and brandished a newspaper in my face. '*Argus*!'

Under the onslaught, ladies clutched at their handbags for security, and at their hats to prevent them cartwheeling into the water. From further along the quay came a squeal of brakes as the mail ship train drew into its siding, ready to take passengers onwards to the diamond fields of Kimberley and the gold mines of the Witwatersrand, where fortunes could be made, according to Father, from a single nugget.

I struggled forward with my case. The Irish wolfhound was barking in the distance. How had the owners exercised it? Many circuits of the first-class deck every morning?

'Anything to declare?' asked a harried official. 'No? Welcome to Cape Town. Move along, please.'

My trunk would be delivered the following day to my Aunt's address.

We were decanted directly into the waiting crowd, made distinct by the pastel dresses of the ladies, and the range of skins from palest white to darkest black. I glanced back at the ship for a moment. Poorer passengers were now disembarking. They were dressed in dull, serviceable colours that wouldn't require much washing on a long voyage, and there were far fewer shouts of recognition as they stepped ashore. I felt a lick of shame. They were much braver than me.

I turned back to the crowd and searched for an elderly lady, resembling Father . . .

'Frances Whittington!' an imperious voice called. A cane waved at me. 'Over here!'

Chapter Eleven

I shall never forget my first view of Protea Rise. Not just because I wanted to paint it straight away but because the place felt, inexplicably, like home.

A home I'd never visited before.

Is that possible?

'It isn't classic Cape Dutch style,' said Aunt Mary Donnelly, with a casual wave at several elaborate mansions as we drove into the leafy suburbs. 'Only a vestige of a gable and too many other influences. English formality, a soupçon of French Huguenot, even a nod to Irish cottage simplicity. Not classic at all. But frankly, who cares?'

This eccentricity was initially a concern for Uncle, she later acknowledged. He was looking for a solid investment. But Aunt was charmed by the place and – she winked – their relationship was at the point where it was important to be seen to be open to wifely suggestion. I could see what she meant as we approached the front of a rambling house, its green shutters set open against plain white walls and its thatched roof perched atop the structure like some extravagant, prickly icing on a cake. But who cared, indeed, when the property more than held its own by virtue of its setting. A vast mountain cliff reared opposite – Fernwood Buttress, waved Aunt – flanked by lesser peaks leading off on one side towards Devil's Peak, one of the outriders I'd sketched on board ship. Determined not to be overlooked, a colourful garden rioted around the house, stuffed with an array of plants I'd never seen. It was surely the most beautiful of eccentric properties.

'Thank you, Samuel.' Aunt Mary climbed out of the car. 'We will not need you further today.'

The black man tipped his cap and carried my suitcase to the door.

In the same way that Protea Rise overturned tradition, so too did its owner. Years at the Cape had weathered Aunt Mary's complexion to more teak than rose, and below her ankle-length dress of blue cotton she wore sturdy lace-up boots that might have tackled Fernwood Buttress in her younger years. Mother would have been scandalised. Aunt's hair was white and pulled off her face into a simple bun, her eyes had a glint that reminded me of Father and she had no truck with fools. She'd kissed me briefly at the docks, leant back, looked me up and down and pronounced that I was my father's daughter, but hopefully more sensible when it came to investments.

'Come along,' she'd brandished her walking cane, 'let's depart. My driver has the motor nearby. I do not drive. Perhaps,' she looked back at me, 'you should learn?'

As we drove around the side of Table Mountain I kept quiet – Aunt, clearly, did not appreciate gush – though I ached to ask the driver to stop so I could grab my pencils . . . that first impression . . .

'Your father says your young man ditched you?'

'Yes.' I turned from the window. 'I was no longer a catch.'

'Good riddance, I say. So, what are your intentions here, apart from being my companion?'

'I'm an artist.' I hesitated, then plunged, as I'd done with Cadwaller. 'I want to make it my career.'

'Excellent. You need something to fall back on when I trundle into the sunset.'

I stared at her. She smiled and patted my hand.

'No intention of doing so just yet. But it's as well to be prepared, wouldn't you say?'

'What are my duties, Aunt?' I asked later over tea at Protea Rise, brought by a smiling brown lady called Violet, and consisting of leaf tea – I'd handed over the Harrods package – and buttered bread cut into triangles and topped with a fruit jam, the taste of which I did not recognise.

'You shall read to me in the mornings, and undertake small chores. Dickens, some Shakespeare. Once you're settled, you might help Violet with the menus. And take over my diary and arrange visits to acquaintances. Your afternoons are free.' She fixed me with a sharp glance. 'But I don't hold with idleness, Frances.'

'I shall draw and paint in the afternoons.'

'Very well. I expect to see your work from time to time. Now,' she got to her feet slowly, 'I shall rest after that kerfuffle at the docks. Lunch is at 1 p.m. and dinner at six-thirty sharp.'

A piping call came from the garden. I left my unpacking, lifted the sash window and climbed outside. A patio ran the length of the house, valiantly holding back shrubs that had spilt beyond their casual borders, some of their blooms petalled, others composed of pin-like tendrils. There was a tree with strokable silver leaves and shiny cones lodged in its branches.

The piping call gave way to a chattering – what sort of bird – I craned upwards—

'You like flowers, miss?' Violet was seated on a rock in the shade, with a sandwich from our tea.

'I do. But I don't know any of these.' I pointed around the garden.

'They're pincushions, Miss Frances. They live on the mountain. Alfius, the gardener, planted them.'

Thin cloud drifted over the mountain cliff. The rock softened as if beneath gauze.

How will I capture such shifting splendour?

'We had a gardener in England. Mr Jacobs. He used to speak to the plants.'

She stared at me and I wondered if I'd disconcerted her. Are the locals godly or do they worship magic? I could offend without realising.

'Miss will like Alfius,' she smiled. 'He talks to the garden all the time.'

'Thank you, Violet.'

I glanced back at my sash window and returned to the house via the patio door.

Over dinner – unsure of the protocol, I changed into a long-sleeved dress in pink and received an approving nod – Aunt announced that she'd taken the liberty of making connections for me with the better families in the area and that a Miss Daphne Phillips, daughter of a friend of her late husband, would be calling on me the following afternoon.

'You can take outings with the Phillipses. They go swimming, I believe, in the summer. And Daphne will introduce you to her circle. She's a dizzy girl at times, but means well.'

'I love swimming. Father used to take me to the coast in the summer. And I don't mind dizziness.'

Aunt regarded me for a moment. She doesn't know me yet, so she can't be sure of my humour.

Daphne Phillips turned out to be a pretty brunette with a smart line in bias-cut dresses. She arrived with her father, a barrel-chested man who, Aunt murmured to me in advance, had grown fat on mining profits since the Boer War.

'So this is Frances!' Mr Phillips boomed. 'Come to find a husband in the colonies, my dear?'

'Father!' Daphne blushed and shot him a furious glance.

'Not at all,' I replied. 'I'm here to be a companion to my aunt. And to further my career as an artist.'

'Well said, Frances.' Aunt frowned at Phillips. 'Careers are not the sole preserve of men, Stephen. Women have also earnt the right to vote, sir, in case you've forgotten.'

'Indeed, Mary. How remiss of me.' He took a bite from a slice of Violet's chocolate cake. 'But you've come at a difficult time, Frances. The Union hasn't been spared from the Crash. There's less money about, so you may find it hard to attract patrons.'

'I'd be grateful for your introductions.' I smiled at them both. 'I know it will take time.'

I will not reveal Father's losses; neither will I reveal that I have yet to sell a single work.

'You really are an artist?' Daphne asked after we left Aunt and Mr Phillips to spar and repaired to my bedroom. 'I can't draw for toffee.'

'You can pick one to keep, if you like.' I spread out a few paintings from my on-board portfolio.

'You mean that? Shouldn't I pay you? If this is to be your career?'

'You could be my promoter, Daphne. If you like my work, you can tell others.'

She glanced at me shyly. 'Mother heard you'd come because of a disappointing love affair.'

'Can you keep a secret?' Surely she couldn't. That might be helpful to me. 'I didn't want to marry the boy who was keen on me. I decided to break away.'

It was a lie. Or was it? Anyway, it was necessary to forestall any pity.

'You're so brave.' She chose a painting of the Bay of Biscay. Grey water. Charcoal-tipped cloud. 'It's beautiful,' she hesitated, 'and a little frightening.'

You're a little frightening, she meant. Tossing aside a suitor. Taking to the high seas. Starting afresh.

'Please take it, Daphne – if it's not too unnerving.' I smiled. 'In appreciation for showing me around.'

'You can call me Daph. All my friends do.'

Dear Mother and Father

I am safely in Cape Town in Aunt's wonderful, eccentric mansion.

There is more here for me to paint than I can possibly manage even if I worked every day for a year!

I met Daphne Phillips, who will introduce me to her set. Cape Town seems about the same size as Southampton but more spread out. I'm working on the geography. Daph often asks me to point in the direction of Table Bay or Hout Bay, say, and you'd imagine it would be easy but it isn't with a peninsula. Only after I realised that Table Mountain faces north, did I get my bearings.

The population of the Cape is mixed. There are those

called Coloured, and some called Malay, descended from slaves brought here in the past. Some even have Chinese features. The black people are the strongest and they undertake the heaviest work. I imagine it must be hard managing such a disparate country. The Argus newspaper reports disagreements over pay to workers of different colours. South Africa seems like a beautiful, volatile jigsaw. You discover, and add, one piece at a time. The final picture is a mystery until the end.

I've been invited to the Races with the Phillipses. My low-waisters are still suitable, Mother, but I'll need to order one or two brighter frocks with my first earnings. Aunt Mary is sharp-tongued but kind.

I think I can be happy here. Thank you for letting me go, Mother.

All my love

Fran

Chapter Twelve

As with the geography of the peninsula, I need to find my botanical bearings. *Leucospermum cordifolium*, a shrub with orange-tendrilled blooms, grows outside my bedroom window. It is known as a pincushion protea. The silver tree I saw on my first day is also a protea, but in a group known as conebushes. Then there are proteas with grey beards and proteas with white flowers and proteas with nodding heads that hug the ground . . .

'Frances?'

Chatter drifted through the open windows. Sugarbirds, the gardener Alfius, had informed me. 'They suck nectar from the proteas, ma'am, when they aren't talking. See how their beaks are shaped?'

'Frances?'

'I'm sorry.' I focussed on the book in my hand. Aunt had requested Shakespeare's sonnets.

'Let me not to the marriage of true minds admit impediments,' I began.

Aunt is canny. This may be a message to me to find a young man who will love me for myself.

'Love is not love which alters when it alteration finds. Or

bends with the remover to remove.'

Or perhaps this is for her. A tribute to the husband lost here, in Africa.

'It is the star to every wand'ring bark.'

Aunt pressed her fingers to her eyes. I thought of Mother and her grief for her son – the brother I'd never met. I waited. The newly familiar chatter echoed from the garden once more. Extravagantly tailed males, modestly plumed females – nature's impish division between the sexes.

'Do you know about the Boer War, Frances?' Aunt lowered her fingers. 'Did they teach you in school? The dastardly Boers, the heroic English? The triumphs and the betrayals? You'll hear different opinions in this country, my dear. Best to keep a closed mouth and an open mind.'

'Father has a poster of Kitchener on his wall. He says it's a reminder to hold powerful men to account, whichever side they're on. To be wary of following blindly.'

'Indeed. A valuable lesson.' She touched a heavy gold ring on her left hand.

'I'm so sorry for your loss, Aunt Mary.'

'Thank you, Frances. Never give all of your heart away. Retain some for yourself. Shall we continue?'

The Kelvin Grove Club, according to Aunt, was the most prestigious club at the Cape and the best place to launch an arrival. It commanded spacious grounds overlooked by Devil's Peak mountain.

Why did it get that name? I wrote in my diary afterwards.

There is so much here that I don't know – quite aside from the myriad proteas.

This place looks and sounds English . . . but I sense

conflicting forces.

A hard segment that wants nothing to do with the home country.

'An Afternoon Tea to welcome Miss Frances Whittington of Hampshire, England, to Cape Town,' the invitation on stiff card had said. 'RSVP Mrs Mary Donnelly, Protea Rise, Bishopscourt, Cape Town.'

Oak trees lined the driveway. I sized them up for climbability.

No, Frances!

The wife of the deputy governor general headed the guest list, flanked by the wives and daughters of other dominion high-ups and the acquaintances of Daphne Phillips's family who represented the burgeoning business community. Regarding dress, the mature ladies wore flowered costumes and a variety of hats ranging from saucer to cloche. Their daughters wore tea dresses and heeled sandals. The waiters wore buttoned suits and mirror-polished shoes, and carried napkins over their arms.

'The cream of young Cape womanhood,' observed Aunt Mary. 'Keen to meet the new competition.'

'Aunt!'

'Forgive me, Frances, but these young ladies are intent upon marriage. They will want to see if you could distract their intendeds. As,' she cast an approving glance over my pink-and-cream stripes and my hair held back by a pair of tortoiseshell combs, 'you most certainly could.'

'Don't bother with the dominion girls,' whispered Daph, 'they're never here long enough. This is Mary Clough,' she guided me to a tiny girl in navy and white spots. 'She's a student teacher.'

'Hello,' the little one said. 'I heard you like to swim?'

Tea was poured from silver teapots, and the napkinned waiters offered trays of cucumber sandwiches and slices of Victoria sponge. The event was as proper as I imagine a tea would be at Buckingham Palace – except for the dark-skinned staff.

'How is the weather in Hampshire?' asked an elderly lady. 'I heard last year was unbearably wet.'

'It was,' I replied. 'We had some local flooding. The Itchen broke its banks.'

'I love the way you talk,' said a girl with a strong local accent. 'My father wants me to take lessons.'

'Is it true the Prince of Wales can dance the Charleston?' asked Penelope Chisholm.

'I believe you sing?' This from a matriarch with a lorgnette. 'We need more sopranos.'

'No, I'm afraid I don't. I draw and paint.'

'Pity.'

'Why, how do you do, Miss Whittington. Welcome to the Cape. Do you ride?'

They assume I come from a privileged background. They believe I'm here to do a little light minding of my aunt before settling down. No one knows the truth, or if they do, they're keeping quiet. Or perhaps they are used to precarious fortunes in Africa.

'Reverend, this is my niece, Frances Whittington, newly arrived from England,' said Aunt Mary on my first attendance to St John's Church in Wynberg, where I recognise some of the girls from the Kelvin Grove. They nod and smile and, if Aunt is correct, they wonder who I'll set my cap at.

'I hope you'll introduce Frances to your young flock.'

'Why, certainly,' replied the reverend, a short man with a rolling gait. 'It just so happens we're having a walk this coming Saturday. Would you care to join us?'

'Thank you, yes. Where do you walk, Reverend? You must be spoilt for choice.'

'We are! This time it's Skeleton Gorge. Meet us at the main gate.'

'The main gate?'

'Kirstenbosch,' said the reverend. '8 a.m. Don't forget to bring a hat, Miss Whittington.'

He moved on down the line of parishioners.

Kirstenbosch.

The name on the card given to me by the man on the *Edinburgh Castle*.

And the place I happened to walk to on my first free afternoon, having seen its grassed slopes from the lower branch of a tree I surreptitiously climbed at Protea Rise. Almost as famous as Kew, Aunt said.

I found shade beneath an arching shrub, fell down on the grass, pulled out my sketchbook and began to draw. A brilliant, miniature bird with iridescent red and green feathers; the backdrop of forested mountains; stands of tree proteas. The heat rose. I wiped my neck and continued. My fingers trembled, not with fear but with greed.

Later, from Aunt's reference book on Cape flora, I identified some of what I'd drawn and felt a secret triumph: *Protea nitida*, a stocky, gnarled tree bearing dried, spiky blooms, contrasting with *Protea repens*, a rambler adorned with thin, pink flowers; all part of the *fynbos*, a collective term for the fine-leaved plants of the paradise kingdom into which I'd tumbled.

And, ornithologically, a handsome double-collared sunbird.

The place seduced me again when I joined the reverend's group.

'Frances Whittington, fresh off the mail ship!' the reverend announced before he and his assistant, Father Ben, led us up Skeleton Gorge between towering yellow-wood trees and mounds of creamy lilies called arums. I touched their waxy petals, ran my fingers along their strappy leaves.

'Look!' Father Ben pointed out a dassie, a lazy, rattish creature basking in the sun.

Silver trees tossed their heads against the sky like attenuated angels. My sinews strained and my heart pounded, not just with the effort but with an overwhelming, joyous relief.

I can be happy here, I'd boldly written to Mother before I knew if it would actually be true.

We stopped at a stream and I followed the rest in cupping the chilly water in my hands and drinking it.

'Purest water in the world!' shouted Father Ben. 'Direct from heaven!'

The group laughed and I warmed to them. Perhaps they also preferred their God outdoors.

'Not far to go!' the reverend mopped his forehead with a handkerchief as we set off again.

Flocks of white-eyed birds swerved through the forest. We pressed ever upwards.

'Can I call on you?' panted Jonathan Pringle, a serious young man reading chemistry at university.

And then the land fell away and we were at the top, easily the highest vantage point of my life. Blue-grey mountains stretched in a jagged spine to the far southerly tip of Cape Point. Treed suburbs graced the foothills;

cupped lakes filled their hollows.

'False Bay.' A girl called Doris pointed to a distant, glittering sweep of sea.

'See the Hottentots Holland mountains?' Jonathan came to stand at my side. 'Far away to the east?'

I was so close to the cliff edge I could feel updraughts in my face.

'Careful, Frances!' Father Ben called.

While the others ate their sandwiches, I pulled out my sketchbook and drew as fast as possible, before anything could escape. The rocks painted with lichen. The arum lilies. The trees draped with what looked like stringy cotton wool. 'Old man's beard,' said the reverend, looking over my shoulder.

Capture the moment – a darting white-eye, a silver protea – fix it in your mind, draw it just so, as Mr Cadwaller once advised.

I have found a hiding place for my diary.

Chapter Thirteen

I've been here for three months.

It feels longer because I find myself deeply at home, especially at Protea Rise.

I yearned for a destination like this from the branches of the English oak, but I never expected it to be so glorious. I've even dreamt of my brother, beckoning me through the riotous garden, and I'm relieved.

I don't want to forget him.

I want him to be part of this future, too.

I wrote to Sue, but it's hard to convey the spectacle without seeming to gloat.

Aunt is a fair employer, tolerant of the young men who call on me, for it appears, once again, that I am popular. Jonathan Pringle is keen. But I don't fall for the early enthusiasts. I know my popularity may not outlast the discovery that I'm actually a poor girl, albeit with a cut-glass accent and good manners.

The Crash apparently claimed victims here, too.

It's just not so obvious amid the splendour, which is free.

Daphne was wearing a new pale blue swimsuit and a matching frilly cap. A gentle southerly breeze met our faces as we got out of her father's motor car at Muizenberg. Children were flying kites along the shore, their colourful, triangular faces dancing in the air, taking me back to the kites I'd drawn for Susan.

'Be careful, girls!' Mr Phillips called as we ran towards the water. 'Not too far, Frances!'

Father used to shout at me in a similar fashion when I fancied I could swim all the way to the Isle of Wight. But African sea is wholly different. I ducked my head under and felt the cool shock of it on my scalp and the tug of its foreign currents. 'Daph! Come on!' I swivelled, treading water, and waved to her in the shallows where several younger children were playing. A swell lifted me with a cushioning surge and deposited me into the following trough. The wave rode towards the beach, gaining height as it approached the shore and broke in a welter of foam.

I struck out into deeper water and flipped over onto my back.

'Aren't you scared?' A young man surfaced next to me. 'Being out so far?'

I blinked water and examined him. He had dark, almost black, eyes. 'No.'

'Why not?'

'If you go beyond where the waves break, you won't get tumbled. And you can float all day.'

He grinned and rolled on his back, too. The sea lifted us up and down and I closed my eyes and listened for the crash of the breakers as they reached the shore. You had to take the risk of getting beyond the breaker line, of course. That required bravery the first time.

'What's your name?' he addressed the sky. 'You're English, aren't you?'

'Yes. Frances. And you?'

'Mark,' he replied. 'Mark Charleson. Was that your father on the beach, talking to mine?'

I heard a call and looked back. It was Daph, bravely swimming towards us.

I waved an arm to beckon her closer.

Mark lifted his head and squinted. 'Watch out!' he shouted.

I rolled over and saw a massive wall of water bearing down. 'Swim!' I screamed. 'Swim!'

Towards the danger, I wanted to shout but the words stuck in my throat, towards the danger!

If he swam backwards in the direction of the beach he'd be caught. But it seemed he knew that already and pulled away in a quick crawl towards the monster. There was no time to dive beneath the rearing wall. I felt myself being borne aloft, my arms flailing as I clawed up the face. Just when I thought it was too late, I was grabbed and hauled over the curling crest. With a mighty roar the wave broke.

I fell into the trough, seawater gurgling in my nose and ears.

'Great!' yelled Mark, letting me go.

I coughed and swiped my hair out of my face. Usually I kept watch for rogue waves, but the sea had seemed too smooth for trouble. And I was distracted, like in the oak—

What about Daphne?

I began to thrash towards the shore. Hands were waving at us and faint calls echoed on the air. The instinct to swim towards the wave had come to me without thinking. Mark had reacted in the same way. Were some people wired with a kind of intuition that saved them?

'Are you alright?' he shouted beside me.

A lone female figure was struggling in the shallows. Every time she tried to get up, she fell down.

'You could say it was my fault,' Mark panted, swimming beside me. 'I made you go too far out.'

I launched myself with the next swell and the wave swept me towards the beach.

Daphne was being carried by her father out of the water.

A woman ran into the shallows and pointed past me.

'Come, Frances.' Mark Charleson took my hand.

We reached hard sand and I let go of his hand and rushed to where Daph was lying on her side, her face white, her hair soaked. There was no sign of the blue bathing cap.

'I'm sorry! I'm so sorry!'

She shook, and began to retch. Seawater dribbled out of the side of her mouth.

'Stand back, Frances,' boomed Mr Phillips, bending over her. 'Let her cough the water out.'

I felt someone behind me – Mark? Mr Charleson? – wrap a towel around me. The kite flyers were pulling in their kites. Someone yelled about an ambulance but Daph, after several minutes of coughing, regained some colour and sank against her father. She lifted her face to me and, in that moment, I thought about the soldier on Father's wall, urging people to follow him. The Kitchener reminder, Father called it. 'I'm sorry,' I fell down beside her, 'I should've come for you.'

A woman screamed.

I turned back to the sea.

A man was carrying a young boy out of the water.

82

His legs were dangling; his head was lolling over the man's arms.

'He swam to you,' the woman yelled, and pointed straight at me. 'You waved and he swam to you!'

I scrambled to my feet. Mark held me back.

'Take him to the first aid tent!' Mr Charleson called. 'Up the beach! They'll help!'

The man struggled across the sand, the woman sobbing at his side, the boy inert in his arms.

'Fran?' Daph whispered, touching my arm. 'It wasn't your fault.'

'Come.' Daphne's father found her sandals and put them gently onto her feet. 'Let's get you home.'

'We'll be going, too.' Mr Charleson squinted up at the cloud beginning to blot out the sun.

'Thank you, young man,' Mr Phillips looked up at Mark, 'you saved Frances from a certain injury.'

'No problem, sir. She's a good swimmer. She'd have made it on her own.'

I opened my mouth to protest but no words came. Without Mark's help I'd have been swept into the depths of the wave and then flung onto the seabed from a height, and perhaps drowned like Daph had almost been. And the boy—

Did God see me? Did he see my moment of distraction?

Why did he choose to hurt someone else?

'Do you come here every weekend?' Mark leant down to me.

'If Daph wants to—' I can barely get the words out.

'What about your parents? Don't they bring you?'

'My parents are in England. I stay with my aunt.'

Mark touched me briefly on the shoulder and gathered his shirt and shoes.

'What about the boy?' I could see a crowd outside the first aid tent.

I began to run. The dry sand was deep and clinging and I stumbled several times.

'Wait, Frances!' He caught up with me, grabbed my hand and we ran together.

'Is the boy alright?' I called. 'Is he alive?'

The crowd turned and stared at me. A few had accusation in their eyes.

'*Ja*,' said an old man in a shabby jacket. 'They saved him. Listen.' He cocked his head and I heard coughing and crying from the inside of the tent and the low murmur of a woman's voice.

I sank onto my haunches on the pavement. The crowd turned away.

It took some time for Mr Charleson and Mr Phillips, supporting Daphne, to reach us. Mr Phillips might not want me to be Daph's friend after this. The Hodgsons avoided me after I fell out of the tree and Mrs Atkins said – I heard this from Mr Jacobs – that young Frances was accident-prone.

'The youngster has recovered?'

'Yes,' said Mark. 'He'll be fine.'

Mr Phillips opened the car door and helped Daphne in. 'Come, Frances. It's time to go.'

Mark guided me in beside her. 'I'll catch you next time.' His black eyes examined me and I thought, for one disconcerting moment, that he was going to kiss me.

I don't remember much of the drive home. I just remember noticing that my feet were covered in sand that was pooling on the floor. I hadn't brushed my feet before getting into the car.

I also knew, as clearly as if he'd been beside me, what

84

Father would say.

There's a pattern here. You're bold, Fran, which is not a bad trait, but you also have a talent for dangerous distraction.

I don't look for trouble, Father, I'd reply. Or lead anyone else into trouble. The wave came out of nowhere—

But that wasn't the whole truth.

I wasn't paying attention. I took the wild African sea for granted.

Mr Phillips glanced at me in the rear-view mirror. 'You need to think before you go too far next time, Frances. There may not be anyone around to save you.'

'I promise, sir. And I'm sorry.'

If Daph or the boy had died, would that make me a murderer?

'Frances!' Aunt Mary came to the door. 'We have a visitor! Go and change, my dear! Goodness, you're covered in sand! Thank you, Stephen!' she called to Mr Phillips who raised a hand from the car. I sent up a silent prayer he wouldn't tell Aunt of my recklessness.

A tall, balding man rose from his chair when I entered the lounge later, my hair still damp from washing.

'Hello, Frances.' He held out his hand. 'It's been a while.'

I had no idea who he was. Maybe it was still the shock, the boy, head lolling—

'Julian McDonald,' he said. 'We met years ago at Southampton docks. When my ship was delayed.'

'Of course. Good afternoon, Mr McDonald.'

The nervous schoolteacher, injured in the Great War, whose parents died of the Spanish Flu.

There was a pause. 'I hope you're settling in well, Frances?'

His gaze travelled over my slightly dishevelled state. 'The Cape is renowned for its hospitality.'

'I am, thank you. How did you know I was here, Mr McDonald?'

He flushed slightly and glanced at Aunt Mary.

'Your father wrote to Julian. Said you'd come to the Cape and to visit next time he was in town.'

Dear Father. Rallying even his most remote contacts to watch over me.

'That's kind of you, sir.'

'Julian, please.' He flushed again, and clasped and unclasped his hands.

'You're rather pale, Frances,' Aunt observed. 'Was the water cold at Muizenberg? Frances is a seal, Julian,' she leant towards him in a confidential manner, 'when she's not painting, she loves to swim.'

'A boy nearly drowned, Aunt.'

'How tragic! Yet he lived to tell the tale!'

Perhaps Aunt feels that young death is more merciful. Less history to be lost.

'He was revived in the first aid tent.'

'Be careful of the sea, Frances,' Julian McDonald admonished. 'It's more unpredictable than at home.'

'Father taught me well, sir.'

But even Father might have been overwhelmed by that wave.

'Well said!' cried Aunt. 'More tea, Julian?'

I glanced outside. A starling had landed on the bougainvillea. Jet-black feathers streaked with scarlet. I've embraced this place, these birds, even the violent sea.

Yet I'm beginning to sense it will be harder to master the

other parts of the country, the parts that hide from casual view or appear in people's expressions or lie beneath the words they use. If I draw and paint, will they reveal themselves to me? What might I find beyond the genteel society to which I've been introduced? What other waves lie beneath its surface?

Chapter Fourteen

When I fell out of the oak it was my own fault. But at Muizenberg, Daphne could have died because of me. And so could that unknown boy, although Mr Phillips told me later that I wasn't responsible. He says the boy's parents were remiss for not watching him.

I'm more careful these days. I look over my shoulder at who's coming after me.

Mark Charleson and I often swim together. It was hard the first time, but Mark encouraged me beyond the breakers and told me we all do things that might have unforeseen consequences.

We talk a lot while we're floating. Mark has graduated as an architect and he knows I want to be an artist. He's handsome in a dark way and he kissed my hand once, when we were at a garden party and he found me alone beneath a jasmine pergola. I like him.

I never told Aunt. Or Daph. Or Sue, in a letter, although she asks constantly if I've found a young man yet. And I definitely never wrote about him to Mother, who would leap into action on my behalf – from a distance – to ferret out the young man's prospects.

Sometimes I wake up early and climb out of my window – to avoid disturbing Aunt – and sit in a shell chair on the paving and watch the world shaking itself awake. If I stay completely still, the smaller birds forget I'm there and approach within touching distance. Dashing orange-breasted sunbirds, shy robins, assured wagtails. When the sun strikes the mountain, the flowers seem to stretch as they await relentless foraging. Nature is untamed here, not constrained by cold weather and encroaching humankind. Sometimes I take my sketchbook, but usually I simply sit and observe and let the place sink into my pores. And I think a bold thought: can I contrive to earn enough to afford a sliver of this paradise for myself?

'Excuse me,' I said to a bespectacled lady assistant in the office at Kirstenbosch, 'could you tell me if this gentleman still works here?' I handed over the card.

She looked at me curiously. 'He does. Do you wish to make an appointment?'

'An appointment?'

'The director is a busy man. You'll need an appointment. Could you tell me what it is concerning?'

'He's the director of the entire Gardens?'

'Indeed he is! Director Compton has been in his post since 1919. What is this about?'

Seize the moment! I could hear Mr Cadwaller shouting.

I opened my portfolio and selected a recent painting. *Erica multumbellifera*, worthy for its name alone, if not for the abundance of purple, bead-like flowers. A type of heather, similar to those from the highlands of Scotland. And a challenge in fine brushwork.

'Would you give this to the director when you next see him?'

She frowned as she examined it. 'The director doesn't take unsolicited work.'

I gave her my most emollient smile.

'Please let me introduce myself. My name is Frances Whittington, from Protea Rise in Bishopscourt. I was on the *Edinburgh Castle* when the director gave me his card. He was interested in my paintings.'

Was he? Perhaps he simply wanted to increase visitor numbers and handed out cards at random.

'Very well. I shall pass it on. But I can't promise you'll get a response.'

'I understand. The director is a busy man, as you said.'

She looked at me closely, alert to the hint of sarcasm.

'You've been most kind,' I went on, with all the sincerity I could muster. 'Thank you so much.'

Daphne is set to marry Trevor Bell, to whom she's been promised almost from birth, on her twenty-first birthday at St George's Cathedral in the city centre. I'm not sure Daph is overly enamoured – Trevor is pleasantly bland – but I suspect her father is keen to have her settled so she'll be less influenced by someone like me, for Daph has taken a shine to me even though I nearly drowned her.

'Where shall we hold the engagement party?' she mused. 'I fancy the top of Table Mountain. Trevor says it can't be done, but Father knows the cableway operator. We just have to hope for calm weather.'

Back in Embury, Phyllis Carter's engagement had been marked by tea at the local public house.

And so I found myself riding the cableway up the face of the precipice I'd first seen a year previously from the *Edinburgh*

Castle. Birds of prey hung in the air, the city slid into miniature below us and I laughed out loud at the audacity of it, and the incongruity of our clothing. The young women, including myself, wore tea dresses and heeled shoes as if we were once again at the Kelvin Grove. The young men, including Mark and Jonathan Pringle, were in suits. Daph wore a corsage on her wrist and a brimmed hat with a silk ribbon to match her frock.

'Will you marry Mark Charleson?' Penelope Chisholm whispered into my ear.

'He hasn't asked me. We're friends.'

'You'd better move fast!' She glanced around to where Mark stood among a group of young men, some of whom were Bell cousins visiting from upcountry. 'He's a catch! Don't let him get diverted!'

'Why does everyone want to marry me off?'

'Because you're beautiful and unattached. Beautiful, unattached girls are dangerous!'

The cable car slowed and lurched between the rails of the upper station. The doors opened and our party teetered out onto the plateau with shouts and whoops, the engaged couple in the lead. Table Bay, foam-fringed, curved into the northern distance while the peaks of the Twelve Apostles rode imperiously above the Atlantic seaboard. The spine of the peninsula – which I'd first gasped at from the top of Skeleton Gorge – wound its sinuous way south to Cape Point.

How is it possible for one place to be so extravagantly blessed? I later wrote in my diary. *Is it fair on the plainer parts of the world?*

The plateau turned out to be mounded with sandstone outcrops and split by rocky crevices. I recalled my lessons with Mr Cadwaller on perspective, the deception created by distance.

'Frances?' Mark appeared at my side.

'Is the rest of the country like this?'

'You mean is it as magnificent?'

'Yes.'

He smiled and touched my hand. 'Outward beauty always catches the eye, Frances. But don't be deceived. The Africa beneath is not so easy to understand.'

'I'm starting to realise that. Africans don't have the vote,' I said. 'But neither did women, until recently.'

He was silent for a moment. A finger of cloud slipped over the far edge of the precipice and dissolved against the cliff face. Mr Phillips says it's due to the temperature gap between land and sea and whether the air will choose to hold its moisture invisibly or transform it into cloud.

'Read all you can, Frances. Then talk to ordinary people, the gardener, the maid who works for your aunt, the local storekeeper. Find out what they think. You'll discover that nothing,' he spread his arms over the vista, 'is quite as it seems.'

Mark has never spoken this way before. If he's right, painting its face may not reveal this country to me.

It will require me to dig deeper, invest more of myself.

Julian McDonald, calling occasionally when he's in town, says the white man will never yield to the black. Mark took my arm and led me along the path to the tea room where I could hear the others laughing.

Chapter Fifteen

I've submitted further watercolour sketches to Director Compton and posted two pencil drawings of *Erica multumbellifera* to Mr Cadwaller. I hope the connection to Scottish heathers will encourage Kew to ask for more, and to pay for the work. Aunt counsels patience.

But without success as an artist, my small salary won't be enough for an independent future. Yet perhaps I won't need it? I'm on the edge of love with Mark Charleson, it just requires me to plunge. He already meets the condition I so brazenly announced to Mr Cadwaller: sufficient means to ensure any future family would be well looked after while I painted. If my Embury vicar could divine my thoughts from afar, he'd accuse me of the unseemly materialism he warned against. But I care for Mark, quite aside from his wealth. We've been courting for eight months.

'May I take Frances for dinner at the Mount Nelson, Mrs Donnelly?'

Aunt glanced at me. I nodded. She should, of course, have accompanied us, but she'd announced, when I was newly off the *Edinburgh Castle*, that she had no intention of policing me.

'Of course. Enjoy yourselves, my dears.'

'I made a reservation,' Mark said, tucking my arm through his as we left Protea Rise. 'For three.'

'You were going to invite Aunt along?'

'In case she chose to join us.'

'Why didn't you invite your parents as well?'

He grinned. 'Don't tease. It's almost impossible to get young ladies on their own.'

'But you often get me on my own,' I laughed. 'In the sea. Unchaperoned.'

'Ah, but that's not the ideal place for serious discussion.' He turned the car through the columned gateway towards the pink façade of the Mount Nelson. 'If I said something dramatic you might take a gulp of water and I'd have to revive you.'

He parked the motor car and came around to open my door.

'So are we to be serious tonight?' I asked lightly, taking his proffered hand.

'Only over the main course. Over dessert, we can be as merry as you wish.'

We sat at a window table from where the inky sky was visible, sprinkled with southern hemisphere stars that were still new to me. We ate fish prepared with a cream and parsley sauce, accompanied by carrots cut into pennies and beans grown in the hotel's kitchen garden. I was relieved to note from the glances directed towards me that my dark blue low-waister was not out of place among the ladies present. My wardrobe, so agonised over by Mother for its relative paucity, has so far stood up to scrutiny.

'You're very quiet, Frances,' Mark said as the waiter topped up my wine glass. A crisp Cape white.

'What would you do, Mark, if you and your family lost everything?'

I want to know if he's aware of my father's losses. I admit it's a roundabout way of asking.

'Is that what's worrying you?' He reached across the table and touched my hair. 'If we lost everything, I'd take more basic work. It would be a challenge to do more with less. Frances,' he took my hand and lifted it to his lips, 'I've fallen in love with you.'

'Would you still love me if I was poor?'

'But you aren't.' He squeezed my hand. 'And if you were it would make no difference.'

I searched his face. 'Truly? It would make no difference?'

'Truly.'

'Then you should know that my father lost his fortune in the Crash.' I paused. 'I came here to make a fresh start. To make my way as an artist and become independent. I didn't expect to be loved.'

The shock in his eyes gave way to something that was not pity. I think it was tenderness.

'But you are loved, Frances.'

He got up from his chair, came around the table and bent down and kissed me on the lips.

A titter of amusement rose from fellow guests. I don't remember anything about dessert.

I told him I loved him too, I admitted later to my diary. We kissed again. But what about the freedom I first scented as the ship pulled away from England? Yet if I hesitate, I might lose him.

This is different from last time. I love him.

And he knows me. He knows I take chances, sometimes without realising. And he understands creativity. I copy from real life but Mark creates from his imagination. Together, we might achieve something special.

He said my poverty would make no difference.

But I'm wary. Time will tell if my revelation cools his ardour.

In the meantime I will have time to reflect as well, while he's occupied with his family's American guests. We will telephone every day, he said.

Dear Miss Whittington, began the letter propped up by my place at breakfast the following morning.

> *Thank you for submitting your painting of* Erica multumbellifera. *Plus the further protea and succulent sketches. All have been properly identified and accurately depicted. If you are in agreement, I will place them in the appropriate portfolios for use as references. You may, of course, retrieve them if you wish.*
>
> *At Kirstenbosch, we collaborate with botanists who study Cape flora and publish in the scientific press. We are often asked to recommend illustrators. I was intrigued with your work on board ship and I am most impressed with this latest offering. There may be opportunities for you in this respect and I shall offer your work as an example.*
>
> *Kindly forward your full details, including the nature of any previous commissions, plus references of published work if appropriate.*
>
> *Yours faithfully*
> *A. R. J. Compton*
> *Director*

I took particular care with my appearance for the Governor General's Ball at the Kelvin Grove: a fluid sea-green chiffon with a dropped waist and a scalloped hem that would float about my legs in the breeze, and marcelled hair that hugged my head in gleaming waves. My green-with-a-fleck-of-ginger eyes looked back at me from the mirror with a certain glint.

'Charming!' said Aunt, who was to be my chaperone. Mark was escorting his parents and their guests whom he'd been required to guide around the peninsula.

'I love your dress!' Daphne exclaimed in the ladies' powder room. 'Will you dance with Mark the most?'

She twirled in front of the mirror. 'I wish I'd been able to choose my beau, like you.'

'Be grateful,' I whispered as we entered the ballroom, 'it's good to be spoken for.'

Chandeliers cast prisms of light over the starched linen. Roses arched from a central vase.

'May I have this dance?' Jonathan Pringle leapt up from his table and held out his hand. Aunt smiled and motioned for us to go ahead. In a moment of candour between Shakespeare readings, she told me a man had to have three assets to succeed in life: honour, money and the ability to lead a lady on the dance floor. She didn't say which was the most important.

Jonathan and I joined the gliding couples in a carousel of whirling colour. Most ladies were wearing traditional long gowns rather than my below-the-knee flapper style. Was it a clever choice or a reckless ploy when discretion would've been safer? We circled slowly, and I tried to spot Mark without noticeably craning my neck. Local friends inclined their heads as we danced by: Penelope Chisholm, clinging a little too hard to her partner in case he might run away in the direction of an unattached girl, Mary Clough, newly married and already cradling a gentle bump beneath her flowing dress. The governor general waltzed past with his wife, who widened her eyes at my dress.

'How lovely you are tonight, Frances,' Jonathan grinned at me. He's continued to call but he's well aware I'm being courted by Mark.

'Thank you!' I managed lightly but I could hardly speak, for there, coming towards us, was Mark with an unknown dark-haired beauty in his arms.

He will stop, I told myself. *He has to stop.*

I edged Jonathan slightly, so as to be in their path.

The violins swooned, Jonathan nodded proudly to acquaintances.

Mark will see me and smile.

And then he will surrender his partner gracefully and we will waltz away together and later he will escort me onto the terrace, where he will ask me to marry him and I will say yes.

Mark raised his hand from the back of the dark-haired beauty to acknowledge us, and swept on. The orchestra changed key from one Strauss waltz to another.

'How strange,' Jonathan murmured, sensing an opportunity. 'Have you fallen out?'

The musicians caressed the opening notes of 'Wiener Blut'.

'Not that I know of.'

We passed again. I tried to catch Mark's eye but he kept his attention on his partner. And then I saw him guide her from the dance floor and onto the terrace.

'Young Pringle, you can't monopolise the prettiest girl in the room!' Daphne's father clapped a hand on Jonathan's shoulder. 'I insist on a dance before she's all taken!'

Jonathan released me with a rueful smile and I allowed myself to be clamped to Mr Phillips's pudgy chest and whisked away. 'What are you doing with yourself these days? Apart from tormenting every bachelor in the Cape or risking life and limb at sea?' He chuckled and pulled me a little too close. 'That was a close call for my Daph.'

'I know, sir.' I wriggled so that I could breathe. 'I'm working on my art.'

'Ah, yes. But I suspect you'll be too busy with a family one of these days!'

'Perhaps.'

'The finest ideal any young woman could aspire to.' He raised our clasped hands to a balding man dancing nearby with a woman taller than himself. 'What do you like to paint? The sea?'

'I paint flowers. Sometimes birds.'

At a table on the far side I spotted Mark, now seated with his parents and another couple.

'Wonderful to have a hobby.' He steered me into a tight turn. 'I keep telling Daphne she needs one.'

'It's not a hobby, Mr Phillips. I'm drawing for the director at Kirstenbosch. It's my career.'

Now Mark was looking my way.

'Come, come,' Mr Phillips exclaimed, 'a career? Whatever for?'

I feigned being out of breath.

'Mr Phillips, you've exhausted me! Thank you for the dance. Will you excuse me?'

'Of course,' he boomed. 'I'll go find Daph.' He planted a wet kiss on my hand and wandered off.

I made my way towards the Charleson table. Mark and

his father stood up as I approached. His mother, who always dressed in black, remained seated. She was in delicate health, Mark said.

'I hope you're well, Mrs Charleson.' She gave a slight smile.

'Mark!' I leant forwards, expecting him to kiss me on the cheek as he usually did, but this time he didn't. Perhaps he felt it was too public a space for such intimacy.

'Frances?' Mr Charleson glanced over my shoulder. 'May I introduce Miss Astrid Fairbrother?'

I turned around.

The dark-haired beauty, older than myself, and dressed in a sleek blue gown that matched her eyes, looked me up and down. 'How do you do,' she said in a strong American accent. She raised an eyebrow at Mark. 'I thought there were no stylish ladies at the Cape.'

I could tell Mark was embarrassed.

'Are you here on a scenic tour, Miss Fairbrother?'

She gave a little smile and a shrug. 'Mark?'

There was a moment of silence.

It was Mr Charleson who broke it. He came around the table and placed a hand on my shoulder. I realised, with a chill, that he was about to console me. 'We're delighted to say that Mark and Miss Fairbrother have just announced their engagement.'

Astrid Fairbrother went over to Mark and stood beside him, close enough to show ownership.

Mark met my eyes and looked down at the table. His mother stared into the middle distance.

'But—'

You lied to me! I wanted to shout. *You said it would make no difference if I was poor! You said I was loved—*

I was aware that my breath was coming fast and shallow.

At an adjoining table, Penelope and Mary were whispering together and looking at me.

Mr Charleson, his hand still resting lightly on my shoulder, guided me away.

'Come, Frances,' he murmured, 'I know you were keen on Mark, but Astrid is a good fit for our family.'

The musicians paused; the dancers on the floor seemed to slow in their tracks and turn, as one, towards me. So, they seemed to be asking, what will you do now?

'She's wealthy?'

He hesitated, and that hesitation told me all I needed to know. Money, and a lot of it, was the only currency in the post-Crash world. It had been true in England with Brian, and it was true here with Mark.

'It's more about a fresh approach,' he said. 'An American angle. Good for Mark's business.'

The orchestra resumed, this time with a jazz swing.

The noise level in the room rose. A dominion girl fluttered her fingers at me and turned around to giggle with her partner, a boy whom I'd ignored a while ago in favour of Mark.

'I see your aunt,' Mr Charleson gestured. 'What a delightful evening this is. Such wonderful music. I wish you well, Frances. Do stay in touch.'

He bowed slightly and turned away.

Chapter Sixteen

Aunt was watching.
She saw Mark ignore me, she saw Mr Charleson escort me away.
She realises that the match would have given me both love and creative freedom.

'What news from the director?' Aunt asked over breakfast a few days later.

'He's promised to refer authors who are looking for illustrators to me. But nothing so far.'

Aunt spread marmalade carefully on her toast.

'We will hold a viewing!' She laid down her knife and clapped her hands. 'In the spring. I shall invite all my friends on the understanding that they will be expected to buy an artwork. Now, Frances, you'll need to draw and paint at speed! And what price shall we set? Nothing extreme, but sufficient to be taken seriously. Violet?' She rang a small bell at her side. 'Bring me my diary, please.'

Though the invitation list would be all female, husbands and partners were welcome. Aunt believes in marketing by stealth: win over the women, and you will get the men in due course.

At no point did we discuss my abandonment by Mark.

Violet baked lemon cake and I helped her to make shortbread biscuits. We dug out the spare silver tea set and I borrowed easels from a local school on which to display my work.

Pencil and watercolour sketches of Table Mountain, as seen from the *Edinburgh Castle*. A sunbird on a crimson hibiscus. Cloud over Fernwood Buttress. And for those after nostalgia, a painting of yellow gorse and purple thistles.

'Where did you study?' asked one of the dominion wives. 'At the Royal Academy?'

'I see the Lord in your work, Frances,' said Father Ben, pointing to the sunbird. 'He is your inspiration.'

'It's all about technique, Father,' I countered lightly. 'I was well taught. And I practise.'

'Indeed! There's no substitute! Whether it is in paint or prayer!'

'Well done, Frances.' Julian McDonald hovered. 'I shall write to your Father telling of your success.'

'It's a start, sir.' I glanced about at the chattering guests. They would buy, but for most it was about the social occasion. 'Will you excuse me?'

'Miss Fran should draw people,' Violet hissed from behind the teapot. 'Show what they think.'

'I'll take the hibiscus, Frances. I have one just like it in my garden.'

'Thank you, Mrs Radisson. I believe you've just returned from India?' I'd learnt the guest list off by heart, along with family details provided by Aunt. 'Do you find the colours here different?'

'India has more orange,' she shrugged. 'It's everywhere. Quite tiresome. Marigolds, for example. They make garlands of them. Do you draw pets, Frances?'

I've no idea whether the knowledge of my penury – apart from a tiny salary – has swept through the Cape in the months since my public rejection. There must have been speculation. Why would Mark Charleson spend eight months courting Frances Whittington only to throw her over for a visitor in the space of a week or so? There must be more to it than a lover's tiff . . .

It's a question I've continued to ask myself. Yet Mark said it would never be about money.

I received a letter from him in the wake of the events at the Kelvin Grove in which he apologised for his behaviour. Circumstances had arisen, he wrote, that were beyond his control and which he deeply regretted he was unable to reveal. I would hold a place in his heart, he ended, for ever.

It's not an answer I understand.

We loved one another. If money was not the issue, what could possibly have arisen to keep us apart?

I'm not angry with him, oddly enough. I feel only confusion and waste, an empty heart – and the disquieting sense that I have now attracted and failed to land two young men.

'A triumph, my dear!' Aunt bustled over at the end. 'You've arrived as an artist!'

'Thank you.' I kissed her powdered cheek. 'You made it happen, Aunt Mary.'

'Stuff and nonsense! Here are your earnings!' She handed over a brass container. 'Not excessive, but you're on your way!'

My dear Frances
I am replying by return post because I sense you require clarity.

> *The news out of Kew is mixed. While they are impressed by your treatment of* Erica multumbellifera

and would like to see more, they cannot commit to an arrangement as yet. I have urged them to offer you payment for a series of illustrations but it will take time to be settled. I suggest you pursue the director at Kirstenbosch with all vigour.

Your work is magnificent, my dear. Have courage!
Yours most sincerely
Raymond Cadwaller

'Miss Fran! Miss Fran, wake up!'

I opened my eyes blearily. I hadn't been sleeping well lately. It started after the viewing, when Daph and Trevor talked of the new pictures I would paint and how eligible young men would surely be queuing up to court the promising artist. The letter from Mr Cadwaller had arrived at the same time.

'What is it, Violet?'

Sun was breaking through the curtains. I can't have voile here because the light is too bright. Even the moon is brighter—

'It's the madam. Come, miss!'

I swung myself out of bed, grabbed a dressing gown and ran after her.

Violet had opened Aunt's curtains. She was lying on her back in bed, her silver hair spread freely on the pillow. A tea tray sat on the bedside table, brought by Violet as she did every morning.

'Let her sleep,' I whispered. 'She's weary.'

'No, Miss Fran.' Violet's voice broke. 'Feel her, ma'am.'

I put out a hand and touched her cheek, her neck, and her age-freckled hands. They were ice cold. I leant down and put an ear to her mouth but there was no stir of breath.

'Call the ambulance, Violet. Quick!'

I held Aunt's hands, massaging them, trying to warm her flesh with mine.

I rubbed her chest, willing it to rise and fall, but it remained still beneath my fingers.

Violet returned and stood on the other side of the bed, tears flowing silently down her brown cheeks.

The clang of the ambulance broke the early morning silence and I found myself wondering if their bell was the same pitch as that on the ambulance that came for me.

'Miss, step aside please.'

The ambulanceman leant over Aunt, tried for a pulse, listened to her chest, performed resuscitation, but Aunt's wiry body lay unresponsive. He lifted his hands away.

'She has gone, miss.'

I took her cold hand in mine. We'd only had a year. I never told her how much she meant to me.

'Just a moment—' I stared into her eyes, milky and unfocussed when they'd always been bright.

I reached down and closed them gently with my fingers.

I telegrammed father.

AUNT MARY PASSED AWAY FUNERAL NEXT WEEK STOP LOVE
FRAN

'Come stay with us,' rumbled Mr Phillips. 'You shouldn't be on your own.'

'I want to be at Protea Rise, sir. It's my home.'

And I had to reply to the cards, scores of them, arriving each day: Deepest condolences . . . a wonderful person . . . a woman of courage . . . she will be missed.

Father telegrammed back.

BELOVED FRAN BE BRAVE STOP LETTER FOLLOWS STOP
LOVE FATHER

At night I see Aunt's face in the darkness. I see the boy, head lolling, being carried from the sea at Muizenberg. I see my brother peering in through the sash window.

Aunt Mary's funeral service was held at St John's, followed by tea at Protea Rise.

'Seek refuge in the Lord,' intoned the reverend, clasping my hand as the coffin was taken away.

Another tea, so soon after my successful viewing. More shortbread, more lemon cake, more people shaking my hand because I am Aunt's closest relative present. And so many donations: the Chisholms brought a stew, Jonathan Pringle's mother baked a ham to be eaten cold, strangers left cake and baskets of fruit as if Violet and I had been seized by uncontrollable hunger. I gave some of it to Alfius and Samuel, both of whom came to the funeral. I insisted Violet sit alongside me.

'I should be at the back, ma'am.'

Violet has started calling me ma'am instead of miss.

'If you sit at the back, I shall come and sit next to you.'

I didn't have a black dress so Violet's sister, a seamstress, quickly ran up a plain black shift.

'I'm sorry,' Julian McDonald said, handing over a small bunch of flowers. 'If there's anything I can do?'

'I'll be fine, sir. Thank you.'

'Call upon us, Frances,' said Father Ben as the last mourners left. 'And hold on to your faith.'

But I don't really have faith, Father Ben. Not like yours.

My faith – my God – lives outside, stirring the leaves on the trees, painting the feathers of birds. Saving me when I fell, but taking Aunt from me without compunction?

Chapter Seventeen

'Miss Whittington? Good morning. I'm Alan Field, of Field and Sons.'

He followed me into the lounge, nodded at the gracious furniture, the verdant garden beyond the sash windows. 'Do accept my deepest sympathy upon the passing of your aunt.'

'Thank you, sir. May I offer you tea?'

'Please.' He opened his briefcase. 'It falls to me to present your aunt's will.'

He waited as Violet delivered the tea tray and closed the door behind her. It's surprising how little our routines have altered. I still change for dinner. But now I dine alone, though I've persuaded Violet to eat with me on Sunday evenings. I hope we can extend that practice to other days, but I don't yet know the boundaries of mistress–maid relations here on the southern tip.

'Mrs Donnelly altered her will soon after you arrived in Cape Town last year.'

'Really?' I never expected any help from Aunt other than what she paid me as her companion.

'Here is a copy, Miss Whittington. This,' he pointed to a paragraph, 'is the relevant section.'

I fingered the sheet filled with Aunt's slanted writing in the sapphire-blue ink she favoured.

Once all expenses have been settled, I wish to leave the remainder of my estate to my niece, Frances Grace Whittington. I was not blessed with children but Frances has become the daughter I never had, and a singular young woman. I hope that her inheritance will give her a measure of independence.

God bless you, Frances. You have brightened my days.

I haven't wept for Aunt in public. She wouldn't have approved of noisy displays of mourning but under the lawyer's sympathetic gaze, I found myself crying for her loss, and the loss of a separate, fledgling love that had promised so much.

Mark had written from America, where he'd travelled to marry Astrid Fairbrother. *I am so sorry, Frances. You are in my thoughts.*

But not in your heart, I wanted to reply.

Alan Field removed the handkerchief from his breast pocket and handed it to me.

'I was very fond of her,' I choked, wiping my eyes.

'Quite understandable. Mrs Donnelly was a remarkable woman.'

'What does it all mean, sir?' I handed him back the handkerchief.

'You may remain in Protea Rise while the estate is wound up. The proceeds from the sale of the property will be directed towards the borrowings that Mrs Donnelly made for maintenance, repairs and upkeep over the years. Once those have been settled, and provision made for Violet, the housemaid, any remaining monies will revert to you.'

For a moment it seemed that the chorus of birdsong from outside had abated.

'Protea Rise must be sold?'

'Yes, indeed. Mrs Donnelly only had a small pension from her husband. She was obliged to take out loans against the property for expenses such as her motor car, rethatching of the roof and general running costs.'

'I'll have to leave?' Suddenly I was back in England, with Father. *I'm so sorry, my dear . . .*

'Yes.' Mr Field hesitated. 'In due course.'

'I don't want to go.' I struggled not to shout out the words. 'This is my home—'

I want the patter of rain on the thatch, I want every bird call, every rampant bloom. I don't need to imagine exotic macaws or jungle orchids any more, my inspiration lives and breathes here—

'I'm afraid that will not be possible.'

'How soon? How soon will it be sold?'

'It's difficult to say. The housing market is depressed due to the ongoing effects of the Crash.'

The Crash, again. Will I ever be free of its malevolence?

He came over to where I was sitting and bent down. It was good of him to try to understand how I could possibly form an attachment to a place I'd only known for a year.

'Miss Whittington, once Protea Rise is sold and all outstanding loans are repaid, you will perhaps have sufficient funds to afford a small property of your own.'

'Thank you, sir. I'm grateful.'

He straightened up. 'My firm will appoint an agent to

handle the sale. In terms of the contents of the house, I suggest you choose any items of furniture or personal effects that you wish to keep. These could be placed in storage until you move into your own property.'

Dearest Fran

Your mother and I are heartsick at the passing of your Aunt Mary. We have not seen her for many years but I know, from your letters, that she became a loving confidante for you. This is a cruel blow, especially as you were starting to find your feet socially.

We have thought long and hard about the position in which you find yourself. I know you stand to inherit from your aunt which should allow you to find accommodation to tide you over. You may choose to return to England, of course, but if you wish to stay in the Cape – ideally marry there – then your mother and I may very well come out ourselves and find a small property of our own near to you and any future family. I realise this is all up in the air at the moment but I want you to know that we will support whatever decision you take.

You've done so well, Fran. We are proud of you. Thank you for laying my sister to rest with such care. I heard from Julian McDonald. He said it was a well-attended service.

All our love

Father

Julian McDonald has been kind. I suspect he is contriving visits to the city in order to check that I'm in good health, and that the winding up of Aunt's estate is proceeding efficiently. He sits on the couch, clasping and unclasping his hands, his face set in a mould of concern.

'These matters always take time, Frances. Patience is required.'

A lack of patience is not my problem. I long for time to slow down.

'I'm in no rush, Mr McDonald.'

He looked at me with surprise. 'Do you not wish to have some certainty?'

'Oh, I have certainty. Protea Rise will be sold. It's just a matter of when.' I looked away from his pale gaze. I didn't wish to explain further.

'I imagine you've grown fond of it.' He swept a hand around the lounge. 'It will be a wrench to leave.'

Why is he telling me what I already know? I mustn't be rude. Yet I'd rather be left alone to wrestle with a future from which Aunt and this special place will be missing.

'Will you excuse me, Mr McDonald?' I rose to indicate I had other pressing duties.

'Julian, please.' He gave a shy smile. 'We surely know each other well enough for first-name terms.'

My pressing duties are artistic.

I'm painting furiously, attempting to capture what I'm leaving behind. My fingers are permanently stained, I rise in the middle of the night to work, I fall asleep at my easel in the grey hour before dawn. And I'm tormented by the story of my life so far: a pattern of leavings.

'Use this tragedy, Frances,' Mr Cadwaller wrote, after hearing from my parents. 'Let this charge your brush with greater determination, greater ambition. Find refuge in art!'

But my hands shake at times, like during the Great Depression. 'Go slowly, ma'am,' says Violet, retrieving my crumpled discards from the bin. 'Ma'am's fingers will come back.'

Last night a long, liquid, bubbling call drifted through the open window.

A coucal, I registered, my eyes straining through the darkness. A secretive bird, heard if there was moonlight, a graceful, low-flying blur of black, cream and burnt orange that I'd yet to paint—

Mr Field called after two months.

'We've received an offer, Miss Whittington.'

'Yes?' I pulled off my apron. I could refuse the offer, stall for ever . . .

'It's not as much as we would like but I suggest you accept it.' He named a figure.

'Why so low, sir?'

'It is the conditions of the market.'

'And the house is eccentric,' I murmured. 'Not true Cape Dutch.'

'Not at all. It's charming. The interested party is keen. Miss Whittington,' he leant forward, 'we could wait, but the imperative is to wind up the late Mrs Donnelly's estate in good order, in good time.'

Rather accept an offer now, Father had said, than wait for one that will not come.

'Very well, sir. Let us go ahead.'

Samuel, whom I've kept on temporarily, drove me into Cape Town to the Field and Sons offices. As we rounded the side of Devil's Peak, gale-force wind tore at the motor car. The

114

cableway was surely grounded. These days I see signs in the weather—

'Miss Whittington. How nice to see you.'

The lawyer's office looked directly at the shrouded face of Table Mountain.

'I have the final accounting of your inheritance.' He gave a tight smile. 'All outstanding loans and charges have been settled and you will inherit the sum of one hundred pounds. Your aunt's wishes have been fulfilled. Congratulations, Miss Whittington.'

Cloud was lowering over the city like a theatre curtain descending after a performance.

'One hundred pounds won't be enough for me to buy a place of my own, Mr Field.'

He gave a sympathetic smile. 'Perhaps not.'

'Definitely not. I've looked at the property listings in the newspaper, sir.'

He blinked. Women weren't expected to search out answers for themselves. But in that respect Father has trained me well. My research also showed the going price for a house such as Aunt's. Mr Field is correct. We've done the best we could. We've sold for a fair price given the circumstances.

'We are,' Mr Field inclined his head, 'at the mercy of forces outside our control. But this settlement will, at least, give you sufficient funds to cover temporary accommodation while you make other plans.'

What other plans, Mr Field?

I am out of plans.

I am homeless.

Chapter Eighteen

'You will come to us,' declared Daphne's father. 'I won't hear of anything else. Then, with your father, we shall consider your options, Frances.'

'Do, Fran.' Daph took my arm. 'We'll have so much fun! You can help me with the wedding!'

They are generous. But behind the scenes, Mr Phillips is surely wringing his hands at the convergence of Mark's withdrawal and Aunt's death . . . and wondering if I am jinxed.

Before any move, however, there is the clearing of Protea Rise.

I sort through Aunt's unfashionable but practical cotton frocks, the sturdy shoes – I shall keep one pair of lace-ups to remind me that mountains can be climbed – and the shawls she'd wrap around her in the cool of evening. I finger each item but without her sharp presence they're imposters, hinting at what she was, a pale reflection of the real person. In her study I find poignant letters in a carved ebony box. *My dear,* Uncle scrawled in faded India ink, *our position is difficult, the Boers are fiendish but we soldier on. I think of you constantly. I dream of being back at Protea Rise.*

I keep the letters, alongside the lace-ups.

And I wander the neighbourhood, sketching anything I find: non-eccentric houses with Cape Dutch gables, brilliant yellow succulents, the purple undersides of *Plectranthus* leaves. Some turn out well once I add paint, some show lamentable skill, all are crammed with a harshness of colour and style that is new and a little frightening. Was it determined distraction? Or the refuge Mr Cadwaller recommended? I'm becoming someone I don't quite recognise.

'Ma'am?' Violet found me one day on my knees, leafing through Aunt's collection of ancient magazines.

How to sew an invisible seam. New ways with parsnips.

'Ma'am? Mr McDonald is here to see you.'

I scrambled up.

'Frances?' Julian McDonald leant through the doorway. He always appeared a little stooped, perhaps from years of bending down to his young pupils.

'Mr McDonald.' I pushed my hair out of my face. I struggle to call him Julian. 'Good morning.'

'Shall I make tea, ma'am?'

'Thank you, Violet. We can still offer tea,' I smiled ruefully, 'our cups will be the last to be packed.'

Julian McDonald was formally dressed in a dark suit and a matching tie. His eyes were pale blue, like the trickle of seawater that remains when a wave retreats.

'What are your plans, Frances, now the house has been sold?'

'I hope to take a small flat,' I said, lifting my chin. 'And pursue my art over the next few years.'

He glanced around at the depleted lounge. 'You must miss how it was.'

'Yes.'

'I've been in touch with your father, Frances.'

'I believe so. He said you remarked favourably on Aunt's funeral.'

'I corresponded with your father more recently, Frances. He shared with me your likely circumstances.'

I found myself blushing at my bold words about finding a flat, pursuing my art. Father's candour would mean that Julian knew it was mostly wishful thinking.

I am out of plans.

'Frances – my dear—' He came across and crouched in front of me as Mr Field had done. 'I have the consent of your father. Will you marry me, my dear?'

'What?' I jumped from my chair.

You're too old, I wanted to shout. *Too old for me! Too reluctant to express an opinion, too quick to defer to those who do – nothing like the young men who've courted me—*

He stood up, reached for my hand and squeezed it.

We stood facing one another, he anxious, myself poised to bolt.

'Frances?'

His skin was hot, I felt stifled, I wanted to be outside.

'My dear?' His voice faltered slightly.

I stared into his face. Julian McDonald was a casual visitor, never a candidate for husband. He possessed a benign face, it was true, with a chin that would soon become a little jowly, and lips that were usually creased into a slight smile. His expression was invariably one of kindness or whimsy, occasional bewilderment, but never ill-temper. I felt no quiver for him, no stirring at all.

'Why do you want to marry me, Julian?'

Confusion flickered across his brow.

'I care for you, Frances. We've known each other for several years.'

I found myself without words. Was casual acquaintance enough for a lifetime?

'I know I'm older,' he gave a tentative smile, 'but I will love you and cherish you as if I were a young man again.'

Shame rushed through me. He didn't deserve to beg. He was honourable, he had enough money to own a good motor car and his own home; he could, presumably, dance . . . even if the setting might be a world away from the Kelvin Grove and the smart folk who peopled it.

'Will you give it some thought, Frances? I know it's a lot to take in.'

He let go of my hand. We remained standing, an awkward distance between us. 'I'll return the day after tomorrow. Will you be here in the afternoon?'

I nodded.

What do you say to a man who has just proposed, when you have no words to respond either way?

He bent down and kissed me on the cheek, then turned and walked away, carefully avoiding the cardboard boxes and the stacked gramophone records that Aunt used to sway to.

I sank onto the chair and listened as his motor car departed. *Love*, Mother once said when she sensed my indecision over Brian Harris, *has nothing to do with marriage*.

'Ma'am?' Violet came in with the tea tray. 'Mr McDonald's gone already?'

'Yes. Thank you, Violet. I'll take my tea into the garden.'

Cirrus clouds traced high patterns in the sky, a sure sign, Aunt used to say, of fine weather to come.

Julian used to call on us whenever he came back to town from his upcountry posting. If I happened to be home, he'd talk to me, admire my drawings, and I'd ask him about life as a teacher out of politeness. Nothing more. He'd always been my parents' acquaintance and Aunt's acquaintance, not mine. 'Come now,' Aunt once teased with an arch glance, 'I always expect you to arrive with a bride, Julian! You're doing well, time is marching on!' And he'd grin sheepishly and scratch his sparse hair and say that he'd never really found the right girl.

If Aunt knew he had his eye on me, she never let on. And I never considered the possibility.

A band of cloud was drifting over Fernwood Buttress.

My spark comes from here . . .

And also, I realised with a tremor that recalled the fall, from the laughing child I still chase in my dreams, and who's somehow followed me across the sea to Protea Rise, to this enchanted garden, to the budding future I imagined with Mark.

Julian lived in a hamlet many miles away. He made his way amid thorn trees and dry riverbeds and people who worked the land and slept with rifles at their bedsides.

What will I do, Julian, in the small town where you live? Who will be my friend?

My sea-green chiffon will be as out of place as a flood in a desert.

And what of my art?

A woman married to a man in a distant, rural area would never gain recognition or attract commissions, or even have time to paint. I would be taken up with running a home, feeding a family – for Julian would want children, maybe a whole pack of them – and my art would wither like the flowers

I try so hard to catch at their peak.

Is that to be my fate?

And yet I would be loved, surely. Julian would be kind, wouldn't he?

This could be a loving rescue. Or it could be a trap from which there'd be no escape.

Chapter Nineteen

When I think back, I wrote some years later in my diary, *this proposal of marriage comes to me in colours and textures. The colours are pale and the texture is, I'm afraid, as thin as an over-diluted watercolour. It reminds me not of dawn and the stir of new life but rather of sunset and leave-taking; an ending rather than a beginning.*

I'm ashamed it should be so.

And I'm still sad for my younger self that I didn't rebel and find my own way when I sensed – though I tried to persuade myself otherwise – that it was more trap than rescue.

Why was I not bolder?

And should I have anticipated there would be other proposals that would carry more fire? My experienced heart says yes.

But when you're young and the road ahead seems to be narrowing, you can't imagine there may be detours that send you in a direction you could never have dreamt.

'Ma'am!' Violet shouted. 'Trunk call! Mr Whittington says to come quick!'

I threw down my brush and rushed to the telephone. Calls from abroad were prohibitively expensive; not even Aunt Mary's death had warranted one. 'Father?'

'Dear Fran.' Father's voice cracked slightly. 'We'll have to be brief. Your mother is listening in. We know you're considering Julian McDonald's proposal.'

'You must marry him, Frances,' Mother chipped in. 'He's a good man.'

'He may be a good man but I don't love him!'

'He's prepared to overlook the lack of . . . support,' Father hesitated, 'and we've no doubt he'll be an honourable husband.'

'Why does he want me, Father? Fifteen years younger and mostly a stranger?'

'Because you're beautiful and accomplished,' Mother asserted, 'and he wants a wife who'll be a fit companion.' Her voice rose. 'This will assure your future, Frances!'

The telephone line crackled with silence.

'Fran.' Father's tone was gentle. 'It is your choice and we will support whatever you decide.'

'Thank you, Father. And Mother. I will write and let you know.'

'God bless you, my dear. We miss you dreadfully.'

There was a final crackle and he was gone. I replaced the receiver and walked into the garden.

Mother was right about my being a fit companion. I'm slender, I've inherited her abundant hair in a shade that turns heads, I can hold my own in conversation thanks to Father making sure I'm more than a decoration. I read the papers, I draw and paint. But, equally, Julian McDonald could find any number of fit companions if he chose to look. There were several young women of my acquaintance who were more beautiful and probably better equipped to be wives than myself.

I picked a silver tree leaf and smoothed its delicate skin.

He returned two days later in the same dark suit and carefully knotted tie. This time I was prepared. Violet brought tea onto the verandah and we sat side by side in the shell chairs and talked about the weather – unseasonably cool – and the garden – particularly lush.

'I'm grateful, Julian,' I began. 'I hope you'll forgive me if I appeared ungracious the other day.'

He smiled and shook his head. Perhaps he had prepared, too, for he seemed more assured.

'I've given your proposal a lot of thought.'

I expected him to nod and make some suitable comment on the wisdom of careful consideration but instead he reached across and took my hand and murmured, 'I love you, Frances.'

How can you say that when we hardly know each other?

But I have no choice other than to believe him. I've made the necessary calculations. Rental and living costs will quickly eat up my inheritance if I have no other income. I visited Director Compton and I telegrammed Mr Cadwaller. I asked the same question – abbreviated in Cadwaller's case, more lengthy for the director.

CAN I MAKE A LIVING RIGHT NOW AS AN ARTIST?

And both replied that it was too soon to say. Art was an uncertain business. The director reiterated that there was interest, as shown by the two sketches I'd been remunerated for in an upcoming publication, but not, as yet, an ongoing demand. Mr Cadwaller telegrammed to say Kew was keen but constrained.

I confided in Daph who said Julian was a good man – is

124

that the only adjective people can find to describe him? – and that I might have more opportunity for adventure in the country than the city.

I loosened my hand from Julian's and lifted my palm to his cheek and leant in and kissed him. His lips were firm but there was no tender frenzy like I'd felt with Mark. I do not love him, and he knows it. But he was prepared to rescue me and give me a respectable future.

'We'll build a life together,' I said with contrived conviction. 'And a family, too.'

He grinned then, as if a great weight had been lifted – why did he doubt, when I had no choice? – and stood up and drew me into his arms. I felt the steady, slow beat of his heart. It would have to be enough.

You'll be able to draw, wherever you go, Mother had said as we stood on the quayside in Southampton.

He released me. 'Shall we marry at St John's, Frances?'

There was no time to waste. 'Yes, thank you.'

'I will speak to the reverend. Arrange for the banns to be read.'

'Miss Frances Whittington?' the telegram boy asked a week later when I opened the door. 'Sign here.'

THRILLED AT NEWS STOP ARRIVING CARNARVON CASTLE FOR WEDDING STOP LOVE FATHER

Chapter Twenty

Ever since Father told me our house would be mine one day, I've thought of my life as a circle. Like the plants I draw. Bloom, die, lie dormant, and then return. But Embury is gone, and Protea Rise, too. And I am marrying Julian McDonald.

Firstly, because I cannot support myself. Secondly, because I don't wish to be a continuing burden on my parents, given that all of Father's assets have been drained from that single, toxic basket into which he placed them and show no sign of revival. And thirdly, because I can no longer be sure that the young men I attract will propose. When it comes to it, they prefer to attach themselves to well-heeled girls.

I bought a second-hand white satin dress and had it altered by Violet's sister, Sophie, who was a seamstress.

'Tighter,' I instructed, 'no one must think the reason for marrying so quickly is because I'm expecting.'

Violet and her sister dissolved in giggles. 'No chance of that, ma'am.'

'It is rather revealing, Fran,' chided Daph, looking at the nipped-in waist and scoop neckline.

'I want Mark – if he's back – and the others to see what they've missed.'

'Fran!'

I might have no need of sea-green chiffon in my new life but I intend to leave this one with a flourish.

My parents, newly off the Carnarvon Castle, were in church to hear the final reading of the banns.

'It will be a solid marriage, Frances,' Mother murmured. 'I knew you'd be sensible.'

Mother and Father have bought a small house in Newlands village from the proceeds of the sale of the Embury semi, and they've taken on Violet. Mother has met an amenable prayer group at St John's and found a suitable hairdresser in Claremont. 'Our future is with you, Fran,' says Father, newly thin. It doesn't suit his height or formerly cheerful untidiness. 'We're here to stay. There are bound to be business opportunities for accountants.'

Julian and I were married on a spring day with waterfalls tumbling off Fernwood Buttress and the magnolia at Protea Rise unfurling buds of the palest pink. I wore Mother's bridal veil over my swept-up hair and carried a hand-tied posy of wild flowers picked on a walk in Newlands Forest.

'Fran?' Father stopped as we approached the church door. 'I hope you can forgive me?'

'There's nothing to forgive,' I said. 'Not any more. Julian will make a fine husband.'

And I'm spreading the risk, as you taught me, Father.

Now I'm in Julian's basket of assets.

His eyes roamed over my face beneath the veil, as if wanting to imprint how I looked at that moment.

'You can still be the person you want to be,' he murmured. 'Marriage will not change that.'

I heard the opening notes of the wedding march.

'Come,' I said, straightening the carnation in his buttonhole. 'Smile, please, Father.'

I took his arm and we paced down the aisle.

Faces turned towards us. Violet and her sister in their best dresses, alongside Alfius in a battered jacket and Samuel in his chauffeur's uniform. Further forward, the Chisholms and the Cloughs sat side by side; Daphne in a frothy hat with her fiancé and her parents – Mr Phillips, if he'd discovered our family's misfortune, likely calculating the cost of even a modest wedding to Father's depleted balance sheet; Penelope and Mary, who'd seen my humiliation at the Kelvin Grove Ball; the Pringle family, including Jonathan, who chose to look at his order of service instead of at me. But no Mark, newly returned from America. He'd sent a note of regret and a glass fruit bowl. Mother hovered in the front row in a tasteful lemon suit and pillbox hat. She'd brought with her a card from Susan wishing me well and insisting that I never cut my hair regardless of the heat or the demands of family life.

My future husband stood at the end of the aisle in the same dark suit and tie he'd worn when he proposed. There was a nervous smile on his lips. The organ reached its climax and faded to a final chord. I turned and looked at Father for a moment and saw tears in his eyes. Later, at the simple reception in the church hall, the guests would recall with fond smiles that the bride's father had been so overcome with joy at the wedding of his only daughter that he'd wept. But I knew differently. Father had cried for me, and for the marriage I'd been obliged to contract.

Did you ask Julian to marry me, Father?

I turned back and smiled at my soon-to-be husband.

With trembling hands, he lifted my veil and draped it behind me.

'Dearly beloved,' declared the reverend, with a surreptitious glance at my expertly fitted outfit, 'we are gathered here today . . .'

Light from the stained-glass windows painted rainbow colours on the floor. Carmine, lapis . . .

'I, Julian Thomas, take thee, Frances Grace,' said Julian after a while, 'to be my lawful wedded wife.'

A fluttering came from outside as doves settled on the roof and began to croon.

'To have and to hold, for richer for poorer,' I heard myself say.

The organ thundered into 'Love Divine', but I couldn't sing.

'In sickness and in health, until death us do part.'

Will God help me love this man I am pledging myself to?

'I now pronounce you man and wife.'

The register is signed, although my hand is shaking so much that Julian needs to steady my fingers.

The organ rings out once more, Julian tucks my hand in the crook of his arm and we process down the aisle past smiling faces and into the confetti-strewn air.

Julian and I left from the reception for our honeymoon up the coast at the seaside town of Hermanus. From there we would travel to our home on the edge of the remote Karoo that I'd never seen.

'Write to me!' whispered Daphne, as I made my way through the crowd of well-wishers.

We hugged and I turned to embrace Mother and Father.

'We'll come to see you soon,' Mother managed in a choked voice. 'Take care of her, Julian.' She reached up and kissed my husband on his cheek.

Father was beyond words and simply held on to me.

'I'll be fine,' I murmured, freeing myself gently. 'Just fine.'

I turned and saw Violet and her sister on the fringes, smiled at them and mouthed 'thank you' and patted my dress. I will miss Violet's quiet influence. Like I miss Aunt's unvarnished opinions. Everything that I've taken for granted, I realise with a catch in my throat, will have to be won again.

Then Julian was opening the door of his motor car and helping me in. My dress spilt over the seat and I tucked it about my ankles. There was no going-away outfit; I wanted to drive off in my satin. The crowd waved and cried 'Good luck! Safe journey!' The traditional tin cans attached to the back bumper clattered as we pulled away. In the rear-view mirror, Fernwood Buttress rose sharply against the afternoon sky.

Chapter Twenty-One

It wouldn't be polite of me to write about my honeymoon other than to say that Julian proved to be a gentle and considerate lover. And, in truth, he was. But seeing as no one will ever read this entry, I will go further.

Let me start with myself. I had an approximate idea of what would take place on my wedding night but was largely ignorant of the mechanics. Mother had mentioned, after a zigzag from botany to zoology which left me mystified, that married life in the bedroom often required time in order to be successful.

If I'd been with a man who stirred me, I've no doubt I'd have been swept along on a wave of desire and my ignorance would have been of little consequence. The deed would have been done with passion. But instead I had a kind, nervous husband who was at pains not to embarrass me or himself.

But first, the drive to Hermanus.

It took us up the winding Sir Lowry's Pass through the Hottentots Holland mountains, peaks that I'd looked at so often from my side of the peninsula. The heaving ocean soon disappeared and fresh, forested country spread before us. We talked but there was a strange tension which was, I suppose, only natural for two people who'd been acquaintances and now found themselves as man and wife. I allowed myself to be distracted by the stands of proteas crowding the lower slopes, until we finally wound out of the mountains and around the curve of a small bay. By the time we pulled into our hotel, it was already evening and neither of us felt inclined for a late supper.

I changed out of my satin, bathed, sprayed myself with perfume, examined my face in the mirror and pinched my pale cheeks, then put on a cream nightgown that Violet's sister had embroidered with pink roses at the shoulder and hem. When I returned to the bedroom, Julian was waiting for me in bed, in his pyjamas. The room was dark, save for the light from a full moon over the sea, visible through the windows we'd left open to catch a breeze.

We'll see each other, I thought, the moonlight will play over our bodies like a blessing . . .

My nerves began to subside.

He lifted the covers for me. We lay, facing each other, for some time. He stroked my face. The sound of the sea came through the window, waves breaking and retreating. He leant forward and kissed me and I moved my lips against his, waiting for the moment when he would, presumably, take the lead. But it didn't happen and so I sat up and began to unbutton my nightgown.

'You don't have to,' he whispered, alarm flaring in his eyes.

'But we are man and wife,' I murmured, reaching down to kiss him.

Yet it seemed he had no wish for that level of intimacy. He only went so far as to remove his pyjama trousers under the cover of the bed linen and lift my nightgown to my waist. With our top halves still clothed, he attempted to make love to me.

I cannot say that the first time was successful, because I was unsure of which position would best achieve that outcome but would not embarrass him.

'I'm sorry,' he muttered, moving off me and hastily reclothing. 'It will take a little while, my dear.'

'Of course,' I replied, slipping my nightgown down over my legs, when what I most longed to do was throw off the garment entirely – and his, too – and sink against his bare body and listen to the sea as we drifted to sleep. And then wake in the night, naked, to try again.

I shall now secrete this diary in the new hiding place I've prepared.

Chapter Twenty-Two

I'm not sure what other couples do on their honeymoons, but ours was, I suspect, overly prim. We walked on the cliff path above the churning waves every morning; we ate locally caught fish in the hotel dining room; we read books from the collection in the lounge in the evening while I waited for the sea air or the rolling surf or the golden sunsets to work their magic on my husband. Perhaps it was because we were clearly honeymooners – older guests smiled and nodded at us – or perhaps it was that he didn't yet know how to handle a wife. A routine of sorts established itself. We spent the mornings together, and every afternoon, while Julian worked on his lessons for the coming term, I sketched the seagulls strutting on the sand, or the fleshy mats of succulents that clothed parts of the cliff, or the subtle layers of rock that gave it such dramatic form. The afternoons, I realised guiltily, were leaving me more uplifted – as fresh subject matter always did – than the nights with my new husband. As soon as we got to our new home, I'd add colour—

'My,' came a voice over my shoulder, 'that really is very good.'

An elderly man tipped his hat at me.

On our outings, Julian and I talked of his school, our house that I had yet to see, the cost of living in the country versus the city, the rise of a toothbrush-moustached man in Germany . . . and in the evening I'd come into the bedroom with an extra button undone in the hope that it would spark his passion and we would consummate our marriage in a blaze of desire.

We did achieve the consummation, but it was not quite the union I'd expected.

He was flushed and spent, but I was left with a sense of incompleteness.

Yet I was happy for him. And when we left Hermanus, he hummed in the car and took his hand off the wheel and squeezed mine. 'Thank you, my dear. A memorable honeymoon.'

Early morning mist was wreathing the valleys as we retraced our route towards Sir Lowry's Pass.

'Can we stop at the crest?'

He pulled off onto the gravel and we got out of the car. The peninsula spread before us, dominated by Table Mountain and the Fernwood Buttress massif. Twin bays – Table and False – cut scoops into the narrow strip of the Cape Flats in the foreground.

'Why, it's an isthmus,' I turned to Julian in delighted surprise. 'Can you see? The only piece of land that stops Cape Town floating off into the Atlantic!'

'Such an imagination!' He smiled. 'Shall we go on? There's much more to see on the way.'

But not this! I wanted to cry. *Not this!*

'Come, Frances.' He led me back to the car. 'We'll spend tonight in Wellington, then go over Bain's Kloof to Worcester, and the following day onwards to the Hex River.'

135

Rows of emerald vines unfolded across the land, white iceberg roses tumbled riotously over farm gates, Cape Dutch homesteads glowed in the morning sun. We managed light conversation about the ordered landscape, rather like the talk that would have taken place if we were brother and sister. 'They don't need much water,' Julian said, for example, motioning to the green expanse. 'Vines are desert plants, my dear. They only need a little of it at the right time. Too much can dilute the juice.' And so on . . .

The transformation into husband, I rebuked myself, required time and a generous heart. I must invest in Julian before there will be a return.

We stayed overnight at a hotel set in an orchard of fruit trees on the outskirts of Wellington town, a small community huddled beneath the shadow of the mountains we were to cross the following day. While Julian checked the oil and the level of water in the radiator, I wandered among the almost-ripe peaches, fingered their soft skins and rehearsed what I would write to Daph.

You will love married life! Will you come and visit me one day? Our new home is beautiful and I've met many interesting people . . .

He was extra solicitous that night, as if he knew my secret dread.

'You'll want a good breakfast,' said Mrs Uys, our hostess, bringing out generous eggs, bacon and sausages the following morning. 'It's a long way. Have you travelled Bain's Kloof Pass before?'

'Oh yes,' said Julian. 'I come this way often.'

'Take spare water,' advised Mr Uys. 'Check your tyres at

the garage before you start.'

'This pass,' Julian changed gears as we headed upwards, 'was built by a Scotsman eighty years ago.'

I clung to the door handle as the road snaked across the face of the mountains, sometimes revealing a precipice yawning to my left, sometimes forcing us hard by the rock wall. The motor car slowed with the gradient and I watched the temperature needle climb. Hot wind whipped through the windows; flags of cloud swirled over the heights. 'Are we overheating?' I shouted but Julian only shook his head, though his hands gripped the steering wheel so tightly his knuckles showed white. Eventually, after more stomach-churning bends, we broke away from the green valley entirely and found ourselves in a landscape of shattered rocks and bushy proteas that were unfamiliar to me. A huge bird of prey sat in majestic stillness on a pole. Julian pulled into a lay-by and I stumbled out of the car. The bird extended massive wings and took off silently. The valley brooded some two thousand feet below us, farm dams glittering like shiny pennies.

'A different world!' He smiled at me.

I nodded and forced myself to breathe deeply. The mountains of the peninsula now scribbled a distant line, Protea Rise hidden somewhere among them. The twin bays were lost in the haze. On the edge of the gravel, a pair of flowers bloomed on an insignificant plant barely six inches high. I knelt down and picked one. Gentian-blue petals, a speck of black at their centre.

You'll be able to draw wherever you go, Mother had said.

'We must be on our way, my dear.' Julian was holding open the car door. 'It's a long descent.'

'Coming—' I took one last look.

My life will circle back. It must. One day.

From the summit we plunged towards a hot valley. Barefoot children waved to us as we went by. The searing wind made my cheeks feel as if they were being steadily flayed. At the foot of the pass, Julian stopped at a farm stall with a petrol pump and bought us glasses of tart, cold lemonade. I gulped mine down in the shade of a pepper tree while he filled up.

'New to this area?' The farmer's wife looked me over, noting my flimsy open-toed sandals. She wore velskoens, like her husband who was handling the petrol pump: sturdy lace-ups made of tanned hide, like the ones I'd saved from Aunt's belongings.

'Thank you for the lemonade.' Julian came over. 'We're heading Hex River way.'

'Hotter there,' she remarked, taking in my flushed face. 'Good luck.'

Worcester, our next stop, appeared like a mirage surrounded by mountains and bisected by a broad, mostly dry riverbed. As we drove down the main street I could see the tarmac melting on the margins.

'Keep the windows and curtains closed,' advised our host. 'Cooler that way.'

'Why don't you rest?' I said to my husband. 'I'll go downstairs. See if they have any ice.'

But there was no one in the bar so I went outside and down the road, keeping to the shade of overhanging trees. Most people were speaking Afrikaans. The only words I knew came from the conversations I'd overheard between Alfius and Violet.

I seem only able to think in short sentences . . .

'Are you lost, ma'am?' A brown lady stopped beside me as

I hesitated on a street corner.

'No,' I glanced back at the way I'd come, 'I don't think so. But thank you for asking.'

She nodded. A thin child ran up and hid in her skirt.

'You got change, ma'am?'

I looked at her more closely. Her cotton dress was torn. Her eyes were not the brazen or affectedly piteous kind that marked the professional beggar. I could tell she was ashamed to ask. I reached into my pocket and pulled out my purse and gave her all the shillings I possessed.

She clutched them, thanked me and walked away. The thin child followed.

In haste, and then I will tuck this away:

Julian is sleeping. The drive over Bain's Kloof Pass was terrifying and yet, in hindsight, exhilarating.

Then the silence when we stopped at the top, the wildness of the place.

I feel a sense of being adrift, cast away from all that's familiar.

It's to be expected, I suppose. It will be better when we arrive and there is some certainty.

I wonder if he's noticed that I have yet to mention the name of where we're going.

Aloe Glen.

Named by a Scotsman like the one who designed the pass and who saw a resemblance with his beloved homeland. It's too small to be on a map, Julian explained to my parents, when Father searched for it in vain in his atlas. But they weren't to worry. After all, Matjiesfontein is more remote and widely known.

Chapter Twenty-Three

Worcester was cooler the following morning but I still chose my lightest frock, a short-sleeved cream low-waister. Mother and I had clearly miscalculated when putting together a simple trousseau for me, centred around unadorned dresses that would not require excessive ironing – but with sleeves for modesty. I would have to unpick those if I was to survive the summer.

'There's a severe drought at the moment,' Julian said as we drove past scores of men at the side of the road, hoping to be picked up for casual work. 'Poverty is rife.'

'I gave all my coins to a poor woman on the street yesterday.'

'Be sensible, my dear. You can't save everyone you pass by.'

'I suppose not.'

This is a different country from what I know.

'Look at the mountains,' I pointed, to distract myself, 'they're a strange shape, not so much peaks as slabs. Could it be from lava that's flowed in waves?'

Julian smiled across at me. 'You have a geologist's eye, Frances.'

The vegetation, too, was altered. No lush Cape flora but a low understorey, in brown and grey, tinged with dusty green. How would I mix such cryptic shades? What would Mr Cadwaller advise? Yet if I only painted the vividness that lay in my memory, I'd be forever looking backwards. A lone car passed us from time to time but the road was mostly empty, a ribbon of grey stretching ever onwards. The sun climbed higher. The heat beat down on the dark metal of the motor car until it felt as if we were in a furnace. There were wine farms but they were dustier, less lavish. I could not conceive of the kind of place that might lie at the end of our journey. We climbed out of the valley and into a new one bounded by slanting, grey mountains on both sides. I tried to evoke interest in the huge vista but the scale was too great and the heat too intense, and after a while we both lapsed into silence. The only relief came from a meandering line of vegetation marking a stream, flanked by sharp green vineyards. Water was the only thing that stood between riches and ruin, life and death.

I thought of Muizenberg and the cool, deep sea. And I thought of Mark.

'Have you noticed the railway?' Julian pointed to one of the few signs, apart from the sweating tarmac, the dusty vines and a telephone line, that man had passed this way. 'We'll follow it all the way home.'

I struggled not to weep.

An animal came out of the scrub, invisible until the moment of impact. One moment Julian was steering the car in a straight line, the next he was wrenching the wheel and there was a glancing blow against my door and I was falling forward and crying and the tyres were screaming and then we were skidding to a halt on the gravel.

'Frances!' I heard Julian shout. 'Frances!'

The engine cut out. Silence crashed about us. The hot wind

died and in its place came a whiff of burning rubber mixed with heat and sweat.

I lifted a hand to my head but there was no blood, just a dull ache beneath my trembling fingers. 'My head,' I heard myself mutter. My head. Again. I became aware that the door was being wrenched open and Julian was helping me out. He was panting.

'Frances? My dear, are you hurt?'

Why does he call me my dear?

'Why don't you call me darling? Mark called me darling—'

'What?' He gathered me against him. 'Are you hurt?' He pushed away my hair and probed my skull. 'No, thank God,' he muttered under his breath, 'just a bruise.'

I tried to walk away but my legs didn't seem to want to obey my brain and crumpled beneath me.

'Careful!' He lifted me in his arms and carried me to the side of the road.

We stayed there, me cradled in his arms, my cheek against his neck, the broiling veld enveloping us. The banging of his heart was the only movement I could sense.

'The car?' I cried out, after a while. 'How will we go on?'

I don't want to go on! I want to turn back, cross the isthmus of the Cape Flats and go home.

'Hush,' he rocked me gently, 'just rest. The car will be fine. We'll be fine.'

His words registered. I'd said those words, they were mine not his—

'That's what I told my father.'

'What do you mean?'

A piping came from the scrub. A robin perhaps.

'I said I'd be fine, marrying you.'

He bent his head and kissed me. Properly. His lips searched mine, mine opened under his.

And then he went back to the car, took the undamaged canvas water bag from the bonnet and let me have a drink. The sun was directly overhead and the heat was radiating off the gravel with a shimmering intensity that was making my eyes water. The scrubby bush offered no shade. There wasn't a tree in sight. We couldn't stay here in the open, not for much longer.

'What happened? What hit us?'

He gestured a little way back. 'An animal. A buck. I'll see if the car will start.'

I stared down the road. A tangle of fur and legs lay on the tarmac. Julian opened the bonnet of the car. I got to my feet slowly, steadied myself, then walked towards the body.

My brother ran away from me through the garden, beckoning me to follow . . .

It was a tiny antelope, a springbok, surely no more than a week old. Its fur was the colour of milky cocoa, its ears were lined with pink skin, and its eyes were huge and terrified, scarred with the memory of the collision.

'Frances?' Julian called from the direction of the car. 'Don't go there!'

There was a dent in its flank and a small amount of blood. Perhaps the damage was worse inside, crushing those delicate organs, stopping its heart. Or perhaps the little creature simply died of fright.

'Frances!' Julian ran up to me and tried to lead me away.

'No.' I twisted away from him. 'Let me look. He's beautiful. I want to remember what he looks like.'

'But it's dead, my dear. Please,' he took my hand, 'come

away now. Staying won't do any good.'

I knelt down and examined the soft nostrils, the curling eyelashes, the hooves so shiny they might have been polished that morning. I never imagined that death could be so beautiful.

'What will happen to him?'

'There'll be nothing left by tomorrow.' He gestured up into the sky. 'Vultures, birds of prey. Maybe jackals from the veld. They'll be here soon. Every death serves a purpose in Africa.'

I looked up at him. I knew so little about this side of him. Or the hard country I'd entered.

'Do you think he suffered?'

'The little buck? No. It happened too quickly. Come, Frances.' He took my hand. 'We've been fortunate. The car will start. And we can get the door panel repaired. If we'd hit a bigger animal, we'd be in a lot more trouble.'

I took a last look.

'Shouldn't we move him off the road? So another car doesn't hit him?'

'Not necessary. There's little traffic and the carcass will be scavenged soon enough.' He pointed skywards. 'Look, they're gathering already.'

There, circling lazily against the burning sky, was a pair of enormous birds, perhaps like the one I'd seen at the top of the pass. Circling and circling. Waiting for us to leave.

Every death serves a purpose in Africa.

I must be careful. Out here, it will be easy to become a victim.

Chapter Twenty-Four

'You were lucky,' observed Mr Pretorius, the owner of Doorns Garage and Panel Beaters, down a side street. 'Could have taken out the whole side.'

'And me,' I put in with a bright smile as the dust from our arrival in the forecourt settled on my sandals.

'It's no joke, ma'am.' He folded his arms across his chest.

'Of course,' I said. 'Just trying to look on the bright side.'

'Thank you, Mr Pretorius,' Julian said hastily, extending his hand. 'I'll bring the car on Wednesday.'

He hurried me away. As we drove off, I waved to Mr Pretorius who raised a hand.

The land changed again. Individual, fleshy plants studded the scrub. Here and there tall spikes rose from their midst.

'Aloes,' said Julian, following my gaze. 'They were the most distinctive plants the railway workers noticed when they were building the line through to Kimberley and the diamond fields.'

'Poor souls!'

He glanced across, unsure if I was being flippant or serious – or momentarily deranged from the bang on my head. Julian doesn't know me yet. He can't pin me down.

One moment I'm lamenting an antelope, the next I seem to be joking. And I hardly know myself in this heat, on this immense plain—

'There was action nearby during the Boer War, did you know that, Frances?'

'Was Lord Kitchener involved?'

'I've never asked. It's best not to get involved.'

'Not involved? But you live here!' I laughed, gesturing at the stark hills. 'Don't you want to know?'

He lifted his hand where it rested on the gear lever and briefly tapped my arm.

'You should tread carefully, my dear. People don't talk to strangers easily. Memories are long.'

'Because of the war?'

Father had cautioned me all those years ago. He'd said nothing was settled.

'Look!' Julian pointed into the distance. 'There it is! Aloe Glen!'

I craned through the fly-streaked windscreen. At the base of a rearing mountain lay a cluster of houses. Julian slowed down as we approached. A dog sidled across the tarmac. Single-storey houses lined both sides of the road, each property sitting at the back of a fenced plot, curtains drawn against the heat, yellowed squares of lawn out front. One place had a formal bed of red roses, but that was the exception. A flag hung limply above a cafe where a group of men turned to stare at us as we went by. One lifted his hat and Julian acknowledged it with a flick of his finger on the top of the steering wheel. Down a side road named Stasieweg, I saw the railway station. A single platform. A peeling sign for the ticket office.

I should say something. But what?

Julian is waiting for me to say something. I should comment on how neat it looks, how friendly those men seem, how I look forward to meeting my new community . . .

If he had borne me off to a place that was small but beautiful, or small but lively, or even small but snowbound I could have been intrigued. Even enthusiastic. But this—

'How charming.' I forced a smile. 'Where is our house, Julian?'

'Just down here, Marico Road,' he said cheerfully, steering the car off the main thoroughfare. We bumped along a gravel track until he stopped at a fence with a gate inserted into it. He got out and unhooked the gate, and we drove down an earth driveway towards a low, white-painted house with a verandah along its length and a single tree planted in the middle of a brown lawn. There were no flowerbeds, no shrubs, nothing green at all apart from the centrally located tree.

'You'll be able to get going on the garden,' said Julian, pointing to the desolation. I doubted even Alfius could coax anything from such barrenness. Julian opened my door, took me by the hand and led me over the heat-crisped grass towards the house. The red corrugated-iron roof glinted in the sunlight. Gutters led to a downpipe that fed a large green tank mounted on a concrete block by the side of the house. There were no chairs on the verandah.

'Do you have chairs? For the verandah?'

I'd want to sit outside. And, whatever the temperature, I'd never allow the curtains to be drawn across the two front windows so that the place appeared blind.

Julian didn't reply, being too busy unlocking the front door.

I wondered if he would lift me across the threshold as Mark would surely have done, but instead he stood aside and allowed me to go inside first. The interior, at least, was cool and through the dimness I made out dark wood furniture, a bookcase, and a sofa upholstered in green. The curtains were an indeterminate shade of beige – indeed much of the house turned out to be either beige or dark green. The only exception was a maroon rug that covered the floor in front of the sofa.

'You must arrange the furniture however you wish,' Julian said.

I nodded. I could even paint it. If I found no real flowers amongst the scrub to copy, I could paint pretend ones onto the furniture in compensation.

No, Frances, I scolded myself. Be grateful.

'It's a good size house, as you'll see,' went on Julian. 'More than we need, but perfect for a family—'

'Middag! Good afternoon!' came a peremptory voice from behind.

I swung round. A substantially built woman in a sun hat was filling the open front doorway.

'Ah, Mrs van Deventer.' Julian went over to her. 'Come and meet my wife. Frances, may I introduce Mrs Ellie van Deventer?'

'How do you do,' I said, offering my hand.

Ellie van Deventer seized it and squeezed hard and stared at me from my uncovered head to my inadequately shod feet. She must have been about sixty, but it was hard to tell. She might have looked the same from the age of thirty, such must be the desiccating effect of the local climate. She wore her hair scraped into a bun beneath the hat.

'My!' she addressed Julian. 'Isn't she a tiny little thing!'

'Do you live nearby, Mrs van Deventer?' I put in, as Julian looked nonplussed. She must have seen us arriving. Or the

148

men outside the cafe had a particularly swift way of passing on news.

'Just up the road,' she said. 'Next to the Vermeulens. I heard you had an accident?'

I caught my breath and glanced at Julian.

'How did you know?'

She could, of course, have noticed the dent in the side of the car but I soon realised this was my first experience of rural gossip. Perhaps it worked as follows: Mr Pretorius from Doorns Garage and Panel Beaters called up someone in Aloe Glen to say we were arriving and that he'd met the schoolmaster's new wife, and by the way we'd hit a buck on the road and the new wife was quite sweet but rather silly.

'Oh,' Mrs van Deventer took off her hat and fanned herself with it, 'you know, word gets round.'

'I'm sure it does. Julian,' I turned to my husband, 'we must invite Mrs van Deventer for tea once we're settled. I hope you will come.' I edged towards the front door and held out my hand once more. 'Thank you for calling on us and making me feel so welcome.'

What will you say to your friends, Mrs van Deventer? That I have good manners but will surely be too fragile for this life?

'No trouble.' She took my hand again in a vice-like grip. 'I hope you get that car fixed, Julian.'

I watched her clump down the verandah steps.

'She means well,' said Julian, putting a hand on my shoulder.

'Of course,' I smiled up at him. 'Of course she does.'

Despite its relatively small profile, Julian was right about our house: it was a good size. It had a combined lounge and dining room, one bathroom and three bedrooms that looked out onto a yard with a washing line and a view of the particular peak that dominated Aloe Glen. The rooms were high-ceilinged and the floors were wooden throughout. All the windows were curtained in the same shade of beige and I wondered – wickedly – if Julian or the previous owners had taken advantage of a job lot of fabric. The whole place was larger than the cottage Mother and Father now inhabited in Cape Town, with a garden bigger than the original in Embury, although whether the latter feature was a bonus was uncertain. Lack of water would surely limit the cultivation of anything bigger than a postage stamp. The contents of the outside tank were surely for household use.

'Shall I leave you to unpack?' Julian hefted the last of my suitcases into the bedroom, where a bed with a brass heading faced a curtained window. 'Use any of the drawers that are free. And the cupboard.' He indicated a wardrobe against the wall.

'Can I take one of the bedrooms for my painting?'

'Of course. Will you be alright here? I'm going to check on the school.'

He pecked me on the cheek.

I listened to his footsteps echoing on the wooden floor and then a double click as the front door closed. Silence filled the house. The bed had a green quilt and I smoothed it. Julian's new school term was starting in a few days' time. He was the headmaster, it made sense for him to check. I waited for a few minutes – no dogs barking, no whistle as yet from a passing train, no children shouting – then ran into the lounge, flung open the curtains, unlatched one of the windows and pushed it wide.

Cool evening air wafted into my face like an unexpected gift.

I breathed deeply, unpinning my hair and shaking it out. The air smelt of dust overlaid with something faintly herbal that hadn't been noticeable during the heat of the day. As I turned away, I caught sight of myself in an old-fashioned circular mirror on the opposite wall. A pale face stared back, dominated by wary eyes and a halo of un-marcelled hair. For a moment I was back in the hospital after my fall, looking at my bandaged head and torn clothing. I looked away quickly – was that really me? – and opened the front door, ran down the steps and circled round to the back of the house and into a barely grassed yard. Beyond the boundary fence the overhanging peak was turning a subtle shade of pink. I sat down on the step outside the kitchen door. The fragrance I'd detected seemed to be coming from the veld and I sniffed but it was elusive. Sage, or perhaps a wild rosemary . . . A heron flapped slowly overhead, its long neck tucked in, legs trailing neatly behind. I unbuttoned the top of my dress and spread my arms wide and closed my eyes and felt the air play over my skin. In my mind's eye I saw, again, the reflection in the mirror. The woman staring back at me was a stranger.

Julian said later that I must have fallen asleep because of the rigours of the journey and the accident with the buck. He suspected I'd gone outside – perhaps to inspect the washing line – and had become overwhelmed with exhaustion. He was initially worried that I'd fallen but he could find no obvious sign of injury. He claimed that he found me slumped on the ground by the kitchen steps, my dress half off, my hair undone and my head resting on my arms. I remember nothing.

Chapter Twenty-Five

'Will you be alright on your own?' Julian asked on the first day of the new term. He is always solicitous – although what he would do if I said I wasn't, I have no idea. What would you do with a young wife, newly married, fresh from Cape Town, who is not alright?

Send her back?

'I'll paint,' I replied. 'And rearrange the furniture.'

And put up my pictures: *Fernwood Buttress from Protea Rise*, some disas in the waterfall gorge above Kirstenbosch, reminders of what I've left behind but also motivation for what I must create here. One day there should be paintings of Aloe Glen on the walls – the peak, the endless veld, the aloes those Scotsmen saw when designing the railway.

'Yes, do,' he said, leaning down to kiss me on the cheek.

That roadside kiss has not been repeated. Perhaps it only happened in my accident-bruised imagination.

I watched him walk down the drive. The school was only a few minutes away. In fact, everything in Aloe Glen was only a few minutes away. And Julian walked briskly, eager for the challenge of his pupils.

The whistle of the morning train broke the silence.

Even after a short time, I've learnt the timetable of the trains and how their passing divides up the day; and the symphony of creaks and groans in the night as the corrugated roof loses its heat.

Julian sleeps untroubled, while I jerk awake and fall into a fitful doze.

I went into the bedroom I'd set aside for my art and found a small square of stiff card and began to draw. The view through the window – I refuse to close any of the curtains save for our bedroom's at night – happened to show the peak at a perfect angle to the morning light. My pencil moved quickly, finding the striations in the rock at its crest and the mounded scrub on its slopes. Draw, Frances! Paint!

From the station came the sound of the engine building up steam for departure.

Once the sketch was finished, I turned the paper over and wrote on the reverse:

With best wishes,
Frances McDonald.

I put on a dress of blue linen with elbow-length sleeves, squeezed my feet into Aunt's lace-ups, grabbed a basket and matching blue straw hat and set off. It was still early, so the heat had yet to build to the crescendo I now recognised every day until the light faded and the veld exhaled its herby sigh of relief.

I walked up the gravel road – Marico Road – towards the van Deventer house. Their lawn was marginally better than ours, and there was a narrow band of shrubs below the front window where the plants gained some shade when the sun swung behind the house.

What was the etiquette? A rusty postbox hung off the wire gate. I dug into my basket but before I could post my sketch through its opening, the front door opened and Mrs van Deventer waddled laboriously down the steps.

'Good morning!' I called. 'I was going by—'

Did she spend all her time staring out of the window in case of passing traffic?

'Come in,' she shouted. 'What's that you have?'

I unlatched the gate and walked towards her and handed over the sketch. Today she was covered in a voluminous apron that stood out from her frame like a tent and her hair was bound in a scarf. Perhaps I was being unfair; perhaps she'd been in the middle of housework and just happened to glance outside.

She stared at the card, at me, at my hat, and then at the peak. She turned it over to see the message.

'Why? Why have you brought this?'

Have I blundered? Are small notes of appreciation not welcome here? I felt a blush rise into my face.

'I wanted to say thank you. Thank you for calling after we arrived.'

I'd hardly been out, what with unpacking, and no one else had called on us. Julian said folk kept themselves to themselves – and most of the population lived on farms anyway, not in the town – and that I'd meet people in due course and I should not try to push too hard in the early days. But I still felt I might have offended Mrs van Deventer by shooing her out that first day.

'You did this?' She tapped a broad finger on my drawing.

'Yes, I did. I – I hope you like it.'

'*Ja*. It looks like that.' She squinted up at the mountain.

'But you don't have to give me anything.'

She handed the card back to me.

'Oh, but I did it for you,' I said, not taking it back. 'As a gift. Please keep it.'

She hesitated, shrugged and pushed it into the pocket of her apron. 'Do you want to come in?'

'That's very kind, but I can see you're busy. I'm on my way to the store. Perhaps another time?'

'Julian said you painted. There's no one here that paints. No time for it.'

I forced a smile and replied with what I hoped was an appropriate mix of confidence and modesty. 'I'm an artist, Mrs van Deventer. It's what I love to do.'

'It's different here.' She looked me over as she'd done that first time, as if my appearance could give some clue as to why I was the way that I was. 'You'll find out. Tell Mr Fourie at the store I'll be in later.'

'Of course. Goodbye, Mrs van Deventer.'

I held my head high as I walked to the gate.

When I turned and lifted my hand in farewell, she'd already gone inside.

Aloe Glen's main thoroughfare was quiet. I passed the white-painted Dutch Reformed church, set back from the road in a rectangle of dry grass with a faded board out front announcing the name of the dominee and the times for Sunday service. I looked one way, then the other. Not a soul or a vehicle stirred. The houses were as closed up as when we first arrived. A little way out of town, a windmill stood motionless.

I straightened my shoulders.

The town store sat between the cafe – no men lounging

outside today – and the petrol station. It was a long, thin shape, with goods packed onto shelves that stretched from floor to ceiling.

I pushed open the door and was relieved to find human life.

'Morning, Mrs McDonald,' said a ferrety man with a moustache. How did he know who I was? Were my looks so clearly urban and my arrival so comprehensively flagged that I could be no one else?

'I'm Mr Fourie. Your husband has an account with me,' he went on, inflating his chest and giving my linen dress a sideways glance, 'so he charges his goods and pays at the end of every month. Choose whatever you wish. Do you have enough sausages? Mr McDonald is always after sausages.'

I'd already discovered that Julian's diet as a bachelor left much to be desired. The kitchen cupboards contained rows of tins and little else.

'Do you have fresh vegetables?'

Mr Fourie looked at me with a mixture of surprise that I didn't know, and defensiveness that I might find his answer disappointing. 'Once a week on Wednesdays. The drought, you know. Or you could grow your own, ma'am. That's the best way, then you can give them the water they need. Hang on.' He grabbed a small ladder and set it against the shelves and climbed up. 'Ah, here they are. Tomatoes. Beets. Lettuce.' He brandished packets of seeds.

'Why not? Thank you, I'll take them. And do you have chicken?'

In the harried run-up to the wedding, Violet had given me cooking lessons and chicken was a dish I'd mastered. 'One chicken like this, Miss Fran,' she advised over a hot roasted bird, its skin enticingly crisp, 'between two people can last way more than one meal, Miss Fran, if you store it in a cold place.'

Mr Fourie reversed himself down the ladder. 'You'll need to speak to Meneer Erasmus. He keeps chickens. His son goes to Mr McDonald's school.' The ferrety face crinkled into a conspiratorial grin. 'He'll be sure to oblige.'

'I see. What fresh food do you carry, Mr Fourie?'

'I'm short right now, ma'am. It sells out quick. Vegetables on Wednesdays like I said, mealies in season, potatoes on Saturdays when old man Viljoen comes to town, and you can order steak or lamb chops. There's more animals being slaughtered right now.'

'Fruit?'

I thought back to the luscious peaches and pears that Aunt's travelling grocer used to deliver to the door of Protea Rise. I'd imagined they came from places like this, beyond the mountains, but maybe those places had more water than here. Maybe their farmers didn't have to kill their animals because they couldn't afford to feed or water them.

'All depends on the season and the harvest. Parsons' farm, down Worcester way, has apples right now.'

Keeping us fed was clearly going to involve time and multiple vendors.

In the end I settled on tinned beef and ham, some potatoes that Mr Fourie found at the back, bread from the previous day, sugar and tea and a bag of dried fruit. In addition, I found out that the doctor visited once a week, the nearest dentist was in Worcester and if my stomach began to trouble me, I should boil our water twice before drinking it.

'Thank you, Mr Fourie,' I said. 'I'll come in first thing on Wednesday for vegetables.'

I left the store with my laden basket and looked up and down the road again.

Still no one.

But there was a brown bird, a very large one, sitting on a telephone pole opposite, its yellow talons curling over its perch. I stepped onto the road and waited. The sun was beating through my inadequate straw hat. I took one more step. I should get a bush hat if I wanted to spend more time outdoors. The bird swivelled its head and stared straight at me. I caught my breath. Its beak was shiny, deeply curved, and its chest was striped in ribbons of cream and brown. I took another careful step forward. The piercing eyes examined me. I'd need to use the thinnest of my sable brushes to capture those stripes, a thicker one for the muscular talons flexing themselves even as I watched. And the eyes—

A blaring horn made me step back in fright.

A car raced past and I caught sight of shocked faces at the window as they shot by. The bird spread vast wings and took off with effortless power.

I watched until it was a speck against the sky.

Chapter Twenty-Six

I have been here for ten days.

Everyone talks about the drought.

It's as if it is a living thing, squeezing the life out of the locals and turning their land to dust and their animals to skeletons or slaughter.

I've never had to worry about water before.

And I've never seen people spend so much of their time looking upwards for the possibility of clouds.

I've written to Mother and Father and Daph, with the cheery phrases I rehearsed while wandering through the peach orchards in Wellington. I'd be more honest if I was writing to Aunt.

I asked Mr Fourie to arrange for a Cape Argus newspaper to be delivered to us once a week.

I am lonely.

Not even my brother comes to me in my dreams.

Aloe Glen woke in the afternoons despite the pressing heat. The cafe was busy, Mr Fourie's store did a steady trade and the petrol attendant at the garage – a large black man called Tifo – ushered farm lorries to the pumps with a flourish. This increased traffic coincided with the end of the school day and the arrival of the afternoon train. I walked along the road, nodding to several pedestrians. I make a point of nodding to everyone. Julian's school occupied the former mission station originally set up as an alternative to the Dutch Reformed Church that held sway in most rural parts. When the missionaries left, their mission either accomplished or their donors fatigued, the church closed but the accompanying school remained open.

A small group of women was clustered beneath a lone tree at the school gate.

A horse was tied up against a post, its head deep in a nosebag.

As the women turned to look at me, I realised that I was utterly wrongly dressed. They wore neutral-coloured frocks and velskoens, or shirts with drill trousers that may have belonged to their husbands. All wore bush hats. My pale blue linen and matching straw, while valiantly tempering the heat, stood out like a delphinium in a rockery.

'Good afternoon.' I smiled and went forward with an outstretched hand. 'My name is Frances McDonald. I've recently moved here.'

They stared and I wondered if they only spoke Afrikaans and therefore couldn't understand me.

After a few moments, a tall woman in dungarees came over and grasped my hand. The others followed, and then averted their eyes or stared at me and my outfit with curiosity. No one spoke. I racked my brain for something else to say – what a beautiful day, I promise to wear something less frivolous next time – when a bell rang. Children of assorted ages raced across the playground as if issuing from a burst pipe. The horse looked up from its nosebag. The youngsters flung themselves against the women, who greeted them in a mixture of Afrikaans and English and then marched them down the road or into farm lorries that drove off in clouds of dust. Older children slung their satchels over their shoulders, clambered onto bicycles and pedalled away. I watched everyone leave, raising my hand in farewell, and turned towards the school. It was a plain, single-storey building of dressed stone with classrooms down its length, their sash windows set wide open to catch any breeze. When I asked Julian about the age range, he said they took pupils up to fifteen. Older children went to boarding school in Worcester. From one of the classrooms came the faint tinkle of a piano in the rhythm of a waltz and my mind shot back to the Kelvin Grove, my expectations as the orchestra slipped into 'Wiener Blut' . . .

There was a net at one end of the concrete playground and two netball hoops at the other, separated by the white lines of a court. Pigeons rooted at the foot of the boundary fence. Two rugby posts marked out a bare pitch beyond the playground. There was no grass. Anywhere.

I crunched my way across patchy gravel and through a door.

'Frances? What are you doing here?' Julian hurried towards me.

His tie was loose and he looked flustered.

'I came to see where you work.' I reached up and kissed him. 'And to meet some of the mothers.'

He took my arm and steered me down a corridor lined with framed class photographs, and then into an office. His jacket was slung on the back of a chair behind a desk laden with neatly piled papers. A window gave a view onto the empty playground. There was another chair by the wall and he guided me to it before closing the door and taking his own seat behind the desk.

'Is something wrong, Julian?'

He passed a hand across his hair.

I'm getting to know my husband's mannerisms. When he's agitated, he touches his face or his hair.

'You can't arrive without telling me,' he said. 'I'd have met you and introduced you properly.'

'But I did introduce myself,' I said, with a short laugh. 'They shook my hand.' Reluctantly, in some cases, but nevertheless they did – though they didn't notice my farewell wave.

He looked at me for a moment, confused. Julian doesn't yet realise that I'm not like him. I may be lonely, but I refuse to be deferential. If I don't take the initiative, I fear I will expire of heat and boredom in a place like this. Daphne would say I'm being brave. Or maybe I'm just not ready to conform.

You can still be the person you want to be, Father had said at the church door. Marriage will not change that.

'You don't need to protect me, Julian. I can take care of myself.'

'That isn't the point.'

'Then what is?'

We'd never had a disagreement before and I could tell he was unsure how to proceed. Julian was always mild-mannered and slow to criticise. Some would say it's an admirable trait and one I should try to cultivate but, to me, it smacks of having no firm opinions of one's own. I got up, went around the desk and leant down to embrace him. 'I'm sorry to arrive unannounced. But no damage was done, was it?'

'Things happen by the book here, my dear,' he murmured, fingering a lock of my hair that fell against his face. 'People don't like to be surprised.'

'Or perhaps,' I adopted a gently teasing tone, 'you don't like to be surprised?'

There came a peremptory knock and the door opened.

'Julian – oh!' A woman stopped in her tracks, hand over her mouth, eyes sparking with amusement.

I straightened up. Julian struggled to his feet.

'Frances,' he cleared his throat, 'let me introduce Miss Laetitia Snyman, my deputy.'

'How nice to meet you,' I said formally, coming around the desk to shake her hand.

Laetitia Snyman was at least ten years older than me, and not conventionally attractive. Her face was crowned with heavy brows that gave her a faintly simian appearance. But there was an energy to her that was reassuring after the inertia that seemed to grip the town, or maybe it was simply a consequence of the temperature.

'*Veels geluk* – best of luck,' she said with a strong accent. 'I hope you'll be happy here.'

'Thank you.' I glanced from her to Julian. 'Do you wish to speak to Julian privately? I can wait outside.'

'It's the timetable. I can talk to him tomorrow. After I've played for assembly.'

'You play the piano? I heard you as I was walking in.'

'Yes. I'm the music teacher. And I do history as well.'

'Ah, yes.' I laughed. 'I spent years with a textbook called *Cross, Castle and Compass*.'

She raised a furry brow. 'I don't know that one. We use Afrikaans books, mostly.'

'Frances is an artist,' Julian put in, now recovered from the embarrassment of being found in a compromising position

163

with his wife. 'She's very talented.'

Laetitia nodded and backed towards the door. 'Nice to meet you, Mrs McDonald.'

'Frances, please.'

She nodded and left the room.

I listened to her feet tapping swiftly down the corridor. 'She seems very enthusiastic.'

'She is.'

'Why did you say that local people don't like to be surprised? She took it rather well.'

'Frances!'

'Oh, come.' I perched on his desk. 'It's not the end of the world to be seen hugging your wife!'

For a moment I thought he was going to protest, but he simply looked at me with those kind blue eyes as if I were a pupil whom he'd yet to figure out.

'Can I tell you something?'

'Of course.' I went back to the visitor's chair and sat down. 'I'm sorry if I embarrassed you.'

He turned for a moment and contemplated the simmering veld beyond the playground.

'No one knows that my grandfather, Hamish McDonald, was a teacher here.' He turned back to me. 'At this very mission station, although at the time the entire school,' he raised his hands to encompass the building, 'comprised only two classrooms. He taught for five years before returning to Scotland.'

'Why didn't you tell me? Or my parents? We always wondered why—'

'Why I'd buried myself in a rural backwater?'

I blushed and sat back in my chair.

'In his day, my grandfather taught Latin. Today, we have children who can hardly speak English, the language of the world. That's why I'm here, to give these youngsters a chance.'

'But then they might leave Aloe Glen—'

'Indeed.' He lapsed into the usual reticence.

Yet perhaps it was a front to shield a determined impulse, one that I would never have considered him capable of. 'You're saying that you're here,' I began slowly, picking my words with care, 'in this mostly Afrikaans place, to give these children enough English to make their way in the world. Yes?'

He nodded.

'And yet doing so may split them from their families, allow them to find work in the cities, in jobs that their parents wouldn't be able to do? Or understand?'

There a pause and I wondered if I'd been too brazen.

'You express it so well, Frances.' He flashed me a shy smile. 'You use words like the paint in your pictures. Yes, I want them to make the most of themselves. Isn't that what education is all about? Even if it means leaving this place.'

I stared at him. He was a radical. He was willing to undermine his community by encouraging a language that many of the locals still associated with the horrors of the Boer War and the hated imperial foe.

From down the corridor came the piano once again, this time with a lively polka. My feet twitched. Laetitia Snyman was a lady after my own heart.

He leant forward. 'Do you know why I married you?'

I hesitated. 'You said you loved me.'

'I do.' He gave me another shy smile. 'But I recognised early on that you had a particular gift, quite aside from art. You said things out loud that I often thought but could never express.

You seemed able to read my mind and translate it into speech.'

He knelt in front of me and took my hand. There was no confusion in his face, now, only certainty. 'You have the courage to say and do what I can't, Frances. I need that.'

The piano stopped. Or maybe the import of what he was saying smothered all other sound.

In that moment, in that small office, I realised I was not the one who had been rescued by our marriage. My husband needed me far more than I would ever need him.

He got up and held out his arms.

Then he kissed me like he'd done on the road with the fallen antelope and the vultures circling.

Every death serves a purpose in Africa.

As we broke apart I wondered if the death that had occurred was also mine: my younger, naïve self.

And I wondered what new self I would grow.

Chapter Twenty-Seven

I like my husband. I'm not in love with him – those emotions remain locked away in Cape Town with Mark – but I care for him in a way I didn't believe possible during the stilted days of the honeymoon and the fumbling caresses beneath our nightclothes.

It's no exaggeration to say that the tone of our marriage changed after Julian's confession.

He was unburdened; I no longer needed to hold my tongue.

Or did I?

I now had the confidence of my husband and yet I was uneasy.

Or perhaps uneasy is the wrong word . . .

Since arriving in Aloe Glen I've begun to feel as if I can't quite trust myself or my opinions. The bold instincts that Father encouraged, Mother rued, and Daphne admired, are being disturbed. Like the disturbance you see in a glass of water placed on a barely vibrating surface. A casual glance shows nothing untoward: the glass is intact, the water has not spilt. But look more closely and you see the perturbations, the tiny circular waves building and crashing against one another.

Is it the heat? The remoteness? The lack of green grass? The accident?

The absence of Aunt and her trenchant opinions?

I can't blame the accident; the tender lump beneath my hair subsided after a week or so.

But the possibility of becoming a victim myself has not. It preys on me.

The innocent buck, the watching veld, the vultures circling overhead.

It is, in its way, a twisted, negative version of the sharpness I felt after falling out of the oak.

I must be on my guard. All is not what it seems.

I am not what I seem.

Chapter Twenty-Eight

'Do you have an art teacher?' I asked Julian over our first roast chicken dinner. Meneer Erasmus had indeed been willing to provide us with a fresh bird every fortnight. And I'd been first in line on Wednesday morning for vegetables, where I met a tall woman in dungarees whom I'd first seen at the school gate. She said her name was Sannie Metz.

'No,' he sighed, 'we don't have the funds for a teacher.'

I waited for a moment, hoping he might follow where I was leading.

'I could start an art class after school. Say, once a week?'

It was, in truth, a selfish offer. If I didn't reach out, I'd be stuck in my house making the same picture of Aloe Peak over and over, because so far Mrs van Deventer was the only person who'd called and there was little housework since Julian engaged a quiet coloured woman called Sipata to clean the place. I wrote weekly letters to Daph, less often to Sue – my life is now so remote from hers I suspect our correspondence will soon evaporate – but words on a page aren't enough.

'What a good idea!' Julian leant across the table and took my hand. 'Do you have enough materials?'

'I do. We could start drawing, and move on to paints later.

I have more than enough to share.'

'My dear,' said Julian, his pale eyes warm, 'I'll announce it at assembly.'

'Why don't you offer adult literacy classes?' From the broken conversations at the school gate it was clear the children weren't the only ones in need of English tuition. 'I'd help with that, too.'

Again, it was a selfish suggestion but you can't expect a town to embrace a stranger until she proves her worth. I was in need of credibility that went beyond merely being the headmaster's wife.

'English classes for grown-ups?' He gave me an amused glance. 'That might be controversial.'

'More than art? Think of all those Rubens nudes . . .'

He gave me a startled glance. 'You wouldn't—'

'Of course not! We'll draw flowers and sunsets – I promise!'

'I can't wait for us to have our own family, my dear. You'll be a fine mother.'

I smiled at him. I had no wish to start a family just yet, even if it would provide welcome distraction. It seemed to me that motherhood in Aloe Glen was a kind of treadmill. As soon as one child was born, the pressure was on to deliver the next, and the next. Mothers at the school gate corralled flocks of children. Julian's reserve in the bedroom, I reflected with some guilt, meant I was unlikely to fall pregnant until his awkwardness – and his technique – improved.

On the first day of my project, I settled myself in the junior classroom with sheets of paper and boxes of pencils and awaited my first pupils. I planned to take the children outside, steer them towards a suitable subject – a shiny beetle, the outline of Aloe Peak, that lone tree at the school gate – and then we'd return to the classroom to capture what we'd seen on paper.

That first, critical glance . . . I heard Mr Cadwaller saying.

'Good luck!' Laetitia Snyman poked her head around the door. 'It's very good of you to make time!'

I have more time than I know what to do with, Laetitia.

I listened to her heels clicking down the corridor. No one came. I sat for an hour. Then I got up and looked in a small mirror on a side wall.

Maybe it was my hair? I refused to scrape it into a bun as was the local style. It was loose, swept back off my face with the tortoiseshell combs Mother had given me for my eighteenth birthday. I gathered up the paper and pencils and put them into my basket and closed the classroom door quietly behind me. Julian was supervising a student teacher and not available. The whistle of the afternoon goods train cut through the quiet. I walked across the playground, down the main thoroughfare and along Marico Road to our house. The odd shout came from invisible children playing in hot backyards. No cars came along the road. I didn't turn in. I didn't want to go home. I kept walking until the road petered out and the veld began. The sun pounded down and I angled the brim of my hat to protect my neck, and picked my way through the low scrub. Heat mirages danced at the horizon. I began to feel light-headed and pulled two sheets of paper from my basket and placed them down, gathered my skirt beneath me, and sat. Ants scurried by my feet, twitched about my sandals, but moved on. Around me, low grey-brown bushes with tiny, hard leaves thrust themselves from the dry earth. Here and there, thin spears poked upwards. Maybe – I leant forward with a stab of interest – they were

171

actually the stalks of bulbs past blooming?

I grabbed a sheet and pencil and began to draw.

A thin black stem tipped with a shrivelled head that I'd have missed if I hadn't been at ground level. I should come back to this spot, watch through the season, wait for their flowers, dry one and send it to Kirstenbosch with a sketch—

'Ma'am?'

I swung round and scrambled to my feet. A woman in a faded dress and a battered hat stood behind me.

'Hello,' I said, wiping my hand on my dress before extending it. 'I'm Frances McDonald.'

She ignored my greeting and bent down and retrieved my sketch from where it had fallen, and examined the drawing as if it were a medium she'd never come across before. Then she knelt and pointed to the plant I'd been copying.

'Yes.' I knelt down beside her. 'I think it's a bulb.'

'Bulb.' She pronounced the word slowly, and nodded her head.

'Does it have flowers, in the springtime?'

'September.'

'What colour? *Watter kleur*?' I reached for my smattering of Afrikaans.

'Purple.'

She had dark eyebrows that contrasted with hair which was almost white, presumably bleached from the sun. Her skin was tanned nut-brown. Then she handed me the sketch and ran off, her bare feet agile and sure over the scrub. She didn't return to the road but instead leapt across the veld like an antelope rather than a human. I had a sudden picture of her running across a road oblivious to an oncoming motor car, and colliding with it.

172

'I'm so sorry, my dear,' Julian said later, over dinner, about my slow start. 'We're part of a rural community. Culture isn't a priority.'

'I'll give it another try. I'll ask Laetitia if she can find a candidate in one of her classes.'

Maybe if one child came, others would join. And this wasn't like swimming beyond the breakers; I didn't need to be mindful of leading anyone into danger. Daph, the unknown boy . . .

'I know these people,' Julian went on, 'they're not easily swayed. If you haven't had any takers, I doubt you will again. Don't agonise, my dear. There are other things to occupy you.'

'What, exactly?'

'Why, this house,' he gestured, 'your own art, a garden with some vegetables, you have the seeds—'

'But I want to make a difference, Julian, like you do.'

I could tell this was an argument I wouldn't manage to translate for him. Julian came from a world where women were supportive, perhaps clever, but not necessarily enterprising.

'I don't want to be a decoration!' I found myself shouting. 'I want to make something of my life here!'

'And you will,' he soothed, patting my clenched fist on the tablecloth. 'Give it time.'

It was what Mother said in her latest letter: It will take time, Frances. You're always too impatient.

I breathed deeply and toyed with my leftover chicken.

'I met a woman today.'

'Excellent!' beamed Julian. 'I'm sure you'll soon have a circle of friends.'

'She ran through the bush. She didn't stay on the path.'

'What were you doing out in the veld? I've warned you not to stray—'

'I was just at the end of Marico. Where it becomes scrub. Looking at the plants.'

'Who was this woman?'

I gathered our plates. There were oranges for dessert. Mr Fourie had kept some aside for me. I'd peeled them and cut them into rounds and we'd have them sprinkled with a little sugar.

'She never told me her name. She had white hair. And she could run fast.'

She was gone before I could pin her down.

Like the child in my dreams slipping away before I could tell if we looked alike.

'I'd rather you didn't talk to strangers, Frances. There are vagrants about, you're a beautiful young woman. And please stay in town, the veld is rife with scorpions and snakes.'

'I could draw them,' I murmured, staring out of the window.

'Frances.' Julian ran a hand through his sparse hair. 'Please, my dear. Don't be irresponsible.'

You're lucky, I wanted to shout once again, and bang the plates I was holding until they smashed. *You're not searching for occupation!*

But I didn't. I reminded myself that he is my husband and a good man. Laetitia Snyman has said that Julian is transformed since our marriage. He's more confident with the staff, more decisive. If I stray, if he loses what I've brought him, that new-found bravery will drain away. Whereas I—

We washed the dishes in silence.

Afterwards, when Julian retired to prepare the following day's lessons, I went out of the kitchen door and sat on the step and watched the mountains change from purple to grey, and sniffed the fragrance rising from the veld. I closed my eyes and conjured up Protea Rise and the sugarbirds hopping in the proteas. And then I imagined myself floating by the side of a dark-haired young man at Muizenberg as the swells lifted us on a turquoise sea.

Chapter Twenty-Nine

Mornings and evenings were the time for subtlety in Aloe Glen. The rising or lowering sun softened the landscape before it succumbed to the harsh glare of yellow sun or the dead black of night. In the weeks after our arrival, I drew Aloe Peak from each of our rooms in the morning and in the evening. Ten sketches so far but none worth posting to the director at Kirstenbosch due to my own failings rather than the mountain's. I looked for bright proteas in the foreground, or towering yellow-woods, or the darting purple flight of a kingfisher, but there were none of those and my pencil faltered. I could have changed subjects and drawn the antelope whose terrified eyes and broken body were still sharp in my mind, but that was too much like trespassing on a tragedy.

Dear Daph, I wrote briefly on a postcard featuring a steam train against a lurid sunset.

I'm learning to love Julian. Time can help! I've met some people and I'm making friends. It's hot and I miss you all, but our house is a good size and I'm starting to paint.

Can't wait to come back for your wedding!
All my love
Fran

On Sunday mornings we attend the Dutch Reformed church. Julian wears a suit and I wear one of my trousseau dresses and heels that stick in the ruts of the gravel road as we walk. Julian feels it is important to show solidarity with the community even if we might not appreciate the more complex sermons. But, in fact, it turned out to be easy. The theme was consistent. I needed to consult a dictionary at first but after a few Sundays I understood.

'*Die hemel en die aarde,*' the dominee thundered from the pulpit, '*behoort aan die Heer!*'

The heaven and the earth, I translated to myself, belongs to the Lord.

'*Bekeer!*'

Repent!

'It's so grim,' I protested as we headed home, Julian nodding and raising a hand to other congregants as we passed. 'Where is kindness and brotherly love?'

'Rural people live at the whim of nature, my dear. Repentance is an appeal to God for mercy.'

'For rain? But isn't that a kind of bargaining? I will repent but then You must bring rain?'

'Hush, Frances.' Julian looked about. 'Don't talk like that in public.'

The following week I arrived at the school gate early with my basket of paper and pencils.

'I hope some of your children will come to my art class today,' I said brightly to the waiting mothers, many of whom I also recognised from church. I was dressed differently. No more low-waisted linen dresses and matching straws. I'd bought a set of khaki boy's dungarees from Mr Fourie – there were no women's and the men's were designed for individuals

177

the size of bears – and paired it with a plain white shirt. But my hair stayed loose. Susan, back in Embury, would approve.

'The classes are free.' I moved to a second group which included a Mrs Engelbrecht whom I'd met at the store and exchanged a few words with about the lack of rain. 'We'll be drawing outside.'

I didn't wait for them to look away or for the school bell to ring, but smiled and marched confidently across the playground towards the classroom that had been set aside.

Let them gossip amongst themselves about this strange wife of the headmaster, I told myself. Let them giggle about how she didn't speak their language . . . but let them also wonder if a child who held back from rowdy games might enjoy a gentler pursuit with pencil and paper.

I set up my easel and began to draw.

A pile of books stacked in a corner.

A world map unevenly tacked on a wooden board so that it looked as if the continents were drunk.

Ten minutes went by. The bell rang. Teachers shouted above the noise of slamming desks. Feet drummed along the corridors and I straightened up and faced the door with a smile.

The noise abated after five minutes and I got up and glanced through the classroom window. A ball was being kicked across the hard pitch by a group of boys in sports kit. The mothers at the gate were gone. The children who cycled to nearby farms were gone. Only a cloud of dust remained, churned up by their various wheels as they drove off.

'Mevrou McDonald?'

I turned.

A young boy was hovering in the doorway. Behind him – and nudging him into the room – was the woman from the veld. She wore the same faded dress but this time she had shoes on her feet and she'd tied her white hair into a loose plait. I couldn't remember seeing her on Sundays. Maybe, like me, the outdoors was her preferred church.

'Hello,' I said quietly to the boy, when I really wanted to embrace him. 'I've been drawing. Would you like to see what I've done?'

I don't know if he understood me, but he edged forward and I led him towards my easel and began to add the outline of a fish leaping out of the sea beside the continents.

The boy grinned.

I pulled up a chair for him, set out fresh sheets of paper and a box of coloured pencils.

'If we make a circle,' I drew one, 'it can be the start.'

I added a second, smaller circle above the first, two tiny ones for eyes, a flick for ears . . .

'*Uil*!' The boy looked at me in amazement, seized a pencil and copied me.

'*Uil*,' I repeated, smiling. 'Owl.'

We will teach each other, this child and me.

I glanced back at the doorway but his mother was gone.

Chapter Thirty

Beloved Fran, Father wrote after their first visit to Aloe Glen. Your mother and I are so pleased you've settled happily into your new home.

Sadly, your mother has been unwell since we returned. A chill, that has taken a while to shake off.

As soon as she's fit, we'll come and see you again.

There's a new president in America who says he has a New Deal to overcome financial woes. Look out for an article in the latest Argus. *Certainly, that would be better than the kind of National Socialism that's being peddled in Germany.*

On a local note, I can understand how you fell in love with the Cape, my dear.

I took a walk to Protea Rise yesterday. I happened to see a brown man working there called Alfius who asked to be remembered to Miss Frances. He said the proteas miss you, which is a preposterous thought, but rather charming.

Your ever loving Father

The leaves on our centrally located tree hung their heads. Sometimes I tugged them slightly to see if they were still attached, fearing that they may only be held on by the memory of sap.

As soon as I collected my new velskoens from Mr Fourie, I headed back into the veld. The vegetation surrounding Aloe Glen seemed designed by God or evolution somehow to survive minimal rain and violent temperatures. Plants had the option of going dormant for a season but most animals interested in self-preservation could only venture out once the heat had abated. So I waited until the sun was striking the mountains at a low angle, bringing out the relief in the topmost rocks and throwing the lower reaches into shadow. If I sat quietly on my folding stool I could disappear into the landscape, become part of the scrub, and wait for it to give up its secrets.

No chattering sugarbirds here. No busy white-eyes. But perhaps, if I was patient . . .

I smoothed my shirt. What would my friends, English or Cape, think if they saw me now? Sitting in the middle of the bundu in a slouch hat, drill trousers and one of Julian's old shirts?

Poor thing . . . what a comedown.

Yet who were they to criticise, I could hear Aunt Mary retort – or, for that matter, Mr Cadwaller. Who among them had the wits to seize such an alien life?

The sun edged further towards the horizon. A whistle and a series of puffs announced the passing of the evening goods train. Soon, if there was no action, I'd need to get back and start cooking. Sipata peeled the vegetables before she left but the main course was my responsibility. Julian's routine was strict: dinner at 7 p.m., two hours of marking, bed by ten. The call, when it came, was quiet, no more than a peep. I strained through the undergrowth. A dun-coloured bird hopped along a track, stopped, and looked at me. Its feathers were the colour of the earth and if it had been motionless I might have missed it entirely except for one, outstanding, feature: a blazing orange throat.

We watched each other, equally astonished I believe, before it flitted off.

'I saw a new bird!' I burst into the lounge. 'With an orange throat!'

'Oh yes?' said Julian, not looking up from his exercise book. 'I hope you didn't go too far.'

'It was such a surprise, that colour amidst the brown—'

'I'm sorry, my dear, I'm rather busy. Don't you need to make dinner?'

I pulled off my hat and hung it on the stand by the front door and waited for a moment.

The eagle on the telephone post on my first trip into town.

The narrow stalk above a shrivelled bulb. A small brown bird with a blazing orange throat.

I'd have to look hard. My subjects would no longer be easy to see or available in great numbers. Colours would be mostly dun, rarely dramatic—

I ran into the bedroom that was my studio, grabbed a pencil and began to draw.

Dinner was late that night.

The woman from the veld was named Truda Louw. Her son, Deon, was my only pupil for a year. I met Sannie Metz and Aletta Erasmus regularly at the school gate or in church but it was only Truda who showed any curiosity about me. Newcomers, Mother had warned me in a moment of insight, hold no interest for incumbents. The Louws lived in a simple cottage close to the railway line and Truda's husband was a wheel-tapper. I knew she could never be a friend in the way that Daph was, but she was willing to speak to me even though we couldn't manage each other's languages particularly well. Yet I've discovered that when there is need on both sides, words matter less than you think.

'Were you born here, Truda? In Aloe Glen?'

'*Ja*,' she said, picking at her nails which were bitten to the quick.

'Look, I brought a flask. Will you have some tea while Deon is drawing?'

'*Dankie*. Thank you. There is enough?'

'Of course.'

We drank in silence. Deon drew, his tongue sticking out in concentration.

'Your hair is *pragtig*,' Truda said, pointing to my combs.

I'm flattered she noticed for I have the sense, when I look in the mirror at home, that I'm becoming just another anonymous Karoo wife in dungarees and velskoens.

My choice of friend did not go unnoticed.

'You want to watch that Truda Louw,' sniffed Mrs van Deventer.

'Why, Mrs van Deventer?'

'They say she's not right.' She motioned to her forehead. 'In the head.'

'She's been kind to me,' I said, lifting my chin. And I may not be right in the head, either.

'Mrs van Deventer says Truda is deficient in some way,' I said to Julian over breakfast. I'd persuaded him to put a small table on the verandah. Sometimes sparrows hopped towards us, eager for crumbs.

'She's had a hard life. Her husband is a mean fellow. Young Deon doesn't say much in class.'

But he must have talked for, at the start of the next year, eight children turned up to my art class.

'Welcome,' I said, speaking in English though by now I could manage simple Afrikaans. 'What's your favourite colour?'

'*Rooi*,' piped up a girl in pigtails.

'Here's a red crayon. Draw me a flag with stripes and spots! Anyone else?' I held up a fistful of crayons.

'Me! Me!'

'Thank you, Mevrou McDonald,' said Sannie Metz later at the school gate.

There was a stir of wind. She glanced up. 'Maybe rain, *mevrou*?'

'I hope so.' I'd already gathered that the Metz farm was in trouble.

'My Toby,' ventured Mrs Engelbrecht from the fringes, miming a child stumbling.

'Clumsy? Drawing would help, *mevrou*. Let him give it a try.'

'You've done well,' said Laetitia Snyman with a grin. 'You hung on till they came.'

There is a further, unexpected benefit: the mothers speak broken English to me because they don't believe I understand any Afrikaans, so each conversation becomes a stealth lesson in literacy.

I'm aiding Julian's quiet radicalism.

While the children drew flags and mountains with the sun

setting garishly behind them, I focussed on the dry veld at the end of Marico Road. I'd always identified my Cape Town plants – *Protea repens*, *Lampranthus vygies*, disa orchids – but my bush selections were a mystery. So I drew them the way I saw them: low, small-leaved plants that grew slowly and bloomed sparingly. I waited to capture flowers that appeared on fleshy stems for a few weeks and then died of heat; I waited until the bulb I'd first seen as a shrivelled stem flowered in the spring.

It took a year.

A year of broiling heat, biting cold, dust-laden wind – and an unsuccessful attempt to grow vegetables that succumbed to either thirst or insects. A year when milky springbok with teetering fawns stepped across the veld, caught my scent even though I held my breath, flicked their ears and leapt away. A year during which I travelled back to Cape Town to Daph's wedding and wore my sea-green chiffon and laughed with friends and said how happy I was and stayed away from Protea Rise lest it undo me.

Three veld sketches, with each unnamed specimen drawn in leaf, in flower, and dormant. Examples of each stage, dried and pressed between the pages of my heaviest book.

I put on my linen dress. It still fitted me; there was no baby yet.

A year's careful work deserved a formal send-off.

'Mr Fourie, I have a parcel for Cape Town that I want to protect from getting bent.'

'Pictures?' He darted a look at me. The fact that I sat in the veld for hours was well known around town.

'Yes,' I replied. 'I'm sending them to the director at Kirstenbosch.'

Mr Fourie rooted beneath the counter and found a set of cardboard inners that he placed around the parcel, then put the whole thing into an oversized envelope, and I paid him for the stamps.

'Thank you, Mr Fourie.'

'Take it yourself, ma'am.' He looked at his watch. 'Train's due in thirty minutes.'

I crossed over the empty main road. Dust devils, those fleeting whirlwinds that rise up in a vortex and die away almost as quickly as they appear, barrelled across the veld beyond the railway line.

I waited for an hour, on a bench on the platform.

A bird of prey circled, joined by another. A carcass nearby, perhaps.

Every death serves a purpose in Africa, Julian had said.

'*Mevrou*?' A man was walking along the railway track. He wore blue dungarees and carried a box of tools. He had a beard that straggled down his chest.

'Good day!' I jumped up. 'How long till the train comes?'

'*Amper*. Soon,' he said, dumping his toolbox on the ground.

I sat down and looked along the tracks but there was no telltale smoke denoting an imminent arrival.

'What do you teach my son, *mevrou*?'

'I beg your pardon?'

'You teach my son.' His words came out resentfully, as if they cost him.

'I'm not a teacher, Mr— I'm sorry, I don't know your name.'

'You are. He stays after school.'

'Ah.' I forced a smile. 'Does he come to my art class?'

The man nodded, coming closer, his hands on his hips, his

186

face scowling up at me.

This must be Deon Louw's father, the wheel-tapper, the man whom Julian described as mean, who perhaps accounted for the way Truda bit her nails and looked over her shoulder even when there was no one there.

'I teach the children how to draw. How to shade. Are you Deon's father, sir?'

He leapt up onto the platform. It was too late to run. I could scream but no one else was about.

'Don't teach my son *Engelse kak*,' he spat, looming over me. 'My boy's an Afrikaner!'

There was still no whistle, no singing from the rails to signal the arrival of the train.

'Of course,' I said, staring at him. 'We draw sunsets and flowers, Meneer Louw.'

'That's what you say,' he snorted. 'It's a trick. Like before, when they took our women and children and put them in camps! Burnt our farms!'

'Come, sir.' I forced a laugh. 'I'm just teaching children to draw. That's all.'

Yet what if he was right? What if my classes – and Julian's – were leading the children into deep water, towards a wave they might not be able to crest? Yet surely they deserved their chance to try.

'*Goeie middag*, Meneer Louw,' I said, standing up. 'Good afternoon.'

'What about that?' He gestured at my package. His eyes were inflamed. He might grab my paintings, toss them to the ground, stamp on them and destroy what has taken me so long to achieve.

'I'll come another day. When I hear the train.'

187

The package could wait for one more day. It had taken a year, after all, to get this far.

I turned and walked away slowly to avoid enraging him further. For Wynand Louw, every interfering Engelse was a fresh assault in a war that still raged, thirty years on. Yet with anyone else I might have been prepared to admit that the classes benefitted me, too. The learning achieved by the others – whether of art or language – builds me, helps me through each dry week.

Dear Director Compton
I hope that you are well. I have no reference book for
Karoo flora, therefore I am unable to identify the plants
I have drawn. They are different from anything I have
ever seen before. Their lives are ruled by a lack of water
so the leaves are small to prevent evaporation, or fleshy
to enable them to store whatever moisture they manage
to find.

I would be grateful if you could write back and tell
me the names of what I have drawn. And if Kirstenbosch
is able to pay me a small sum for my work, then I
could save up to buy a reference book. I could seek out
unusual specimens at your request. The aloes, higher up
the mountain, are specific to this area, I believe.

Thank you for your previous encouragement and
support, sir.
Yours sincerely
Frances McDonald

Chapter Thirty-One

Imagine, if you can, a landscape of pitiless thirst: roots scrabbling through dust, rocks cracking, a sense of unforgiveness. Perhaps this is what the dominee plays on when he exhorts us to repent: our tears, to part-quench the thirst beneath our feet. I've begun to walk further. Not just into the veld but to the northern edge of town where coloured folk like Sipata and an increasing number of poor whites live in simple shacks. They nod to me and I nod back to them. The men from this community work on the farms or maintain the railway line, and the women work for white people who can afford to pay them. No one makes much money these days, and even white skin doesn't exclude you from poverty. I don't come here to stare at the community, although I often bring clothes to donate to the dispossessed families or a pumpkin that we've been given that is too big for us to eat once I've given Sipata a share. I come here to see Aloe Glen's thirst, from a unique vantage point. And to try to understand.

Unlike the oak in England, it's not a vantage built on height, but rather on geography.

To my right the land is succumbing to Karoo semi-desert; to my left it still has elements of the lush peninsula. To my right, sheep browse the scrub and dust stirs over the brown veld. To my left, the river still carries enough water to turn the bordering land green enough to support vines. Above this divide reigns Aloe Peak, directing what little rain there is to one side or the other.

I paint the divide. And I see the desert encroaching.

I had to wait to show Father my vantage point until Mother recovered from her illness and the season was favourable. Winter in Aloe Glen was too cold and summer too searing for comfort. They arrived by train on a cool autumn day with the dust devils quiescent and a farmer driving sheep to the train for onward journey to market. Bleating and not-quite-muffled curses echoed along the platform as Mother and Father alighted. The conductor threw up his hands at the chaos and climbed back on board. Mother frowned at my bush shirt and trousers while Father raised his hat to the farmhands as if they were besuited mail ship passengers. 'My,' he shouted, watching the loading operation with interest after we'd hugged, 'so this is how we get our mutton!'

I drew him hastily away. Father wasn't to know that the railways had introduced cheap rates for farmers forced to send their entire flocks to slaughter. This was one such tragedy visited upon Sannie Metz and her family from the drier side of town. I tucked Mother's arm through mine and led her to the motor car. Normally we'd have walked from the station but Father had written to say Mother wasn't yet strong enough for any distance beyond one hundred yards on foot.

'You can drive, Frances?' She looked at me uncertainly from the front seat.

'Yes, I took my licence in Worcester.'

'Bravo!' called Father from the back seat as we lurched

off. The train whistled and departed to a further chorus of bleating. I wondered how Mr Metz could bear to watch. There was no sign of Sannie. Men loitering in front of the cafe turned to look at us as we drove by and I nodded to them out of the side window. Mrs van Deventer, on her knees in the vegetable patch, raised a pudgy arm. She'd been more forthcoming of late, since I'd managed to harvest six unblemished tomatoes from the straggly crop nurtured beneath our bedroom window.

'How are you, Frances?' Mother asked later, patting a hand over her hair and examining me closely.

'I'm well,' I said as I poured tea on the verandah. 'Julian and I are content.'

Mother's anxiety centres around the fact that there is no baby. I'm also beginning to wonder, for Julian is more accomplished than before. Perhaps my qualified affection is the reason I've not yet conceived.

'Indeed.' Mother pulled her cardigan closer. 'You must look after yourself.'

Mother is also disconcerted by the thirsty land about us, but she's reassured by the number of people with whom I'm on nodding acquaintance. And as regards my personal view of Aloe Glen – should either of my parents ask – I'm prepared to defend what I at first derided, mainly to save Father from residual guilt, but also because I don't want to be pitied. And also because Director Compton has written back to say that at least one of my specimens was unknown to Kirstenbosch and could I send more paintings?

We can pay you an honorarium, Mrs McDonald, for similar work. I am particularly interested in the aloes.

I danced around the house, holding the letter.

Our quiet Sipata broke into a giggle as she polished the furniture. 'Ma'am is happy?'

And mostly I am, although just when I believe I've forgotten my old love, I see a particular shade of dark hair or I recall the touch of lips that are not my husband's – and I'm wrenched back.

Is this a kind of adultery of the heart?

Father and I set out early the following morning towards the lower slopes of Aloe Peak. I was wearing dungarees and velskoens, to Mother's distaste. At some stage I must point out that tanned hide, rather than patent leather, convey both status and practicality in Aloe Glen. We climbed steadily, Father and I, him using his stout walking stick on the uneven path. The sky stretched overhead, bare of any clouds; I've come to expect that they will occasionally build up only to melt away in teasing fashion. Sometimes there is lightning, sometimes distant thunder brings folk onto the streets, but rain rarely falls. The air is so clear that the horizon appears infinite in a way I never knew in England, extending far beyond the crisp line of the valley or the distant plain that leads to Kimberley and, conceivably, all the way to Cairo.

'It's certainly dramatic, Fran. And tranquil.'

We stopped and looked back. A train crawled north under a head of smoke; the mountains thrust sharp profiles into the blue. Father didn't need to know the unease I still feel, the vibrations beneath the surface that emerge when I meet someone like Wynand Louw who regards me as the enemy.

Am I safe here? I asked my diary that day.

'At least we don't have to climb a tree,' Father gave a quick grin, 'to get a view.'

'It's all in front of us,' I nodded. 'As far as the eye can see.'

He unbuttoned the leather case he was carrying around his neck and passed me the latest set of binoculars. I adjusted the focus and traversed the mountainside. Grey-brown *bossies* struggled to survive amid tumbled rocks of grey and ochre but also – my heart quickened – a pinkish aloe, its tentacled leaves clasped around its heart as if in prayer.

'Your mother is dying, Frances.'

I pulled the glasses from my eyes.

'No! It can't be—'

Mother, carefully set Mother? Who tried and failed to mould me in her likeness, whom I've loved but never really understood—

'I'm afraid so.'

Father, his face suddenly haggard, put his hands on my shoulders and drew me into his arms. 'They say it's her lungs.' He rocked me gently, the glasses pressed between us. 'It may have started even before we left England. There is no cure, my dear.'

I didn't cry.

I sat down on the stony ground and Father levered himself down beside me. He pulled his watch out of his waistcoat and looked at it, as if the time mattered.

'Will she have treatment? Is there a chance?'

'Dr Reed says they'll try, but it's already too late. We must be strong, Fran.'

The sun crept higher across the face of Aloe Peak, illuminating clefts that had earlier appeared flat.

'How long does she have, Father? How long do we have?'

I measure time by the seasons that pass without rain.

'Months. Maybe a year.'

Mother may not live to see whether I have a child.

'Will you tell me my brother's name?'

Father didn't answer for a while. But I had to know. I had to talk to Mother about him so that he could live on even when she was gone.

'Gideon. His name was Gideon.'

'How old was he, when he died?'

'Four years old, Fran.' Father closed his eyes for a moment. 'He died of tetanus.'

The disease that comes when children run and fall and scratch themselves.

'That's why, when you fell, Fran, your mother—'

'She thought I might die, too.'

Father put his arm around me. How often have we sat, side by side at a vantage point, while he taught me about what I was seeing or what history lessons I should heed or the value of a solid investment? But never before about my brother. Or Mother's fear that I might die like him.

A rock kestrel hovered over the veld, then dived, then pulled up and hovered again.

'What will you do, Father?'

'I will carry on.' Father straightened his shoulders. 'Just as you will. I will seek out new clients, and you will paint more pictures.'

I stared straight ahead. I didn't want to see his face, or show him mine. The sky was turning more white than blue as the day warmed. Soon, the kestrel might decide to return to its nest and wait for the cool of evening before beginning its hunt for food once more.

Father got to his feet and held out his hand to me. 'Shall we go back?'

'Just a little further, please, Father.'

When we reached it, the aloe I'd spotted through the binoculars looked as if it had been rolled across the veld by the wind and somehow anchored itself just before falling down the mountainside. From that precarious attachment, it didn't then stretch out its spiked leaves for balance but bundled them together so that they resembled a kind of circular arrangement of barbed wire. And it was a shade of dusty pink. An armoured, pink plant that would require the blending of rose madder, viridian and ochre, along with brushwork of the utmost precision to reflect its harsh lines. I knelt down and examined the plant-ball, avoiding the razor-sharp leaf margins. No sign, as yet, of a flower stalk.

I could wait. I'm always waiting in this place.

I'd sketch it now and then come back when it sent up a flower.

And Mother might die before that happened.

But this could be a slow leaving. Unlike Aunt, who was torn away from me overnight.

Chapter Thirty-Two

'Throw them out!' shouted a man from the back of the school hall. 'Throw the government out!'

Mrs van Deventer, seated along from us in a knitted hat and matching shawl – there was snow on Aloe Peak – worked her eyebrows at me. Her grandson, Frans, is one of my art pupils, so I've risen again in her estimation following the success of my tomatoes.

Julian took my hand. 'Don't react.'

Under my coat I was wearing a plain blue skirt and a white shirt, an outfit carefully contrived to fall between bush clothes and Cape Town formality.

The member of parliament held up his hands.

'*Dames en here*, ladies and gentlemen, let us be calm.'

'Why? *Waarom*?' shouted random voices, and I could understand their outrage. I'd visited farms whose vines had died after years of dessication. My tiny vegetable patch outside the kitchen door was rock-hard. The Metz children's school uniforms were threadbare, my art pupils drew riverbeds that were dry.

'We have a coalition government,' the MP said soothingly. 'We must be patient.'

'Smuts is a traitor! We need to follow Germany!' came a voice that I recognised. I looked around and saw Wynand Louw on his feet and Truda cowering in silence beside him. Wynand has picked up English from Truda who is a regular at the literacy classes Julian and I run once a week, when I am not in Cape Town visiting Mother who is now confined to bed.

'He admires Herr Hitler,' Truda whispered to me last week. 'He says he will save Germany.'

'We will make representations, you may be sure of that,' the MP said hastily.

The rumble of dissent rose until half the audience was on its feet. Only representations!

'What about the poor whites on the edge of town?' a woman's voice called.

'It's the *Engelse*!' yelled someone. 'They want to use the *droogte* to steal our land!'

'Shut up,' shouted another. 'We fought in the Great War while you were hiding away!'

'Did your mother die in the Boer War camps?' came the swift rejoinder.

I sensed the intake of breath around me. Kitchener's concentration camps and his policy of scorched earth was forever branded on the soul of these people. But this harking back would do nobody any good. Where was the thundering dominee? Why didn't he take charge with the authority he dispensed from the pulpit?

'Say something!' I hissed to Julian. 'This is your place, you teach children to debate without shouting!'

But it was not Julian's style to impose himself.

I stood up and clapped my hands above my head.

There was a surprise lull. The headmaster's odd wife, I

197

heard them thinking. The one who draws, who looks as if she will fall over in a strong breeze.

Julian looked up at me with an expression of horror.

'The headmaster has something to say,' I said.

I smiled and gestured for him to stand up.

For a moment he hesitated but then I saw the cloak of schoolteacher drop around his shoulders and he rose and stepped into the aisle. His voice, when it came, was steady. The whimsical smile I used to find so annoyingly deferential now seemed the perfect foil to the emotions sweeping the hall.

'One of the first lessons we teach our pupils is how to attract attention.' He lifted an arm into the air. 'It's to prevent uproar in class and give everyone an equal chance to be heard. We also have rules about language.' He gave an exaggerated wink and the audience grudgingly nodded. 'Shall I therefore play schoolmaster and give everyone a chance to speak, one by one? Mr Louw, will you allow Mrs Engelbrecht to begin? Thank you, sir. Madam, over to you.'

It was the turning point.

Cora Engelbrecht received a round of applause after asking for help for the poor whites on the edge of town. Abel Metz said there should be an increased police presence to stop sheep rustling. Mr Fourie stood up nervously and said that the morning train was often late and that it was a disgrace that his customers had to wait so long for their goods. The audience nodded in agreement.

There were no more yells about bringing down the government. Afterwards, the member of parliament asked Julian if he'd ever thought about a career in politics.

The dominee appeared from the back of the hall and said he was just about to intervene when Julian had done so. Mrs van

Deventer said it was just as well Julian had intervened because that Wynand Louw was ready to turn the place upside down. Laetitia Snyman grinned and said she'd play me a military polonaise next time I was at school. And a previously silent mother from the regular group at the school gate approached me as I was pouring tea and said her name was Anna Visser and she wanted to thank me for standing up and making the men quieten down.

'I don't know what to say, my dear,' Julian confessed as we walked home, 'you are my better half.'

He stopped on the corner of Marico and bent down to kiss me with the same passion as when we were crouched by the roadside after the accident with the young antelope. Julian is most aroused when we are in danger, or at a moment of revelation. It's when we're both most alive, when our marriage might be more than a habit, when I might conceive Julian's child.

'You bring out the best in me,' he murmured against my mouth. 'And you terrify me.'

Chapter Thirty-Three

There are parts of me that my husband doesn't know. He doesn't know about my brother, who died before I was born and yet who lives in my dreams, a laughing child just out of reach.

In a small town, little is private. There is speculation about why I have not had a baby.

I sense Julian is anxious. He sees a family as the ultimate expression of unity.

My barrenness can no longer be put down to a tentative husband. Julian has learnt how to love me and there's no reason, according to our family doctor whom I visited quietly in Cape Town, for me not to fall pregnant. Daph has two children already. Susan, in England, has twins.

I'm ready for a child. I've made my peace with this place. I have banished – I think – the unease, the vibrations that once disturbed me and I don't go looking for trouble.

I grow vegetables in our plain garden with mixed success, but at least I try.

The Afrikaans woman, Truda, has become my friend. We are in tune despite her husband's antipathy

*towards me. And I know a dozen women by name who
will speak readily to me and who I hope, this year, will
accept an invitation to tea.*

*Just as I've waited for the veld to bloom, so I have
waited for the first shoots of friendship.*

I'm writing this on the train. Snow speckles the very tops of
the Hex River mountains. The vines are winter-bare against
the earth.

The sidings trundle by, Orchard, Sandhills . . .

North-west to Tulbach to avoid the gradients of Du Toit's
and Bain's Kloof, south to Wellington.

The first sight of Table Mountain.

I see Mother once a month. When she has gone, there will
be less excuse to visit Father and my beloved peninsula so
frequently.

'She's better today, Miss Fran,' Violet murmured. Mother has
replaced Aunt Mary in Violet's affections. 'She always is when
she knows you're coming.'

The velvet curtains were half-drawn – Mother finds
daylight too bright – casting the bedroom into permanent
twilight. She was propped up against the pillows, a shrunken
figure but still carefully coiffed. Violet sets her hair for her
every other day. I wish Sipata was more like Violet, more
like a friend.

'Frances!' Mother held out her arms.

I went over and embraced her gently. Mother still doesn't
do fulsome hugs, but she's more emotional than she used to
be. She cannot close doors behind her any longer.

'How was the journey? How is dear Julian?'

'It was beautiful, Mother. Snow on the mountains. Julian sends his love.'

She sank back against her pillows. 'I'm so relieved – every day, Frances – that you have Julian.'

'He's a good man,' I replied.

'It was the right decision. For you to marry him.'

I won't be drawn, so I nod and press her hand. Under my coat I'm wearing the blue linen low-waister with elbow-length sleeves, one of the few trousseau dresses that I haven't cut the sleeves off. I'm so accustomed to trousers that a dress and stockings feels restrictive and I can't wait to throw them off. But for Mother, I always wear a dress.

'You look lovely, Frances.'

I waited a moment, then took her thin hand. The veins stood out like blue cords. If I didn't distract her, she would ask if I was well and that would lead to whether there was a medical reason why I was not yet a mother. I used to wonder whether a medical reason prevented Mother from having another child but I decided it was because she was choosing to keep Father at a distance. Yet perhaps she did want one but her body betrayed her, wouldn't stir to her desire.

'Will you tell me about my brother Gideon?'

It's the first time I've used his name.

Mother glanced out of the window. 'He liked trains.' She looked back at me. 'Your father ordered a set from Harrods. Gideon would set it up in the lounge, and drive it around on the floor making chuffing noises. But most of all, he loved to run. He never climbed like you, Frances, he preferred to run.'

A child ran away from me, beckoning me to follow . . .

'I've seen him in my dreams, Mother. Running. And laughing.'

She smiled and a single tear slid slowly down her cheek.

'Then it wasn't a teenage fantasy? You truly saw him?'

'I did. Rest now.' I leant over to kiss her. 'I'll be back in a while and we can talk some more.'

I helped her off the pillows and eased her flat.

Her body felt light, breakable. If I held her too tightly, those blue veins might rupture.

I left the door slightly ajar and joined Father in the lounge.

Rain, blissful rain, pattered against the windows.

'Fran?' He looked up from his newspaper.

'She'll sleep for a while. I'll go back in again later.' I paused. 'How is work, Father?'

He's told Mother little of the difficulty of building a reputation in the Cape. He let her believe he was in demand, that only her illness was stopping them from adopting a more lavish lifestyle.

'Business is fair, my dear.' He removed his glasses. 'Good enough to support us and employ Violet. I couldn't manage without her, Fran. And the reverend is most kind. We have much to be grateful for.'

I glanced about. There was no study so Father spread his papers on the dining table when necessary.

'Where is Kitchener, Father?'

'Haven't you spotted him?' He shot me an amused glance. 'In the spare bedroom.'

'Still as an omen? A warning?'

'Indeed. Ever necessary, I believe.'

'Don't be silly, Fran,' exclaimed Daphne when I had tea with her. 'Smuts won't stand for any pro-German trouble. We're a dominion, allegiance to the king and all that. Maisie! Share those blocks with your brother! Now have you heard,' she leant forward, 'Penelope Chisholm's husband has run off with his secretary! Mary says it was on the cards all along, Penny was too possessive.'

Daph has never visited me in Aloe Glen. She says the climate wouldn't suit her and, in any case, she was doing me a favour: if she didn't visit me, then I'd be forced to come to Cape Town to visit her which would be less of a hardship all round.

'Mrs McDonald!' The director greeted me with a firm handshake. 'How is the Karoo treating you?'

'It's not quite the Karoo, sir, it's on the cusp. I see two vegetation types.'

'Ah,' said Compton with satisfaction. 'Variety, then?'

'Yes. And I think I may have found a rare type of aloe.'

His eyes sparked. 'Is that what brings you to Cape Town?'

I glanced out of the window. Cloud was wrapping itself around Devil's Peak. Cloud, mist, fog, drizzle . . . words that have disappeared from my vocabulary.

'I'm here to visit my mother. She isn't well.'

'I'm so sorry.' He inclined his head. 'But you do have something to show me?'

I opened my portfolio case and took out three sheets.

The first showed the complete aloe, pinky-green leaves erupting from an untidy stem clinging to stony ground. The second was a leaf detail, showing the toothed margins and the broad, fleshy connection to the stem. The third was the flower spike, with multiple orange flower heads, incongruously airy above the thuggish whole. I'd waited a further year for those.

'Enviably precise,' Compton remarked. 'We'll be able to gauge the response to your work at the upcoming exhibition.'

He was being careful not to raise my hopes too high.

I reached into the portfolio again and took out a final sheet and placed it in front of him. It was a risk, of course. I wouldn't have hesitated with Mr Cadwaller but maybe it was unwise to show it to the director. After all, what could he say? But I have no one else to ask. And it's time.

'This is just for me, sir.'

He lifted it and held it to the light. I'd deliberately made it pale, with a wash of colours that met and drifted apart and coalesced again into the central image. Was it an image?

Perhaps it was simply a blend of colour and water that only I would recognise.

'*Mevrou*?'

'Yes, Deon?'

Back in Aloe Glen we're drawing sunflowers with great yellow heads and lanky stems. And landscapes of emerald-green grass and steel-grey mountains and bright blue rivers . . .

'Have you ever seen the sea, *mevrou*?'

We are, young and old, obsessed with water and the possibility of its abundance.

'Oh, yes,' I smiled. 'I used to swim at Muizenberg. And with my father in England.'

'My father doesn't take me anywhere,' said Deon, bending back over his picture.

I knelt down beside him. We had taught each other, this boy and I, just as I predicted. Since the owl, Deon had deconstructed the world into mathematical shapes in a way I'd never imagined: mountains were interlocking triangles, river meanders described semicircles, railway lines were parallels disappearing into the distance. Deon taught me that art could spring from the most rigid of origins.

'Well,' I said quietly, 'it's because he's busy. Soon you'll be at boarding school in Worcester.'

'I'm not going there. Pa says I have to leave school.'

The clumsy Engelbrecht boy dropped his crayon and fished for it on the floor.

I got to my feet and clapped my hands. 'Time to finish up, class!'

The youngsters raced across the playground to their waiting mothers. Truda was there and I waved to her and she waved back but hurried Deon away. I've learnt not to be offended when she doesn't engage. Usually it's when she's bruised, which she blames on tripping, but the Truda I know, the one who runs through the veld like a gazelle, is the most sure-footed creature I've ever come across.

'You cannot allow this, Julian,' I said later, over supper. 'Deon must stay in school.'

Of the bruising I say nothing and I'm ashamed. But my acceptance in Aloe Glen is still partial, even though I attend church, say nothing controversial, wear the right clothes and endure the same drought. I have not yet gained the right to interfere.

'Wynand Louw wants his son to join the railways.' Julian reached for a baked potato. 'At least we've equipped the boy with enough English to make his way in due course. You can't get too attached, my dear.'

'Is it money? They can't afford the boarding school fees?'

'Perhaps, although there are bursaries available. Deon's results are far better lately. You may have thought you were only teaching art, my dear, but the children's English has leapt ahead. You're our secret weapon, Laetitia says.' He nodded at me. 'Take credit, Frances.'

'We could help the Louws,' I said slowly. 'You and I. Couldn't we?'

I want to do more than just show Truda sympathy, and pretend to ignore what I see.

'You have a generous heart, Frances. But we must set money aside for our own family.'

I stared at him. We'd just passed our seventh wedding anniversary.

He looked away and smoothed his thin hair. Julian knows there have been several times when I hoped for good news, but then my cycle returned and our chance was gone. Sometimes I wish he'd rage and shout at the unfairness of it, and I would then rage and shout with him and we'd clear the air and go on again, but that is not his way.

I stared past him towards Aloe Peak, rearing through the window.

Somewhere up there are the aloes I'm drawing for Kirstenbosch.

My legacy, perhaps, if there is no child.

'It might not happen, Julian. Have you considered that? I might never have a family.'

I thought, later, that this could have been one of those moments that spurred his passion – like the accident with the infant antelope or the time when he told me I'd rescued him – and he could sweep me into his arms and kiss me and we might be lucky. But after we'd done the dishes, he settled down to marking books. I went outside and threw some water on my carrots and sat on the kitchen step. Stars pricked through the darkening sky as if peeking through velvet curtains in a bedroom. I closed my eyes. A child appeared, not the one that

I chased through the grounds at Embury and Protea Rise, nor the boy I'd taught to draw, but another child, different from either of those.

'They say,' said Mrs van Deventer through tight lips, leaning over her fence, 'that there will be a war.'

'Oh, surely not?'

'Just as long as they don't take my boys, they can make as much war as they want.'

But whose side, I wanted to ask, *will we be on? Will we join the British, still seen as the foe around here? Or will we make common cause with Hitler and his jackboots?*

'My husband says we need to stand up to Germany, Mrs van Deventer.'

'Why should we do that?' she snorted, folding her arms. 'It's not our fight!'

'I suppose,' I said carefully, 'that our loyalty as a dominion should be towards Britain.'

She looked at me with displeasure and hoisted her sagging skirt.

'You stand behind your people in England, I know that. But this is your home now,' she pointed to the baking veld, 'if you draw our aloes and take credit for them, you should side with us.'

I stared at her.

'Anyway,' she leant over and placed a thick hand on my arm, 'it will be up to those *domkoppe* in parliament what happens. But I tell you this, they're not taking my boys. Or anybody else's boys round here. We'll hide them away. And no one,' she wagged a finger, 'no one better tell.'

* * *

Dear Mrs McDonald

I am happy to report that in our latest exhibition, your paintings attracted widespread attention. We offered them for sale as you directed, and all were sold to collectors and enthusiasts of Karoo flora.

I enclose a cheque for the proceeds.

I hope one day to come and see the Pink, Armoured Aloe. It is indeed a most impressive plant.

Please do continue with the Aloe series, and also if you find succulents in the genus Lithops, *formerly* Mesembryanthemum. *These resemble nothing so much as stones on the ground, until they flower.*

Yours most sincerely

A. R. J. Compton

Director

Chapter Thirty-Four

If, as an artist, I am profiting from a landscape, what is the correct compensation for that?

I owe it my respect, certainly. My allegiance, up to a point. But do I owe allegiance to those who, like my neighbour, believe they own it because they've been here longer than me?

Still no rain.

Every day I tap the water tank to monitor its level.

Every day I tap lower and lower.

Germany has invaded Poland.

Father, calling from Cape Town, says it will be war.

It has become, as with the Great War, a matter of honouring alliances. What will our country do? Hertzog's party in the coalition prefers neutrality or outright support for Hitler, Smuts's party says we owe loyalty to the king and must ally with Britain.

I don't want our young men to die on a distant battlefield, either.

But I know that fascism is an evil thing.

'Please come in,' I said, holding the door open. 'Welcome!'

I'd had Truda to tea but never a group, mainly because

it took so long for my tentative acquaintances to agree to socialise with me. My previous invitations had been greeted with polite thanks followed by a range of excuses from rug-beating to birthing animals. So I waited inside until I saw them at the gate – shades of Mrs van Deventer – and then flung the door open. Truda Louw, Sannie Metz, Aletta Erasmus, Cora Engelbrecht and Anna Visser trooped in, wiped their velskoens and glanced about, shyly eager to see what the headmaster's house looked like.

'*Magtig*!' gasped Cora, clapping a hand to her mouth, and began to giggle for I'd kept my truculent promise to paint the furniture. All the dining room chairs bore green vines curling up their wooden legs and creamy jasmine twining across their backs. Julian hadn't minded, Mother thought it outrageous, and Father chuckled and said it would surely start a trend. Blooming Desert, he called it. Soon they were all giggling at the English woman and her strange habit of painting perfectly good wood in all the colours of the rainbow. I couldn't have planned a better ice-breaker. Once calm was restored, they expressed their best wishes for Mother's health and then settled down to lemon cake – Violet's recipe – and syrupy koeksusters – Sipata's – washed down with tea. At first there was light talk of children and, inevitably, the prospects for rain.

'What will happen if there's a war?' Anna broke ranks over the second pot of tea.

'If the drought breaks, our men need to be here,' Sannie said firmly. 'There'll be heavy work.'

'Smuts doesn't care about our farms,' put in Aletta, 'he only wants to suck up to the British.'

They glanced at me. The local newspaper, prominently

on display in Mr Fourie's store, had been trumpeting similar comments for weeks.

'More tea?' I offered the pot around.

'My husband won't fight,' said Aletta, stirring in her sugar vigorously. 'He says it's not his business. But what about Mr McDonald?'

I glanced out of the window. Aloe Peak stood proud, but its slopes were brown. Much of the scrub I'd drawn was barely alive. Orange-throated longclaws, flapping herons, birds of prey, were rare. Even my joyful, agile springbok had vanished. Nature was on the cusp of giving up. There'd be death here before there was war abroad.

'Julian will want to do his bit,' I said carefully, 'but he sees his job as headmaster to be the most important contribution he can make.'

'Do his bit?' Truda wrinkled her forehead.

'It means to do his share. To make a difference.'

'*Verstaan*, understand. Like helping even if you don't have to.'

'We have our own problems,' said Cora, setting her cup down. 'Drought, white poverty—'

'But Wynand is angry,' interrupted Truda. 'He says Smuts will call people traitors!'

She was wearing one of her faded dresses that left her arms bare and her neck exposed.

'Wynand is always angry,' retorted Sannie to general nodding. 'Don't listen to him.'

Truda glanced at me. I knew her fear of Wynand was greater than her ability to ignore him.

'What will you do if there's a war, Frances?' asked Cora softly. 'Will you support your people?'

'My people?'

'*Ja*,' she said with quiet doggedness. 'The English.'

'But I'm not just English, Cora,' I replied gently. 'You are my people, too.'

They nodded and smiled but they didn't believe me. Mrs van Deventer wouldn't, either. I've earnt their provisional friendship, but when sides are eventually cemented and there can be no fudging, they won't expect me to take theirs.

'What will you do?' repeated Cora. 'If it comes to fighting?'

I shook my head.

It was weak of me, and they knew it.

For a moment I felt a tremor, a spasm of the unease I thought was gone.

'Dearly beloved,' intoned the reverend at St John's in Wynberg. It was Father Ben, newly promoted to Reverend, who'd led the mountain hike when I stood close to the precipice. 'We are gathered here today to celebrate the life of Emily Frances Whittington, devoted wife, mother and friend.'

I took my Father's hand.

Since the Aloe Glen tea party, which broke up with kisses on the cheek and what I hoped was genuine warmth, the world had teetered and then reeled into conflict. It began with the declaration of war, the split in the government and Smuts prevailing narrowly to take the country onto the side of the Allies. Eight months of phoney war followed during which we hoped peace might somehow be salvaged. But then Germany swept across Belgium, Holland and France and within weeks Britain stood alone. The phone call came as Julian and I sat by the radio, listening to news of the French surrender. Father was telephoning to say I should come because Mother had

213

weakened and Dr Reed was not sure how much longer she had, and she was asking for me. I threw a change of clothes into a suitcase and raced for the late train. As the rails clicked, I muttered to myself.

Live. Breathe. Don't go before I'm with you. There are things to be said.

Don't go . . .

Father met me at the station in central Cape Town and we drove as fast as his motor car would allow.

'War latest!' shouted the paperboys on the corner. 'Read all about it! War latest!'

'Oh, Miss Fran.' Violet met us at the door, her eyes red. 'The Lord kept her for you.'

This would be different from Aunt Mary, who would have abhorred a deathbed scene.

'Mother?' I murmured close to her face. 'I'm here. I'm with you now.'

A faint smile etched itself on her lips. There was almost no substance to her these last few months, just parchment skin over bone, shakily connected by veins of cobalt blue.

'Frances?' she whispered, opening her eyes. 'Will you forgive me?'

A frail hand felt for mine. I held it, careful not to squeeze.

'Whatever for, Mother? There's nothing to forgive.'

'Water?' she managed.

Violet appeared at my side with a glass. I lifted Mother's head and dribbled a little into her mouth.

'I couldn't let myself love you openly,' she murmured. 'Not after losing Gideon. I couldn't do it again.'

The detachment, the attention to trivialities lest heartbreak intrude, the absence of a sibling for me.

'It wasn't because I didn't care.' She tried to raise herself up. 'It meant I cared too much!'

I gathered her small frame against me.

'I know. I loved you then, Mother. I still love you. There's nothing to forgive.'

She sank back. I stroked her forehead.

'Open the curtains,' she said faintly.

I got up and pulled the heavy velvets aside.

'You loved to look out at night,' she whispered. 'I couldn't understand why.'

She closed her eyes. Father came in, and Violet too, and we waited until the dawn broke and birds called sharply through the open window and she slipped away from us.

I shook myself in the front-row pew.

That had happened a week before. I cashed my cheque from Kirstenbosch and went to Stuttafords in Adderley Street to buy a black dress and a small veiled hat and black heeled shoes of a quality that Mother would have approved. We found Father's darkest suit and I bought him a black tie.

'I don't see how I can come, my dear,' Julian said down a crackling party line from Aloe Glen. 'Will you forgive me if I stay here? I shall be with you in spirit and you have your father—'

It was exam time, the school was short-staffed and Laetitia was ill with bronchitis.

'I'll be fine,' I said. 'We will bury Mother and I'll return in a few days' time when Father is settled.'

'Thank you, my dear. I knew you'd understand.'

And so here I was in the church where I married, with Father and Violet, the Radissons, the Pringles, several of Mother's Bible study friends, recent work colleagues of Father's whom I didn't know and of course Daph, with her husband and parents.

'So sorry,' she whispered, clinging to my hand, 'will you have time for tea with me? And this war, I'm so frightened – I love your hat—'

Doves landed on the roof and began to croon. I found myself borne backwards in time.

I, Julian Thomas, take thee Frances Grace . . .

In sickness and in health, until death us do part . . .

Light fell through the stained-glass windows and alighted on the floor. Carmine. Lapis.

We stood to sing 'Abide with Me'. I glanced at Father. He'd struggled with his tie and it had come loose. Mother would never have allowed him out of the house like that.

'Emily lived for her family,' said Reverend Ben during his eulogy, although he did not know the whole of it. 'A devoted wife, a devoted mother. She knew pain and she knew joy, as we all do in this life.'

After the funeral, we hosted tea and refreshments at the cottage.

'My condolences, Gerald,' intoned Mr Phillips, clapping Father on the back and leaning down to kiss me on the cheek. 'Where is that husband of yours, Frances?'

'He couldn't get away, I'm afraid. Can I offer you a slice of cake?'

'You need to come back to Cape Town,' Mr Phillips said in a low voice. 'Gerald needs you now.'

'Yes, do!' Daph appeared at my side and deftly took her father's plate. 'None for you, Father, think of your waistline. Julian could find a position here, don't you think?'

'Perhaps.'

'A reasonable eulogy,' said Thelma Radisson, who'd bought an early painting from me and later adopted Mother into her knitting group. 'But there should have been something about her brother. She clearly adored him. Have you seen the papers? They say Hitler's massing troops at the Channel.'

'Will you move?' I overheard Mr Finlayson, a new colleague, say to Father. 'Why not find a flat? Consolidate your position. No need for full-time help, either, I would've thought.'

Reverend Ben approached, his eyes appraising.

'Ah, Frances, still drawing I believe? Still finding inspiration in the works of God?'

'Yes,' I smiled. 'Aloes in the veld. And rare bulbs. Beauty amid the drought.'

The following morning I put on my velskoens and bush trousers and walked to Kirstenbosch. The air smelt of moist earth and newly bursting jasmine. Fernwood Buttress rose above a filmy belt of cloud.

'Good morning, ma'am,' said the attendant at the gate. 'You're our first guest of the day.'

The tears began to well as I climbed the path beneath the camphor trees and found myself at the tangle of Van Riebeeck's ancient hedge. I'd like to say I was weeping over Mother, but I wasn't, and I don't think she would have minded. To my right a *Protea repens* heaved with sunbirds; further on, the stream that once defied all my attempts to copy it ran swiftly over its pebbled bed. I pulled off my velskoens, dabbled my feet, ran barefoot across the yielding grass . . . then wiped my eyes and put my shoes back on and climbed up to a bench near the upper boundary, not far from the path that led up Skeleton Gorge. In the distance rose the Hottentots Holland mountains, in the foreground spread the leafy suburbs. I'd deliberately not brought Father's binoculars with me because the temptation would have been to search out the thatch roof of Protea Rise . . .

I closed my eyes and let the sun warm my face.

'Frances?'

Mark Charleson stood in front of me, astonishment on his face, one hand outstretched as if he needed to touch me to see if I was real.

'I heard you lost your mother. I'm so sorry.'

I longed to reach out to him, too. Feel his skin under my fingers. Twine my arm with his—

'Thank you. She passed away last week.'

He might touch my hair, like he used to—

He sat down at the far end of the bench and said nothing. I remember this. He was happy with silence. A pair of sunbirds darted among shrubbery, their iridescent feathers catching the light.

'Hard to paint,' he murmured, 'like the flash of a prism.'

'Cadmium orange, green sharpened with yellow. My old teacher said it's all about technique.'

'It is,' he smiled, 'but you bring more than that.' He turned to face me. 'I bought one of your paintings, you know. A strange plant with thorns that draws my attention every time I pass it.'

I glanced away from him. Beyond the horizon lay Julian and the rough veld I've embraced.

Go, I told myself. *Go now before this becomes another memory that will never let you go.*

'Why are you here so early, Mark?'

He hesitated. 'I wanted to savour it while it was quiet. I came to say goodbye.'

'To Kirstenbosch? You're moving?'

'More than that. I'm about to leave for America.' He cleared his throat. 'My wife never settled here.' He shot me a glance. 'She returned with the children to Texas when war broke out. I've sold my practice and I'll join them shortly.'

For the first time we were looking at each other squarely. He was older about the face but still dark-haired and dark-eyed. I glanced down at his hands, fine-boned yet strong enough to haul me over a breaking wave. Did he still turn towards danger to save himself?

'Good luck, Mark,' I said, standing up and holding out my hand to him. 'I wish you well.'

He rose, too, and took my hand briefly. His eyes roamed over my face. I blushed for my bush outfit.

Why don't I break through this careful courtesy?

Ask him if he feels our meeting must be more than a coincidence? Perhaps, then, we can laugh and blame it on a God who's chosen to tease us, bringing us together on the cusp of his departure.

We began to walk down the slope.

'Are you happy, Frances?'

I stopped and searched his face. 'Are you?'

He had children. He surely loved his wife for that.

But he didn't reply, just touched me on the arm.

'I have a flat, in Bella Vista Mansions in Claremont. Number 30. Will you come and sign your painting?'

Don't ask to see me again. Please.

'I don't think so, Mark. I have to sort through my mother's belongings. As you can imagine.'

'Of course.'

'I think,' I went on with a bright smile, 'if you will excuse me, I'll go back via the herbarium.'

219

Again, I offered him my hand. He took it and squeezed gently.

Then he bent down and kissed me on the lips, briefly, tenderly, and walked away.

Chapter Thirty-Five

Father said a diary is a friend. I could tell it anything.
  But I cannot. Not yet.
  It has rained. Violently.

'There's an emergency town meeting,' Julian said with noticeable agitation when he collected me from the station and I wondered at the crowd marching towards the school. Rare, heavy cloud obscured Aloe Peak. Water was collecting in the ruts of the road, where my Cape Town heels once snagged. 'The local commandant is speaking. It's about the war. I have to be there, there may be trouble—'

'I'll come with you. Let's drop my case at home and go. Should I quickly change?'

I was in Cape Town clothes – low-waister, stockings, heels.

'No time. Are you sure, my dear?' Julian shot me an anxious glance. 'So soon after your mother?'

'Of course,' I said. 'This is my town, too.'

By the time we arrived, the school hall was packed. Several of the men were armed, I noticed, adding to an undercurrent that reminded me of the earliest days of my unease. The dominee was in the front row, talking seriously with his neighbours.

'Take your seats, *dames en here*!' shouted Abel Metz who had the loudest voice in these situations.

'Over here!' beckoned Laetitia Snyman. 'I saved you seats.' She paused. 'I'm so sorry about your mother, Frances. I hope she got a good send-off?'

'We could have done with some of your lively music.'

The commandant rose. He was in his fifties, I guessed, dressed in the uniform of a regiment that had served in the trenches of the Great War. He spoke in a mixture of English and Afrikaans.

'*Dankie*, ladies and gentlemen, thank you for coming.'

Rain began to drum on the roof. The farmers in the audience exchanged glances.

'We are here to talk about our role in the conflict unfolding overseas. The war against Germany and Italy. A war that involves us all.'

'We don't want to fight,' came a shout from the back. 'Not for the British!'

'One moment, sir!' The commandant held up his hand. 'There is no conscription for now. We are on the side of Britain and the Empire, but you won't be asked to fight unless you volunteer.'

'We won't!' yelled several more.

'Hitler has invaded peaceful countries,' the commandant went on more forcefully, 'he has bombed civilians, thousands have died or been imprisoned. The Italians have joined his wicked Axis alliance!'

His voice rose to a crescendo. 'We cannot stand by! We must play our part!'

Wynand Louw leapt to his feet, screaming. 'Never! *Nooit*!'

Mrs van Deventer raised an angry fist and shouted about

222

her boys. Meneer Erasmus, the taciturn farmer who supplied our chickens, waved his arms in the air. Here and there, amid the melee, the odd person remained quiet. Mr Fourie from the store, who had the misfortune to resemble Hitler, remained seated, perhaps calculating the loss to his business if the area was emptied of his hungriest, fighting-age customers. Truda Louw, by the side of her raging husband, caught my eye and gave me a frightened smile. Cora Engelbrecht had her hands over her mouth. Anna Visser's baby started to cry and she slipped out. By my side, Julian clasped and unclasped his hands in his lap. I wondered who would restore order. The dominee, belatedly? I couldn't intervene this time. I was one of the *Engelse* and my loyalty, as Mrs van Deventer had harshly pointed out and my tea party ladies had alluded to, was still seen to be with my people in England.

The commandant held up his hands once more.

The hall calmed slightly. Thunder rolled in the distance.

'I know many of you lost loved ones in the Great War,' he bowed his head in respect, 'but this time we are directly threatened. Italy and Germany seek to expand in Africa.'

He began to build to a climax even as the shouts rose against him.

'We must defend our country, our continent and our sea route! We need good men and true to stand up for what is right!'

I felt a movement beside me. Julian had risen to his feet.

There are some people who naturally command silence. Julian was not one of those but he was, nevertheless, the headmaster. And he'd also been recognised for his deft handling of the previous meeting. Yet I never expected this. Julian was a follower, not an initiator. He'd needed me to set him up last time.

I looked up at him. He rested a hand on my shoulder.

'Thank you, Commandant. I have Scottish roots – as some of you also have – and I support Britain and the Empire. Not blindly, for I recognise the injustices of the past, especially in this country.'

There was a grumble of agreement. Anna's baby had stopped crying and she returned to her seat.

'I support Britain because I believe we can be a beacon to the world. And no peace-loving country deserves to be trampled underfoot by a tyrant.'

They were silent, now.

'I'm forty-five,' Julian grimaced and smiled, 'I've survived one war and I'm not the aggressive type.'

There was grudging laughter.

'I've decided to volunteer. I'll play my part in this war, in whatever capacity I can.'

I heard jeers and gasps, one of them my own. He sat down. Unexpected tears spilt onto my cheeks. Perhaps for Mother or for this intransigent town and my upright husband? Or perhaps they sprang from guilt that had nothing to do with either.

'*Foei tog*,' said Laetitia, putting an arm round me. 'Don't cry, now. Your ma is in heaven.'

Julian took my hand in his and lifted it to his lips. I searched his face. Had he truly found his voice – and his conviction – independently of me?

If not, then I had emboldened a cautious man merely by sitting at his side.

And now he is going to war.

* * *

'They won't let me fight,' said Julian after we'd dashed home through the downpour to a scratch supper. 'I'm too old. It will be Intelligence, probably. Or Signals. Come, dry your hair, Frances.'

'You don't need to,' I pleaded, grabbing the towel and rubbing it over my hair. 'You've already proved your bravery the last time. Let younger men volunteer.'

'You're not advocating neutrality, are you, my dear? I thought you'd have applauded.'

I threw down the towel and looked at him. Julian is strangely buoyed by his decision. He's not dismayed by the overall tenor of the gathering, especially when no one stood up after him in support. If anything, the mood descended into sullen refusal and the meeting broke up with no clear outcome and left the commandant standing alone on the stage as the crowd filed out into the rain.

'Your place is here,' I tapped the table, 'with your pupils. You can do more by educating the next generation than serving in a war that will take its course without you.'

'Ah, that's where you're wrong, Frances. I'm setting the example that some things are always worth fighting for. However old you are. However unsuited you may be.'

'An example that younger men should set, Julian.'

He once said I brought out the best in him but also that I terrified him.

I fear what I have sparked.

'Now,' he went on, standing up and holding his hand out to me, 'shall we leave the dishes for Sipata? I've missed you so much, my dear, while you've been away.'

I can't say why I did it.

Was it because it carried an element of danger that I

knew was wrong but couldn't help wanting? There was no calculation involved, not like the calculation of my younger self in planning to marry well.

It would haunt me, that I knew. However innocuous it turned out to be.

All I can say is that I borrowed Father's car, telling him I wanted a drive to clear my head – after Violet and I had spent a sad few hours sorting through Mother's belongings – and I drove to Claremont and knocked on the door of number 30, Bella Vista Mansions.

Chapter Thirty-Six

The rain, having held off for so many years, continued to pour down as if rebuking us for despairing that it would ever do so again. The dominee held an emotional service of thanksgiving while the children played outside, sliding in the mud and dirtying their shoes. Rivers rose from their dusty beds, Marico Road became a quagmire and Julian filled sandbags and placed them at the ready in case the waters approached our door. I ran into the rain every day and stuck out my tongue and felt its stinging drops and even rejoiced when my vegetable garden was washed away. Our lone tree put out several new branches. And, through the deluge, the familiar whistle of the morning and afternoon trains were joined by whistles from the extra services taking volunteers to mustering and training points near the coast. Sometimes I grabbed an umbrella and sloshed to the station to watch the trains passing through and waved at the young men hanging out of the windows despite the wet.

'It's gathering pace,' Julian said with quiet satisfaction. 'I knew we wouldn't be found wanting.'

But few trains stopped at Aloe Glen. And the dominee said nothing to his flock about their Christian duty to fight fascism, or, at least, to oppose its cruel agenda. Repent, repent, was what we got on Sunday mornings, but for no particular sin.

Julian's orders arrived.

'It's Intelligence,' he said with quiet satisfaction. 'To Durban for initial training, then we sail for Cairo.'

I fingered his new khaki uniform as we sat on the verandah, the flashes proclaiming his South African regiment rather than his Scottish one from the Great War.

'You'll continue our good work with the art and literacy classes, my dear?'

'I should do more,' I said restlessly, 'not just paint or teach English.'

'But you'll be keeping alive what I started, Frances.' He knelt by my side, his pale eyes looking at me tenderly. 'My radical project, as you call it. It'll be your contribution, your war.'

He was right. It could be my war. I touched his cheek in a kind of apology. He was so decent, so reliable, while my own emotions see-sawed with every fugitive memory of Cape Town.

The last thing Julian did before he left was to arrange a bursary for Deon Louw.

'Our job is to present the opportunity, Frances. It will be their decision as to whether to take it.'

So, one early evening, he took off his tie and rolled up the sleeves of his shirt to convey informality and we walked to their cottage by the railway station. I was wearing bush clothes and carrying a tiny mountain aloe for Truda to plant. She'd never invited me to her home because, she said with a blush that reached through her tan, it was too plain. And it was: a shoebox of a place, a bare patch out front, burglar bars prominent against the permanently drawn curtains. No wonder she ran away into the veld whenever she could.

'Headmaster?' Wynand Louw opened the door halfway, suspicion clouding his face.

'May we come in?' Julian put on his broadest smile. 'We have some news for you.'

'Truda!' He turned and yelled into the gloomy interior. 'It's the headmaster.'

She appeared, followed by Deon. I'm always struck by the way she visibly shrinks in her husband's presence. She folds that gloriously rangy body in on itself until she's almost crouching. Deon stands upright but says nothing at all when his father is nearby.

'Good evening, Truda. How are you? And Deon?' I smiled at them both. 'I've brought you an aloe.'

'Thank you.' Truda's eyes briefly flickered with warmth.

'Invite them in,' Wynand Louw said to his wife gruffly.

'Come,' Truda cast me a desperate glance, 'please come this way.'

We sat down on a small, sinking couch. They sat opposite, on separate chairs, Wynand lounging in his, Truda on the edge of hers. Deon hovered in the doorway.

'I'm happy to report that Deon,' Julian inclined his head to the boy, 'has won a bursary to board at the high school in Worcester. Congratulations, Deon!'

There was silence. I smiled and clapped my hands. 'Well done!'

Julian got up and went over to the boy and shook his hand and then re-joined me on the couch. My husband was the best kind of schoolmaster: ambitious for every child. But he'd gambled with these parents. He'd congratulated Deon as if his departure for high school was already a foregone conclusion.

'Who says he's going to Worcester?' Wynand duly turned to glare at Truda. 'Did you do this? Did you?'

'It's standard practice, sir,' Julian interrupted smoothly. 'Promising pupils are always put forward.'

That was a lie. An application was usually initiated by the parents in agreement with the school.

Wynand Louw flexed his fingers. A clock ticked loudly.

I felt the place closing in on me; its darkness, the barely concealed rage from the man opposite.

'He must go!' Truda jumped up and rushed over to Deon and put her arm round him. 'It's his chance!'

From outside came a volley of barking and Wynand Louw burst out of his chair and wrenched the curtains open and screamed *voetsak!* before turning back to us. Deon shrank against the door jamb.

'It's a wonderful opportunity.' I forced the words out quietly. 'You must be so proud of your son.'

'What else must be paid? For the school?'

'Nothing else, Mr Louw. The bursary covers uniform, tuition and accommodation. My wife and I,' Julian looked across at me and smiled, 'would like to sponsor any sports kit Deon may need.'

'*Asseblief*, Wynand,' Truda's voice trembled, 'let our boy go. These people are kind. Let him go.'

Wynand made to march towards the doorway where his wife and son stood. I tensed and moved forward on the couch. I wanted to run to her and promise to look after her when Deon went away; I'd find a means to divert Wynand's savage attention. Let her go, too . . .

'You must leave,' he growled, turning to us and gesturing towards the front door.

'We understand,' I said, rising. 'You need to discuss this as a family. The Inspector of Schools is keen for Deon to progress. Have you met him, Meneer Louw?'

'No,' he replied sharply and again gestured towards the door.

'Ah,' I said. 'His brother is chief of the railways.'

He gaped at me. I put a hand on Deon's shoulder, smiled warmly at Truda and offered my hand to her husband. He took it briefly, nodded to Julian and pushed open the front door.

'Good evening,' Julian said. 'I'll see you tomorrow, Deon.'

'And I'll see you too, Truda,' I added, 'don't forget it's your turn in the library.'

We walked down the path. The door slammed shut behind us.

I don't often pray, even in the Dutch church where the dominee watches us closely. But as we crunched over the gravel I prayed that Truda would not be hurt that night.

'Inspector?' Julian stopped and stared at me. 'Railways chief? Whatever are you talking about?'

'If it encourages him to agree, I'm prepared to tell any lie that is necessary.'

'And the library? She works in the library? I had no idea—'

'She doesn't. But if he thinks she'll be on display and therefore refrains from beating her, then a phantom job will have served its purpose.'

'Frances.' Julian shook his head and permitted himself a sly smile. 'You're shameless.'

On the day Julian left, the railway station was crowded with farmers and their families travelling to Worcester to a stock sale. The generous rain meant that grazing had recovered enough for the land around Aloe Glen to be restocked. His military uniform stood out among the bush clothes, and murmurs followed us as we made our way down the platform. At first no one came over to wish him well and I felt like shouting at them for being so ungrateful, so callous towards a man who'd taught their children. Julian brushed a hand over his head, his face set with its usual gentle smile.

I said nothing, just stood by his side and stared, daring them to ignore him.

'*Veels geluk.*' Abel Metz eventually broke away and approached us. He gripped Julian's hand, clearly torn between respect and dismay. Several others took his cue and came over as well although with no great enthusiasm. The cafe men only nodded from a distance.

Cowards! my younger self wanted to shout. *Cowards!*

'Frances?' Laetitia Snyman linked her arm with mine.

She'd made no judgement on Julian's choice, she simply said she would carry on until he returned and he was not to worry; and that she would encourage the continuation of the art and literacy classes.

'Thank you for coming,' I said with feeling.

The train rolled in, the station staff bustled to refill the water tank and check the coal. The farmers and their families got on board with much jollity. Laetitia shook hands with Julian and retreated a few steps away. Julian bent and kissed my cheek and I put my arms about his neck and felt the steady beat of his heart. For a moment, I was back on the side of the road and he was kissing me under a broiling sun. 'Goodbye, my dear,' he whispered against my cheek.

On the night he volunteered, when we left the dishes for Sipata, I hoped for a similar meeting of heart and body, but he was tired from the strain of his decision and fell asleep before I got into bed beside him. I lay awake for hours as the roof creaked.

He picked up his bag and climbed aboard the train. The conductor shouted and waved his flag. A gust of wind brought a flurry of raindrops that splattered onto the platform like soft bullets. I watched him find a seat by a window and turn to me. The engine exhaled steam and the train began to move in a squeal of metal. He touched a hand to his lips and mouthed something and then the train gathered speed and he was gone.

The platform emptied.

I watched until the rear light disappeared into the greening veld, and turned away.

At the far end of the platform, Wynand Louw was watching me.

Chapter Thirty-Seven

I lied to my diary. I have never done that before. So, I must set this record straight, although no one will ever know.

I did calculate. Mark was leaving. No one would discover. How could they?

And if it produced an unexpected outcome, Julian would rejoice along with me. I got out of the car in front of Bella Vista Mansions. The forested slopes above Kirstenbosch were falling into afternoon shadow. I examined the front windows of the block for a twitch of lace curtain, a curious face at a window. I locked the car, and walked up the path. I told myself that I could always stop him, and stop myself, but I knew I wouldn't.

Why? Why did I do it? Perhaps it was the buildup of emotion from Mother's death. Or perhaps it was the sense that my life needed at least one moment of defining passion.

They came together as I knocked on his door.

He opened it and said nothing, just held out his hand and drew me inside.

* * *

Julian's departure coincided with the transformation of Aloe Glen.

We have grass on the school playground, the river in the valley flows at speed, the scrub has erupted into colour. Lilac *vygies* sparkle in the sunlight, unknown bulbs wave delicate spires of blue and white, eagles soar, kites hover, weaver birds appear where before there were none. The wild sage and rosemary float their invigorated perfume about my legs as I wander in their midst.

'It's a miracle, Mrs van Deventer!' I called as I passed her house. 'The veld is alive!'

'*Ja,*' she sniffed and went inside.

With no husband to care for and only my weekly lessons to organise – although the numbers at the literacy class have dropped – I've been painting constantly. No more scrubby ochre and sienna but shades unused since Cape Town: fuchsia pink, magenta, the palest primrose yellow. I know the bounty won't last so I've been up at dawn to catch the early light and stayed out all day, shifting my folding stool every hour or two to a new location and fresh subjects. Mr Cadwaller would be proud of my diligence. Truda appears silently behind me, watches me sketching, touches my shoulder, and runs away. She doesn't speak but I know she comes to tell me that I'm not alone. I've never had a friend who is so special to me and about whom I know so little, and she so little about me. My hands are brown, my hair is being bleached like hers, I'm stiff from crouching over. Sipata watches with astonishment and makes me soup that I heat up whenever I return.

'Ma'am must eat. The flowers must wait while ma'am eats.'

'Where have you been, Fran?' shouted Father over the telephone. 'I never find you at home.'

'Father!' I caught my breath, for I'd rushed in only moments before. 'You won't believe it!'

'It's Julian? He's not going after all?'

'No, no! It's the veld, Father, it's a miracle!'

Sometimes families of springbok *pronk* – a kind of kicking up of heels – as they race past me. Perhaps they see me so often they now accept me as part of the landscape.

'But what news of Julian, Frances?'

'He's arrived in Egypt. I received a letter. He can't say where he is, exactly. Father, the flowers—'

'But not near the front lines?'

'No.'

'Just as well. The Italians are attacking.'

My weekly newspaper and the evening broadcast on the radio kept me in touch, but news reached the town at large only belatedly and the locals maintained a stoic indifference because none of their own were involved. Julian, it seemed, did not qualify.

'I heard from my husband, Mr Fourie,' I said when visiting the store. 'He sends his greetings.'

He gave me a brief nod. Perhaps newly aware of his resemblance to Herr Hitler, he has shaved off his moustache. 'What is it that you need today, Mrs McDonald?'

He is not usually so brusque.

And my tea party ladies have failed to reciprocate my hospitality. Aletta and Sannie wave from a distance but do not come over to talk to me or enquire after Julian's well-being. Cora Engelbrecht is busy with a creche for toddlers in the poor white area on the outskirts of town.

'Can I help, Cora? I could do a morning or two?'

'Thank you,' she said, colouring slightly. 'But I have enough help. And you're busy with your pictures.'

I am being shunned. Ever so slightly. But shunned

nevertheless. It's a feeling I'm familiar with. In this case it may not be a concerted action, one that the ladies have discussed amongst themselves and which has led to a collective decision, but rather something more opaque: they don't know how to deal with me now we are clearly opposed over this war. My husband, who gave us both legitimacy in the community, made his choice and is gone. I'm on my own and the barriers I broke down are being raised once more, slowly and steadily.

'Frances?'

Truda materialised beside me on bare feet. Lately, she is miraculously unbruised and Deon is to go to high school in Worcester. Julian's tactics and my lies worked. I laid down my pencil and she squatted beside me on the ground.

'No one wants to talk to me any more, Truda.'

'*Ja*,' she nodded. 'They say you'll leave.'

'But why? This is my home.' And it is, for all its testy drawbacks.

Truda picked a stem of grass and nibbled on it. I'd like to paint her one day, although I know little about portraiture. She is so wild, a creature almost always in flight.

'They say you're different. They know you're clever,' she pointed at my sketch, 'and so you'll leave. They say you'll take with you what you got from us, and leave.'

You'll take with you what you got from us and leave.

I stared at the page. My art and literacy classes, my determined engagement, my devotion to Julian and the school . . .

Truda placed a sunburnt hand on my head. 'Your hair,' she murmured, 'it's getting like mine. And you're kind, Frances, you're the kindest in the world.'

She jumped to her feet and ran off.

Chapter Thirty-Eight

He drew me inside and we kissed and I was back at the Mount Nelson, his lips warm on mine.

We did not speak of his wife. We did not speak of his children.

We did not look at my painting on the wall.

I said nothing about why I'd come. There was no need.

Even though it had been ten years, there was no hesitation, no awkwardness. It was the consummation I'd longed for on my wedding night, tender, urgent, overwhelming, and the tears that flowed were drops of gold I wanted to hoard for ever.

We talked afterwards, when I lay in his arms and the sun painted shadows on the opposite wall and I told him that love was surely the colour of the sea we once swam in, a rich turquoise tinged with cerulean.

'I dream of you constantly,' he murmured. 'I dream I proposed to you, and that you said yes.'

'I would have.'

He bent down and kissed me. As he lifted his face from mine, I could see there were tears in his eyes, but they were tears of sorrow rather than the ones of joy that had earlier mingled with mine.

'What is it?'

He brushed his eyes. 'I've never forgiven myself,' he looked down at me, 'for not telling you why. And sooner.'

'Then tell me now, and never again.'

'My family also lost money in the Crash. My mother needed expensive medical treatment abroad that my father couldn't afford.' He grimaced.

'They made me choose. My father agreed with Astrid's family that if I married her, the Fairbrothers would fund the treatment in the United States.'

I caught my breath. It was an arranged marriage. Both of us supposedly rescued or obligated. Both of us entrapped.

'At first I refused. I said I loved you. But I could see my mother was deteriorating.'

'You don't have to say any more.'

He kissed my neck, my breasts . . .

Later, he told me he loved his children – two girls – but not his wife. And that he would enlist on the British side if America stayed out of the war.

And I told him that I was fond of my husband and would never leave him because he needed me. I also said that I had a brother called Gideon who died before I was born but I see him when I dream.

I said nothing about why I had no family, and he did not ask.

When I write these words, I am filled with a glow that is him, and will be him for the rest of my life. I know that what I have done is wrong, but I cannot regret it.

And I couldn't help it.

Chapter Thirty-Nine

'Ma'am?' Sipata came over to where I sat in front of my easel. 'Ma'am must eat.' She put down a plate of sliced melon. Since the rain, there is fruit in abundance.

'Thank you, Sipata.'

I feel different, but I suppose it's because I'm alone.

'It is what ma'am has been hoping for.'

'I don't think so.'

I laid down my paintbrush and looked at her. She's been a quiet presence in my life for a decade.

'It will be, ma'am. I see it in your face.'

I got up and looked in the mirror. Sipata was imagining what was not there. Titian hair greeted me, now bleached by the sun; extra freckles across my nose from my hours in the veld; green eyes with a hint of ginger . . . and wariness, for I've travelled this road before.

'Father,' I said a few weeks later over the telephone, 'I thought I'd come and see you.'

'Oh, do!' his voice echoed down the line. 'We'll go to the docks, like old times.'

'Are you leaving?' Mrs van Deventer shouted from her garden when I walked by with my suitcase.

'No!' I shouted back sharply. 'Why should you think that? I'm visiting my father. Back in a week.'

I hefted my case to my other hand and walked on, aware of her eyes following me.

A tiny little thing, she'd called me when I first arrived.

'Return to Cape Town,' I said to the ticket master at the station.

'It's running late,' he replied with a shrug. 'Given way to a troop train from upcountry.'

The stations and sidings ticked past – Worcester, Goudini, Artois Mill – amid rows of vines that marched on either side of the track like soldiers on parade. Water glimmered in the distant, newly full Brandvlei Dam, naked children waved as they splashed in streams turned brown with silt. We turned south. The peninsula hove into view above a layer of low cloud, a many-turreted ship rising from the ocean.

'Frances!' Father hugged me on the platform when I arrived. 'Don't you look well!'

'And you, too, Father. Sorry I'm so late.'

'Not to worry.' He leant down and whispered. 'I found a couple of new clients while I was waiting. But such grim news, Fran.' He gestured at the sombre billboards. 'There's still talk of invasion.'

'No one talks about the war in Aloe Glen. It's as if it's not actually happening.'

'And that's the problem.' Father tapped the wheel impatiently. 'The country's divided. Troublemakers are agitating against Smuts. It's outrageous.'

'I know one of them.'

'You do?' He shot me a horrified glance. 'Come home!

241

Leave that backwater while Julian's away.'

'It's my home, Father,' I said firmly. 'Backwater or not, it's where I've made my life.'

'I'm sorry, Fran. I know it's not really a backwater but I still feel some responsibility—'

'Hush! Look at the mountain! I want to paint while I'm here.'

Violet noticed straight away although she didn't react until Father was out of view and earshot.

'Oh, Miss Fran!' She swiftly pulled me into her arms. 'Praise the Lord! And just before Master Julian left! If only your dear ma and your aunt could be here!'

'I don't know, Violet,' I whispered. 'It's early days.'

'Ja, but I can see it. A woman knows.'

'You're looking wonderful,' exclaimed Daph the following day, running her eyes over me. 'Who would've expected lonely country living to suit you so well? Now, shall we take the children to Muizenberg? Not to swim,' she cast me a warning glance, 'but to fly kites. What do you say?'

We went on a day of low swells. Ideal conditions, I reflected, for a freak wave.

'Trevor's begun flight training,' Daph confided with nervous pride while the children unpacked their kites. 'The Commonwealth plan to boost the RAF. I'm hoping the war will be over before he has to fly combat. What news of Julian?'

Waves crested and broke against the shore. I closed my eyes briefly.

'Fran? Are you alright? Is it Julian?'

'No.' I shook myself. 'He's fine, he can't say much. He

complains about the heat and the flies.'

'Maisie! Give your brother a chance! I'm so pleased you're back, Fran.'

'I'm only here for a week.'

'I don't believe it,' laughed Daph. 'I said to Penny you'd surely stay now Julian's overseas.'

On the way back, I took a detour past Protea Rise. The owners had built a wall around the property that hid all but the prickly thatched roof. I braked and brought the car to a standstill. Somewhere behind the wall was the orange pincushion protea. I didn't need to see its blooms, I could copy them from memory.

'Congratulations, Frances,' Dr Reed said after examining me. 'You've always been healthy – it just took time. The human body follows its own rhythms.'

I smiled at him and nodded. Dr Reed may be experienced but he is, in this instance, wrong. It took a different lover for me to fall pregnant. I hugged the enveloping warmth. I wasn't barren, I would have a child to carry our family forward—

'Let me book your confinement,' he went on, consulting his diary. 'Now, eat sensibly and rest well. Come and see me every month. I presume you'll stay in Cape Town?'

I will tell no one. This will become Julian's child, conceived before he left.

'Frances?'

A joyful surprise for him, a life-long secret for me.

'I'll be going back to Aloe Glen,' I said. 'I may have the baby there.'

'I'd be happier with you here,' he countered. 'Those

rural areas may not be well served.'

'Shall we decide nearer the time, Doctor?'

This baby should be born in Aloe Glen. It will be the seal on my belonging there, and a riposte to those who expect me to retreat to the soft comfort of the Cape.

'Very well.' He came around his desk. 'Take care of yourself, you're going to have a beautiful baby.'

I walked out of the surgery and sat down on a bench outside. I will have a beautiful baby who will never know his or her real father – but will adore Julian. I'm shameless, Julian has said so himself – in jest, it's true – but this time he'd know I'm being serious. My husband deserves this child and I have no intention of taking that reward away from him. Mark has a family already, and his greatest gift to me will be one of my own.

The sun warmed the back of my neck as I walked along the treed streets to Father's house.

I once wondered what would become of me after I went to live in Aloe Glen.

I know, now, and it's a surprise: I'm no longer sad at having been taken away from all I loved, and I no longer feel cheated of passion. This new self isn't a victim, either, as I'd once feared in that tiny hardscrabble town. I will return to Aloe Glen and produce this baby and show that I can be a worthy part of the community. I'll teach, I'll speak out when I see a friend abused, I'll paint aloes and stone plants and *vygies* and send the work to exhibitions and build my name.

And, when that has been achieved, I may choose to leave with my family.

I opened the gate. Violet waved to me from the front door.

Will Gideon come back to me in my dreams more often?

I want to tell him he may soon have a nephew or niece to chase in a drier garden than he ever knew.

Chapter Forty

I don't intend to tell anyone yet and I'm not showing, so there's no rush. I confess I want to savour this baby alone for a while. I've waited so long.

I hope my pregnancy may change the minds of those who are carefully shunning me.

But if the dominee congratulates me will I be able to resist a little wickedness? I shall adopt a pious expression and say that 'Die Here' looked down on us and saw our dutiful churchgoing and chose to reward us for our patience.

I will not confess that this child was conceived with a love such as I have never experienced before. Or that my husband played no part.

I will not say that I committed adultery. I won't repent.

Will God – the kinder one in whose church I was married – forgive me?

'*Mevrou*?' The boy looked about the classroom but the other pupils were bent at their work. He leant towards me and hissed '*Dankie* – thank you, *mevrou*.'

'For what, Deon?'

'For the bursary. For talking to my pa. For saying I must go to high school.'

I smiled at him. 'You deserve to go.'

'*Ja*, but—'

'What is it?'

'It's my ma.'

'I'll watch over your mother, Deon. I'll make sure she's safe.'

'If Meneer McDonald was here—'

'I know, Deon. But you'll have to trust me. I won't keep quiet about it any more. I'll get help.'

It wouldn't be easy. The nearest police station was at least twenty miles away.

'*Mevrou*?' Lottie Engelbrecht raised her hand. 'I saw a ring around the sun yesterday.'

'That's called a halo,' I said.

'Like you get on Jesus,' piped up Frans van Deventer.

'Yes,' I said. 'But when the halo's around the sun, it's made from ice crystals reflecting the light.'

The children looked at one another and I wondered whether the dominee would have some tricky questions to answer. The schoolmaster's wife, he'd glower, unsettling things again. So often, and mostly by accident, I find that my classes go beyond art or literacy. While we're learning to draw or to write grammatical sentences, we stray into fresh territory.

'Let's look at "either . . . or", and "neither . . . nor",' I said to my small group of ladies at our early evening literacy class a month later. 'One gives us a choice, the other gives us none.'

'Mostly there is no choice in life, Frances,' laughed Sannie Metz, who has recently relented, as have the others. Maybe they sense the coming baby. Maybe, this time, their forgiveness will last. 'Mostly we must make do.'

247

'Ma'am!' came a shout and we all turned. 'Ma'am!'

Sipata stood in the doorway, her eyes wild. 'You must come! Hurry, ma'am!'

'What is it? Why are you here?'

'The house, ma'am! I was almost home. Come look!'

I jumped up and ran out of the classroom, the women crowding out behind me. A plume of black smoke was rising into the air above Marico Road.

'Truda,' cried Sannie Metz from alongside me, 'go to the station. We need the water trailer!'

The smoke was coiling into the sky like a snake.

I've seen a cobra rise up and inflate its golden hood. We watched each other. I wasn't frightened. I stepped back and it sank down and slithered away.

Truda sprinted across the playground, feet hardly touching the ground.

'Go, Frances,' Sannie Metz pushed me, 'go save what you can! Take her, Sipata.'

The other women ran to their cars or bicycles. They needed to get home to ensure their fire buckets were in place and their hoses connected. From the direction of the station I heard shouts.

'Come, ma'am,' Sipata was urging quietly, 'we will go there. I will help you.'

Why are the shortest journeys often the longest? The procession down the aisle on my wedding day, the walk to the entrance of Bella Vista Mansions. But the dash to my burning house was the loneliest because there was no Julian or Mark at the end of it, or even a whistle from a passing train, no sound at all other than a distant, obscene hiss. Mr Fourie's store was closed, the petrol station was deserted, no one was hanging about the cafe.

Can't you see my house is burning? I wanted to yell. *Doesn't anybody care?*

I stumbled on the uneven road surface and Sipata's steadying arm stopped me from falling.

'Careful, ma'am. I will help you,' she panted. 'I will help you.'

The gate stood open. There was a livid reek of burning. Figures, dimly visible through the whirling smoke, were filling buckets from our newly full tank and passing them hand to hand. One of our lounge windows was smashed and the curtains that I liked to keep open were burning. Deeper inside, orange flames licked at my painted chairs, the maroon rug on the floor, the single place setting laid for me at our dining room table. I must try to save something, anything – my diary—

Julian's walking stick was propped against the verandah wall.

'No, ma'am!' screamed Sipata.

I beat open the front door. It swung back, smoke billowed, the fire flared with the extra oxygen. Heat struck my face, smoke caught in my throat. I clutched at my stomach. The baby—

'No!' A man hauled me out of the doorway. 'Wait for the water trailer! It's on its way.'

He had a branch in one hand to beat the flames should they jump outside the house. I nodded dumbly and allowed Sipata to guide me away from the wall of heat. The bucket fillers were tossing water through a second smashed window, the one through which I'd first drawn Aloe Peak. But I recognised none of them, they were not my neighbours. And there was no sign of Mrs van Deventer. A van roared through the gate, with a water trailer hitched to it. Two men got out and began to unroll a thick hose and connect it to the tank. Several others joined them and began to pump. The hose filled, like a worm slowly inflating.

'Thank you!' I shouted, although they surely couldn't hear me. 'Thank you!'

The man in charge ran towards the house with an axe and began to smash the intact windows.

'Why are you doing that?' I screamed, rushing after him. 'Why?'

'To get the water in!' he yelled.

The men led the hose closer. An arc of water gushed from its end and began to play towards the house, seeking the gaping windows as a route to the furnace inside. Smoke and flame erupted into steam. The fire, I realised, would only do part of the damage. The water would ensure that anything left unburnt would be drowned. My precious Cape Town paintings, the aloe flowers pressed between the pages of my heaviest book, the bush clothes that have helped me to fit in here, the city clothes that have made me stand out, Julian's wedding suit, the melon that Sipata cut for me this morning and that I would have finished tonight . . . and my precious diary, the passage of my life—

'Come, ma'am.' Sipata drew me away.

I turned to stare at a crowd that was now gathering at the gate: the neighbours, late to arrive.

You didn't run to fight my fire. You left it to strangers.

I teach you English, I help your children, but you didn't run to fight my fire.

The smoke seemed to be abating, or perhaps it was simply less visible against the darkening sky. Orange flames still darted but the hungry roar was giving way to a smouldering rasp. Through the gloom I saw that one of my paintings was still on the wall, its frame buckled, its glass cracked, its subject – a disa, I think, although I've lost my bearings – streaked with soot.

How much time has passed?

Mrs van Deventer lumbered over and spoke some words that I couldn't hear.

The strangers who'd been filling buckets of water stopped, came to my side, and muttered about how it might have started. A lamp knocked over, maybe. I wanted to retort that there'd been no one in the house, and Sipata knew never to leave a lamp lit, and then I realised that these were not strangers. They were Sipata's neighbours: poor men of all colours, fallen on hard times. Their clothes weren't just ragged from their efforts to help, they'd been ragged before they ran across town to fight a fire in a home far wealthier than their own.

'Thank you for helping, sir. Thank you,' I spread my arms, 'to all of you—'

'You can rebuild, ma'am.'

Rebuild? Was this not a signal to leave?

What sort of foundation was this for Julian and me to rebuild upon? For our child?

I pushed my hair from my face. The heat blast must have blown out my combs. Abel Metz came towards me, his eyes red from the smoke. 'Sannie fetched me, I was nearby. I'm sorry, Mrs McDonald.'

'Frances!' Truda's eyes were bloodshot, too. 'You must come home with me, Frances.'

I stared at her and then back at the charred house. My heart was throbbing as if it had been physically struck. I'll have to tell Julian, even as I've been savouring the moment to tell him about the baby—

'The ceiling's gone.' Abel Metz, again. 'We'll get the

engineer from Worcester to come and look.'

'We'll watch it for a while longer, Mrs McDonald,' said the man on the hose. 'You go now, ma'am.'

The remaining water throwers shrugged on their thin jackets, tipped their caps to me and left quietly.

'Ma'am must lie down,' said Sipata in a stronger voice than normal. 'Ma'am must eat.'

The baby. My child. A house is just bricks and glass. A child is far more fragile.

'Go with Truda Louw,' ordered Mrs van Deventer. 'You must rest.'

Does she know? Can she tell?

They are looking at me curiously, sympathetically and, in the case of Mrs van Deventer, with some impatience. She's probably thinking I will never survive this blow. And maybe I won't, although she never thought I'd last this long from the start.

'Come, Frances.' Truda took my arm.

Why were two of the windows already broken when I arrived?

Chapter Forty-One

I don't remember much about the rest of that night, other than my dreams. I know that Truda and Sipata walked beside me to Truda's house, and then I was drinking hot tea and Truda ran a bath and left me some nightclothes and led me to Deon's room – Deon who was now at school in Worcester thanks to Julian – and I sank onto his narrow bed and slept.

The dreams pursued me all night. I saw my brother Gideon running away from me while Protea Rise burnt in the background.

I saw a child – my child – smiling at me while Aloe Peak disappeared behind a wall of smoke.

I saw Julian in the desert, amid a bombardment of guns and tanks, their cannons spitting orange flame.

I saw scorched paper, seared trousseau dresses and blackened wood . . .

'Frances?'

I jerked awake.

'Frances, I've got tea.' Truda stood in the doorway in a short cotton nightgown, her white hair cascading, a cup in her hand. 'And I fetched your bag from school.'

'Thank you,' I whispered and levered myself up. The nausea

rose in my throat. I rushed down the corridor to the bathroom and retched. Truda's hand stroked my back.

'It will be alright,' she murmured. 'It's a good sign.'

'You know?' I wiped my face and raised it to her.

'*Ja*,' she whispered and gave me a gentle smile. 'When you came back from Cape Town.'

I sat down on the floor and leant back against the wall. 'Where is your husband? I can't stay.'

Truda's gaze slipped away from mine. 'He's gone.'

'Gone?'

'*Ja*. He said it's work up the line. The railway tunnels. You can stay.'

'Only for a day.' I got up slowly. 'Thank you, Truda. Then I'll find somewhere else.'

'Come drink your tea. Then I make eggs.'

Truda still struggles with the small words, the pronouns, the definite and indefinite articles. But I secretly enjoy her English. It's plain and all the more expressive because of that.

She held out her arms and embraced me.

'Thank you,' she muttered before releasing me, 'for being my friend.'

After breakfast I put on my smoky bush clothes, ignored Truda's pleas to rest, and walked to my house. The baby felt heavy in my stomach.

Hush, I whispered, stroking the gentle bulge, trying to calm us both. *You and I are well . . .*

Is this fire a tragedy or an opportunity? I've seized opportunities before.

In daylight, the house appeared almost intact until I went closer and saw the glassless windows. The front door was ajar. I knocked – why? This was my house after all – and went in.

Ash stirred around my velskoens. Ceiling panels were strewn across the floor or propped at odd angles against half-burnt furniture. The corrugated underside of the iron roof was exposed, like human ribs stripped of their covering of skin. In front of me, three chairs had somehow survived and their decorations were still visible in blistered paint: a bunch of sepia jasmine, a twist of pockmarked vine.

A sob caught in the back of my throat. Is this God's punishment for my sin with Mark?

The once-beige curtains lay in a charred heap beside the windows. The fireplace was as empty as it had been yesterday, for we only laid fires in the winter. The table, sideboard and sofa were blackened hulks, not quite destroyed but surely unrecoverable.

I shook myself. I had to get to the bedroom. The door was jammed and I kicked it until it yielded. The brass heading on our bed had been broken by a descending roof beam. Debris littered the bed linen but my bedside oil lamp stood curiously untouched. I rushed into the corner and stared down at the floorboards, then looked about and grabbed a broken stick and levered one up. It was there – unburnt, intact. I pulled it out and pressed the floorboard back. *Thank you, thank you—*

'Hello? Anyone there?'

'Yes,' I shouted, shoving the diary into my pocket. 'In the bedroom.'

'Mrs McDonald?' A young man stood in the doorway. 'Peter Webb, ma'am, engineer. Abel Metz called me. I'm here to assess the damage.'

I spread my hands towards the chaos.

'It always looks worse than it is,' he said cautiously, 'but if

255

the structure is sound, you can rebuild.'

'Thank you for coming so quickly, sir.'

I picked my way to the kitchen where a single upturned saucepan lay on the floor, surrounded by a stain that was perhaps the soup Sipata usually left for me. I pushed open the back door and went down the steps and lifted a small rock. There, underneath, was her key.

And now, the studio – my refuge – which I'd left until last.

The door opened reluctantly, its lower edge grinding. I stopped on the threshold, my fingers shaking on the handle. If I'd come upon the room as a stranger, I might have wanted to paint the bizarreness of it.

A snowstorm of charred paper was spilling from the open door of the cupboard, eddying around the pile of sticks that was once my easel. My paintbox had sprung apart from the heat, scattering single cakes whose melted trails marked the floorboards in a random, abstract pattern. I stepped inside and picked up a pot of carmine red that I'd brought back from Cape Town. It was slightly warm. I rolled it into the corner and watched the contents ooze.

I'm not quite right in the head at the moment, even though I haven't fallen or been in an accident.

What about the painting I showed the director?

I scrabbled frantically through the fallen papers but it wasn't there. Instead, my hand fell upon glass. Two distinct heaps, one on the floor by the window and one scattered in the centre of the room. Some of the shards were curved, not flat. I went over to the window and examined the frame. It still had a few pieces of glass clinging to it. They were flat.

'Mrs McDonald?'

Why did it matter? My paints were melted. My work was

destroyed. The special picture I sought was gone. I was back in England, searching for glass from Father's smashed binoculars as a way to atone—

'Mrs McDonald.' Peter Webb stood in the doorway. 'I'm happy to say the walls are sound, but the roof beams need examining and new ceilings must be installed. The floorboards can be sanded down, apart from where they've been too badly burnt.' He looked up from his clipboard. 'The priority is to replace the glass to render the property watertight.'

I fingered the curved shard in my hand and held it out to him.

'Where did you find this?'

'Here.' I gestured. 'In the middle. And in the centre of the lounge. It's not window glass, is it?'

'No, ma'am. It doesn't appear to be so.'

He left the room. I followed and found him bent down over the half-burnt maroon rug, probing shards of glass with the point of his pencil.

'You can contact me at my office, Mrs McDonald.' He stood up and handed me a card. 'In the case of house fires,' his kept his tone neutral, 'the police are obliged to investigate.'

'Thank you, sir. I'm most grateful.'

'Mevrou McDonald!' came a call from outside.

'Take some time, ma'am, to decide what you wish to do. But get the place glassed as soon as possible.'

'Mevrou McDonald.' The dominee lifted his hat and crunched over the uneven floorboards.

Mr Webb nodded to me, glanced at the dominee and stepped away.

'So very sorry for what happened.' The dominee reached out and clasped my hands. 'The ways of the Lord are not for us to question.'

'Thank you, Dominee. Why are you here?'

'To give comfort.' He looked at me in surprise. 'To pray with you, *mevrou*.'

'I don't need prayers, sir, I need somewhere to stay.'

He looked uneasy. 'I will ask my congregation. But you could return to your family in Cape Town.'

'No,' I said. 'This is my home. And I'm having a baby.'

His eyes widened. I imagined the thoughts whirring through his head. The outspoken English woman, whose husband had sacrificed himself to go and fight for the British, was expecting a child and her house had just burnt down . . . I saw a flicker of shame cross his face. He'd never defended Julian's dedication to the town, he'd never spoken out from the pulpit against prejudice at home or abroad. And now he was being asked to house the tricky wife.

'You should return to Cape Town, Mrs McDonald. It would be sensible.'

That's the adjective Mother deployed when advising me to marry Julian.

'I don't wish to be sensible, sir. I've learnt to appreciate Aloe Glen. I want to have my child here.'

He looked doubtfully at the tumbled ceiling panels, the blackened furniture.

'I'd also like to know how the fire started, Dominee.'

'Fires are often acts of God, Mrs McDonald.' He raised his eyes skywards. 'Not for us to understand.'

'On the contrary, I believe we should try to understand.'

He regarded me with narrowed eyes. The dominee is used to being the fount of all ecclesiastical wisdom, so he finds dissenting opinion difficult to absorb. 'I don't follow, ma'am.'

'According to the engineer, the police are required to

investigate all house fires.'

'Only if there's evidence of foul play, Mrs McDonald.'

I bent down and picked up a piece of the rounded glass.

'The police may have an opinion about this, sir. I have no glass like this in the house.'

'A milk bottle, surely?' He smiled. 'A simple but sad explanation. Shattered in the fire.'

'I don't drink milk, sir. I take my tea black. We have not had milk in the house since my husband left.'

He stared at me. The dominee is not a bad man, just a blinkered one. 'I will contact the police, ma'am, on your behalf. I am sure, however, that the fire was an accident.'

'Possibly it was. But I'd like an opinion. Thank you, Dominee.'

He lifted his hat and turned towards the front door, but halted and turned back. 'Please join my family for dinner this evening, Mrs McDonald.'

'Thank you,' I said. 'That is kind of you but I'm staying with Mrs Louw. She will give me a meal.'

I went back into my studio and touched the empty spaces on the wall where my paintings used to hang.

Am I safe here? I've asked my diary repeatedly.

No, I'm not.

'Sorry!' shouted Tifo from his petrol pump as I hurried past. 'Sorry for your fire, ma'am.'

'Mrs McDonald,' Mr Fourie came out of his store, his hands clasped together as if in prayer, 'a tragedy, especially with Mr McDonald away. At least you have a home in Cape Town, ma'am.'

I kept going until I reached the outskirts, the vantage point

Father and I had looked down upon from Aloe Peak, where tin-roofed shacks and mud huts and simple cottages crowded close to one another. Small children of all colours were playing on the bare earth. I counted the dwellings down a rutted path and knocked on the door of a modest cottage.

'Ma'am!' Sipata gasped, looked beyond me fearfully and then pulled me inside.

'What is it, Sipata? Why are you afraid?'

She shook her head and gestured to the only chair. 'It is not safe, ma'am.'

'What happened yesterday? When did you leave the house?'

She looked down for a moment and then back up at me.

'I laid a place for ma'am at the table. I left soup in a pot, off the stove. The sun was going down. I closed the door like always. I left the key under the stone at the kitchen door.'

'I know. It's still there.'

'I walked along the road, ma'am, and then I heard a noise. I looked, ma'am, but I saw nothing.'

'What noise?'

Her eyes became defensive. 'I don't know, ma'am.'

I leant back and closed my eyes. Nausea rose in my throat.

I felt Sipata's hand on my arm, gently. 'The baby, ma'am? Ma'am has eaten today?'

'Yes, I've had breakfast, thank you Sipata.' I opened my eyes. 'What did you hear? Or see?'

'I don't want trouble, ma'am,' she murmured. 'I only saw smoke when I was nearly home, ma'am.'

There was a knock on the door. A white woman I didn't recognise came inside, carrying a small paper bag. She nodded to Sipata and held the bag out to me. 'I'm sorry about your house, Mrs McDonald.' Her voice was hesitant but her English was good. She wore tattered khaki trousers and a man's shirt. She was very thin. I opened the bag. Inside were two small apples. 'For you, ma'am. To help.'

I got up and embraced her. Hot tears spilt onto my cheeks. Sipata and the unknown woman guided me back to the chair.

'I'm sorry,' I managed, wiping my face. 'Thank you for the gift. You are too kind.'

'What is your name?' I asked the woman when I left.

'Lena Fuller.'

'Thank you, Lena.'

A small crowd had gathered. A barefoot girl ran up and clutched at Lena's leg as she went to stand next to a coloured man. I recognised him, and several others, too. These were the men who rushed across town to throw buckets of water on my fire.

'Thank you.' I shook hands with each in turn. 'Thank you for saving my house.'

I found myself wanting to paint them, to tell the story of their lives written across their worn faces.

And I think I know why Sipata is frightened.

'Fran, my dear, how lovely to hear from you. I have news!'

'Oh, yes?'

'Indeed! You'll be proud of me. I've volunteered!'

'But aren't you too old, Father?'

He chuckled. 'I shall never take up arms, my dear. More likely to shoot my own side than the enemy. No, I'll be joining Logistics, here at the Cape. Managing the flow of troopships through the harbour, organising hospitality for the young men while they're on a stopover.'

A black crow alighted on the railway track and began to

rifle in the dirt. I saw, once more, the ash, the melted paints, the scorched paintings.

'Fran? Are you there?'

'There's been a fire, Father.'

'Oh, I'm so sorry, my dear. I thought the veld was green after all the rain.'

'It wasn't the veld. It was our house.'

There was silence down the line and Father's voice, when it came, was clipped of its earlier cheer.

'You must come home, Frances. You cannot stay there. I will come and fetch you and bring you home.'

'No, Father,' I said. 'Not yet. I need to be here to see what can be saved.'

I'm not succumbing to distraction, Father. I want to find out what happened. How a house could burst into flames on its own without a lightning strike or an overturned lamp. And with an oven and a fireplace that were both stone cold.

Chapter Forty-Two

My dearest Frances

As ever, I cannot say where I am. I can only say it is very hot. But your artist's eye would be intrigued by the endless sand, the stars at night, the palm trees by the river.

Morale is good despite the reverses you surely know about. The enemy is dogged but so are we.

This is hard terrain to fight over. Just providing the forces with enough water to drink – let alone to shave – is a mighty task. Here, drought is permanent.

I think of you so often, my dear. I know that you've grieved over not having a family but I want to reassure you it no longer matters. We have each other, and our work, and a comfortable home, and that is surely more than enough.

I love you. I know that it has taken a while for you, but I do believe that we are now one.

Ever your

Julian

'Good day, Mrs McDonald. Can I get you anything, ma'am?'

'I'll take some tinned fruit and ham. And a half dozen eggs.

Please put it on our account.'

'That won't be necessary, ma'am,' Mr Fourie muttered. 'I will not charge you.'

I waited a moment before replying. I think I'm becoming a tiny bit vengeful.

'That is very kind, Mr Fourie, but I insist. The bank did not burn down, sir.'

I left the store and looked up and down the road.

Where are my tea party ladies with whom I believed I was reconciled? My literacy students? They ran home to check on their own fire preparedness – as I would have – but they never returned and their husbands never offered help. Of all our acquaintances, only Truda and Abel Metz assisted me in the aftermath. The flames may have been doused but a different fire is stifling Aloe Glen.

Shame? Embarrassment?

The dominee called to say that despite putting out an appeal for accommodation, he'd received no offers as yet from the townsfolk or from those on nearby farms. Laetitia Snyman apologised that she couldn't offer me a place because her parents' property had no spare room for guests.

'Stay, Frances,' repeated Truda. 'I will look after you.'

Lena Fuller appeared in Truda's doorway and said she had a fold-out bed if Mrs McDonald required it and though her shack was small, I was always welcome.

'Mrs McDonald, are you there?'

I came out of my burnt kitchen where I'd been sorting pots and pans. The young policeman ran his eyes over my blackened bush trousers and stained shirt.

'Ma'am, I'm here to investigate the fire. The dominee said it might be foul play.'

I blinked. Perhaps I was misjudging the dominee.

'Yes. Come this way, officer.'

I led him to the lounge and showed him the pile of thick, curved glass; then led him to a similar pile in my studio, hidden among the loose papers strewn across the floor. I'd left the mess in place, to avoid disturbing potential evidence.

'Both windows were broken, sir, when I arrived on the scene. If you go into the other bedrooms, where the firefighters smashed the windows deliberately, you'll find only window glass.'

The officer knelt down and felt the shards between his fingers.

'I don't drink milk, sir. There are no glass bottles or vases of that sort in the house.'

'Was anything missing, ma'am? Was anything stolen?'

'You mean, was the house burgled first and then set alight?'

He reddened slightly. 'Robbery could be a motive, ma'am. A fire would cover the robbers' tracks.'

'Nothing was stolen, officer.'

I rescued my most valuable possession, sir, although a second – but lesser – treasure is still missing.

'If it wasn't robbery,' he held his pencil above his notebook, 'who would want to set fire to your house, ma'am? You have a maid?'

'Yes, she raised the alarm. If it weren't for her, the entire house might have gone up.'

'You can't be sure—'

'She's my friend, officer. She'd never do me harm. The oven was off, there were no lamps left burning. You can speak to Sipata, sir. She lives on the edge of town.'

The policeman looked me over again and made a further

note. I wonder what he makes of me, an Englishwoman in an overwhelmingly Afrikaans community, an Englishwoman dressed in the clothes of a farm worker and claiming her maid as a friend.

'Is there anybody in town who would wish you ill, ma'am?'

'You want to know if I have any enemies?'

I have been strong so far. There was only the single sob when I saw my blistered chairs, melted paints and blackened pictures, and my brief breakdown in Sipata's cottage at the woman's, Lena's, kindness.

But now, as he watched me, the weight of Aloe Glen's judgement crashed down, a decade's worth of suspicion, partial approval and, since the fire, only silence.

I sank onto the charred floorboards.

'Please, ma'am,' he squatted down beside me and patted my back awkwardly, 'please don't cry.'

But I couldn't stop. I wept for my good-sized house that might never be rebuilt, I wept for Julian and his belief that we were one, I wept for the lost image I'd drawn of my brother and which only I could recognise, and I wept for the hopes I'd had for my place in this stubborn town.

He put an arm about me kindly, and murmured that it would be alright and that he would do the best he could and that my house could surely be repaired.

After a while, I sat up and wiped my face.

'Officer, I don't think this was an accidental fire.'

'Because you're English, ma'am?' His brow furrowed. 'Because your husband volunteered?'

'Perhaps,' I nodded. 'He was the headmaster of the school. He felt it was his duty to go.'

'But who would be cruel enough to do this when you were alone?'

'You can find out, sir.'

He flushed and helped me up.

I reached into my pocket for a handkerchief and blew my nose. My hands were filthy, my handkerchief now had black fingermarks over it, my untethered hair was falling about my face. For all I knew, even my teeth might be black.

'I will make enquiries, Mrs McDonald, but I can't promise anything. Without witnesses . . .'

I watched as he left, picking his way through the debris. Sipata wouldn't identify anyone, or admit to the sound of breaking glass even if she'd been close enough to see or hear. She was too frightened of the consequences if she did. A coloured maid possibly fingering a white perpetrator . . .

I gathered up the scorched bed linen and dumped it onto the growing pile outside. I'd moved our motor car, thankfully undamaged, into the backyard to pack it with items for the local rubbish dump but I'd have to get a man with a lorry to take away the furniture.

'Hello? Anyone here?'

'In the backyard,' I called.

'Henry Venter.' A large young man in bush shorts marched through the kitchen door and extended a meaty hand. 'I'm a builder. Abel Metz sent me. Could have been worse, ma'am.'

'I'm pleased you say so. To me it looks unrecoverable, Mr Venter.'

He followed me back inside.

'Nah.' He rapped his knuckles against the passage walls. 'Takes a lot to bring down these old places. You'll need new ceilings of course,' he stared upwards, 'but the beams can

267

probably be saved. I'll do a walk around and then I'll send you a quote, ma'am.'

'Can I ask you to look at something in particular?'

'Certainly.'

I led him first into the lounge and then into the studio and showed him the piles of curved glass. 'When I arrived soon after the fire started, these two windows had already been smashed. But this is not window glass, is it?'

'No.' He looked about and sniffed. 'And the firefighters broke the rest of the windows, did they?'

'Yes, to spray water inside.'

He fingered a glass fragment. 'Did you have any cushions here, ma'am? Or a carpet?'

'In the yard. I was going to throw it away.'

He strode outside and rummaged through the pile of linen and pulled out the maroon rug. He shook it and proceeded to sniff, concentrating on the parts that were unburnt.

'Smell, Mrs McDonald. What does that say to you?'

A sweet fragrance, overlaid with smoke, pricked my nostrils. Suddenly I was with Julian, driving over Bain's Kloof Pass, the motor car struggling with the gradient; then I was drinking cold lemonade at the farm stall, and there was a sharp whiff as he filled the tank. I sniffed again. It was unmistakable – but only when lifted up to the nose.

'Petrol,' I said. 'It smells of petrol.'

'Do the police know, ma'am?'

'The officer didn't see this, Mr Venter. But I'll telephone him and let him know.'

'Do that, ma'am,' Henry Venter said with brisk sympathy. 'Could be arson.'

* * *

By the time he left, the wind had risen and was blowing through the broken windows.

A surviving sheet of white paper lay on the floor. I picked it up and walked into the lounge. The circular mirror that had reflected me on the night I arrived in Aloe Glen still hung on the opposite wall. A hairline crack ran down its centre. I walked closer. A face looked back at me.

Who is she?

Thin, gaunt almost. Wild hair, blonder than before. Green eyes with a hint of ginger and a sheen of defiance shading to despair. I placed the paper on the blackened table, and bent down and picked up a sliver of burnt wood.

Charcoal.

I looked across at the mirror one more time and began to draw.

A face emerged. My face. Angled cheeks, straight nose, billowing hair, lips set in a line. No sign, as yet, of any bloom, any softness, from my pregnancy. I reached down and rubbed my finger through the ash on the floor and stroked it below the lines of the cheekbones to make hollows, and under the eyes to make shadows. I'd scratched the index finger of my left hand by accident and a bright spot of blood welled. I smeared it on the paper, in the background, to denote fire.

Then I picked up the charcoal sliver and tapped it to make the point sharper.

I drew a line down the centre, slashing my face in two just like the crack bisected the mirror.

Chapter Forty-Three

The dawn was yellow-pink when I set out the following morning towards Aloe Peak. Silvery rain clouds drifted over the heights. There's an other-worldly beauty to the desert when it's been given a reprieve.

It took about an hour but I eventually found the armoured aloe. The recent rain appeared to have had no effect on the plant; it still clung precariously to the slope, although – I leant closer, careful to avoid the spikes – there was evidence of tiny, swollen leaves sprouting from its heart.

I must start my art afresh. Father will send me replacement supplies. I will sell my paintings as soon as the paint is dry.

I sat down beside the aloe's thorny mass and stared at the town below.

Where would I live? I couldn't stay with Truda for much longer. Wynand was due back soon. The charcoal portrait was under my bed, along with my diary. I must find a new hiding place.

I'd brought a sheet of cleanish paper, a pencil and a square of unburnt cardboard on which to press.

Dear Julian

I imagine the Sahara is a dryer and vaster version of the land around Aloe Glen and that lets me feel closer to you.

I have news which is both joyful and shocking.

There has been a fire at our house. The ceiling has come down and much of the furniture has been damaged. I don't think it's useful to agonise over how it started, but rather be grateful I wasn't home at the time. The building is sound and Abel Metz can recommend a builder. If we can afford to repair it then I will do so, if you agree.

And that brings me to my joyful news. You're going to be a father! Yes, dear Julian, I'm expecting a child. Dr Reed in Cape Town is happy with my progress and the baby will be born early next year. We'll be a family at last! I may go back to Cape Town for a while, but Aloe Glen is our home and it's the place where we'll be reunited once this hard war is over.

The art and literacy classes go on.

With all my love

Frances

I reached out a finger and touched one of the armoured leaves. A spot of blood welled on my fingertip. The fire in my portrait . . .

I folded the letter and put it in my pocket.

The house must be swept of ash. The burnt furniture must be removed.

And later I must call Father and tell him I'm having a child.

And then I must find somewhere to stay.

A dark shape was drifting over the facing slope. Even without binoculars I knew it was a black eagle, conspicuous white 'V' on his neck, feathery wingtips splayed to ride the currents and stay aloft.

I have to learn to fly on my own.

Aunt Mary would agree. Indeed, she'd be outraged if I gave up.

Mrs van Deventer came out of her house as I hurried by, the first time I'd seen her since the fire.

'You should go home, Frances,' she shouted from her front step.

I unhooked the gate and walked towards her. Usually, I wait politely before being asked to enter.

'There's a police report due, Mrs van Deventer.'

'Why?' she retorted.

'The fire may have been set deliberately.'

She placed her hands on her hips and pursed her lips. 'Now who would want to do that?'

I turned and stared towards my house and then back at her.

'I've never been accepted here. However hard I tried.'

She opened her mouth but I held up my hand. 'When Julian chose to fight on the side of the British, someone wanted to tell us we're no longer welcome.'

She stared at me, her hands now fidgeting beneath her apron.

'I intend to stay. I will wait and see what the police find.'

'You don't give up,' she muttered.

'No,' I said, lifting my chin. 'I don't. And I'm also expecting a baby, Mrs van Deventer.'

'*Ja*,' she nodded, her face softening slightly. 'I saw. Frans?' she yelled into the interior of the house.

Her grandson appeared. 'Hello, *mevrou*.' His face fell. 'Sorry about the fire, ma'am.'

'You go with Mrs McDonald,' said his grandmother, giving him a slap on the shoulder. 'You help her to lift things in her house, you do what she tells you to do. Now go! Make yourself useful.'

The boy nodded and ran to the gate, and waited for me to follow.

'Thank you, Mrs van Deventer.'

She shrugged. 'We're neighbours. We do what we can to help.'

But not neighbourly enough to offer help until confronted.

'Look here,' she placed a rough hand on my arm, 'I know you don't fit but I don't hold with driving you out.' She snatched her arm away and went inside, banging the door behind her.

Between them, Sipata and young Frans van Deventer moved the burnt furniture into the backyard while I removed the paintings from their frames, keeping what could be saved and reluctantly jettisoning what was too damaged onto the rubbish pile.

A *Long-tailed Sugarbird atop Protea repens*, smeared with soot.

A *Fernwood Buttress from Protea Rise*, whose upper edge was blackened.

A stained *Aloe Peak at Sunset*, where I'd experimented with a shade of violet I'd never used before.

'Ma'am can make more pictures,' said Sipata, coming into the bedroom. She held out a handful of dry paint cakes. I fingered my blue linen low-waister. It was intact, but the matching straw hat had collapsed. The sea-green chiffon from the Kelvin Grove – never worn in Aloe Glen – was gently tinged.

'Have the police spoken to you, Sipata?'

'Yes, ma'am.'

'Did you tell them about the noise you heard?'

'Yes.'

'Was it breaking glass, Sipata?'

Her eyes widened. 'I can't say for sure, ma'am. I'm sorry, ma'am . . .'

Once they'd gone I looked again for my lost painting and then left, closing the front door behind me. There was no need; anyone with a desire to snoop or loot could have pushed it open and taken whatever they pleased.

A car was parked outside Truda's house and a policeman was sitting on the couch in her front room. Truda sat opposite, weeping.

'What is it?' I rushed over and knelt beside her. 'What happened?'

But I knew. The police had uncovered what I suspected.

'It's Wynand,' Truda muttered and pushed back her tangled hair.

I turned to the policeman. He was older than the man who'd called on me.

'Officer? I'm a friend of Mrs Louw's.'

He shifted on the couch. 'Mr Louw has been detained, ma'am. I'm Captain Ellis.'

'On what grounds?'

'Sabotage. Interfering with the railway line to cause derailment of troop trains.'

I sat back on my heels. 'But he set fire to my house!' I blurted.

274

'No!' Truda gasped. 'Not the fire?'

The captain shrugged. 'I'm not aware of any fire, ma'am. This is about the railway track. It's a pattern since the declaration of war. Transport interrupted. Telephone lines cut.' He got to his feet. 'I'm sorry for your difficulty, Mrs Louw. Your husband will be detained until he's no longer a threat to the country. Good day, ma'am.'

'I'll see you out, Captain.' I led the way out of the front door and closed it behind me. 'Sir? Will you listen to me for a moment? There may be more to this.'

'We know Louw belongs to a pro-Nazi organisation, ma'am. One of his crew confessed so we have evidence of his wrongdoing.'

'Sir, my concern is a different matter. Right now, your colleagues are investigating a fire at my house on the day Wynand Louw left town to inspect the railway tunnels up the line.'

'Go on, ma'am.'

'There's evidence of a possible firebombing, sir. Two windows were broken. There are glass shards that don't match the window glass. The soft furnishings smell of petrol.'

'Who is the investigating officer?'

'Sergeant Roland, from Touw's River Police Station. If Wynand Louw set fire to my house then he shouldn't simply be detained, sir, he should stand trial.'

The captain regarded me closely. 'Why do you live here, ma'am?'

'I beg your pardon?'

'Why do you live here?'

'My husband is the local headmaster. I've been here for ten years.'

275

'And where is your husband, Mrs—?'

'McDonald. Frances McDonald. My husband volunteered. He's in North Africa with the Allied forces.'

I could tell he was putting the pieces together. Reluctantly. Perhaps even sceptically. A Nazi sympathiser, bent on sabotaging the railway line, decides to inflict a further slice of damage by tossing a petrol bomb into the house of a man who's fighting against the nation he admires.

'It makes sense, does it not, Captain?'

'Maybe, ma'am. But national security takes precedence in a time of war.'

'You will speak to Officer Roland?'

'I will. But we'd need to find witnesses placing Louw at the scene, or evidence he assembled a firebomb at home, for example. Otherwise there's no case.'

He glanced back at the tiny house, the barred windows, the bare front patch, the weeping wife inside.

'We'd have to search Mrs Louw's home. And question her further. Do you want that, ma'am?'

I hesitated. Truda had offered me shelter as soon as I found myself homeless. Sipata is too frightened to speak, and the neighbours – if they saw anything – will never implicate one of their own. I stared along the railway line. No recent whistles, no smoke.

It was true. The line was out of action.

'I'd be grateful,' I said slowly, 'if you would investigate as far as you can without involving her.'

I went back inside and made tea and sandwiches with the ham I'd bought from Mr Fourie.

Truda remained crouched in the armchair, hugging her arms about her body as if waiting for a physical blow from a husband who could no longer threaten her.

'He made fire at your house?' she whispered over lunch.

'No,' I said firmly, 'I jumped to a conclusion that wasn't fair.'

'A conclusion?'

'Yes. I thought it might be him because he left. But I was wrong. He was up the line.'

Truda relies on her instincts. She's at one with the veld and with wild creatures. I've seen her get so close to a scrub robin she could almost stroke it. She senses I'm lying.

'Why don't you rest?' I led her gently to the bedroom.

Perhaps, once she's rested, she'll realise she ought to be relieved.

Wynand, by his malign actions, has let her go.

Set her free.

This is my first entry since the fire. I did not seek out danger. It found me. And I drew what it did to me. But I've been unable to write anything until today. I'm living in a house with a friend whose husband threw two petrol bombs into my home.

My maid is frightened because she saw him and knows that if she identifies him, he will come for her. If not now, then when he's released.

I know he's the culprit and Truda knows it, too.

But we cannot speak about it because then we'd destroy the affection we hold for each other.

I need Truda, and she needs me. Together, we must navigate our way in this town, past this fire. I have never had a friend like her. Or Lena and Sipata. Their friendship is elemental, like the landscape.

What happens when the war is over, I don't know.

I've found a hiding place where this diary will never be found.

The baby moved inside me today. A fluttering beneath my ribs.

I live for the promise of new life.

Chapter Forty-Four

My meeting with the bank manager, Mr Porter, was memorable, mostly for the dramatic view of the Worcester valley and surrounding mountains from his office.

'Mrs McDonald, your husband does not have extensive savings.' Porter's tone was mournful. 'His funds went to pay off your property and to the purchase of a new motor car. You say you don't have insurance?'

'That is correct.' I hesitated. 'My husband believed it was too expensive.'

Julian was so cautious in his habits, I assumed he was right to consider it unnecessary. I trusted him over money, but then I'd trusted Father, too. If this fire has taught me anything, it has taught me to ask questions, demand answers, and never to acquiesce again.

'While he's up north, most of Mr McDonald's war wages are being paid into your account, to cover your living expenses. But there are insufficient funds for major works at 10 Marico Road, Mrs McDonald. And I regret the bank is not in a position to offer a loan.'

Worcester's mountains, I noticed, were more settled in the landscape. Aloe Peak and its neighbours rose out of the earth in defiance, clawing at the sky, desperate for rain, for respite.

'What do you suggest, sir?'

He leant forward and clasped his hands together. 'I recommend you sell, madam. The land will be worth a fair amount; property prices have gone up since your husband bought fifteen years ago. And then you can purchase afresh when your husband returns.'

'I don't think the market is buoyant in Aloe Glen at the moment.'

'It is the war, I agree. Most buyers are waiting.'

'Then I shall, too,' I said, gathering my bag.

'You have family in Cape Town, I believe?'

'Yes,' I said. 'Why does everybody want me to leave the place I vowed to make my home?'

'I thought, madam, with your background,' he glanced obliquely at my last remaining smart dress, 'you'd be happier in the city.'

'Thank you, Mr Porter,' I rose and held out my hand, 'I shall bear your advice in mind.'

'Any help,' he said with a concerned face, 'don't hesitate to ask. Such a tragedy for you.'

I held back a retort. I've no patience, any longer, with contrived sympathy. Yet I have no ammunition to counter it other than with words.

Or with my art.

On my final visit to Marico Road, I rescued my folding stool and spent an hour scrubbing it clean. Sergeant Roland and Captain Ellis found me in the yard. The local rubbish man had just taken away the sofa, the chairs and our bed, which turned out to have a broken frame.

'Sergeant? Captain? There's news?'

They exchanged glances.

'Good morning, ma'am. Our investigations confirm there's petrol on the rug. It's possible the curved glass and smashed windows point to a petrol bomb or bombs being thrown into your house.'

'That's progress, isn't it, Sergeant?'

'Yes,' he nodded, 'but there are no witnesses, ma'am. Your housemaid saw no one. Neither did the neighbours. And it seems there were no passers-by that day.'

'Wynand Louw could have done it before he went up the line—'

'He could have,' Captain Ellis put in, 'but we can't confirm his movements, ma'am. Someone else may have attacked your house, not Mr Louw.'

I sat down on the stool. The nausea grabs me every so often and it's best to sit down. From the sky came a series of cries. Wheeling jackal buzzards, back since the rain.

'Are you alright, ma'am?' The young Sergeant advanced and crouched down next to me.

'So you're not going to charge him. Or anyone else.' My voice was hoarse and I cleared my throat.

'Mrs McDonald, we don't have the evidence to lay charges.'

'You've questioned him?'

'He's refusing to speak, ma'am.'

'Even about his sabotage?'

The captain looked at me with pity, mixed with some impatience.

'We can't discuss that, ma'am. I can assure you the sergeant will follow any leads. But at this time we can only

281

say your fire could have been arson, perpetrated by unknown individuals.'

'Wynand Louw is not a suspect?'

'No, ma'am. He is a threat to law and order and is being detained for that reason.'

A house fire was a peripheral offence when compared with sabotage.

'I see. May I have a report, Sergeant? Of the investigation? I may need it in order to apply for a loan.'

It was a lie, of course, but he wasn't to know. I intend to leave the house as it is, blackened, abandoned and yet not abandoned. A rebuke to all who pass by.

The sergeant glanced at Captain Ellis, who nodded.

I followed them round to the front. The collapsed ceiling panels were clearly visible through the open door. Jagged glass clung to the lounge window frame. The burly Henry Venter was coming to board up the windows at the end of the week.

'Would you have pursued this investigation differently in peacetime, sir?'

'Let it go, Mrs McDonald,' Captain Ellis replied with a hint of irritation. 'National security takes priority.'

It was clear. There would be justice only if the perpetrator gave himself up and confessed.

'Will you and the new baby stay with me?' Truda asked.

She knows I want to remain in Aloe Glen, she knows that the veld has captured me even though I find the town unforgiving. Mark understood this, too. Before I left Bella Vista Mansions, he said that my aloe painting showed not just skill, but heart as well.

Yet what would you tell me now, Mark? Now that I

282

carry your child within me?

'I'll stay for a while, thank you. But only if I pay rent. I insist on that.'

'Yes,' she nodded. 'Some money will help me, too.'

Truda needs income. Apart from the company I can provide now, she's alone.

I will paint every day.

I'll force confidence into my fingers and build up my portfolio from its ashes while I wait for the baby. Mr Cadwaller would expect no less. And if the police make no progress, I shall let it be known in the wider community that the evidence points to my house being burnt on purpose.

Chapter Forty-Five

Dear Mrs McDonald
Following on from the success of our last exhibition, we
are planning a new one for early next year.

If you wish your work to be included for exhibit and
sale, then kindly forward it to us by end of November
to allow for the timely preparation of the catalogue.

As you know, your paintings garnered considerable
interest and I have no doubt that future work of yours
will do so, too. I suggest, in the light of your previous
success, that we raise the asking prices by a modest
percentage?

Yours sincerely
A. R. J. Compton

Director Compton imagines I have a stash of finished work
ready to send him. I could make the excuse that I'm waiting
for my child, that I'm too shocked by the fire to come up with
fresh work . . . but I need the exposure as well as the money.
After paying Truda a fair rent and replacing my most severely
smoked clothes, there won't be much left in our account.

The partly damaged paintings may still have a use: I could
copy them to create new versions.

I waited in the classroom after school on the usual afternoon.

The bell rang.

Children ran down the corridors, bicycles whizzed off, farm lorries manoeuvred in a cloud of dust.

No one came. Then—

'Mrs McDonald?' Frans van Deventer poked his head around the door. 'Have you got any crayons left, ma'am? Or did they all burn up?'

'Not all of them, Frans,' I replied. 'And we do have paper – look!' I brandished some grey, creased sheets. 'We can draw very good storms over Aloe Peak with these!'

'Yes, please,' Frans said, coming in and sitting at the desk next to mine.

Footsteps came down the corridor. Toby Engelbrecht sidled in and gave me a shy smile.

The early evening literacy class did not revive at all.

I waited in the classroom, with Truda alongside me, but no one came.

I'm being shunned again, but this time it's more serious. Supporting the wrong side in the war made for awkwardness, but now my house has burnt down. Do the mothers look me in the eye and pretend nothing has changed? Do they proclaim their regret and offer help?

They do neither. They prefer to disengage entirely.

'Father,' I said over the telephone. 'I have more news.'

'Ah Fran, I'm so relieved. You've decided to come home?'

'Not just yet. I'm expecting a baby, Father.'

'Good God!' he shouted down the line. 'How wonderful!'

'Yes, after all this time.'

I waited as Father calculated his next line of attack. Father and I are alike in the way we reason – he taught me – although he betrayed his own advice.

'You've a duty to protect this child, Frances. Julian would agree. And your mother would've insisted.'

'I'll be back for regular check-ups, Father. I may decide to have the baby in Cape Town.'

'Excellent. That would be for the best. Julian knows?'

'I wrote to him.' I glanced out along the railway tracks. 'I haven't heard back yet.'

'A baby.' Father's voice softened. 'I'm so proud of you, with this fire, the war—'

'Thank you for sending the paints,' I said gently, into the pause. 'I'd love more watercolour paper, too.'

'It'll be here when you return. Now, when can I drive up and fetch you?'

'I'll drive myself, Father, when the time comes.'

'Don't be stubborn, my dear. I insist.'

'Father—'

'No, Frances, I mean it. This is no time for heroics or distraction.'

'You'll have to trust me. I want this baby as much as you do. I love you, Father, I'll see you soon.'

'Be careful, Fran. Definitely no more expeditions, please. No climbing for aloes.'

I went into the veld today. Not up the Peak in defiance of Father but to my usual spot at the end of Marico Road. It's hard not to be drawn to my boarded-up house but I only stop to check the postbox every day for a letter from Julian. There's been no reply, but the mail is constantly disrupted by sinkings that I read about in my weekly *Argus* long after they've happened. In wartime, news – and death – comes in arrears.

It's the first time I've been sketching since the fire and I find my eyes blinking at the transition from soot to colour. A second wave of plants is in flower. They didn't erupt immediately after the drought broke, but took their time so they'll need to race to set seed and thrive before the next dry spell. There's a pale iris-like plant; a dark geranium; some jewel-toned *vygies* that Truda recalled seeing as a child but never since.

I unfolded my stool and sat down.

These sketches won't be perfect – my fingers are stiff, I don't have pristine paper, most of it is grey – but perhaps I can make a virtue out of that. These could be my fire drawings: a series created in the aftermath, drawn on damaged paper. I like the contrast of burgeoning growth on singed paper. I feel a movement and clutch my stomach. The baby is moving inside me in agreement. I laugh out loud, the first laugh in weeks.

I pick up the pencils I've rescued and begin.

Delicate lines for the geranium flower, serrated for the leaf margins, narrow on the stem . . .

Tomorrow, I'm taking the train to Cape Town for my next visit to Dr Reed.

I plan to remain for a week and then come back. Father will no doubt try to persuade me to stay for good, as will Daph, who sent me a frantic card to say how horrified she was to hear about the fire and that I must come back especially – oh, Fran, such excitement! – with a baby coming.

Am I being stubborn for no purpose?

No one is talking to me.

Why don't I say good riddance, wipe the dust of Aloe Glen from my velskoens and leave for good?

But if I leave, isn't that running away? Being cowardly?

I could make it safer – and more tolerant – for the next newcomer if I stay.

I stopped for a moment in mid pencil stroke and stared down at the scrub.

Surely it can't be . . . I bent closer . . . A colony of tiny stone plants, Director Compton's longed-for *Lithops*, crouched in the soil just beyond my feet. Almost invisible, their miniature bulbous leaves split down the centre to reveal the start of a thin stalk that would become a flower if I waited and checked every day. The leaf colour would need a blend of cream, umber, sepia . . .

'Mrs McDonald!' The dominee hurried across the station platform the following day. 'One moment, ma'am. You're not leaving, are you?' He glanced at my suitcase.

'No,' I said cautiously. 'I'm going back to see my father for a few days.'

He'd prefer it if I went; no more wrestling with the possibility that one of his flock might have set my house ablaze.

'I've found you accommodation,' he announced. 'Above the petrol station. There's a small flat with a bathroom and a second bedroom. It would be available for a modest rent.'

The train drew into the station on squealing brakes. Smoke swirled along the platform. I closed my eyes for a moment against the chance of cinders.

'Why, Dominee? Why do you want me to stay?'

'I spoke to the sergeant.' The words came out of him reluctantly. 'He says the fire was probably arson.'

I stared along the railway line towards the tunnels where Wynand Louw was supposed to have gone on the day my house burnt.

'Do you have any idea who did it, Dominee?'

'No.' His face was tight. 'But I regret it's happened in our town.'

The conductor came down the platform and blew his whistle. 'You getting on board, ma'am?'

'Yes.' I bent to pick up my suitcase. 'Thank you, sir. I'm grateful. I'll take the flat.'

A place where I could be on my own, where I could grow my baby quietly. I love Truda but there'll be no space for me when Deon comes home for the school holidays. She says he can sleep on the sinking couch, but that's not fair.

The dominee nodded, took the case from my hand, opened the carriage door for me and handed it up.

'You've been badly treated, Mrs McDonald. There will be justice for the culprit. A reckoning.'

'When, sir?'

'If not in this world, then the next. The Lord sees all.'

'That may be too late for me, sir.'

'Ah, Mrs McDonald. Welcome back!' Director Compton, greyer than when we first met, came out of his office at Kirstenbosch and shook my hand. 'You have some new paintings for me?'

'Not quite yet. I'm busy with a fresh series, sir.'

He has no idea of the fire, he has no idea how many paintings I've lost, how bereft I am.

He ushered me to a seat across from a desk piled on one side with papers and on the other with botanical specimens. A dried sprig of Erica, a silver tree cone.

'I came to tell you, Director, that I've found some *Lithops*. I'll be making several sketches of them.'

'Ah, stone plants. Excellent!'

I glanced over his shoulder. There it was: a framed *Pink, Armoured Aloe*, the same one as Mark's.

He followed my gaze and nodded to me. 'The most extraordinary plant, rendered with immense skill. You've made further studies of it?'

Should I tell him? If I let it be known, that might help my cause.

It will also enrage my neighbours if they come to hear of my plan. Art as revenge . . .

The deadline is tight. I must paint and grow my child simultaneously.

And force my community to look me – and themselves – in the eye.

Chapter Forty-Six

Fran, my darling Fran, there are no words to describe how I feel!

To think that we will be having a baby, a child of our own, is the greatest gift I can imagine.

I sit here at my desk, looking out over the great river, and long to be back with you.

Please go home to your father and allow him to take care of you as I would if I were there.

I know you don't particularly believe, but perhaps the Lord did indeed decide to bless us.

Take a rest from your painting, my dear, and enjoy waiting for the little one.

This child is the certain fruit of our love for each other.

Ever yours
Julian

I pray to Julian's Lord that He won't punish me for deceiving my husband, that He will keep my secret.

I'm in the flat above the petrol station. Tifo, the petrol attendant, is my closest neighbour, apart from the men who hang about in front of the cafe and pretend not to notice me. It's livelier here than Marico Road. Cars whizz by heading north, lorries pull in to fill up with a crunch of tyres, the whistle of the trains is a blast that I fancy rattles my windows. I've lost my views, but there's an oblique slice of Aloe Peak visible from the tiny bathroom. I never imagined being reduced to this – Father would be horrified, I've exaggerated the flat's dimensions for him – and yet I feel strangely liberated. I've arranged my own insurance, paltry though it is.

I only go back to Marico Road to clear the postbox and tend my vegetable patch.

I like the contradiction of green growth against a blackened, empty house.

It's a further rebuke to my neighbours.

As an arrival gift, Mr Fourie gave me a bag of oranges that I shared with Sipata and Lena, and Mrs van Deventer sent Frans along with a meat pie. The dominee offered extra chairs but the simple furniture and bed will serve me well until Julian returns and we move somewhere bigger. My cutlery and pots have been scrubbed and are usable. My bush clothes are stained but clean. While I was in Cape Town, Violet's sister sewed three maternity dresses for me, one for the current winter, and two for the heat that will follow, along with instructions to eat pickles when the time came.

'Are you sure, Frances?' Truda hovered in the doorway once I was unpacked.

'Yes!' I embraced her. 'And you can come here, too, whenever you wish.'

She needs to know she has sanctuary with me if she needs it. I will shelter her, like she sheltered me.

'Wynand says it's not over,' she whispered. 'He says in his letter that many more like him are still free.'

'They won't hurt you, Truda. Their quarrel is with the government, not with you.'

'What does Julian say,' her faced softened, 'about the baby?'

'I think he cried. He can't wait to come home.'

She nodded and touched my hand.

Julian wrote nothing about the latest blows against Allied forces.

'Egypt and Suez are the prize,' said Father tersely over the phone. 'They can't be allowed to fall.'

Julian had also written to Father, telling him to insist I return to Cape Town.

'In time, Father. Don't worry.'

'But I do, Fran,' he said crisply. 'I've always supported you but you're being mulish.'

'I have to stay. I must prepare for the exhibition.'

And nature, it turns out, is conspiring with me. The *Brunsvigia* lilies are flowering in an abundance I've never captured before. Multiple pink trumpets radiate from a central stalk to resemble fragile globes held aloft. Once the petals fade, the entire head breaks off and rolls away like tumbleweed, scattering seed in a final, dramatic flourish. I sit on my stool at the base of Aloe Peak every day and sketch them on the new paper Father bought for me. Sipata and her neighbour, Lena, come to watch. A few days later, some of the poor men who fought my fire appear. Perhaps they came out of curiosity: the sight of a lone woman, making pictures in the midst of the veld, or perhaps they want to protect me, although I don't know why when Wynand Louw is detained.

Sometimes the men tell me how beautiful my sketches are. But not always.

'Paint a picture of your house, ma'am,' one man said quietly. 'Show it like it is.'

In their own quiet way, they are urging me to reveal what no one wants to acknowledge. And I suspect they know who did it.

Afterwards, I go back to the flat and mix colours and build up the full effect of the lilies. I decide on well-diluted pyrrole red for the petals, ochre for the skeletal remains.

I work long into the night.

'Ma'am must eat,' Sipata says.

She still comes to help even though I can't pay her as much as before. She makes soup and we share it together. Sipata and I are now friends. The fire has brought us together, as it has forced others away. If I happen to see Cora or Sannie at the store, they smile and compliment me on my pregnancy and then they leave before we can have any kind of conversation.

There are many plants, of course, that aren't in flower at the moment. I have sketches of them, damaged in the fire, that I plan to copy in the evenings. But I find that it helps to be outside for the light and the sense of movement in the veld. So I attach a damaged sketch to my new easel – sent by Father – and clip a fresh sheet on top and set off.

'Ma'am?' Tifo came over to me one day as I headed out. 'There's a place you can sit.'

He led me round the side of the petrol station to a patch of grass. Aloe Peak reared in perfect symmetry against the sky, its slopes clothed in familiar scrub. If I sat with my back to the building, I could catch the light and the movement without having to walk so far.

'Thank you, Tifo. What a good idea.'

I might even see springbok in the distance. Agile, fleeting beauty.

'My,' a voice intruded over my shoulder a month later, 'what a beautiful picture. Do you sell any?'

She was wearing exotic wide-legged trousers and a broad-brimmed hat with a velvet ribbon.

'Yes, in Cape Town. I'm preparing for an exhibition at the moment.'

'Phillip?' the lady called over her shoulder. 'Come and look!'

It's Tifo, I realise. He sent them from the forecourt.

A man in military uniform came around the side of the building, jangling his car keys in his hand.

'We can't stop now.' He gave my picture a cursory glance. 'We're late as it is.'

'I take commissions,' I said. 'My name is Frances McDonald. If you give me your details, I could paint whatever you wish. Or you can see my work at Kirstenbosch in the new year.'

'I'll be gone by then.' The man gave a brief, wry smile. 'But my wife holds the purse strings.'

'Just as well,' the lady teased. 'My taste is far better than yours!' She twiddled her fingers at me and they turned away.

I heard the sound of their motor car pulling out of the station. Once upon a time I could have been that woman: well-dressed, handsomely married . . .

But she – and Tifo – have given me an idea.

I begin to dash off a few smaller drawings, first impressions like Mr Cadwaller once urged. Reflect what the eye sees!

A wagtail scratching at the base of the building. A bird of prey silhouetted on a telephone line.

A few lines, quickly rendered. A moment captured, just so.

Chapter Forty-Seven

My hands are shaking as I write this.

I went back to Marico Road today with a torch, and stood in my ruined studio.

Sipata and I hadn't moved the cupboard because it stood flush against the wall and anything on top of it would have fallen to the floor and been found.

I crouched down and played the beam of my torch between the wood and the wall.

There were a few sheets of paper lodged in the tiny gap.

I stood up and began to pull on one side of the cupboard.

Why did I do it? What if it had fallen on me?

But then it gave slightly, sufficiently, to allow the papers to escape.

Two preliminary sketches of my aloes. One of the bird with the orange throat.

And, between them – I sat down and wept – the precious image of Gideon, the one I showed to Director Compton. It is remarkably undamaged.

Since the fire, my brother had disappeared from my dreams.

Perhaps now, he will return.

Three months, ten watercolour paintings, ten pencil drawings. A sheaf of damaged work. A slim portfolio of what I call my 'Cadwaller Sketches'. The picture of my brother. My diary. The charcoal portrait. My easel, my paints and pencils. My brushes. A set of Cape Town outfits.

And a decision to leave Aloe Glen and have my baby in the city.

Why, after I vowed to stay?

Because there will be no second chance if I happen to stumble in the veld or pull a cupboard onto me in my haste, for I know, as surely as I know the identity of the father, that this will be my only child.

I need to be in a safer place.

Once the decision was made, Father refused to allow me to undertake the journey alone. 'Bain's Kloof ought not to be negotiated in the final stage of pregnancy. I will come up by train and we'll drive back together. No arguments, Frances.'

The dominee stopped by last evening to wish me well.

'We shall pray for you, Mrs McDonald.'

It is kind of him to make the offer. I notice of late, when I attend church, that he's careful to pray for all victims of the war. I feel the glances of my fellow congregants on the back of my neck as he speaks.

The early train drew in beneath a cloud of smoke.

'Fran!' Father bustled out of his compartment, tie flying about his face. 'How well you look! And the countryside,' he threw his arms wide, 'so lush, my dear. Extraordinary!'

'The car's packed, Father. We can go straight away.'

The word has got around that I'm leaving. My informal protectors have been quietly tipping their caps at me and shaking my hand whenever I encounter them around town. Mr

Fourie has wished me well and cancelled my weekly newspaper. The art class has been suspended. Laetitia embraced me and told me not to stay away for too long.

'Good luck, ma'am, good day, sir!' shouted Tifo, as he attended to his petrol pump. I'd asked him to carry my suitcases and easel downstairs so that Father would not need to see my tiny flat.

'Good day!' Father lifted his hat. 'Friendly fellow! Ah, Mrs Louw, how nice to see you again.'

'And you remember Sipata, Father? And may I introduce Lena Fuller?'

'Indeed I do. How do you do, Mrs Fuller. I know you've all been very kind to Frances.'

'We brought tea.' Truda handed me a basket with a flask. 'And Lena made sandwiches.'

I embraced them both and felt Truda shiver slightly. 'Maybe you won't come back,' she murmured.

'Ma'am will be back,' said Sipata quietly. 'The veld will bring her back.'

'Goodbye, ma'am,' came a voice from behind. It was Toby Engelbrecht, a teenager now.

'Shouldn't you be in school?'

'It's breaktime, ma'am.'

I put a hand on his shoulder. 'I'll be back in a few months, then we'll do some more drawing.'

The youngster nodded, blushed, and ran off, nearly tripping over his feet.

Father held open the passenger door. I took a last glance up the road that led north between the slabbed mountains towards the flat plains of the Karoo. I want to introduce my child to that infinite horizon. I climbed into the car and Father closed the door and raised his hat to the three women. We nosed out onto the road and I waved.

'I'd like to see your house,' Father said, turning down Marico Road. 'Do you mind, my dear?'

From a distance the place looked blind, like the houses I'd seen when I first arrived in Aloe Glen, their curtains tightly drawn against the heat. But my house was blind because its windows were boarded up.

'Oh, Fran.' Father put a hand on my arm. 'A tragedy—'

'Can we go, Father?'

He turned the car around and we drove past the van Deventer place where Mrs van Deventer was surely watching. She'd given me a pair of knitted bootees when she last saw me.

'I made a mistake about you, Frances McDonald.' She sniffed. 'I didn't think you'd last this long.'

'Thank you, Mrs van Deventer. For the bootees as well.'

She gave a grudging nod. 'I will see no one interferes with your house.'

'That is kind, but Sipata promised to do that for me. And the men who helped fight the fire.'

She looked at me, affronted, but I'm not ready to give her any reprieve.

Not yet.

Not after what I now know.

Last week I attended the church ladies' morning for the first time since the fire.

Cora, Sannie, Aletta and Anna were there, the tea party ladies who laughed at my painted furniture and kissed me on the cheek when they left my home. I sat at the back of the hall so they didn't notice me.

An expert cook demonstrated how to carve tomatoes to look like roses.

An up-and-coming soprano sang folk songs.

We ended with a reading from the Bible that was, I think, about faith, hope and charity.

'I'm leaving to have my baby in Cape Town,' I said when I found them together at the end. 'Before I go, I wanted to ask what I'd done to make you avoid me since the fire.'

Cora gulped and rearranged a chair. Sannie blushed. Aletta looked at her feet. Anna stared at me.

'I'm not leaving until you tell me. Or maybe the dominee knows?' I pretended to look about for him.

It was Anna who was the bravest.

'It's not you, Frances. It's just—' She glanced desperately at the other three and then back at me. 'We didn't know what to say.'

'Why? You could at least have shown more sympathy, Anna.'

I sensed their shame – but for what, exactly?

'We know who did it,' blurted Sannie.

My head pounded and I saw again the orange flames, the cracked mirror, my ruined pictures.

'Why didn't you tell the police?' I shouted.

They looked at one another, and then around the hall but it was, by now, empty.

'Because,' Cora put a hand gently on my arm; I've missed Cora's softness, 'most of the men – our husbands – belong to the same organisation as Wynand Louw. It favours Germany. It's responsible for the sabotage. If we tell the police about Wynand, they'll want to know how we found out, and they'll detain our husbands, too.'

'So we kept quiet,' said Anna. 'We stayed away from you to save our men.'

'And what if I now go and tell the police?'

'They won't believe you,' asserted Aletta, speaking for the first time. 'They won't believe the whole town knew and did nothing to stop it. It would be your voice against the rest.'

The whole town knew and did nothing to stop it.

I felt behind me and sat down on a chair. 'But your husband helped me, Sannie! He called the engineer, he recommended a builder!'

She knelt at my side. Tears slid down her cheeks.

'He was ashamed. He thought it was wild talk. He never expected Wynand to go through with it.'

'Did you know,' I stared at each one in turn, 'what was planned for my house?'

'No!' they exclaimed.

'Abel told me afterwards.' Sannie wiped her tear-stained face. 'I told the others, but not Truda. We swore to keep the secret. We thought if we left you alone, you'd leave. It would be safer for us if you left.'

'But I didn't.'

I felt the baby heave beneath my flowing dress. My head was aching.

Cora ran to the kitchen and poured me a glass of water. 'Here, drink slowly.'

I held the glass against my cheeks for a moment and then drank.

Their English is much better these days. Both in vocabulary and grammar. I have, at least, achieved that.

'We were caught, Frances,' Anna said quietly. 'Caught between keeping our men out of jail and being friends with you.'

I couldn't really blame them.

I stared around at the church hall, at the framed photographs of past lady members smiling on the walls.

If it had been me, would I have endangered my family's unity by being honest?

Pulled my own house down for the sake of an outsider?

Chapter Forty-Eight

'Mrs McDonald! Look this way, please!'

Flashbulbs exploded.

Father took my arm protectively and beamed his old, expansive smile. A young *Argus* reporter elbowed his way over.

'What is the background to the so-called Fire series?' His pencil hovered above his notebook.

I glanced inside to where my paintings hung.

A Pink, Armoured Aloe. The same one Mark bought, its tentacled leaves clasped about its heart.

Fernwood Buttress from Protea Rise, repainted from memory.

Aloe Peak at Sunset, based on the first sketch I made in my new home.

The *Lithops* drawings, some on tinged paper, some on fresh.

'Mrs McDonald?'

'There was a fire,' I replied. 'A number of my pictures were burnt. Some were saved.'

'Fran!' Daphne waved at me frantically over the heads of the crowd.

'But why, ma'am, would you choose to exhibit ruined work alongside pristine?'

I know how I'd like to answer his question, but I also know my reply is not for sharing. The whole town knew and did nothing to stop it.

Better to stress the artistic contrast and leave it at that: new paintings, elegantly framed alongside grey, creased versions, un-glassed and pegged beneath simple metal hangers. Father, after initial qualms, said that there was no such thing as bad publicity and I should stand firm.

So did Mr Cadwaller, to whom I'd written for advice.

Ignore the naysayers, he wrote back, *art is all about risk. Hold your ground, Frances!*

But the director and his committee had been nervous.

'I don't wish to discard the damaged paintings, gentlemen,' I persisted. 'They highlight a fresh approach in the later interpretations.' After lengthy deliberation, they finally gave cautious approval – even to the text for the catalogue: a unique opportunity to showcase an artist's response to tragedy – after which there'd been a tricky discussion about pricing. Director Compton suggested the price for each new painting should include its damaged equivalent if I insisted on showing it alongside.

'But they took the same amount of work, sirs,' I said. 'And they tell a story which has a value, too. May I suggest the same price for each?' There was an intake of breath. The committee members are botanical experts, not necessarily art lovers or businessmen. And I'm discovering a commercial bent. 'If,' I added with a smile, 'a buyer wishes to purchase both versions, then the damaged painting will be reduced by half.'

'Very well,' said Director Compton, hastily. 'I think we

can agree to that.'

But they wonder at the wisdom of making a political statement at an exhibition, although arson is never mentioned, and they doubt anyone will buy damaged goods. Maybe they're right? Yet the newspapers describe ongoing sabotage around the country. Pylons brought down, trains disrupted. For those who suspect the fire may have been deliberate, my warped pictures show the price of disunity.

'Come,' said Director Compton, fending off the reporter and ushering Father and me through the door.

Another flashbulb exploded.

The crowd parted.

I see some familiar faces – the Chisholms, the Pringles, Thelma Radisson in a vast hat, but mostly it's a gathering of well-dressed and hopefully wealthy strangers with a sprinkling of military uniforms. And it's an approving crowd. I've become so used to being the interloper, the outsider, that I don't expect to be welcomed.

'Here you are!' Daph wormed her way through the crush. 'Hello, Mr Whittington. Aren't you proud?'

'Ladies and gentlemen.' Director Compton ascended a small dais and clapped his hands. 'Good evening and welcome to our latest exhibition. It is most gratifying to see such an enthusiastic audience, despite the constraints of wartime. Tonight marks the opening of our dedicated space devoted to the work of the artist Frances McDonald who, I'm delighted to say, is with us this evening.'

Daph squeezed my arm. Mary Clough gave me a tiny wave.

'Go,' whispered Father, resplendent in hired black tie. 'Take care up the steps.'

I'm wearing a new dress Violet's sister made for me at the

last moment. It is ink blue, the colour of the upcountry sky before darkness, with a crocheted, white collar. My hair is pulled back with a set of velvet-covered slides Violet found when sorting through Mother's drawers, perhaps being kept as a gift for me. Director Compton led the applause as I walked forward. The clapping fragmented in my ears, lifting me back to the English oak and the sound of breaking lens glass and a sharpened view of the world. But there was no need for tremor. The faces looking up at me were smiling and nodding.

Where had they come from? I've only ever sold perhaps a dozen paintings. Should I bow—

Director Compton held up his hands. The room quietened.

'I first saw the work of Frances Whittington, as she was then, when she was twenty years old, on board the *Edinburgh Castle*. She later submitted a sketch of Erica multumbellifera, from specimens here at Kirstenbosch. The detail was astounding. From such beginnings,' he flourished a hand around the room, 'Frances has gone on to become a superb botanical illustrator and a watercolour artist of rare quality. I hope you enjoy viewing her work and hopefully acquire a painting to cherish.'

More applause.

It was a long way from a folding stool in the veld.

I waited for a moment.

'Thank you, Director Compton, ladies and gentlemen, I'm honoured to be here. Many of the works you see showcase the plants growing around Aloe Glen, a small rural community on the edge of the Karoo.'

I paused. 'When I first moved there, over ten years ago, I struggled to see anything worth painting. But then I began to look more closely and found aloes, stone plants, and rare bulbs. It made me realise that there is beauty in the most remote place, if we're prepared to look hard enough.'

The audience were nodding.

I remember the moment when I asked Mr Cadwaller if I could be an artist.

I plunged, again.

'But for me, these paintings reflect more than their subjects. They show the passage of drought, fire, flood and war. And the journey I've been privileged – and challenged – to take.'

The thunder of applause took my breath away.

'Bravo!' someone called.

Director Compton took my hand and led me off the dais.

'Frances!' A greying Mrs Phillips caught my arm and embraced me carefully around the baby. 'Your mother would've been so thrilled. Many congratulations, my dear! I want one of the *Brunsvigias*.'

I glanced at the three paintings, one in close-up, one showing pink globes strewn across the veld and the final one of the tumbleweed stage.

'Such brushwork,' a woman in a turban said. 'Exceptional, Mrs McDonald!'

'Will you excuse us, madam?' Director Compton steered me away. 'Well spoken, my dear.'

Father followed, discreetly. He's ready to rescue me in case I get overwhelmed.

'May I introduce Major Owen Jefferson?'

'How do you do,' said a tall man in a bemedalled uniform. 'I'm intrigued by this aloe—'

'Why, Frances.' Daphne's father barrelled up. 'You said you wanted to be an artist and here you are!'

'Thank you, Mr Phillips.' I extricated myself. 'May I

introduce the director and Major Jefferson?'

'Pleasure,' said Mr Phillips and planted a kiss on my cheek before heading across to the wine table.

'This aloe,' Jefferson repeated, examining it in close-up, 'you observed it in the wild or in a collection?'

'In the wild, sir. I only paint from wild specimens.'

The director slipped away. Perhaps his role tonight was to introduce me to potential buyers. The heat in the room was increasing. I felt the baby move. I'd need to sit down soon.

'I plan to buy this one,' he gestured towards the aloe in flower, 'and the fire-damaged one.'

'Thank you.' I paused. 'Why do you want them both, sir, if you don't mind my asking?'

'Placed side by side, Mrs McDonald, they're a powerful statement. They tell us to be vigilant.'

An omen. A warning. I glanced at Father. He nodded.

'Ma'am.' The reporter, again. '*Studio with Glass Shards*? What message are you conveying?'

For a moment I was back in my burnt house, touching the floorboards streaked with melted paint, discovering the glass piled in the centre. If you didn't know, the scene might have been staged as an example – a foretaste – of modern art. Or a novel reflection on war: chaos rendered in primary colours, within a frame of fashionably charred wood.

'I paint what I see, sir.'

Mark said my paintings showed where my heart lay.

But my heart is not whole, not concentrated in one place or with one person or on one subject.

It's divided. Protea Rise, Aloe Glen, Julian, Mark . . .

'Frances?' Director Compton reappeared. 'Will you excuse us, Major? And,' to the hovering reporter, 'Mrs McDonald has answered enough of your questions. Frances, a gentleman is interested in Fernwood Buttress from Protea Rise. He wants to know the date of the painting.'

I held out my hand to Major Jefferson who clasped it in both of his. 'Stay safe, madam.'

'Stunning detail,' I overheard as I followed Compton. 'Have you looked at the *Lithops*?'

'I want *Aloe Glen at Sunset*. The original and the smoked one.'

'Congratulations, Frances.' Preston Bell, Daph's father-in-law, intercepted me.

The director led me into a quiet corner where an old man sat in a wheelchair.

'My dear Mrs McDonald.' He peered up at me through filmy eyes. 'I have an interest in your two paintings of Protea Rise. Forgive me for not getting up. How do you know it?'

'I lived in Protea Rise for a year, sir, after I arrived from England.'

'When did you create this particular work?' His hands were trembling on the arms of his chair.

'Recently, but it reflects the house and garden from about a decade ago. You know the house, sir?'

'Indeed.' He tried to still his hands. 'I designed it, before the turn of the century. Part of the specification was to preserve the wild *fynbos*. The *proteas*.'

I felt my head begin to spin.

'Frances?' Father hurried to my side.

'Is there a chair nearby, Father? I'd like to sit down.'

He dragged one from the side and placed it next to the wheelchair. I sat down and breathed deeply.

'Father, this gentleman is the architect of Protea Rise.'

'Why, what a pleasure, sir!' Father leant down and shook his hand. 'You must be Maurice Benjamin. My late brother-in-law was the first owner, I believe.'

The old man nodded. 'He was. The latest owner has, disgracefully, built a wall around the property. I'm keen to acquire this painting so I can see elements of the garden which I remember with great fondness. It was laid out by a young, coloured man under my instruction.'

'Alfius,' I put in, smiling up at Father. 'He used to talk to the plants.'

But Father wasn't paying attention. He was staring across the room at one of the Fire series.

'I shall buy both of them, Mrs McDonald.'

Father hadn't seen any of the pictures before tonight.

He left my side and hurried towards it, pushing through the crowd, oblivious to outstretched hands or smiles of congratulation. That particular painting didn't have any spectators, probably because it was difficult to make out. No one knew who it was. I'd been unsure whether to include it, and stipulated that it wasn't for sale. But I wanted it to be seen.

'Frances – so sorry, Mr Benjamin – may I borrow you?' Director Compton again. 'We have a question about technique on the *Lithops*.'

I stood up from my stool. Father turned and looked back at me.

Even from a distance I could see the tears in his eyes.

Father had recognised Gideon.

Chapter Forty-Nine

I've taken risks in my life. Some have been physical ones like climbing trees and swimming past the breaker line. Others have been outwardly trivial, like wearing a flapper dress to the Kelvin Grove instead of a ball gown. But some have been bolder and required more of myself.

Like standing up in a combative meeting and daring my husband to take charge.

Or giving myself to a man to whom I am not married.

The greatest professional risk I have taken was to hang ruined paintings in an exhibition and ask people to understand why . . .

Do I regret what I've done?

Not so far.

But is there a cost? A cost to whatever – or whoever – will follow?

Violet's sister told me to eat pickles when the time of my confinement was near, but it wasn't necessary. Outside events accelerated the process. Firstly, every painting and sketch in my exhibition, both pristine and singed, sold. There was no adverse publicity. Major Jefferson sent a note of appreciation.

Maurice Benjamin sent flowers. I received several letters from visitors who wrote that the singed work was not just a reproach or a 'beautiful revenge', as one writer put it, but a cry for justice that hadn't be served.

I opened a new, private bank account to take the proceeds as I waited for the baby. I am saving, but I will not say for what.

And then . . .

'Fran,' Father rushed into the lounge and twiddled the knobs on the radio, 'listen!'

Crackling filled the air, followed by an American voice.

'A date which will live in infamy,' President Roosevelt announced. There had been an attack on a place in the Pacific called Pearl Harbor. America was declaring war, the same America that had caused the Crash but would now, hopefully, rise up and save the world a decade later. If he was not already in the forces, Mark would be called up. Both fathers of my child would be in danger. My own father was exultant: as far as he was concerned, the war was all but won. And then the troublesome pro-Germans in South Africa would be forced to slink home and bury their guns and their inflammatory rhetoric for good. The fighting men would return from abroad to rebuild the peace.

Hamish Gideon McDonald was born in late January 1942.

I named him after Julian's grandfather, who heroically taught Latin in Aloe Glen in the 1800s – the first radical in the clan; and for my brother Gideon, whose portrait now hangs in Father's bedroom.

'How do you know what he looked like?' Father had choked to me amid the buzz of the exhibition.

'He's been in my dreams, Father,' I leant against him. 'Ever since I fell out of the oak.'

'Dear Fran.' He wiped his eyes. 'You've given him back to me.'

And to me, too, Father.

Gideon's nephew arrived on a sunny morning with a southeaster screaming over the Cape Flats and a pile of cloud heaped above Fernwood Buttress. I've seen eggs crack and baby birds appear, tiny beaks yearning for their mothers. I have seen newborn antelope stagger to their feet and run on green legs almost immediately. The birth of my son took longer than that, and there were times when I wondered if it would ever end and whether the baby I'd got so joyously had no desire to face the world.

Violet was with me. She wiped the sweat from my face and gave me ice to suck as the hours went by.

'Breathe, Miss Fran. Long and slow. Think of Master Julian.'

But I don't want to think of Julian. I want to think of Mark, who is my forever love.

'I love him,' I moaned. 'Forever.'

'Yes, you do,' murmured Violet, unknowingly. 'And soon there will come his baby.'

The wind rattled the windows, like it rattled the windows at the Kelvin Grove when I wore sea-green chiffon and hoped for a proposal. But I will have a part of Mark from now on, a part that will never leave. Dr Reed told me to bear down and I felt my body gathering itself for a final surge and I cried out, and then another cry came, a baby's cry. I was shaking from the force of it and the nurse was handling a little wriggling body and placing it in my arms and I saw it was a boy.

A laughing child, a different one, running ahead of me at Protea Rise . . .

Violet was crying. The nurse took my baby and weighed him and then wrapped him in a blanket and gave him back to me. I can see morning sun through the window, striking the mountains yellow when the cloud shifts. It's shining for me and for this little one.

'A healthy boy, Frances!' Dr Reed leant over and pressed my hand. 'Rest now. You've done well.'

I stared down at the baby and felt a wondrous recognition.

He opened milky eyes and looked at me.

He is, without doubt, Mark's child.

'Such hair!' gasped Daphne, arriving at the hospital the next day with a vast bouquet. 'So black!'

'I know,' I smiled, holding the tiny bundle close. 'Perhaps Julian was dark-haired as a child.'

Coal-black hair, dark eyes, and the making of fine-boned hands. I felt no qualms whatsoever. After all, who but me knows?

'Clever Miss Fran!' Violet hugged me and tickled the baby's cheek. He yelled lustily.

'Great lungs!' exclaimed Father, peering at his grandson's open mouth. 'Perhaps he'll be a tenor?'

'Stay,' whispered Daph, 'your father needs you, Fran. You can paint all you like, Violet will help.'

I know she will. It will be the easier path.

In the week before Hamish was born, I received several letters from Aloe Glen.

The police wrote to say that no further progress had been made in the matter of my house fire. Most residents of

Aloe Glen and surroundings, Sergeant Roland explained, are convinced Mrs McDonald was the victim of a tragic accident, and wish to convey their sympathy.

The town's pact of silence had held.

Lena Fuller wrote a surprisingly eloquent page to send Sipata's best wishes because Sipata was unable to write, and also to say that she was visiting Mrs Louw from time to time because Mrs Louw was alone. My friends are caring for each other.

Cora Engelbrecht sent a card saying that the veld was still soft and she'd taken an English book out of the travelling library for the first time and read it cover to cover. She ended with the hope that I and my child would be happy in Cape Town.

My top-floor hospital window looked north, towards Bain's Kloof Pass and the road to Aloe Glen.

'Here's a hungry boy, Mrs McDonald!' Nurse Metcalf bustled in holding a crying Hamish.

I lifted him to my breast and felt the sharp tug of his mouth and the answering response of my body.

'Shall I teach you, little one?' I whispered. 'Teach you both worlds?'

I thought of Aunt Mary and her question soon after I arrived. *What are your intentions here?*

'Well done.' Nurse cast a brisk eye over my technique. 'I'll be back in half an hour. Oh, forgive me,' she pulled a telegram out of her pocket, 'this came for you. Shall I open it?'

'Yes, please.' I glanced down at Hamish. His black eyes were fixed on me, his mouth working. Dr Reed says there's no reason I shouldn't have another baby when my husband returns. The body, he believes, becomes accustomed. Seasoned.

'It's easier the second time round, Frances.'

The nurse ripped open the envelope and held it in front of me.

WONDERFUL NEWS SO PROUD LOVE YOU ALWAYS JULIAN

'You'll stay, of course,' said Father when I brought Hamish home a week later to the nursery he and Violet had prepared in the spare bedroom. A wicker crib; a changing table and easy chair; bright, butterfly-printed curtains sewed by Violet's sister; a teddy bear that once belonged to me and had been kept by Mother; everything we might need if I stayed for good. And, between Father's work and my art, probably enough money to get by.

'Aloe Glen is my home, too, Father.'

'You belong here, Fran. And, professionally, this is where your market lies. You do realise that?'

I do.

But, equally, Father should realise that the inspiration for my most profitable work no longer lies on the peninsula. Collectors have an appetite for what they can't see around them every day: unusual aloes, cryptic *Lithops*, veld lilies. They lie beyond the mountains, where the desert encroaches. A card from Truda arrived in the post with a pressed geranium bloom and a scrawled signature. Laetitia sent a package containing a knitted matinee jacket and the news that the aloes were in flower. The dominee wrote a note rejoicing in the Lord's generosity in granting me a child and Deon Louw sent a formal letter with a question: how should he respond to his school friends who think his father is a hero for sabotaging the railway line?

Please, ma'am, write back. I can't ask Ma about this.

While I pondered my answer, Director Compton phoned to congratulate me on the birth of my son and said he'd had a request from the Royal Botanic Gardens at Kew, in London, via a Mr Raymond Cadwaller, for a set of paintings of an aloe known as a quiver tree, an odd plant whose tentacled leaves erupt from the apex of a pale, ridged trunk.

'I believe they are endemic further north, Frances, but perhaps you may find some.'

Today I took out the charcoal portrait and compared it with myself in the mirror.

Pregnancy and new motherhood has softened my face. But there's a restlessness, too.

Long ago, when I was a child, Father didn't understand that my attachment to our English home would always be about more than its value as an asset. So he fails to realise that my allegiance to Aloe Glen is about more than it being a source of inspiration and, thereby, income. Aloe Glen isn't beautiful – unless you have patience – but it's where I shed my entitled youth and grew up. It's where Julian most needs me. It draws me back. And I have unfinished business there.

Chapter Fifty

I'm watching my beloved Cape through a child's eyes.

Hamish follows the flight of a fiscal as it dives to the ground, picks up a worm and flies back to its perch. Is there a whisper of me in his interest? Does he want to know how feathers layer along a wing or how stripes on a flower petal lead to the nectar at its heart?

'Look,' I say, as I lift him out of his pram at Kirstenbosch, 'these stiff flowers are called proteas. If we wait a while, we'll see sugarbirds with long tails jump onto them.'

Hamish blinks his dark eyes and looks up at me and smiles gummily.

Or maybe he won't care for nature at all and prefer languages, like his acquired father.

He's six months old and I'm still in Cape Town.

I've learnt how vulnerable a young child can be. Hamish became ill one night and I rushed him to Dr Reed who diagnosed croup and advised that it would need watching but wasn't life-threatening. As I drove home, close to tears of relief, with Violet holding a coughing Hamish upright as the doctor suggested, I imagined a journey of twenty miles or more on largely empty roads through bare countryside to the nearest medical help. So I'll stay until Hamish is robust enough – and I'm confident enough – to manage both of us in a place that would prefer me not to return. Truda says the tea party ladies keep assuring each other that Cape Town suits me better.

I now paint Aloe Glen from memory, like I once painted Cape Town.

Pink-green aloes, miniature stone plants, a nondescript brown bird with a blazing red throat.

'Excellent,' said Major Jefferson, who wishes to collect more of my work. 'Could you do *Aloe ferox*?'

Layered cloud was piled atop Table Mountain as I drove into town.

'Good morning, Mrs McDonald.' Alan Field came around his desk to shake my hand. 'Many congratulations on the birth of your son. Please, do sit down. How may I help?'

'I need to make a sworn statement,' I said.

'In connection to what?' He pulled a legal pad towards him.

'It will name people who are implicated in, and responsible for, a fire that destroyed my home.'

I could tell he was taken aback. The publicity around my exhibition was considerable but it was not common knowledge that the fire mentioned in the catalogue was arson.

'Shouldn't this information be disclosed to the authorities?'

I noticed he'd written nothing down.

'Sir, there's no evidence placing the suspect at the scene. And he's currently being detained anyway.'

'For another crime?'

'For anti-government activity. For sabotage.'

'Ah.' The lawyer grimaced. 'Then what is the intent, Mrs

McDonald, of this statement?'

'It's insurance, sir.' I thought back to the bank manager who'd lamented the lack of cover on our house. But this was different. This insurance would be a challenge to those who believed I'd never dare speak out. 'I may need to reveal its contents at some stage.'

'To pursue a court case? For compensation?'

'Maybe,' I paused, 'only for persuasion.'

The cloud layer began to dissolve, tumbling over the precipice into warmer air.

'As your lawyer, I must advise caution. You should speak to me in advance of any accusation.'

'I'd prefer not to use this information at all, Mr Field. But I'd like to place it on the record.'

I suppose most men see me as a small, slender woman distracted by my art. They assume I'm fragile. They do not see the steel.

'Very well. I assume you've written down what you'd like included?' His eyes flashed amused respect.

I smiled and drew a handwritten page out of my handbag. He read it, made a few notes in the margin. Then read it again.

'Is it your intention to return to Aloe Glen, Mrs McDonald?'

'In due course.'

'Leave this with me. I'll rephrase one or two sentences for clarity.' He flipped open a diary. 'Can you see me next Wednesday morning at 10 a.m.? We can sign and witness the document.'

He stood up and came around the desk and shook my hand.

'I've seen your work, Mrs McDonald. You have a rare gift. There are other communities where you could exercise it and be more warmly received. Sometimes it's best to move on.'

'One more thing,' I said on an impulse. 'Do you still have connections with the property market?'

'We do.'

'I want to buy a house, sir. I don't have the funds yet so it will have to be a future purchase.'

'You're very wise to plan, Mrs McDonald. We can assist you as we did over your late aunt's property. Let me know when you're in a position to go forward.'

Chapter Fifty-One

I have a sense that there is a further war in the offing, I wrote in my diary.

> *Father does not see it yet.*
>
> *It will emerge after this war is over. It will be a local war, and not overtly about gold and diamonds.*
>
> *I saw it in my face after the fire, and in the charcoal self-portrait.*
>
> *I heard it in the words of the women who confessed that their men knew about the potential petrol-bombing of my home and did nothing to stop it.*
>
> *I saw it in the discontent of the poor folk on the edge of town who fear they will always be second class.*

Father and I drove to Aloe Glen on a late summer's day when the air was heavy with cloying heat and a belt of haze hovered over the isthmus of the Cape Flats. Hamish slept in his basket in the back of the car, his face flushed, his black hair sticking to his forehead. Father took us on the scenic route via the coast of False Bay, the road squeezed between rolling sand dunes and the vast, flat stretch of Muizenberg beach. I'd swum there a few weeks before, striking out beyond the breaker line, relishing the frisson of danger, while Father watched Hamish. He is quietly dangling before me the diversions I'm leaving behind.

'I need more bush subjects, Father,' I countered. 'And I promised Julian we'd be reunited there.'

The Americans have landed in North Africa, Montgomery has won at El Alamein, and Julian's tour of duty is coming to an end. And while I've loved the unfettered warmth of family and friends, I'm craving a little adversity. I want a harder environment.

And I want my son to know the veld, smell its aroma, marvel at its pinched vitality.

We stopped in Wellington for the night and tackled Bain's Kloof Pass and Worcester early the following day, arriving in Aloe Glen in the afternoon, just in time for Father to board the last train for Cape Town. Truda, Sipata and Lena met us, and Tifo helped with my luggage.

'Frances!' Truda hugged me hard, her white plait falling over her shoulder. '*Welkom terug!*'

'Beautiful baby!' Sipata whispered, while Lena stroked the child's kicking legs.

I left Hamish with them and walked Father to the station. Aloe Peak loomed overhead, the grey-green veld stretched to the horizon and a pair of jackal buzzards circled.

Father glanced about, unnerved by the emptiness, the quality I've learnt to value.

'I worry, Fran—'

'Don't.' I reached up and kissed him. 'Thank you, Father, for bringing me. For understanding.'

324

Am I safe here? I remember writing in my diary in the early days.

After a week I realise that, finally, I may very well be – by force of circumstance.

I know the truth, and the town knows that I know.

They watch me, I watch them.

There's also an ingrained respect for motherhood that I first sensed at the school gate: they won't touch me if to do so would put my child in harm's way. This tentative truce does not yet stretch as far as outright approval, for word has got back that I hung burnt paintings alongside pristine ones at my exhibition. They sense implied criticism. When my acquaintances – are they friends? – drift back, they do so cautiously.

'Welcome,' says Cora Engelbrecht, avoiding my eyes, bending to coo over my son.

'Lovely to see you, Frances,' says Sannie, while Aletta and Anna smile nervously.

Why have you come back? they surely wonder.

Some are generous straight away. Mrs van Deventer waddles down the road with a meat pie, clucks over Hamish, glances at my inadequate frame and shakes her head. 'Eat, Frances. For the baby.' The dominee's silent wife appears at my door, hands over a knitted romper, and slips away before I can invite her in. 'Good day.' Mr Fourie comes around the front of his counter. 'How may I assist you, Mrs McDonald? And what news of your husband?' The poor whites and coloureds from the edge of town are ever welcoming. I feed off the warmth in their eyes.

In the early morning, I lay Hamish on a blanket and tie him on my back and walk into the veld with my folding stool and sketchbook. I draw, then return to the flat above the petrol station during the heat of the day, add paint to my sketches while he naps and, as the sun loses its fierceness, set out again to capture the same scene with the sun in the opposite quadrant. It's an echo of my morning-and-evening sketches from the bedrooms at Marico Road; a new series, Dawn-to-Dusk, capturing the transition.

After a long trek around the circumference of Aloe Peak, I found a group of three young quiver trees on the driest slopes where it seemed nothing of tree size could possibly grow. I smiled and touched their rough bark. *Aloe dichotoma*, sometimes known as upside-down trees because their thorny heads resemble roots. Birds cluster on them, especially when they're laden with yellow tubular flowers that poke between the limbs like multiple candles.

'Frances!' Truda bounded across the veld and stopped beside me, panting. '*Kokerbome*!'

'Yes. I'm drawing them for people in London.'

'The Bushmen use the trees. They make holders out of the old wood for their arrows.'

I remember Julian's words over the dead antelope. And I modify them.

Every life, every death, serves a purpose in Africa.

Seven youngsters came to my revived art class.

'Today, we're going to use pastels,' I said, handing out the chalks. 'Now that the drought is well and truly broken, we can make softer pictures. And you can smudge them with your fingers or a tiny piece of paper, like so.' I demonstrated, drawing the outline of Aloe Peak in navy and then adding lines of green and brown for the lower slopes and blending them in.

'Now you try.'

'Are you famous, *mevrou*?' asked Toby Engelbrecht. 'My ma says people pay you for pictures.'

'It's my job, Toby. Like your father is a sheep farmer and gets paid for his wool? I'm an artist, and I get paid for my paintings.'

'*Mevrou*,' muttered Frans van Deventer after the lesson, when the younger pupils had left, 'I saw him.'

I glanced up from Hamish's basket. He'd slept all the way through. 'Saw who?'

Frans looked at the others and they nodded at him: Magda Metz, Toby and his sister, Lottie, who'd once asked about the halo around the sun that I'd said was due to science and not necessarily to God.

'Mr Louw. I saw him at your house. When the fire started.'

I sat down at the desk.

Scorched linen, broken ceiling panels, the smell of petrol on a purple rug . . .

'I saw him, ma'am. He had a cloth tied around his mouth and nose.' Frans hauled a grubby handkerchief out of his pocket and held it over his face to demonstrate. 'But I know it was him. I told no one, not Ma or Pa or Ouma van Deventer. Only my friends.'

'Tell about his coat,' hissed Toby, and reddened. There's a doggedness to Toby. Others will abandon a messy drawing but Toby will erase his mistakes, drop his pencils several times, pick them up and keep going until he's satisfied with the result.

'*Wag*!' Frans flapped an impatient hand. 'Wait, Toby!'

He turned back to me. Magda came closer to my desk; Lottie hung back.

'He had a package, ma'am, under his coat. I thought he

327

was delivering something, ma'am.'

'Where were you, Frans? How did you see this?'

'I was in Ouma's back bedroom. I saw him take a bottle out of the package, bend down and light it, and then throw it through the front window. Then he went round the side and I heard a crash and that must have been the other window, ma'am. And then he walked away fast. He didn't look back, ma'am.'

Frans paused for breath. 'I didn't see the fire at first. Then I saw flames inside and then the coloured people and the poor whites came and started throwing water, and then you and Sipata came and I,' he stopped and blushed, 'I stayed inside until my ouma woke up. She was sleeping before supper like she always does.'

Here was the evidence the police were waiting for: the perpetrator, identified at the scene of the crime.

'We didn't tell any of our parents,' Magda whispered, looking around at the others. Frans stuffed his handkerchief back in his pocket and rubbed his face. Lottie examined her fingers and shot a glance at me from beneath her fringe. They were teenagers, now, these children whom I'd first taught ten years ago. They'd grown up while I was away.

'No one else knows?'

They shook their heads.

'Thank you, Frans.' I got up from my chair. 'Thank you for telling me. Mr Louw is already in prison. He can't do any more harm.'

They looked at each other and then back at me.

'But that was for the railway, ma'am!' burst out Toby. 'Not the fire. And you said Mr Louw wasn't a hero, you wrote to Deon—'

I caught my breath.

I can't tell you how to answer your friends, I'd written from Cape Town in reply to Deon's letter, *when they say your father is a hero for sabotaging the railway line. I can only say that heroes should inspire the best in each of us.*

'We must tell the police,' Toby said stoutly.

Frans nodded. 'Mr McDonald would say the same if he was here.'

'Honesty will never be punished,' put in Magda. 'Mr McDonald told us that.'

Oh, dear God, forgive me. Forgive Julian. What have we unleashed?

If there's evidence that Wynand Louw threw petrol bombs into our house, it should be revealed. But the witness is a teenager. He'd be testifying in open court against the wishes of his parents. When his testimony is shredded by a determined lawyer – how far away were you, it was early evening, how can you be sure? – I must step up to defend him. I must submit the sworn statement of the wives' confession to me. Not just because of my burnt house but because of the courage of a young man.

'I don't want to hurt Mrs Louw,' I said slowly. 'Can you understand that?'

Rain splattered against the window. It's still a surprise, as is the grass on the sports pitch

'The fire wasn't fair, ma'am,' said Lottie, speaking for the first time. 'Mr Louw must go to prison for it.'

I smiled. The young see events in primary colours, they don't notice the shading, the blending of colours that make the truth and its consequences more complicated, more dangerous. Frans, Toby, Lottie and Magda are seeing the world like I did after the fall. Sharply. Clearly.

The fire is their equivalent epiphany.

I've learnt, slowly, sometimes painfully, to temper my zeal. And what would Julian say? Would he be pleased that his pupils – the product of his quiet radicalism – are planning to betray their parents?

Would he be proud of their independence?

The youngsters grabbed their satchels and ran out.

I went over to the window and watched Toby battling to keep up, Lottie sweeping her hair out of her eyes as she galloped, long-legged, across the playground. They were shouting and laughing, as carefree young ones do, through the softly falling rain.

Their mothers kept the secret to save their fathers.

The children are about to pull the house down on both.

Hamish woke in his basket and began to cry.

I went over to him and lifted him out and held his warm body against mine.

Chapter Fifty-Two

My dearest Fran

I can't wait to be with you. It's been a difficult few months but I've been holding onto the prospect of seeing you soon, and lifting my beloved Hamish in my arms for the first time. I'll telegram my arrival. We won't be separated again. I'm determined about that, especially now we're a family.

All my love

Julian

I could have gone to Cape Town to meet him, but Julian was insistent we should be reunited as we'd planned in Aloe Glen. I brought in an extra bed and squeezed it alongside mine. One of the quiver trees was still in exuberant bloom and I sketched it while Hamish toddled precariously on the stony ground. 'Your daddy's coming,' I sang to him, 'Daddy's coming home!'

I hung the painted version above our beds.

'When will Mr McDonald be here?' Frans van Deventer asked at the art class.

'Soon.'

I've no idea if he's been to the police and I won't ask.

It's not my position to encourage or forbid, only to stand by him if need be.

It was winter when Julian arrived. Light snow dusted Aloe Peak, softening its outline and brightening the cliffs. A bitter wind drove across the veld, blowing the last of the dried *Brunsvigia* heads on their seed-scattering path. The station was empty but I found myself looking over my shoulder for Wynand Louw. The train was late and I waited on a bench, with Hamish squirming by my side in his best dungarees, a woollen jumper knitted by Violet and a felt cap. 'It's Daddy,' I whispered.

'Dada,' he tried to say, to copy me, but he's not used to the word or the possibility of a father.

Hamish loves the station.

He loves to shout at the whistle and jump up and down as the brakes squeal.

I'm nervous; it's been more than two years. Will Julian like this version of me . . . the version that carries a secret so deeply, yet so brazenly by my side, jumping up and down at the arrival of the train?

I stood up.

A carriage door opened.

Few passengers get off at Aloe Glen on a Monday so this must be him.

I lifted Hamish and hurried along.

I knew the moment he took his first hesitant step down. Julian was using a stick. Not a walking stick for the mountains, but a stick to help him on the flat. His hand fumbled slightly on the door. His uniform hung off his frame in folds. He turned, his eyes lit up and I ran to him and he shakily swept Hamish and me into his thin arms.

'Dear Fran,' he muttered, burying his head on my shoulder. I felt his chest heaving against mine.

I pulled away gently, and lifted Hamish to him. Julian gathered the boy and stroked his head, tears coursing down his face. I expected him to be sunburnt from the desert sun but he was pale. He put Hamish down. I knelt beside my son. 'This is Daddy,' I said and pointed. 'Daddy.'

Dark-haired, dark-eyed Hamish looked up at Julian for a moment and then hid his face against me.

'Give him time,' murmured Julian, ever the patient schoolmaster.

I carried Julian's bag and he took Hamish by the hand.

Father should have told me. Julian had spent a day in Cape Town; Father should have sent me a telegram to warn me but perhaps Julian insisted there was no need.

The boy's toddling pace was perfect for Julian's difficulty and we slowly made our way the short distance to the flat above the petrol station. 'Welcome, sir!' boomed Tifo, bounding across the forecourt to shake Julian's hand and take the bag. 'Let me, I will carry the boy upstairs for you. Miss Frances has been painting, right here!' He pointed to my spot around the side of the garage, to where he directs passing motorists to view the famous artist, as he calls me.

'Thank you,' Julian said, and I took his arm to help him up the stairs. He had to stop a few times to catch his breath. 'Why, this is charming, Fran,' he managed when we came through the front door. I'd hung more pictures, and I'd paid Lena to crochet a bright blanket to cover the small couch.

'Mama?' said Hamish and tugged on my hand.

'Why don't you rest? Through here. I'll bring you tea—'

'Mama?' Hamish looked at me and then at Julian. He's

only ever seen women here.

I knelt down to him. 'Why don't you show Daddy your ball?' He grinned and ran into his room and came back and held out his knitted ball.

Julian sat down on the bed and smiled. 'Can you throw it to me?'

Hamish threw it and Julian caught it and threw it back to him. Hamish giggled.

Julian has always needed me more than I will ever need him. I turned away to put the kettle on, to hide my tears.

Julian slept for much of the next week.

He said his weakness was due to a bout of seasickness on the troopship that left him unable to eat or sleep. That, he smiled wearily, explained the weight loss. He'd be fine, he told me, touching my hand, once he was rested. Sipata made soup and I cleaned Mr Fourie out of eggs and made nourishing omelettes and roasted a chicken and cooked green vegetables and made scones from Violet's recipe. Julian tried to eat but his stomach was often upset and he returned from the bathroom grey and sweating. Hamish took to lying down beside him for his nap.

'Dada's tired,' he would say. 'So tired, Mama.'

'Frances!' Laetitia appeared at my door with a pot of honey. 'You're hiding Julian away!'

I pulled the door closed behind me. 'He's not well,' I murmured. 'He needs to rest a little longer.'

She stared at me. 'Can I help? Do you need the doctor? He's coming next Wednesday.'

'Maybe. Will you keep this quiet at school? I'll be back at art class next week.'

'*Sterkte*, Frances.' Her heels clattered down the stairs.

Strength. Fortitude against the odds.

But I don't know what the odds are.

'It's because of the cold,' diagnosed Truda, after visiting briefly. 'The winter here after the hot desert.'

The dominee made a formal call and sat on the couch beside Julian and said he prayed every Sunday for an end to the war and the restoration of peace both abroad and at home.

'As we all do, Dominee,' I said. 'To heal the divisions.'

He inclined his head. I can read the dominee's reactions these days. Perhaps he realises he's on shaky ground. He may have discovered that Frans van Deventer either has identified – or is about to identify – Wynand Louw as the fire-bomber. His congregation could be on the edge of notoriety.

'I shall pray for you, Mrs McDonald,' he said as I showed him out after we'd had tea.

'Pray for my husband, Dominee. And Aloe Glen. Not for me.'

It was provocative, I know, but irresistible. He'd said there'd be a reckoning. Perhaps not in this world, he'd added. But, to my mind, justice ought to come sooner. Or at least genuine remorse.

Yet is there a cost? I reflected once more. A cost to whatever – or whoever – will follow? My child. Frans van Deventer, Magda, Toby, Lottie . . .

I must not let rancour take over my life. Or my art.

Each night, as Julian drew me against him, I pondered whether to tell him the truth. But his body felt worryingly frail and I kept silent. And so did he, revealing nothing about the war or the real reason for his illness. We were caught in a trap of our own making, I realised: both of us with so much to tell, yet so little that could be shared without consequence or hurt.

I'd been shaken by tragedy and new life; he'd been devoured by another war, as I feared.

Yet who was I to hold it against him? He felt he had no choice.

And neither did I, Julian. Under different circumstances.

And neither do the youngsters.

Toby came to our door. 'Frans van Deventer has told the police.'

He stumbled back out and down the stairs before I could respond.

A month went by.

'What's wrong?' asked Mrs van Deventer when I came across her at the store. She'd told me earlier that it was no surprise to her that Julian's health had been ruined in the wilds of the Middle East.

'Your husband is better?' asked Cora Engelbrecht with a penetrating glance.

'You aren't painting, ma'am,' observed Sipata. 'Leave Mr Julian with me. I will take care of him.'

My hands were becoming stiff and out of practice. I could start with the quick Cadwaller Sketches that sell easily by the side of the petrol station. We could do with the extra income.

And my husband retches in the bathroom every morning.

'Tell me what's wrong, Julian. Please. It's time I knew.'

This was no brief illness. My husband has become an old man; his remaining hair is completely white.

'It's my stomach. I ate something in Egypt that didn't agree, my dear. The doctor said it would resolve itself in time. I feel better already just being home.'

His tone was mild. I detected no fear. That was the essence of Julian: quiet acceptance, no fuss. Julian would never smash the china, as I'd once wanted to do. Instead, he spent each day in our tiny lounge, reading to Hamish, who fetches book after book until Julian falls asleep.

'Dada thleeping,' Hamish lisps and lies down beside him.

'Let's go to Cape Town,' I said after another long fortnight. 'Dr Reed will recommend a specialist.'

Hamish stared up at us. Julian stroked his hair and smiled at me.

'I'm getting better, Fran. I'll be back at school in a month or so.'

I lie awake at night and listen to his restless breathing. Once he's asleep, I creep out of bed and open the curtains so I can watch the stars wheel slowly across the sky. I wonder if Mark looks up from whatever battlefield or ocean he traverses, and remembers our single afternoon together. I pray – yes, I do – that he's safe. His daughters deserve to know their father into old age.

'Can we look at the house?' Julian asked one winter day. He'd shown no interest so far so perhaps it was a positive sign. We left Hamish with Sipata and drove there because he'd struggle to walk the distance, and also because I didn't want others to see the extent of his weakness.

'Oh, Fran,' he muttered, and passed a hand across his forehead as we approached. I stopped the car and leant across and kissed his cheek. This was his house before it was mine. He'd worked hard to pay for it, he was proud of its good size.

'Shall we go in? Or would you rather not?'

The lone tree was doing well but I'd allowed the vegetable patch to go fallow. And, after two years, the boarded-up windows have sunk into the walls with a permanence that seems irreversible.

He stood on the wispy grass, leaning heavily on his stick, and I wanted to weep for him.

'Let me see,' he said, struggling up onto the verandah.

The ash, debris and glass had been cleared away but that didn't lessen the shock.

I followed him as he made his way slowly from room to room, his stick tapping the floor grimly, his shoulders bowed. When he came to my studio, he turned to me with horror.

'Your pictures? Oh, my darling—' He let go of the stick and bent over, his head in his hands.

I remember when I got angry that he didn't call me darling. I put my arms around his thin frame. 'I've painted new ones,' I murmured against his bent back, 'and exhibited some of the damaged work.'

He straightened, took up his stick and pointed at the trails of melted paint on the floor. It's as well *Studio with Glass Shards* was bought by a private collector. I wouldn't want him to see it displayed.

'How, Fran? You never said how it caught fire.'

Maybe I'd been wrong to protect him. Maybe he needed to be taken out, pushed beyond what he appeared capable of.

'It was foul play, Julian.'

'What?' he gaped. 'How? Who?'

I took his arm and led him to the single dining room chair that remained. He sat down heavily.

'Someone threw petrol bombs, one through this window,' I pointed, 'and one into my studio.'

I could see he was unable to conceive that anyone could do such a thing.

'The police found the culprit?' he asked eventually, his voice shaking.

'Not yet.'

If the truth fails to come out, I will not tell him. Seeing the damage has been enough of a shock. I will bear it alone. He once called me his better half; now I must be his stronger half.

The cracked mirror is still on the opposite wall but I don't dare look at it.

I don't want to see either of us reflected in its unsparing surface.

'We should sell, Fran. Get rid of it. Let someone else make repairs. It's too upsetting—'

A pair of cries reaches us through the open door. Crows foraging in the bare vegetable patch.

'Let's wait and see.' I helped him up. 'Let's get you well before we make any decisions.'

I have an idea. Crazy. Provocative, again. Part of the unfinished business before we move on.

And I will need the house to bring it to fruition.

Chapter Fifty-Three

Julian is convinced that Hamish is his biological child. And so, it seems, is everyone else. Only Daph, puzzling over the infant's jet-black hair, shot me a questioning glance. Julian even recognises traits of his own in Hamish: the boy's attention to words, his earnestness. I play up each tenuous connection. Hamish is my gift to Julian.

For my part, I find Mark in Hamish's every feature, every movement. And I secretly rejoice. The long fingers. The fascination with blocks, with building. I hope he'll also have Mark's acuteness – his wiring – for danger.

And I adore him, he is funny and serious. He puts his arms around me and I give him my whole heart.

I'm still waiting for the reckoning which is to come in Aloe Glen, when my ammunition may be needed. But I wonder if the moment has passed. I used to be much more impatient than I am now. Mother, dear Mother, would be relieved. I'm on to the third volume of my diary. The other two remain safely in their hiding place, along with the fire portrait. Sometimes I take out an earlier one and open it at random. The words are often more relevant now than ever: There are parts of me that my husband doesn't know.

'Ma'am!' Tifo shouted. 'You have a visitor!' He led a tall man around the corner of the building.

'Mrs McDonald? Please don't get up.' Major Jefferson, newly unrecognisable in civilian clothes and a deerstalker hat, came over and held out his hand. 'Forgive me for interrupting you.' He peered down at my sketch. 'That is most impressive. *Aloe dichotoma*?'

'Yes.' I put down my pencil and shook his hand. 'For Kew Gardens. What brings you to Aloe Glen, sir?'

'Why, this, of course!' He held out his arms to the landscape. 'I'm in Worcester for a few days.'

He unfolded a shooting stick, pressed its point into the ground and settled onto the leather seat.

'One of your paintings is in a gallery in New York – were you aware there were overseas collectors at your exhibition? And they contacted me about new work. I thought I'd visit you.'

I stared over the veld. It was shaping up to be a hard year. Rainfall was low and dust devils were frequent. I don't know if I have the patience, the resilience, for another drought. For the waiting.

'Are you no longer in the army, sir?'

'Put out to pasture,' he chuckled, 'not before time. And with the war grinding to an end I'm happy to say the art world is reviving, hence the queries from abroad.' He paused and watched a black-and-yellow butterfly with scalloped wings. 'In civilian life I'm a curator-cum-consultant for hire, so to speak. Helping my clients build collections.'

'Could you make me famous, Major?' I murmured with a half-laugh. 'Surely my desert plants, my chronicling of drought and scarcity, are too niche? Too stark?'

'That's where you're wrong. The plants you paint are so unusual they're an instant talking point.'

I glanced up in the direction of the flat.

'My husband hasn't been well. I haven't painted as much recently, but I'm hoping that will change.' Julian was back at school twice a week. It's a start. 'Do you wish to commission specific work, sir?'

'Well,' he folded his arms, 'they're highly impressed with your botanicals, of course. And the landscapes. But a Mr Cherriot, the American owner of the famous Cherriot Gallery in London, wonders if you've ever considered portraiture?'

'No,' I replied. 'Never.'

Major Ferguson nodded. He contemplated Aloe Peak, cocked his head at the distant sound of a whistle.

This is a strange conversation.

He's come all this way to talk about a genre in which I have no experience.

'I'm working on a Dawn-to-Dusk series, Major. I've completed one pair, a stand of eucalyptus trees planted at the time the railway line was being built.'

'Mrs McDonald, I must come clean.' He extended his hands in apology. 'Your father kindly invited me to tea last month and he showed me a work you painted some time ago. It was part of the Fire series, on display but not for sale. An extraordinary piece. That's why I've come to see you.'

'Gideon,' I murmured. 'My brother Gideon, who died before I was born. It's not for sale.'

'I understand. But if you paint more—'

I packed away my sketches and my pencils, and collapsed the easel. 'May I offer you tea, sir?'

'That is most kind.'

If Major Jefferson was surprised at our modest accommodation, he was too discreet to say. Sipata kept Hamish amused in the bedroom while we spoke. I showed him the eucalyptus and he said he'd be interested in any other paintings I made of the quiver trees that were not earmarked for Kew.

A key scratched in the door. Julian stopped on the threshold in surprise.

'Julian, may I introduce Major Owen Jefferson? He's a collector. He's interested in my recent work.'

'Mr McDonald, your wife's desert subjects are highly regarded. But perhaps,' he looked at Julian with a brisk compassion, 'you'd be more comfortable in Cape Town?'

'Frances loves the veld.' Julian looked across at me and smiled. 'It's her inspiration. And Aloe Glen is where we can make a difference. Where our son can run free.'

'Indeed.' Jefferson rose. 'Thank you for the tea, I must be getting back to Worcester. Do let me know if you contemplate portraiture, Mrs McDonald. In the meantime, I look forward to your new work.'

'Portraits?' Julian looked across at me as the door closed. 'Whatever is he talking about?'

'He was misinformed. How was your day?'

Julian sank onto the couch. 'I think I'll rest for a while. It went well, just a little tiring.'

'Dada,' shouted Hamish, racing out of the bedroom, followed by Sipata. 'Let's throw, Dada, throw!'

'Daddy's tired.' I scooped him up in my arms. 'We'll go throw your ball outside.'

I grabbed my smallest sketchpad and a pencil and stuffed them into the pocket of my bush trousers. Sipata gathered her bag. Hamish and I often walk her home. It's rather a long way for his little legs and sometimes I have to piggyback him, but he's getting stronger. There are no trees for him to climb, so his challenge is one of stamina rather than altitude. He skipped along between Sipata and me as we deviated through the church grounds. I don't think the dominee minds; sometimes he comes across us and pats Hamish's head and says that the Lord looks kindly on all those in His garden.

I stopped and pulled out my pad and pencil.

A quick sketch, a moment captured, just so.

The boy throwing a ball, little arms raised; Sipata picking it up. A few pencil strokes and there he is: my child. And the bent outline of Sipata by his side. Caring. Vigilant. On a whim, I flipped over the page to a fresh one.

This time, closer: wavy hair framing plump cheeks, a button nose, dark eyes, the faint arch of brows.

The makings of a portrait—

'I must go, ma'am,' Sipata said, leading Hamish to me. 'It's getting late.'

I turned the page back and tore out the first sketch and gave it to her.

'Thank you, dear Sipata.'

'Ah.' She smiled at the drawing. 'I'll put it on my wall. Goodbye, ma'am.'

Hamish tugged on my hand. 'Home, Mama? See Dada?'

'Yes. Wave to Sipata!'

A policeman was exiting the church. I put my hand up against the lowering sun to see more clearly.

'Sergeant? Sergeant Roland?'

He hesitated, then approached me. 'Afternoon, Mrs McDonald. And this is your boy?'

'Yes, this is Hamish.'

The sergeant bent down and shook Hamish's hand gravely.

'Have you made any progress, sir? It's been over two years.' I don't intend to let such a fortuitous ambush fade into pleasantries.

'Mama?' Hamish pulled on my hand. 'Go home, Mama.'

'I believe you may have received further evidence, Sergeant.'

'What kind of evidence, ma'am?' he hedged.

'A witness, sir. Someone who saw Wynand Louw at the scene.'

Were he and the dominee conspiring to muzzle Frans van Deventer?

'Mama!'

I lifted Hamish and settled him on my hip.

'The witness is a minor, ma'am. His evidence may not be reliable.'

'And why is that?'

'Perhaps you could visit the police station, ma'am. It would be better to talk there.'

I must be careful. I must not get angry. And I must remember Mr Field's advice. The sergeant smiled at Hamish, raised a hand to me and began to walk away.

'It's not easy for me, sir,' I called. 'We must speak now. When the war's over, will Wynand Louw be prosecuted for arson?'

He stopped and turned back to me.

'No one else has come forward to confirm the boy's evidence, ma'am. It's slim. I'm sorry.'

'If others knew Mr Louw was involved, would that make a stronger case?'

We were fencing with each other. The sergeant is more

experienced than he was when we first met.

'It would have to entail credible eyewitness accounts, ma'am. Do you know of such witnesses?'

He thinks I may be bluffing yet he can't be sure.

'I may do, Sergeant.'

Sipata.

But she'd never testify. And if she did, they wouldn't believe her: a semi-literate, coloured woman.

No. Any new evidence would have to be prompted by what was told to me. My ammunition would have to be revealed before Frans was taken seriously.

Hamish had fallen asleep against my neck. I could feel his warm lips against my skin.

'What, for argument's sake, Sergeant,' I held his gaze, 'if I was informed that local people knew Wynand Louw was considering fire-bombing my house and failed to stop him? Or warn me?'

Alarm sprang into his eyes. This was becoming awkward. Yet I'm determined to lead him to the intelligence that I hold about Aloe Glen: I have been told the town is culpable.

'You'd have to swear to that in court, ma'am. You'd have to name the persons who informed you.'

The sun slid down below the horizon. A wisp of cloud flared.

'I understand, sir. I've delayed you long enough. Thank you for the clarification.'

I'd have to bring their houses down.

346

Chapter Fifty-Four

It's been another good year for my tiny population of quiver trees. I suspect they're flowering so prolifically because they know that dryness is to come. I can feel it in the air and on my skin, and in the crisp leaves of the low *bossies* around my feet. I blend blues and greens to create the malachite sunbirds that gorge on the quiver blooms, but the glitter of their wings defies my brush, which is as it should be. Real life holds miracles that no likeness can capture.

'Beautiful, Fran,' said Julian when I showed him. 'You show their elegance, their greed.'

Julian is still thin. I see his weariness at the end of the day. And so I'm painting as much as I can.

The annual exhibition is upcoming at Kirstenbosch. There are special commissions for Major Jefferson and his New York clients – it turns out that America, which gave birth to the Crash that overturned my life, is wooing me as an artist. And I produce a raft of Cadwaller Sketches to sell beside the petrol station. Presumably some townsfolk disapprove, but I don't care. I'm working so Julian can reduce his schedule. There's also the matter of a new home for us. Mr Field says that the property market will pick up after the war and if I wish to

347

invest I should do so sooner rather than later.

'Frans,' I held the tall youngster back at the end of the art class, 'Mr McDonald doesn't know about Mr Louw and the fire. I'll tell him when he's stronger.'

Frans stared down at me. He's about to leave for high school in Worcester.

'Will the police do something, ma'am, about what I saw?'

'I don't know, Frans. If they do, it'll only be at the end of the war.'

He nodded, hefted his satchel and walked away.

He'd meet Deon Louw at his new school. Will he tell Deon what he saw?

'Mama, look!' Hamish ran out of the classroom with a wildly coloured sheet. Hamish loves to sit alongside the bigger students and make his own pictures. He chatters in English to Julian and me, and in Afrikaans to everyone else. Father, initially taken aback, now thinks the boy may be advantaged. 'It's the way politics is going, Fran. It can't do him any harm.' Truda giggles and says it serves me right for coming back. I'm raising a child I won't be able to understand. My tea party ladies are confused.

'Don't you mind,' asks Cora, 'don't you want him to be English?'

'Oh, he is,' I reply. 'But it shows that this is our home, too, doesn't it?'

'Let's drive up to the Logan garden at Matjiesfontein,' I suggested to Julian. 'Before it gets too hot. I'd like to draw their Crassulas. We'll take a picnic. And Director Compton says there are walks we can do.'

'Yes,' shouted Hamish, jumping up and down. He loves to

go out; our flat is too confining.

'Perhaps next weekend, Fran.' Julian looked up from his books.

All week Hamish talked of the upcoming trip. I showed him a picture of the flower I wanted to draw. *Crassula columnaris*, a strange plant, low-growing with packed leaves on a central stem. It puts up a single flower head containing hundreds of tiny blooms. 'Like Dada's shaving brush,' Hamish said, and ran into the bathroom to fetch it. He's observant for a three-year-old.

'I feel a little tired,' murmured Julian over breakfast on the designated day.

'I could drive,' I offered.

Hamish nodded and patted his father's hand. 'Mama will drive, Dada.'

Julian looked across at me for a moment. He doesn't often ask for anything for himself.

'Let's go up Aloe Peak instead.' I turned to Hamish. 'You and me. We'll look for scrub hares and see if we can spot the black eagles. What do you say?'

Hamish looked from Julian to me, and trailed into his bedroom.

Children pick up when adults mask the truth. I used to, with Mother and Father.

'I'll make us a picnic,' I said quickly. 'You rest, Julian, don't do too much marking.'

'Thank you, my dear.' He touched my arm. There's been no passion between us since his return, only fondness. Julian falls asleep the moment his head touches the pillow. I lean over and kiss him but he doesn't stir. I reach back to the memory of Mark while my husband sleeps.

I made sandwiches and packed a flask of tea and my sketchbook. Fat cumulus clouds studded the sky.

'Will they make rain?' asked Hamish, kicking his little boots against the dusty earth.

'No,' I said, squinting up. 'They're just teasing us.'

'Clouds don't tease, Mama!' he giggled. 'They can't think!'

We reached the end of the road and struck uphill. I could show Hamish the aloe that has become my signature. A gallery in New York has bought two new works, and I'm busy with a third one for a private individual in London. Major Jefferson is right: collectors are attracted by unusual species, drawn in situ.

'Look!' I pointed at two soaring birds. 'What do you think they are?'

Hamish shaded his eyes. 'Black eagles, Mama?'

But their undersides were pale fawn, not the distinctive charcoal and white. I pulled a pair of binoculars from my rucksack. A gift from Father.

'Can I see? Can I see?'

I focussed. They were broader in the body, and their wingtip feathers, those fringes designed for uplift, were more pronounced. They floated, executing only the gentlest of turns on those massive wings.

'Come.' I lowered the glasses. 'Sit down here, on this rock. You can look.'

I looped the binoculars carefully around his neck and helped him to lift them to his eyes.

'Point the glasses towards the birds, Hamish, look over the top and then look through. See them?'

The little fellow waved the glasses about for a while and then got the idea. I helped steady his hands. 'Put your finger on

350

the focus; now turn gently to make the picture clearer.'

His body stiffened. I smiled. I knew the feeling.

'Mama!' he yelled. 'So big, Mama! Oh, now I've lost them!'

'No matter.' I took back the glasses. 'Watch with your own eyes, Hamish. You'll see just as much.'

'What kind of birds, Mama?'

'They're vultures, Hamish.'

Vultures search for prey that is already dead, like an antelope accidentally killed by a car. I felt a clutch at my heart. I'd had an intuition about becoming a victim, too.

'Mama?'

'I think we should go home.'

'But we haven't had our picnic!'

'I know. But don't you think it would be nice to surprise Daddy and have it with him?'

'I want to go there.' He pointed to the crest of Aloe Peak. 'Right to the top!'

'Next time. I've got an idea. Why don't we play at Sipata's for a while and then go home for our picnic?'

He grinned and began to skip along in front of me.

Sipata's street was busy. I smiled and nodded at the folk I knew. The Nationalists say they can lift poor whites out of poverty if they win the next election, but they don't say what they'll do for the poor coloureds or blacks who live alongside them.

'Ma'am?' Sipata opened the door in surprise, then bent to hug Hamish.

'Can I leave him with you for an hour or so? I need to check on Julian. Will you bring him back?'

'Of course, ma'am. Is everything alright?'

'Yes, fine. You can share our lunch.'

Sipata nodded and gathered Hamish to her. 'Come, little man, we'll play together.'

Julian was where we left him. On the couch, but now sleeping. I felt a wash of relief. A school exercise book had slipped out of his hands and onto the floor. His arm had fallen, too, and his fingers were dragging on the carpet. I picked up the book and placed it on the side table. His eyes were closed but his head had lodged into an unnatural angle. He'd have a stiff neck when he woke up.

I knelt down by his side. I wish I loved him like I love Mark. I care for him but it's not the same, and maybe he knows. His slow recovery could be partly because of me. Perhaps he knows I found my love while he was away. I'll try harder.

I touched his face. He didn't stir. I shook his shoulder.

His chest wasn't rising or falling.

'Julian! Wake up!'

I felt for a pulse but there was nothing, no flicker, no beat beneath the skin.

But he wasn't cold like Aunt, not yet—

I began to press on his chest as I'd been taught during first aid lessons, and breathe into his mouth. Press several times. Breathe. More presses. More breath.

Cars drove into the petrol station. I heard Tifo's cheerful voice. A train shunted.

But there was nothing from Julian.

I rested my head against his, let my hair fall across his face.

Why do you want to marry me, Julian, I'd asked him when he proposed.

I care for you, he replied. *I will love you and cherish you as if I were a young man . . . You have the courage to say and do what I can't, Frances. I need that.*

I did love him, in my own way.

And I gave him a child to hold close.

I picked up the telephone, cranked the handle, and called an ambulance.

Chapter Fifty-Five

I was not prepared.

With Aunt it was a hammer blow. With Mother it took months of unhappy decline, and then days of drift between coma and lucidity. With Julian, it was different again.

He died as modestly, as quietly, as he'd lived.

'Dada!' shouted Hamish, breaking free of Sipata and racing through the door. He wouldn't know what the emergency vehicles meant but he must have sensed, with childish intuition, that something was wrong. Sipata followed behind, hands clasped over her mouth. I quickly gathered Hamish up and swung him away from the couch so he wouldn't see the men slowly manoeuvring Julian onto a stretcher.

'We'll take him to Worcester, ma'am,' the ambulanceman said quietly. 'They have the facilities.'

Hamish twisted in my arms. I felt his heart hammering against mine. His skin was clammy.

'They'll call you later, ma'am. I will ask the funeral people to call you.'

'Why is Dada sleeping, Mama?' His voice rose to a scream. 'Why are they taking him away?'

'Come, little man.' Sipata lifted him out of my arms.

I'm not crying. That will come later. I must be strong now, for my son.

'Wait, Sipata, put him down.'

She hesitated, then set Hamish gently on his feet.

I led him to the stretcher where Julian lay, as if he were asleep. The men stood back.

'Let's kiss Daddy goodbye for a while, Hamish.'

The boy leant over and put his arms around Julian and squeezed. 'Dada, come back soon.'

I nodded to Sipata. She picked him up and carried him to the bedroom and closed the door.

'Where, Sipata?' I heard him cry. 'Where's Dada going?'

The Aloe Glen wives have been generous. They've delivered stews and home-made cake and pots of soup. Father, who is squeezed into Hamish's bed while my boy sleeps alongside me, has not gone hungry. I'm reminded of Aunt's funeral and the mountain of donated food and, in truth, I'm grateful. I have no desire to cook and in any case I'm busy. The day after Julian died, I walked to the dominee's house and asked him whether he'd be prepared to lead a service, in English, that would pay homage to Julian's Presbyterian roots.

'Otherwise I must take him to Cape Town, Dominee,' I said, as I sat in his cavernous lounge. 'And that would be wrong. This is where Julian served, where he gave of himself to his community, his students.'

'I understand.' He inclined his head. 'I will be honoured to conduct the service.'

He may see it as atonement. So may others.

'I'll help you, Dominee. I will write about what Julian

stood for. We can collaborate.'

He nodded. He knows I understand more Afrikaans than I let on. And I know that the congregation will understand more of the English than they'll let on.

Every morning for the next week, I spent two hours with him in a study lined with heavy Dutch and Afrikaans tomes, converting my words and translating his church phrases into the kind of tolerant message Julian would have admired and understood. And one afternoon, when I returned home, the medical report from the authorities in Worcester was waiting for me. It stated that Julian died of natural causes, aggravated by an infection of the intestine. Dr Reed, calling a day later from Cape Town, said Julian consulted him after he disembarked and handed over a letter from a surgeon in Egypt who believed it was inoperable cancer of the stomach. Julian had sworn Dr Reed to secrecy and promised to return to Cape Town for palliative treatment if he became too ill. Until then, I was not to know. And he wished to be cremated when the time came. 'I'm so sorry, Frances.' Dr Reed's voice cracked with sympathy down the telephone line. 'I had to abide by his wishes.'

'I understand. Julian was much braver than he gave out.'

'And you have young Hamish,' the doctor went on, 'who'll carry Julian's values forward.'

'We are gathered here to mark the life and work of Julian McDonald,' the dominee pronounced on a glaring morning when the heat seemed to travel in translucent waves across the veld.

'Julian was a husband, a father, our headmaster and friend.'

The church was full. There'd been a moment, as Sipata

stood at the door with Lena and her coloured partner, when I thought they'd be barred from entry and I would have to intervene, but the dominee himself appeared and ushered them in. He knew I wouldn't accept a colour bar at my husband's funeral.

'Julian was born in Scotland, but his life's work was shaped here,' the dominee spread his arms, 'in the heartland of this country, where his teaching influenced the lives of hundreds of young people.'

He'd asked me whether there was a particular theme I wished for the eulogy.

Language skills, I'd replied. And the ability to think and reason independently.

'We all know,' the dominee went on soberly, 'that Julian loved the English language. His pupils learnt to love it, too. He believed that, along with their mother tongue, it would take them into the world and help them find their way. The Lord teaches us to love our neighbours. Julian believed we should learn to speak to them, too, in their language as well as our own.'

I smiled. If he were here, my husband would be smiling too. I didn't dare look behind me.

'And,' the dominee paused, 'as important as language, Julian taught his pupils to think for themselves. To reason and come to their own opinion. To make up their own minds.'

I fancied I could feel the mixed emotion of the congregation battering my neck.

'Please stand for the next hymn.'

The organ played the introduction to 'Onward Christian Soldiers'.

'A great tribute, my dear,' whispered Father.

As the grand tune rang out and the singing rose to the roof, it seemed that, for the first time, I was properly at home in this severe church among these stubborn, hard-working people. I thought about Hamish, being babysat by Lena's teenage daughter. One day, I'd describe this final acknowledgement, the collaboration it had involved, the reconciliation it tacitly encouraged.

'It is fitting that our final reading today is by one of Julian's pupils.'

Laetitia had said she would arrange this with the dominee.

A tall boy in school uniform walked past, stopped and nodded to me, then ascended to the pulpit.

I felt tears, then. For the first time.

Deon Louw. If we were searching for a legacy for Julian, this young man embodied it. I reached a hand over my shoulder. Truda was seated directly behind. I felt her take my hand.

For me, Deon's slow, careful recitation of the lesson in perfect English – I don't remember the contents – was the climax, and a blessing that went far beyond the hymns, the prayers, the eulogy.

Over tea and sandwiches in the hall, the Metzes promised to ask me to lunch. Anna and Aletta looked me directly in the face and said that Julian would be missed, while their husbands nodded. Cora pressed a small bunch of wild flowers into my hand. Toby and Lottie said they were sad for me and slipped away. Deon Louw came over and I reached up and hugged him. 'He'd have been proud of you,' I whispered, while Truda openly wept. Mrs van Deventer approached in a voluminous black dress and ancient hat. 'He did his best, that's all you can ask.' The dominee's wife squeezed my hands and said not a word as she manned the tea table. A considerable number of those who approached me were strangers. They said Mr McDonald had taught their children and they would always be grateful. I smiled through my tears. Father stepped in when I could manage no words. 'We're most grateful,' he said to them and shook their hands.

By lunchtime it was over.

'Thank you, Dominee,' I said. 'You did well for Julian. And for me.'

'I shall pray for you and your family, Mrs McDonald.'

I wonder what goes on in his heart. I wonder how he judges his flock.

'Aloe Glen does have a certain attraction,' Father remarked as we walked home, gesturing at the endless bush, the rearing mountains. He's trying to distract me.

'It's a harsh beauty, Father. It only rewards grit. And persistence.'

'Qualities you possess, my dear.'

I linked my arm with his. Dear Father. We slowed for a moment as a pair of guinea fowl scuttled ahead of us across the road and towards the station. They roost in the pepper tree on the far side of the line and their chicks learn to hop onto the platform to peck at discarded crumbs.

'Will you scatter Julian's ashes in Aloe Glen, Fran? It would be fitting.'

'I think on the Peak where we walked, Father, do you remember? Where you told me about Mother.'

'I do,' he paused, 'and where you showed me that extraordinary aloe.'

Later, as we sat down to supper, I turned on the radio.

Julian always liked to hear the evening news.

A sonorous voice filled the air.

'From the headquarters of the Supreme Commander in Europe, General Dwight D. Eisenhower, in Reims, northern France. Germany has signed a document of unconditional surrender.'

'Mama?' Hamish lifted his fork. 'Can I have more 'tatoes?'

'Hush! Listen . . .'

'The Ministry of Information in London has confirmed that an official statement declaring the end of the war will be made simultaneously in London, Washington and Moscow tomorrow.'

There was a pause, as if the newsreader needed to gather himself.

'I repeat, Germany has surrendered.'

Chapter Fifty-Six

Hamish misses Julian more than I do.

I wonder if he dreams of Julian, like I dream of my brother.

Since Father returned to Cape Town, he's stayed in the bed next to mine.

He says he's keeping it warm for Dada and I don't have the words – or the heart – to explain that Dada will never return and that the bed will always be cold.

My weekly newspaper showed grainy photographs of crowds singing outside Buckingham Palace.

Father said there were celebrations in the centre of Cape Town and that the ships in the harbour hooted long into the night, and flares were set off.

In Aloe Glen, the end of the war was greeted with no particular fanfare.

It has always been seen as a foreign nuisance that was bad for business.

There is no longer any reason to hide this diary away.

I shall keep it at my bedside from now on.

Is Mark alive?

I checked the postbox on Marico Road and then walked into the veld, sat on my folding stool and got out my sketchbook. Sipata had arrived before breakfast to stay with Hamish. I pulled my coat tighter and watched my breath frosting. I've come to capture the mountain in its winter mood against a sky flushed by weak sun. It's an oddly gentle sight. The outlines are familiar but the colours are particular. They must convey both granite permanence and soft flux. I'm thinking of slate grey for the rocks – a shade called ardoise, named after the place where the rock is mined in France – and a highly diluted mix of cadmium red and yellow for the sky.

A movement caught my eye.

Grey against grey-green, only becoming apparent when it moved. It was walking towards me, long-legged, a gait of extraordinary elegance. It turned side-on and I saw a crest of feathers. A secretary bird. Mainly earthbound, though it will fly if it can't outrun its pursuer; named after the habit of human secretaries to tuck quill pens behind their ears. I quietly turned to a clean page in my book and began to draw. An eagle-shaped beak, black along part of the wing, a tail that extended at least half its length and brushed the ground.

It turned – did it see me, smell me? – and strode away across the veld.

I watched until it disappeared. I'll show Hamish the sketch when I get back, then we'll look up the bird in our reference book. I'll bring him here to see if we can spot the elegant creature again.

But I know it won't be enough.

We need to leave Aloe Glen and make a fresh start for my son's sake.

And for my own. Now Julian's gone, the fierce inspiration

of the veld is not enough. I will miss my true friends – Truda, Sipata, Lena – but they will understand. I turned at a thudding behind me.

'Frances!' Truda raced towards me, her feet ungainly in boots. 'You weren't at home—' She skidded to a halt. Her hair was bundled beneath a woollen cap and she wore builder's dungarees. I've tried to paint her but she's too transient to pin down, too fragile to capture.

'It's Wynand. They let him out!'

'He's here? In Aloe Glen?'

'*Ja*. He came last night.'

I couldn't help looking at her neck. Her face. We haven't ever spoken out loud about the bruises.

'Deon is home. He slept outside our bedroom door.'

She looked down and twisted her fingers. Truda's nails have been whole for some time. She's become warmer; she even teases me sometimes. And she doesn't look over her shoulder as much.

'Deon won't always be here, Truda. If Wynand hits you, you must tell someone. Me. The dominee. The police.' But I may not be here either. I may not be here to save her, as I promised her son I would be.

'He said he's sorry for what he did. And I must keep quiet. He's going to stand for parliament.'

I stared at her. The other war, the one I believe is waiting in the wings, has begun.

And this time, we'll all be at the fighting front.

'Mr Field,' I said on a hastily arranged visit to Cape Town, 'I have a particular property in mind. Is it possible to find out if the owners would sell?'

Field regarded me cautiously. 'It's not currently for sale?'

'I don't believe so.'

'Then you risk driving up the price, if I may say so, Mrs McDonald.'

I nodded and glanced out of the window. No troopships in the harbour. And, on the street, no cries of 'War Latest'. Now it was all about the forthcoming election.

'I can't afford to buy just yet, sir, but I'd like to plan for the future. Even if it risks escalating the price.'

'You'd like a third party to engage with the owners, sound them out?'

'Yes, I'd be most grateful.'

'When do you intend to come back to Cape Town for good?'

'Soon, sir.'

Hamish and I will stay with Father; he's already said that his home will always be our home. The more Hamish laughs with Grandad, the more the memory of his father being taken away on a stretcher dims.

But I'm also ambitious for our small family.

'Major Jefferson? Good morning. It's Frances McDonald.'

'Ah, Frances.' His warmth came down the telephone line. 'Are you in Cape Town?'

We know each other well enough, now, for first names on his part.

'Yes. I wonder if I could visit you. I have some new work you may find interesting.'

'I would be delighted. Come for tea.'

The major is a wealthy man. He lives in a splendid house in Constantia which appears to serve as an informal gallery, or perhaps a clearing house. Its interior walls are covered in art, its tables groaning with miniature sculptures and artefacts destined for collectors around the world. I dressed for the occasion: a blue dress with a fuller skirt than the previous dictates of wartime austerity. Violet swept up my hair and pinned it in the latest style.

'You're still offering botanical art to Director Compton?' he asked over tea and Victoria sponge cake.

'Yes, but this particular work is different. A single piece, not part of a series. And a departure from my normal style.'

I reached down and drew the fire portrait out of my portfolio and handed it to him.

He took it carefully. For several minutes he said nothing and I wondered if he was disappointed and didn't know how to break it to me. I realise it is unconventional. Mr Cadwaller always said art was about taking risks and I have done that. First with the exhibition. Now, potentially, with this.

'The medium?' he murmured.

'Charcoal, from the fire. Ash. And blood.'

Chapter Fifty-Seven

We're back in Aloe Glen. The pace is quickening. Major Jefferson says the fire portrait is 'remarkable'. He has taken a photograph of it. He will send it to London to the gallery owner who is keen on portraits. So often, remarkable things spring from blows.

To the head. Or to the heart.

I left Sipata that evening with strict instructions that she open the door to no one. Maybe I was being overdramatic. But it wouldn't hurt to be careful.

Aloe Peak glowed in the moonlight. I could attempt a painting in the style of Van Gogh. The sharp outline of the peak against the moon, the grand sweep of the Milky Way. But I don't work in oils, and you need their density to invoke the hard glitter of the stars, the thick flow of their reflections.

I smiled.

Shall we consider oils, Mr Cadwaller?

By the time I arrived, the hall was almost full. In place of the school flag, huge National Party banners swung alongside the flags of the former Boer republics. A display of rifles and vintage uniforms decorated one side of the stage, while the other was occupied by a group of young boys in khaki shorts

and shirts, leading a rousing chorus of 'Sarie Marais' – the
Boer War anthem. I didn't recognise any of them; they were
not local. And neither were the men seated on stage, with
the exception of the speaker and the dominee, who sat with
folded hands, nodding at the enthusiasm of the crowd.

'Frances.' Truda appeared at my side. 'Sit with me?'

'Don't you have to be on stage?'

'I won't go there,' she muttered.

She was wearing a new dress, a severe navy affair, not at
all like the flowing ones she wore when she ran across the
veld. I was in red, made for my latest exhibition in Cape
Town. 'So you'll be seen,' insisted Violet's sister. 'You need to
stand out, Miss Fran.'

The boys finished, came to attention, and gave salutes.
The audience roared.

What would Julian make of this?

It was certainly patriotic, but a narrow patriotism.

'*Dames en here*, ladies and gentlemen.' The chairman
stood up and clapped his hands. '*Welkom*!'

The noise abated. He spoke mostly in Afrikaans and I
translated it in my head.

'It gives me great pleasure to introduce the speaker
this evening, our candidate for member of parliament for
this constituency in the upcoming general election. Please
welcome Wynand Louw!'

Wynand stood and held his arms aloft like a boxer
celebrating victory. Truda shrank into her seat. Despite his
years in detention, he appeared prosperous. I'd only seen
him at a distance since his release. Truda says – with relief,
I suspect – that he's been away in Cape Town and Pretoria
for political meetings. So far, none of the previously detained

men have been charged with crimes related to sabotage, or individual acts against their fellow citizens.

In fact, in some quarters, they're being feted as heroes.

I glanced around and caught the eye of Sannie Metz, sitting with Abel and Magda.

Wynand Louw began to speak. The resentment that I remember so well was still intact, but better presented. He'd clearly been schooled in a particular way to address a crowd: identify yourself as a victim, show how you overcame the odds, promise to fight for the similarly victimised in your audience. But while these might be noble sentiments for any aspiring leader, from Wynand's mouth they emerged loaded, bent on vengeance.

Yet am I any different? I've wanted my own, private redress. But since Julian died—

'Like many of you, I was raised hard,' he shouted. 'We were poor! The land was dry. We went hungry!'

He moved on to his family's travails in the Boer War. 'They took my grandmother, put her in a camp!'

Later, he struggled to find work on the railways; then he was unfairly incarcerated during the war.

'I was a patriot and they locked me up!' He struck his fists.

'Shame! *Skande*!' yelled the crowd.

It spurred his devotion to the cause of Afrikaner nationalism.

'I'm a *Bittereinder*,' he cried, 'and proud of it! This land is for the Afrikaner! We are the chosen ones, the only chosen *volk*! I will fight for you!'

People clapped Truda on the shoulders and shouted their congratulations as he ended. She cowered next to me. If

Wynand was elected, there'd be no more running barefoot across the veld. Deon, at university in Stellenbosch, would have to answer those who praised – or questioned – his father's path from disgraced saboteur to mainstream politician. I listened to the ecstatic applause and glanced down the row at Abel Metz. He'd been ashamed of Wynand Louw. Surely he'd want a less divisive vision of the future?

'Ladies and gentlemen,' the chairman held up his hands, 'Mr Louw will now take questions.'

'What if he wins?' Truda whispered. 'What will I do?'

'You'll manage,' I said. 'I'll help you. We'll still be friends.'

She won't survive. It will be like confining a wild animal to a circus enclosure.

'Blacks are taking our jobs!' someone yelled. The audience rumbled in assent.

'What about wages?' a man called from the back of the hall.

Wynand Louw now became less confident, less practised. He ducked several issues and didn't appear to understand land title, a crucial matter for an MP representing a farming community. The chairman began to sense that the momentum was being lost.

'Last questions,' he called.

I stood up. So far, members of the audience had stayed seated while shouting out their questions. A murmuring filled the hall. They recalled my previous intervention, folded their arms and looked at me with resignation and some sympathy. The headmaster's odd wife, now a widow, I could imagine them sighing. The one who paints and refuses to leave.

I waited.

'You have a question, madam?' the chairman asked with

369

a hint of irritation.

I knew it wasn't wise, this old hankering for a challenge, for danger. Julian would call it my ability to say or do things he would never have tried.

'You wish to speak?'

'Yes, sir.'

I reached down and touched Truda's shoulder in mute apology.

'Mr Louw, why did you throw two petrol bombs into my house in 1941?'

For a moment there was complete quiet. Then the noise crashed about my head and I thought I'd be swept from my feet. All sympathy gone, the crowd screamed for me to leave, to never come back, that I was a disgrace. Hands clutched at me, trying to pull me down onto my seat but I twisted away from them. A man whom I didn't recognise lunged at me. Truda got up and shoved him away.

'Please, ladies and gentlemen!' The chairman waved his arms. 'This is surely a misunderstanding. Mr Louw, will you respond?'

I stared at Wynand Louw. He glared back at me.

'I don't know what the lady is talking about. There's no proof!' His words dripped disdain.

'No proof!' yelled the audience, roused once more.

'It's time to close the meeting,' the chairman shouted. 'It's been an honour to hear Mr Louw tonight—'

'There is proof,' came a strong voice from the rear of the hall. 'I saw you, Mr Louw.'

I turned around. Frans van Deventer, eighteen years old, soon to attend university, was on his feet.

'Frans!' came a querulous cry from his grandmother.

The chairman leant towards Wynand Louw and exchanged a few words.

'Then why, young man,' he called, 'didn't you report this to the police?'

The audience quietened. Frans was one of their own. He wasn't a mad widow. But I could sense their anger that he'd stepped out of line. They'd want him punished for such audacity—

'I did report it. The police didn't believe me.'

A red flush spread from Wynand Louw's neck to his face.

The dominee stood up and walked to the front of the stage. 'These are difficult times,' he held out his hands in supplication, 'we are all sinners in this world. There must be a reason, Frans, why the police did not take the matter further. I think we should pray, ladies and gentlemen, for our nation—'

'I'm not the only proof,' called out Frans. 'There are others who know the truth.'

I caught my breath. Here was the challenge to his friends, his family, his community.

'Then show yourselves!' The chairman came forward belligerently to stand beside the dominee. 'Let us end this attack against our prospective member of parliament!'

Frans and I were still upright.

The crowd was still.

Then, slowly, from along the row, I felt a movement.

Magda Metz stood up.

At the front of the hall, Toby Engelbrecht and his sister, Lottie, got to their feet.

A shiver ran through the audience, as if someone had opened the back door and let in a blast of cold air. If my child had stood up for the truth – a truth I also knew – would I leave him to stand alone?

Five people stood before Wynand Louw. One adult and four young people.

Yet . . . The whole town knew.

Wynand Louw folded his arms and stared at his shoes.

Then . . . Cora Engelbrecht got to her feet between Toby and Lottie.

Sannie Metz stood up and took her daughter's hand. I saw Abel shudder and bow his head.

There was, for a full minute or so, a terrible, threatening silence.

The mood shifted. A low mutter spread around the hall. I became aware of a scraping of chairs.

People were leaving.

Some of them stared at me, but most of them kept their eyes on their feet. It was not a stampede for the doors, more an embarrassed shuffle. *Cowards!* I wanted to shout, as I'd wanted to shout when they saw Julian go off to war without a second glance. I bent down to Truda. She was weeping.

Two poor whites, who'd been at the back of the hall, fought their way against the departing mass and shook my hand. I recognised them. They'd fought my fire. Will I ever understand this place?

'Mrs McDonald?' Frans towered over me.

'Thank you.' I reached up and embraced him. 'That was brave, Frans.'

It would cost him. His outspokenness would be remembered.

'I followed your example, ma'am. Mr McDonald would have, too, if he'd known.'

Lottie Engelbrecht slipped past, gave me a shy smile and took Frans's hand.

Julian's lessons were complete.

And I'd done what I said I would.

I'd forced my community to look me – and themselves – in the eye.

Chapter Fifty-Eight

After the war, Sergeant Roland was promoted to a new position in Bloemfontein. When I enquired as to the status of the investigation into my house fire, I was told that the case had been closed for lack of verifiable evidence. Captain Ellis, who'd prioritised national security over criminal activity, left government service and joined a gold-mining company, presumably to stop the theft of its product.

Is it enough, Julian? I asked my husband as I wandered through the veld.

Or should I use my ammunition beyond Aloe Glen? Tell the newspapers what happened?

A parting shot after I leave.

A final bombardment that will publicly devastate the community . . .

I didn't expect to be torn. I thought my thirst for justice was unquenchable but instead it's faded – even as my country lurches towards greater division. Wynand Louw's campaign for parliament continued with barely a hitch after the school hall meeting. Frans van Deventer is occupied at college and unlikely to be interviewed again by the police, many of whom support Wynand Louw's politics. Deon Louw, who might have wanted his father curtailed, has graduated as an engineer and is hoping for opportunities abroad.

What benefit would my parting shot bring?

What will it change?

'We'll miss you, Frances,' murmured Lena. 'You never looked away from us.'

'The veld will miss you, too, ma'am,' added Sipata. 'You tell its story.'

The *Brunsvigias*, the secretary bird, the quiver trees, the pink armoured aloe . . .

A date of departure was fixed. Truda can barely look at me.

'You've been my dearest friends.' I took their hands in turn. 'You stood by me.'

Yet it is I – or perhaps my precarious life in this place – that has been the cement holding our disparate friendship together. If Wynand Louw and his party triumph, the edge-of-town community may be broken up. It may not be possible for any of us to remain close.

'We'll miss you, Frances McDonald.' Mrs van Deventer leant over her gate when I visited Marico Road for the last time. 'You and your ways.'

'What will you do with the house?' asked Cora over tea with Sannie, Aletta and Anna at the Metz farm.

I hadn't expected an invitation or any sort of rapprochement; I'd lain awake after the political meeting, fearing the confrontation between husband and wife in the Metz and Engelbrecht households, and between the children and their parents.

My house still burns, the fire still has consequences, I wrote in my diary.

The ladies had taken trouble with their outfits, and I'm

touched. A floral dress for Cora, a blue blouse for Anna, print skirts for Sannie and Aletta. I'm wearing a Cape Town exhibition frock and heels.

'I'll hold on to Marico Road for now, and wait for property prices to pick up.'

They nodded. They're uneasy. The house is a tie to Aloe Glen they'd rather I sever.

'We're grateful you never went to the police.' Anna shot me a glance over the top of her teacup.

I chewed my cake slowly.

A gentle lob, Frances. Not a bombardment.

'I made a sworn statement to my lawyer about what you told me at the church ladies' morning.'

Sannie gasped, alarm flaring in her eyes.

Anna clattered her cup back onto its saucer.

'Why?' Aletta rasped, rising to her feet. 'Why did you do that? To get at our husbands?'

'Wait.' Cora reached across and gently made Aletta sit. 'Let Frances finish.'

I glanced out of the window. The Metz farm has recovered. The land was dotted with sheep. I will miss these kinds of vistas, the meandering animals, the hard-slabbed mountains, the unexpected blossoming.

'I never want to use the statement,' I turned back, 'especially since everything came out at the meeting. But it still has value. I'll release it if Frans, Magda, Toby or Lottie are ever punished for speaking out. Or,' I looked at each in turn, 'if you're threatened by your husbands for standing by your children.'

I watched their fright ebb into something bordering on respect, perhaps even gratitude.

Cora hesitated, then got up and came over, bent down and

kissed me on the cheek. 'Thank you, Frances. We understand. You taught us a lesson.'

The others nodded, got up as well and gave me shy kisses.

'Not me, Cora. It was your children.' I smiled. 'They taught us to be true to ourselves.'

Hamish and I drove out of Aloe Glen on a day when the tarmac threatened to melt.

'Will we come back, Mama?' Hamish craned backwards as the town receded.

'Maybe one day.'

I wound down the window fully and let the hot air play over my face. The land began to soften and green the further south and west we went; thirsty scrub gave way to fruit orchards and clumps of sugarbush proteas and rushing, unpaintable streams.

I stopped the car at the top of Bain's Kloof Pass.

Vineyards rolled across the valley floor in patchwork squares; the sea glittered in False Bay. The distant, jagged spine of the peninsula drew the eye.

My life will circle back. It must. One day.

'Look!' I bent down to Hamish. 'See Table Mountain? Lion's Head?'

'I wish Daddy was here, Mama.'

'Yes.' I kissed him. 'But we're near to heaven so maybe he's looking down on us?'

Hamish gazed up into the sky. 'From where the angels live, Mama?'

'Yes, I'm sure.'

It was evening by the time we arrived at Father's cottage in Newlands.

'Frances!' Father hugged me and leant down to swing Hamish into his arms. 'At last, my dears!'

'Welcome home, Miss Fran!' A grey-haired Violet drew me close. 'We're all ready for you. Miss Daphne's coming for lunch tomorrow with the children.'

There was a letter waiting for me in my bedroom.

Dear Mrs McDonald

I have had a positive response to the photograph of your Fire Portrait that I sent to London. Mr Cherriot is interested and would, I believe, make an offer.

However, I consider it may be worth selling the painting at auction in London. That would potentially realise the highest price. I have connections with a prominent auction house and I could arrange for suitable publicity in advance. There is much interest in art made in Africa at the moment. The war has changed perspectives, collectors are looking for fresh inspiration and novel subjects.

Do contact me when you arrive in Cape Town and we can progress this.

Yours etc

Owen Jefferson

'Fran,' whispered Daphne, 'Trevor knows a charming man in his office – you need to look about—'

'It'll be a close call,' said Father to Preston Bell, who'd joined us for lunch. 'Surely Smuts will prevail?'

'Oh, hush about the election,' Daphne pouted. 'I'm tired of all the talk!'

'Milk tart?' Violet offered slices. 'I've kept some aside for the children, Mrs Bell.'

'The writing's on the wall,' said Preston Bell. 'Look how they threw out Churchill. Smuts will lose.'

And he was right.

Later, after they'd left, I propped up the Fire Portrait on an easel in the lounge.

'Major Jefferson believes it could be successfully sold at auction in London.'

Father is not usually lost for words but for a good minute or so, he simply stared. 'I should've come at once. I should never have left you alone, Fran.'

I sat down on the side of his chair and put my arms around him. 'It's not your fault, Father. I drew what I saw.'

'But this,' he motioned at the portrait, 'this shows alienation. Division.'

'Yes,' I said. 'And it may show the future.'

'Major Jefferson, I have one condition for the London auction,' I said, as I sat in his elegant Constantia lounge. He crossed one immaculately clad leg over the other and nodded for me to continue.

'I'm only prepared to sell the Fire Portrait if the new owner puts it on permanent public display.'

'And why is that, Frances?'

Why do I want my private agony visible for all to see?

'Because bigotry shouldn't win, sir. Anywhere, not just in Aloe Glen. And being drawn in charcoal, the portrait can depict anyone's face. From any background. Any colour.'

'Universal suffering?' Jefferson mused. 'The lessons of the war?'

'And the conflict to come, sir.'

'Ah.' He appraised me carefully. 'Between English and Afrikaans? Since the Nationalists took power?'

'It will be about more than language, sir. It'll be about skin.'

'Why not sell it in this country, then? Display it here?'

'Because,' I hesitated, and wondered at my conceit, 'I think it's bigger than here.'

Is this a quiet extension of the revenge I decided to shelve?

Or perhaps it's simply commercialism: I need the money.

Chapter Fifty-Nine

Everyone continues to find a resemblance – or the evidence of shared traits – between Hamish and Julian.

The secret lives within me, never to be revealed. But Julian is gone. Hamish no longer has a father by his side as he grows up.

There is an ache inside both of us.

I ache for Mark.

Hamish aches for Julian.

It was a gamble. I used my private account to buy a return voyage to London. If the portrait didn't sell, or went for less than I hoped, my gamble would be in vain.

'I can't advise you, Fran,' said Father. 'But you have my blessing. Some risks are worth taking.'

'You deserve some fun,' laughed Daph. 'Whatever happens, you'll have a wonderful trip!'

Major Jefferson was already in the capital, making the arrangements for the auction, stirring up publicity. He didn't have the portrait with him; I was bringing it with me in a specially made portfolio that would protect the charcoal. I trusted Major Jefferson, but if anyone was going to lose this portrait to deterioration, thieves or the Atlantic waves, it would be me.

'Take no chances, Frances,' the director had said after viewing the image. 'This is a seminal work.'

'What do you see in it, sir?'

He looked at it with his head on one side. 'Honesty. Contradiction. Warning.'

'I want to come!' shouted Hamish, jumping up and down. 'Why can't I come, Mama?'

I gathered him in my arms and covered his face with kisses.

'We'll be waiting for Mama right here when she gets back,' said Father, patting Hamish's head. 'And think what fun we'll have, you and I, while she's away? Trips on the train to Simon's Town. Picnics!'

A southeaster was blowing as the ship slipped her lines and edged away from the quay. I pushed to the side of the deck. Way below, among the crowd, I spotted Father raising his hat while holding fast to Hamish. My son was waving a huge flag we'd crayoned together, a mountain with a red sun setting behind it, a black bird in the sky, a blue river in the foreground. Hamish loves bold colours.

'Goodbye!' I shouted even though they wouldn't hear. 'God bless!'

I stayed on deck until Table Mountain faded to a scratch on the horizon.

The portrait is in the ship's safe.

I paint, as I painted during my passage to Cape Town to be Aunt Mary's companion. Strangers come up and make comments and I hand out a card from the set Father had printed for me.

Frances McDonald.

Botanical illustrator and landscape artist.

'Art is your business, Fran. Never let a potential client get away.'

I find myself rushing, though, as if my sketches are somehow preliminary, awaiting the affirmation that might come in London. They are not my best work.

Major Jefferson met me at a wounded Southampton, gouged by bombs and heaped with debris. We said little as the London-bound train drew out past pristine villages and damaged ones, and cut through green fields incongruously pitted with craters. I craned out of the window for the winding road to Eastleigh, for the spire of Winchester Cathedral, for Embury, where it all began: the sharp awareness after the fall, the yen for danger and the discovery that I could, perhaps, draw well enough to be an artist. But the rain sifted down to obscure all but the closest landmarks.

In truth, I don't want to see Embury.

Susan wrote after the war to say that it had taken a 'pasting', as she called it. Perhaps in error, after the bombers missed Southampton and jettisoned their loads indiscriminately. Susan has moved with her family to Wales, too far away for me to see her on this short visit.

I don't want to discover that our road is gone, that the oak was pulverised. Although this is not my home any more, it still stirs my heart.

I was to lodge with the major's unmarried sister in Kensington.

'Welcome,' she trilled, opening the door on a grand but

slightly frayed interior. 'You're going to be famous, my dear. I'll be able to boast to all my friends that you stayed with me.'

'Only if the work sells, Miss Jefferson. Only if it sells.'

'Of course it will! Owen has an unerring eye. And I'm Constance, please. Now, will you have a sherry?'

For the first few days I wandered the city with my sketchbook, my throat rasping with the grit that seemed to rise up constantly from the rubble. Stray dogs rooted through fireweed growing in the shells of grand buildings. Proud Londoners carried on past the obstacles, and red buses navigated their way across crevassed intersections. I drew, reaching for the same techniques I employed for botanicals; collapsed steeples and broken masonry demanded at least as much precision. St Paul's dome, miraculously intact but surrounded by devastation, rose like some huge, elaborate flower head beside the Thames.

As my pencil flew, I thought of Mark. What would he rebuild, what would he design afresh?

On the fourth day I took a bus to Kew Gardens.

'Mrs McDonald,' Miss Channing, assistant to the director, greeted me with enthusiasm, 'we're so grateful for your collaboration on the aloes. Mr Raymond Cadwaller first drew our attention to your work. We plan to show them alongside other selections once visitor numbers pick up. The war has limited the ability to travel, as you can imagine.'

'I have another one for you.' I opened my portfolio and handed over my latest painting. A malachite sunbird, perched on the flower stalk of a quiver tree, its feathers glistening in shades of blue and green, its beak imbedded in a bright yellow tubule. 'The emphasis is less on the plant, as you can see. I realise you may not want this because it's primarily about the bird—'

Julian had been too ill to walk with me to the quiver trees, so I painted them for him while they were in bloom and crowded with malachites. He said I captured the birds' elegant greed.

'My,' Miss Channing murmured, 'how utterly captivating. We shall be honoured to add it to our collection. Now, may I offer you tea? And a walk, perhaps? The rain is holding off. I'd like to discuss some new commissions with you.'

The Cherriot Gallery turned out to be untouched by bombing, although adjoining buildings had been hit.

'Welcome!' cried the flamboyant American owner. 'We were spared from the carnage! I'd be delighted to display your portrait, Mrs McDonald. Take your time to look around.' He spread his arms to show an eclectic mix of work. Landscapes, pen-and-ink drawings, oriental scrolls, small sculptures, portraits of every style. Mr Cadwaller would've been enchanted by the range but perturbed by the lack of focus.

'Why do you want the *Fire Portrait*, Mr Cherriot?'

'It's a forerunner. The war has upset old notions, old conventions. Art is on the cusp of vital change.'

I hid a smile. I should have brought along a second *Studio with Glass Shards*.

'And where art goes,' Cherriot waved a hand as if there were no other safe predictor, 'so goes society.'

'Or the other way around, sir?'

'Indeed. Your country is set on a particular path. You have brilliantly reflected that ambiguity.'

Major Jefferson arrived to fetch me early on the appointed morning.

I cannot say I slept much the previous night.

I was wearing my red dress, black court shoes and a small red-and-black hat I'd found in a cubby hole of a shop on Oxford Street. 'How chic,' was my hostess's verdict. 'They'll want to buy you, too.'

Banners hung outside the auction house and a crowd milled through the ornate interior. A man in formal dress guided us to seats in the centre of the room. The director of the auction house hurried over and shook my hand. 'A pleasure to meet you, madam. We shall do our best with your work.'

Mr Cherriot raised a hand to us from his position near the front.

There were several lots before mine, which was just as well, as the process was conducted with such speed it took me a while to follow. The auctioneer was at the podium. 'And now,' he said, as his assistant brought in an easel, set it under the angled lights and uncovered my piece, 'we come to a self-portrait by the English-born South African artist, Frances McDonald, rendered in charcoal, ash and blood.'

The audience murmured. The auctioneer inclined his head.

'A unique treatment, indeed. This *Fire Portrait* was created in the aftermath of a conflagration that took place in the artist's rural studio in 1941. Apart from the advance viewing this past week, it has never been seen in public and the artist stipulates the work should be made available for public display after it has been bought. Ladies and gentlemen, shall we start at two hundred?'

'Here we go,' Major Jefferson whispered in my ear.

I stared at my face. The slash from the cracked mirror.

The blood. The defiant, despairing eyes.

Do these brave, war-weary Londoners understand? Do they see themselves? Do they see others?

I sensed Jefferson's excitement next to me and concentrated on the podium.

'Five hundred, I have. Five fifty? Thank you, sir, on the left. Six hundred. Seven hundred, thank you, at the front. Eight hundred. Am I bid one thousand pounds?'

It continued.

And finally, when I could hardly bear the tension: 'Two thousand going once, twice, going to Mr Cherriot of Cherriot Gallery. Congratulations, sir.'

Two thousand pounds!

With two thousand pounds I can secure what I lost.

The room burst into applause. Major Jefferson hugged me.

Mr Cherriot turned to me and clasped his hands together in salute.

Random people came up and shook my hand and affirmed their congratulations. Several asked what my next work would be. A gallery owner from New York said he'd seen my pieces there and to alert him when I produced fresh portraiture. The curator of a private collection asked for preferential notice of upcoming Cape watercolour landscapes, of the peninsula in particular.

As the crowd began to disperse, I noticed an elderly, white-haired man on the fringe.

He smiled and raised a pair of bushy eyebrows.

'Mr Cadwaller!' I rushed across and embraced him. He is smaller than I remember.

'You've outdone yourself, my dear.' He patted himself

down once I let him go. 'Our early work was merely the curtain raiser. This,' he motioned towards the *Fire Portrait*, where Mr Cherriott was holding forth, 'is your true vocation.'

'I'm not sure, sir. It took too much from me.'

'And so it should! Art does not come without a price, Frances!'

I smiled. Always exhorting me, never giving ground.

'Thank you, sir.'

'You have a story to tell.' He fixed me with a penetrating stare. 'And more work to do.'

He turned away, raising a paint-stained hand.

In celebration, the Jeffersons took me to tea at Fortnum's and then dropped me at the National Gallery where I spent the afternoon in awe, staring at the works I'd only seen in reference books.

I left London a few days later.

The portfolio that carried the *Fire Portrait* was stuffed with fresh work. A London series. A city rebuilding, hauling itself out of the endless debris. I had only lost a studio . . .

Meanwhile, the *Fire Portrait* is on prominent display in the Cherriot Gallery.

Mr C, as he wishes to be called, says it's already causing a stir. He hopes it will cause so much of a stir that buyers will purchase other work from him while they're there. And who am I to object to such a pragmatic instinct? It's close enough to my own.

I called in to look at it one last time. Several people were gathered around.

'Grim, I call it.'

'But you don't want to stop looking. Her eyes—'

'Why the score down the face?' asked a lady in a plaid skirt and matching beret.

'She's two people,' murmured her companion after a moment. 'She's torn by what she's seeing.'

Chapter Sixty

I've been away for seven weeks. Seventeen to twenty-one days each way by sea, and just over a week in London. It's a long time for a boy to be without his mother. We won't be apart again.

I packed the night before we were due to arrive and set my alarm clock for dawn.

I've learnt new colours in London. Not just shades of grey from the rubble but also nuances of red: the particular flush of sunset found in Turner's work. How long did it take the great artist to get it right? Mr Cadwaller once goaded me by saying I could settle for being an educated admirer of the Masters if I didn't want to put in the work on technique. Talent alone would not make up for laziness.

And still he pushes me onwards . . .

I stared at the southern horizon for the first pucker of Table Mountain.

Brightening stained the east.

Other passengers were coming on deck, now. They've often seen me painting during the voyage and they smile and mostly leave me alone. I've handed out the last of my cards and directed the keenest to my exhibitions at Kirstenbosch.

The city appeared below the mountain, intact, shining, blessedly untouched by war. Sun began to catch the gorge slashing the tabletop, exposing the relief in the cliff face. Two tugs curved into the bay to guide the ship to its moorings. I packed my easel and ran to my cabin to stow the pictures.

Slowly, the great vessel eased towards the quay. My fellow passengers waved and shouted and craned down to spot their families. Ropes snaked over the side, the ship was tethered, the gangplank was lowered. Through the noise I heard paperboys shouting '*Argus*! Best paper in town!' A whistle sounded from the mail ship train. Would travellers bound for the diamond and gold fields look up from their newspapers and idly wonder what went on in tiny, thirsty stops like Aloe Glen?

'Fran!' I heard Father shout. 'Over here!'

And then came my boy, flinging himself against my legs.

'Hamish!' I buried my face against his neck.

'Look, Mama,' he shouted, thrusting a picture at me. A boat. A stick figure waving. 'That's you, Mama!'

'Of course it is, clever boy!'

'Fran, my dear!' Father still dresses formally with a hat and a pocket watch although the fashions for men have moved on.

'Did you get my telegram, Father?'

'Indeed, I did!' Father's eyes gleamed. 'A triumph, my dear!'

'Mr Field,' I said over the telephone. 'I'm now in a position to go ahead.'

'Excellent. I will arrange a viewing. The owners are still in two minds, but I suspect if you confirmed your generous offer, they would succumb.'

Fernwood Buttress stretched into a clear sky as I parked the car.

The gate opened with a squeak. The thatched roof still looked like prickly icing, the shutters were still bottle green. And the garden? Abundant, branching proteas filled the borders. A mass of strappy clivias nudged up against the last of the summer's daisies.

The air left my chest and I sank onto the grass.

'Mrs McDonald? Are you alright?' A young woman bent over me. 'Do you need help?'

'No!' I laughed and got to my feet. 'Protea Rise always does this to me.'

'Well,' she looked at me curiously, 'I suppose if you grew up here, perhaps it would. Do come in. I'm Madge Carter; my late father bought the house from your family. I live here with my husband.'

The interior had been updated since Aunt's time. A smarter kitchen. New panelling in the study.

We sat in the lounge at either end of a large couch. Mrs Carter poured tea. I listened for the chatter of sugarbirds, the bustle of white-eyes.

'I believe you wish to buy our house.'

She spoke bluntly, but that suited me. If she didn't want to sell, then there was no point in continuing. Despite the briefest glance before my momentary imbalance, I'd committed the garden to memory. I could paint its latest style even if there was no hope of a return.

'I've been living upcountry, Mrs Carter, but recently returned to Cape Town.'

'I know. And I've seen some of your artwork. Aloes. Proteas. They're stunning.'

'Thank you.'

'We inherited this house but, frankly, we'd prefer to be

nearer the sea. We don't have a family so we're not bound to schools. We would,' she looked straight at me, 'be willing to consider the offer on one condition. Mr Field said it would be up to you.'

'Oh yes?'

'I want one of your paintings please, Mrs McDonald. Of the mountain, done from the garden.'

'*Fernwood Buttress from Protea Rise*,' I murmured.

'I saw it at your exhibition. The one with the burnt paintings.'

Everyone remembers the burnt paintings. They, and the *Fire Portrait*, may end up as my true legacy.

'It will be my pleasure.' I smiled and held out my hand to her. 'I'll paint a new one, reflecting the garden and the mountain as it is today. To make it personal for you.'

And so it was done.

'Are you sure, Fran?' Father asked as we sat in his Newlands cottage. 'You might marry again, you don't want an old man cluttering up the place.' He pulled out his watch and looked at it.

'Protea Rise will be our home, Father. Yours and mine and Hamish's. And I won't marry again.'

'Why ever not? You're a catch, my dear!'

I smiled and ruffled Hamish's hair as he played on the rug with his interlocking blocks. Towers and bridges. Just like his father. I don't know if Mark is alive. I may never know.

I did one more thing while we were waiting to move in.

I wrote to England with a query for the parish records office on births and deaths from the early 1900s. And I found that Mother had been pregnant with me at the time Gideon died. Somehow by intuition, imagination or a twist of science yet to be discovered, I peered out of my mother's womb and saw my brother.

A laughing boy, running before me through the garden.

'Long ago,' I said to Hamish some months later as we sat in the garden of Protea Rise, 'I had a brother called Gideon. He went to heaven before I was born. But I saw him.'

Hamish stared at me with coal-black eyes. 'How, Mama?'

I wrapped my arms about him and rocked him against me.

'I dreamt of him. In a garden just like this.'

'I want to stay here for ever, Mama.'

Chapter Sixty-One

The press are clamouring for interviews. The success of the *Fire Portrait* has spread across the ocean and arrived in Cape Town.

I sat down in a private room at the Vineyard Hotel with the man from the *Argus*, ready to be honest – but not too honest. 'No politics,' warned Owen Jefferson when he set up the interview. You may see the portrait as a blow against bigotry, Frances, but local readers do not necessarily wish to embrace that.

'Mrs McDonald, the art world – and, indeed, the general public – has been buzzing with reaction to your *Fire Portrait*, now on display in London. What does it say to the viewer, in your opinion?'

Mr Cherriot says it shows ambiguity, Father sees alienation, I see the future . . . 'I think it tells us to be aware of the price of suffering.'

'Your suffering?'

'Yes. And viewers may identify with that, in the wake of the war.'

The reporter, Mr Arthur Conradie, waited for me to elaborate. I smiled. He consulted his notes. 'There's been speculation that the fire which destroyed your studio, and which led you to create this work, was set deliberately. Is there truth to such rumours?'

There's no doubt that the whiff of arson has fanned the flames – No, Frances! – of publicity.

I composed myself.

'The fire was a personal loss, without a doubt. But out of loss comes reinvention, don't you think?'

'Reinvention?' Conradie looked sceptical. He's older than the young thruster who covered my first exhibition. He's after a scoop, a revelation that will lift this piece from the supplement pages and into the more lucrative realm of hard news. 'In what sense, madam?'

'I'd never contemplated portraiture, Mr Conradie. My speciality was botanical illustrations and landscapes.' This was easier ground. 'For most of my life I've drawn and painted the flora of the peninsula and the area around Aloe Glen, on the edge of the Karoo, where I lived for many years.'

'So this event, this fire, was so dramatic it spurred you to a new genre?'

'It did. In such circumstances, I would suggest that anyone – even yourself, sir – would be affected.'

'Indeed. To what do you ascribe the popularity of the work, given that it is deeply disturbing?'

I have prepared answers, but how do you describe in words what can only be felt? The woman in London was drawn to the eyes; her companion, to the sense of being torn. We see ourselves in that face. We see our actions.

'I think people have responded to its authenticity. It shows a moment of private crisis.'

Why? I asked myself when I decided to reveal the work.

Why do I want my private agony visible for all to see?

'And the score down the middle?'

'I drew what was in front of me, sir. My reflection in a cracked mirror.'

'Is there a political message inherent in the portrait, madam?'

I hesitated. Careful . . .

'I hope it encourages us – wherever we live, whatever our background – to be tolerant of others, especially if they're different from us.'

'Are you saying that you oppose the government's policy of racial segregation?'

'I'm an artist, sir. A fire led me to create a portrait that's changed my life. It happened during a war that cost many lives. I hope we can learn to live alongside one another again.'

The telephone call came a year later. I'd already received letters from Cora to say that more travellers were stopping off in Aloe Glen. They wanted to look at the Fire House, as they called it. And to see the aloes I'd painted. The Metzes had opened a bed-and-breakfast cottage on their farm to take advantage of the visitors, and Lena Fuller's partner was guiding them up Aloe Peak.

We're grateful, Cora wrote. *Even though you aren't here, you still make a difference.*

'Is that Mrs Frances McDonald, the artist?' The speaker had a strong accent, like the ladies in my literacy class years ago, before we worked on their pronunciation.

'Yes, it is.'

'I am the parliamentary secretary to Mr Wynand Louw. Mr Louw invites you to meet with him next Wednesday morning, madam. At 10 a.m., if that is convenient.'

I sat back on my stool and placed my brush on my palette.

'To what end? Why does he wish to meet?'

'Mr Louw is the Member of Parliament for Aloe Glen. He wishes to seek your views on its progress.'

'Where will this meeting be held?'

'In parliament, madam. In his office.'

I stared out of the window. My studio is now where Aunt's study used to be. It looks directly towards the face of Fernwood Buttress. I paint the mountain constantly, in every mood.

'Very well. I will meet with Mr Louw. But only if the door to his office is left open. Good day.'

I will not give him the chance to insult me in private.

I wore red, my talisman colour. And the hat I bought in London.

'Mrs McDonald.' Wynand Louw came around his desk as his secretary ushered me through the door. He's grown even more prosperous. I heard he had the ear of the prime minister and was destined for a departmental ministry. He held out his hand. I looked down at it, smiled, and briefly gave him mine. He gestured to a seat and went back behind his desk.

'It's been a while. You are very successful – if I may say so, Mrs McDonald.'

'Thank you.'

Under the suit and the good haircut, he still carries resentment. I can tell. It's in the overly broad smile. And he's nervous. I felt it in the dampness of the palm that I so reluctantly clasped. I wonder—

'Why have you asked to see me, Mr Louw?'

He glanced at a photograph on his desk, angled slightly towards me. Truda and Deon. Nervous smiles.

'I would like to apologise. I think it is time.' He creased

his brow, nodded to himself.

'For what, in particular, Mr Louw?'

'The unfortunate incidents that occurred in Aloe Glen during the war.' He smiled again.

'You mean when you bombed my house?'

I said it clearly, so that it would carry through the open door.

His lips tightened for a moment. I've always got under his skin. Don't teach my son *kak*, he'd spat.

'I'm grateful for what you've done for Aloe Glen, ma'am. Jobs have come to the town because of you.'

I waited for a moment.

'Are you worried, sir, that I still have the ability to expose you as an arsonist?'

Rage flickered briefly over his face before he beamed as if I'd complimented him.

'That was in the past!' He waved a hand. 'We've all done things in the past that we regret!'

'Indeed. Thank you for your apology. I will accept it under certain conditions.'

He stared at me.

'What conditions?'

'That you treat your wife kindly, Mr Louw. Do not beat her or belittle her. And do not harm the prospects of the young people who called you out.' I paused. 'Not now. Not ever.'

I could see the calculation going on in his head. Dismiss her with contempt? Or use her?

'Of course,' he said, colouring. 'I'm a different man, Mrs McDonald. They have nothing to fear. Now, shall we have a photograph together?'

'Good day, sir.' I stood up. 'This has been interesting.'

I held out my hand, and left.

Chapter Sixty-Two

In the end it's taken three years, I wrote in my diary.

*I've always had to wait . . . for the veld to bloom or for life
to turn – just a little – towards me.*

*Three years while I painted intensely and tasted
increasing success.*

Three years while my son grew into a fine young lad.

Three years while my country turned against its own.

'Mr Venter,' I said down the telephone. 'Can you do it by
September?'

'Let me confirm, Mrs McDonald,' I heard the rustle of
paper as Henry Venter got out his workbook, 'you want the
wooden boarding taken down, the windows put back in, the
ceiling panels replaced and the whole place painted?'

'Yes, that's right. I'd like the interior to be a light cream
colour.'

'And the floorboards?'

'You can leave them as is.'

'But some are scorched, ma'am. And there's paint all over
one of the floors. It won't look good.'

'I know. But it will add,' I hunted for a word, 'character.'

I could almost hear him scratching his head. And then deciding all artists were probably a little daft.

'You can pick up the keys from a lady called Sipata who lives on the edge of town. Once you've finished, she will go in and clean. I trust her completely.'

'The police know who did it, ma'am?'

'Yes. But he was never brought to justice.'

'It's a disgrace, Mrs McDonald. But I will fix the house as you say. You should get a fair price.'

The light was striking the mountains at a low angle as I drove with Father and Hamish to Aloe Glen on a mild September morning. I'd chosen spring so that – if there'd been rain – we might see *vygies* in bloom, or even irises waving fragile wands above the scrub.

'Look, Hamish,' I pointed, 'see how the rock folds and splits? Aloes can grow up there.'

'Can we go to the top of the peak, Mama?'

He hasn't forgotten we were meant to go there on the day Julian died.

'Yes, perhaps we can.'

I could show him the spot where Father and I scattered Julian's ashes. He's old enough, now.

'There's a particular aloe high up,' Father turned to Hamish in the back seat, 'that your mother has painted many times. We'll see if we can find it.'

I glanced in the rear-view mirror. Thick, tousled black hair, lively eyes. Does he ever sense, somewhere inside, that he's missing a part of himself? I understand what it's like to be deprived of someone at a young age. Gideon meant so much to me even though I never met him. Will I be judged for depriving my son of a unique, loving father – if he's alive?

'Hamish! Over there, see? A secretary bird!' Father leant out of the window. 'What a sight!'

'He's almost as big as me!' shouted Hamish. 'Slow down, Mama!'

I braked and we watched the bird pace languidly across the veld.

The road curved, and the familiar cluster of houses emerged at the base of Aloe Peak.

'Ah,' Father exclaimed as we jolted down a dirt track on the outskirts. 'How charming, Fran! Authentic farm living! This belongs to Julian's colleague?'

Laetitia had offered us accommodation in the cottage-for-hire her parents had built.

Stay with us, Frances, she'd written. *You'll be most welcome. I will bring you dinner.*

Later, when Hamish was asleep and Father was reading the paper, I sat outside on the small verandah and watched the mountains succumb to the night and smelt the herbal tang of the bush.

I miss it, I miss the starkness. This place will always unsettle me. Draw me in and then push me away.

Streaks of cirrus cloud flew high above Aloe Peak as we drove into town the following afternoon.

'No rain,' I said to Father, glancing out of the window. 'Trust me.'

'The clouds are teasing us!' Hamish grinned.

The roads were busier than I remembered. An extra pump had been installed at the petrol station – I rolled down the window and shouted hello to Tifo – and there was a new shop selling knitted goods and souvenirs next to the cafe. Cars and lorries were parked along the side of Marico Road as we turned.

The gate to number 10 was open.

I slowed down and drove up the earth driveway. Henry Venter had done a fine job. Glass gleamed in the windows. The outer walls were clean. The central tree was now encircled by a wooden bench around which milled a large and disparately dressed crowd.

'Why,' exclaimed Father as I parked, 'it's a triumph! And you were worried no one would turn up!'

'Fran!' Daphne waved, picking her way across the thin grass, followed by Trevor and Maisie.

I hid a smile. It was Daph's first – and probably last – visit to Aloe Glen. Her pink silk tea dress and delicate heels might never survive. I was in a white blouse, a full khaki skirt, block heels and my hair was loose. 'It's so different,' Daph murmured after we hugged, casting a nervous glance at the men in sturdy trousers and shorts and their wives in variations of the same, interspersed with the odd frock. Cora in plain blue, Aletta waving at me self-consciously in a print skirt and velskoens.

'Congratulations, Frances.' Owen Jefferson, impeccable in a light linen suit, elbowed his way through and kissed me on both cheeks. 'I've been given a preview. Stunning. Thought provoking. As I expected.'

'Ma'am?'

'Oh, Sipata!' I hugged her. 'How can I thank you?

'My pleasure, ma'am. And Hamish?' She gasped and took his hand. 'So grown up!'

They embraced, a white boy and a coloured woman who'd cared for him from before he was born.

'*Welkom.*' Mrs van Deventer hobbled over and grabbed my hand in a fierce grip. She'd jammed her purple hat onto her head for the occasion. 'I thought you were gone for good.'

'Not quite, Mrs van Deventer.'

'Frances!' Truda hugged me and offered a pair of mauve flowers, the product of the bulbs I'd been drawing when we first met. 'God bless you for what you've done!'

'Who planted those?' I pointed at a small collection of aloes in a simple rockery.

'Truda and I did.' Lena appeared at my side in a cream shift that accentuated her height. 'We thought you should have aloes.'

'Thank you.' I gathered the women to me. 'Thank you.'

'Oh, ma'am,' Sipata whispered, 'we're so proud to do this!'

Folk I recognised – and some I didn't – came forward and reached out their hands to clasp mine. Mr Fourie had a new, less Hitlerian moustache; the dominee's wife was still silent; Abel and Sannie Metz wore warm smiles. A group of poor whites edged in, alongside Lena's coloured partner.

'Shall we start?' she whispered.

I nodded and led the way.

I'd sworn Henry Venter to secrecy, so no one was expecting the scorched but polished floorboards, or the single, blistered chair now varnished to a shine and, in the bedroom, a collapsed roof beam as a horizontal mount for a line of landscapes.

A rising clamour followed me.

I glanced across the lounge.

There it was, on the opposite wall: the mirror, cracked on the vertical.

'Ladies and gentlemen!' Raymond Cadwaller raised his arms. 'Your attention please!'

Director Compton was too infirm to travel, so I invited Mr Cadwaller to South Africa as my guest, and to preside if he felt strong enough. The dominee glanced at me and stepped alongside Cadwaller. 'Will you help, Dominee?' I'd asked. 'If you're involved, then it will be a success.'

'My name is Raymond Cadwaller. I was Frances McDonald's first art teacher and I'm delighted to say she has surpassed all my expectations. Frances spent more than fifteen years in Aloe Glen, painting the scenery and the flora of this magnificent region, to international acclaim. On these walls you can see the results.'

He paused and the dominee translated.

The crowd murmured and stared at the paintings.

Aloe Peak from Marico Road.

Eucalyptus Trees at Dawn.

Lithops: Four Pencil Studies.

Aloe Microstigma in Flower.

Father, by my side, put a hand lightly on my shoulder.

'I'm honoured to be in your vibrant community,' Cadwaller beamed at the farmers, labourers, railway workers, housewives and probably a few of my residual enemies, 'to open the Marico Road Gallery.'

Light applause.

'Thank you, ladies and gentlemen, thank you. This gallery will be used not only for the display of Frances's art but also as a working space. Classes will be held here for schoolchildren to develop their interest. Frances has endowed a bursary scheme to support promising students.'

They clapped more enthusiastically.

'The gallery will be managed by Lena Fuller, assisted by Sipata Pumile,' he enunciated carefully.

I sensed a slight stiffening among certain of the guests. But I don't intend to lend them any comfort. This space is also designed to disconcert.

'We're privileged,' Cadwaller kept his tone neutral as I'd insisted – but why, Frances, the man is a criminal – 'to welcome here today the local member of parliament, Wynand Louw.'

The audience gaped. *The man who bombed the place*, I could hear them think. *Is Frances crazier than we supposed?* They craned around. Wynand Louw, who'd slipped in at the back, gave a tight nod.

When I invited him, I made it clear he would play no active role in proceedings.

'Frances,' Mr Cadwaller gestured to me, 'will you say a few words?'

I took my place alongside him.

'Thank you for coming, ladies and gentlemen.' I smiled. 'When we see drought, poverty and war all about us, art can seem unimportant. But I hope my pictures show the triumph of nature over some of those troubles. Life may be harsh at times, but nature has the power to lift and inspire us.'

No haranguing, I reminded myself. No *Bekeer*! Repent!

Instead, a subtle nudge.

'I want to pay tribute to this community. You made my years here memorable – and productive.'

They exchanged glances. I think I heard Mrs van Deventer sniff in the front row.

'I must also thank my father and my son, Hamish, for their love through difficult times.'

Father flung an arm around his grandson's shoulder. Hamish grinned and I saw Mark in his face.

'This gallery will be a meeting place for people who love

art, and who love the veld that surrounds us. I hope it will bring more visitors – and more jobs – to town. Now, you may wonder why the house has not been completely restored. My studio, in particular,' I motioned for Lena to unlock the door, 'has been left almost the way it was after the fire.'

Surely they knew enough of me by now to know there'd always be a twist?

'I left it like that deliberately.' I paused to give the dominee's translation extra weight. 'I hope its destruction will show the price of discord and the need for reconciliation.'

From the back of the room, burly Henry Venter lifted his hands above his head and clapped. Poor Henry, I'd duped him into thinking he was preparing the house for sale.

Mr Cadwaller glanced about at the smarting audience and encouraged the applause.

The dominee joined in, his face flushed. I stepped away from the centre.

The crowd pushed towards the studio.

I knew what they'd find.

Trails of paint swirling across the floor, melted and smeared by the fire. A series of singed paintings hanging on the wall including a new version of *Studio with Glass Shards*. My easel, its wooden struts scorched, reconstructed and standing by the window. The blackened cupboard that once housed my paper supplies and hid the portrait of Gideon, left open and empty.

Some guests bent down to touch the solidified paint, and then read the captions on the wall in both English and Afrikaans. Cora had her hand over her mouth. Anna Visser, with the latest baby on her hip, glanced back at me and nodded. Sannie Metz stood before one of the paintings and wiped away tears. Lena moved through the crowd, guiding and explaining. She once used to hide her erudition out of shame for her poverty. No longer.

Truda turned to me and smiled. I invite her regularly to Protea Rise when parliament is sitting in Cape Town. We don't speak much; it's enough for her to be away from her husband. And we've mostly said all there is to say. She still wears floating, escapist dresses, but these days they are unfrayed. She spends time with Deon who's doing postgraduate studies in America. Julian's bursary has stretched a long way. Truda likes the Americans; she likes their open spaces.

I glanced around.

So many different souls. Wealthy Owen Jefferson. The poor men who fought my fire. Obstinate Ellie van Deventer. Dear, frivolous Daph. And others who aren't here, like Frans van Deventer and Toby Engelbrecht, ever-cheerful Tifo on duty at his petrol pump. Deon Louw. Aunt Mary. Julian. Mark.

The diverse colours of Africa.

Epilogue

The painting hangs on a side wall in my Dallas office, but always draws attention.

It's become a reference point for me, and an incitement to break boundaries. It shows, without compromise, the ability of nature to take circles and lines and twist them into a shape that holds not only life, but beauty within its distortion. A rare thing.

If I can harness that odd, thorny symmetry, I can design structures that will both challenge the mind and lift the soul.

Astrid knows it was painted by the 'flapper girl', as she calls her. But she doesn't care, even though Frances is now world-famous. Not for the aloe and similar, exquisite work, but for the *Fire Portrait*. It hangs in a gallery in London. I went to see it on a recent trip and had to queue.

It's been widely reviewed in the global press.

A modern classic, is the consensus.

A Mona Lisa for the age of the Cold War, budding civil rights, uncertain freedom.

HAUNTING PORTRAIT HINTS AT TURMOIL, headlined one newspaper.

FRACTURED SOCIETY, says another.

AN OMEN, says a third . . .

Is Frances happy? She said she would never leave her husband, but I know he has died and that she has a son.

I'm tempted to go back.

Acknowledgements

The Fire Portrait required background research that ranged from steam trains to The Great Depression; from wartime politics to the finer points of botanical illustration. Aloe Glen, the fictional town at the heart of the novel, is set along the railway line between the lush town of Worcester and the vast semi-desert of the Karoo. Heading in the latter direction, the Railway and Transport Museums in Matjiesfontein helped me to understand the role of the fledgling Cape railway in rural communities, while the Marie Rawdon Museum offered a glimpse of historical family life. Railway specialist Jamie Hart offered advice on the development of the early Hex River tunnel system and its later enhancements. For a sense of Cape Town in the early-to-mid twentieth century, I'm grateful for the assistance of the National Library of South Africa, the South African Maritime Museum and the Iziko South African Museum. For advice on house fires and the evidence left behind, I was guided by an officer at my local Fire Station.

Much of the novel centres around the heroine's development as an artist and botanical illustrator. I was lucky enough to receive expert advice and a watercolour lesson from Cape Town artist Christine Thomas, who also introduced me to the possibility of charcoal as a medium. Kirstenbosch National Botanical Garden in Cape Town and the Karoo Desert National Botanical Garden in Worcester provided living examples of the flora that Frances painted, while the Royal Horticultural Society's Lindley Library Digital Collections allowed me to view the work of professional artists over the years. Heather Thomas, no relation to Christine, offered valuable creative direction in the development of the cover.

As ever, I'm indebted to my family for their support throughout the research and writing of this novel. None of this would have been possible without their enthusiasm and encouragement.

BARBARA MUTCH was born and brought up in South Africa. Before embarking on a writing career, she launched and managed a number of businesses both in South Africa and the UK. For most of the year the family lives in Surrey but spends time whenever possible at their home in Cape Town.

barbaramutch.com